A Mistaken Life
Distance of Mind

Antonio L. Bugarin

Thanks to my friend, Tori Peterson, for her interest and desire to get involved, for her spelling and grammar checking, and most of all, for her enthusiasm and advice in the creation of my book.

Contents

To choose my reality. In my mind, everything is like it used to be. All alive, all young, all, and everything unchanged. Is it possible that the only thing that exists between today and yesterday is distance of mind? If so, shouldn't I be able to go back to yesterday? To get a little slice that's unchanged, untainted, that looks, feels, and smells like yesterday?

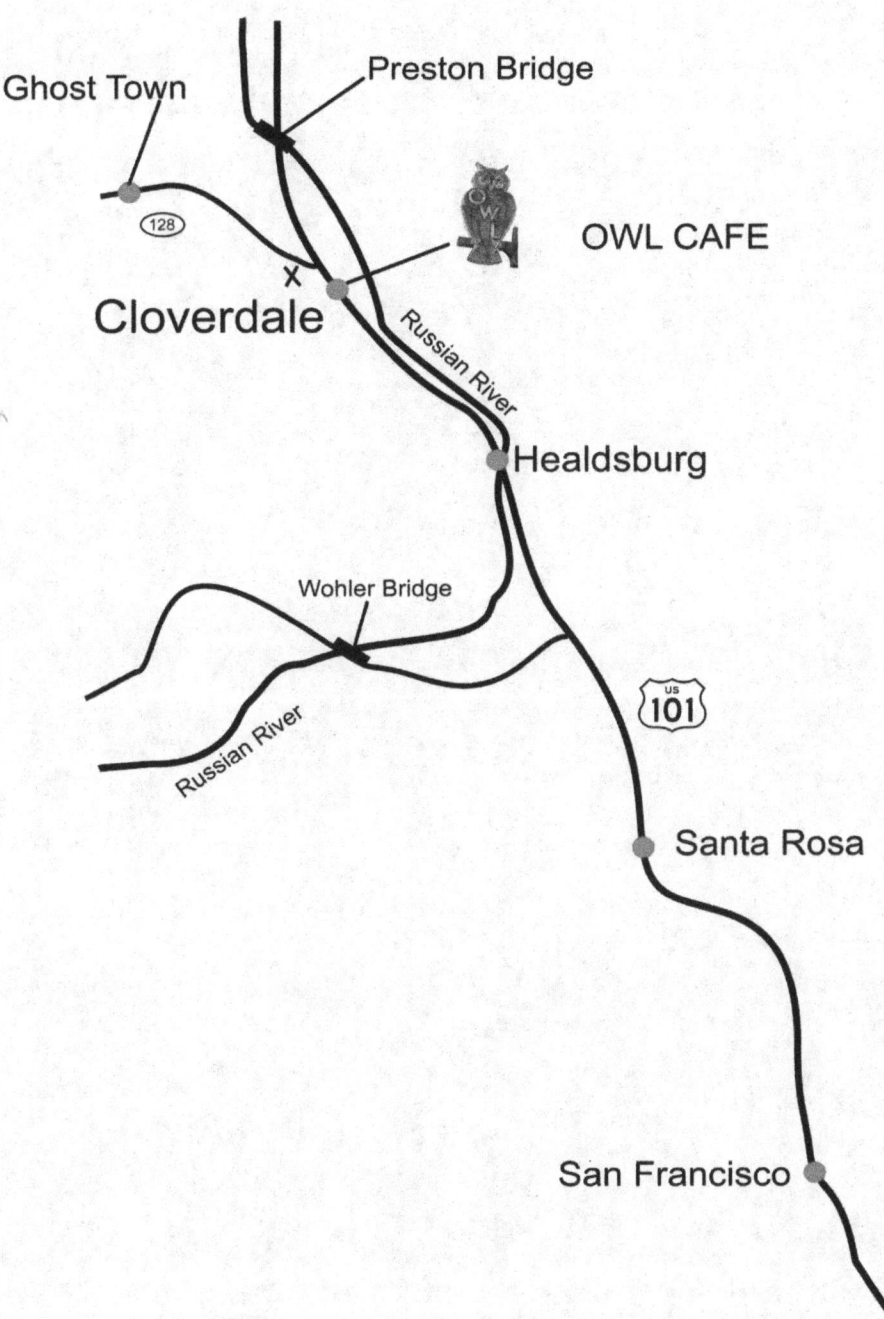

1. THE SOUND OF ANOTHER PLACE

As I stood among friends I didn't have, I found it impossible to look forward. As I thought of the future, it always took me to my past. It felt like my thoughts were escaping. Strange, when you really think about it, something within me was escaping. Stranger than that is that at times, I felt as if I was escaping them. And on that night, it was no different, for there I was, once again, staring at my yearbook. I kept it with me everywhere I went. I don't know why. Maybe it's because it made me feel good, comfortable was more like it. There was something about its smell, the feel of it as it touched my hand. Just open me, I could almost hear it say, and all shall be here, rain or shine, day or night no matter what.

As the minutes became hours, or the hours minutes, I

found myself staring at the picture, and I mean the picture. For there were many, but on that night, it was one that kept me where I wasn't. It seemed like another world, but then again, maybe it was. Who's to say that it isn't? And with that, I turned the pages, and it all came back. There it was, willingly, without a hint of hesitation, an undeniable familiarity. As I looked at the black and white picture of the Owl Cafe, for reasons I couldn't begin to explain, it slowly transformed into the full spectrum of color. There it was, perfectly centered on the flat roof of the two-story building, "DAN'S OWL CAFE" in blue and red neon. Underlined with white neon that extended beyond the letters to the full width of the building. I had no idea who Dan was, but Dan most definitely knew what he was doing. Beyond the right front corner of the building, as if he was hovering in midair, a six-foot tall owl traced in red neon. Diagonally across its chest in capital letters was the word, OWL, also in red neon. It was as if he was waiting to greet all that came in and out of Cloverdale, an hour north of San Francisco in Northern California, on Hwy 101. To the right and left of the owl were many vertical baby blue neon lines. These lines had a purpose. They lit up the entire building and pointed you to the windows and the front door.

"Wow, what a design," I said to the empty space around me. My heart started pounding, its echo in my head, and silence all around me. There it was, on the picture, a phone number, right there in plain view. How can this be? I didn't see this before. The next thing I knew was the ringing of a phone on the other end. What if someone answers? What am I going to say? Maybe I should hang up?

2

Hurry, hang up, I heard in my head. I then heard a woman say. "I really like talking to you, can you hold on?"

"Can I hold on?"

"Yeah."

"What do you mean?"

"I need to do something. Can you hold on?"

"Ah, yeah, sure," I said.

"Okay, I'll be right back," and she placed the phone on hold.

I heard her voice in my head. "Can you hold on?"

I thought about that and realized that I couldn't remember her answering the phone, let alone having a conversation. Maybe she picked up the wrong line and thought she was talking to someone else. I looked down at my yearbook and turned the page to see a picture of Cloverdale Liquor. Boy, do I have some memories of this place. I placed the phone on the counter and picked up the yearbook to get a closer look, and there they were on the page.

Two Georges standing behind the liquor store. The caption read.

"Owner of Cloverdale Liquor, George #1, and George #2, you know who", or, as he was known around town, Drunk George.

As if I didn't have a choice, a long ago memory came calling on a friend. It was a Friday night after a basketball game in ninety seventy-six. I was a senior in high school. Pat Daly and Cathy Crittendon, and I sat in my Dad's truck behind the liquor store waiting for Drunk George to come back with our beer.

"What the hell is this?" Pat asked. "You call this music? Come on, put on some real rock."

Pat ejected the eight-track and pushed in Steppenwolf.

"Here comes George," said Cathy.

"It's about time. I'll be right back," I said.

I opened the door to meet him, but he signaled me to stay put. Drunk, as always, and not noticing that my door was half open, he walked up and handed me the case of beer through the window of the half open door.

"Here you go, don't have too much fun, you little punks." He slurred.

"Thanks, George," said Cathy.

"Yeah man, thanks a lot," I said as we shook hands.

"Why you thanking him?" Pat asked in a dismissive tone. "He's a bum!" He added.

George leaned into the truck and looked at him.

"A bum and proud of it, and you're following my footsteps you little shit, you just wait and see. But you know what?"

He pointed at me, "you are welcome," he pointed at Cathy, "and you are welcome." He looked at Pat, "but you? We'll just see you out here on the streets in a couple of years. Just like me. You little shit." He burst out laughing, turned, and walked away.

"What is your problem?" I asked Pat.

"Oh, shit," Cathy said.

I turned to see what she was looking at and saw a short, fat policeman come around the corner of the liquor store.

Pat looked and instantly said, "oh shit, hurry, take off."

"Oh, man he's coming right at us, I can't take off now,"

"Take off, hurry," Pat demanded.

"I can't, it's too late."

"We're dead, I can't believe it," said Cathy.

"I'm in deep shit now," Pat said under his breath.

What the hell are we gonna do? I better think of something fast. It would be a disaster to get arrested for buying beer. I looked down at the case of beer on my lap, and it hit me. I placed it between Cathy and me. I took my jacket and placed it on top of the beer.

"Okay, now lean toward me," I said to Cathy, "more, more, Jesus."

She realized what I was doing and leaned on me like we were boyfriend and girlfriend, covering the beer between us. As the policeman approached us, I realized who he was.

"Oh my God," Cathy whispered.

I could feel her leg shaking. I tried to calm her. "Don't worry, we're cool."

"That was a hell of a game tonight, you guys really pounce them," he said in his weird accent. He reached out to shake my hand.

"Thanks," I said, "it was a tough one, but we managed to beat them."

"Managed to beat them? You guys destroyed them."

He looked at Cathy. "And what is your name, little lady? I have a hard time keeping track of you all."

"Oh, hi, I'm Cathy."

"Oh, that's right. You know what? I'm invited to your daddy's party next week."

"Oh, good." Cathy managed to say.

"Say hello to your daddy for me, will ya?"

"I sure will." Said Cathy.

I could see her brain working as she thought, how am I

5

going to explain this to Dad?

The cop leaned in and looked at Pat. "Pat, are you hiding from me?"

Pat, leaned forward and looked at him. "No sir, just relaxen over here."

The policeman hit me on the shoulder. He laughed and said. "Ah, can you believe him? I can't believe this guy. Relaxen? Pat, Pat, Pat, is he funny or what?"

I tried to laugh but only smiled.

He looked at Pat. "You behave yourself, Pat. You know, your mama told me to keep an eye on you. Yes, she did. She said keep an eye on my boy for me, will yeah? I don't want him relaxen too much."

He hit me on the shoulder again and laughed even louder. "Look at him, look at him." He pointed at Pat, "ah, just kidden Pat. Relax! Oops, too late, he already done that."

All three of us laughed. He caught his breath and looked at me.

"So, how many points did you score tonight?"

"Sixteen."

"Sixteen! Wow, great job. You know what? Now that I have you here and all. I wanna thank you for coaching my two boys. They really do look forward to basketball practice with you, you know?"

"No problem, I enjoy it," I said and reached for the ignition.

Surprised to see me reach for the ignition, he turned his whole body to the left and looked around, pretending to keep an eye on things. Like he was back on duty. I observed his body language and thought it was funny. He added.

"Okay, it's busy out there tonight, so you guys be careful out there, will ya?"

6

I turned the ignition and the truck started. He backed away and said, "alright, you kids take it easy." He looked back into the truck.

"Pat?"

"Yes, sir."

"You better get yourself some coffee, you hear that?" He once again laughed and hit me on the shoulder.

"Yes, sir," said Pat.

I grabbed the stick shift, pulled it into reverse, and started backing up.

"Bye, bye," said Cathy.

"Say hello to the boys for me," I shouted.

"I'll tell them you said hello, you can bet on that."

I snapped out of my memory to find myself in a void of reference, beyond the bounds of time, traveling without distance in the midst of the absence of presence. Was it a minute, or was it an hour? Was it day or night? Why would anyone want to know? As I looked at that picture, that could very easily be my reality. Why not? After all, they were the good old days. It was a simpler time back then. A couple of beers, a friend or two, and the party was on.

But was it really simpler? Or is it that I was simpler? Have I changed, or did the world change? How can one go from that to this? But what is this? I knew what that was, I think. But were they really the good old days? Maybe I, or we, forget the bad ones. We put them in the back of our brains, out of reach, and that's why we reminisce about the good old days. But then again, maybe we don't forget, it's a survival instinct and not something that we choose. It chooses us. It's an evolution in our genetic mutation instilled by nature. We acquire it along the way by trial and error. By exposure to the elements of life, failure, sadness, rejection, and most of all, regret. All the bad elements that grind away at us, a minute, a day, a decade at a time. Eventually evolving into some kind of instinctual mechanism, the ability to forget, to erase is more like it. Some handle the elements of life better than others, or worse depending on how we look at it, and are therefore the happier ones. Now I have to ask, which memories escaped me and how is it that some memories have the relentless ability to hold on to me, to haunt me is more like it. And with that, came this. Did I choose them, or did they choose me, and if so, why? What is it about certain memories that have the ability, the determination, to control us? As if they were entities capable of choosing, and making decisions.

I opened the yearbook again, and it all seemed like a reflection of a once upon a time, of a once upon a little town, where I can only assume that it was there where my past resides. How long have I been gone? Better than that, why did I leave? Is it possible that I left for reasons I can't remember? How can one not remember something so important? Maybe one of those instinctual brain deletions to protect me from something gone wrong? One of those decisions I made only to regret. Only to find myself years later in a reality I can only assume that it is here in Southern California where I'm supposed to be. As if trying to find the distance between this, and my thoughts, I snapped myself out of that to see the phone on the counter.

"Oh my God, what happened?"

I picked up the phone, "hello, hello, oh no, I can't believe it." I redialed. I heard the phone ring.

"Owl Cafe, can I help you?"

"Oh, hi. We were talking earlier."

"Oh hi, I'm so glad you called back. What happened? Did you hang up on me?"

"No, no, I don't know what happened."

"You know what?" She said, "I've been talking to you for about an hour, and I don't even know your name. What is your name anyhow?"

I heard a bell ring.

"Boy, your timing stinks, you know that?" She yelled. "I'm sorry, not you, the cook over here. Look, don't hang up. I gotta pick up my food. I'll be right back, okay?"

"Oh, sure, okay."

"Remember, don't hang up, I'll be right back."

Instead of putting me on hold; the sound of the phone and the object on which she placed it made its way to me. It was at that precise moment that I realized I could hear the sound of another place. That's kind of weird when you think of it that way. The sound of another place. I guess when the tree falls, it makes a sound. Who was that guy who asked that question? He must have been stupid, or he didn't have a phone. Maybe he said it before they invented the phone. Or, the tree didn't make a sound until they invented the phone. How would we know? But now, it makes a sound, it has to. For I am hearing the sound of another place. I could hear people talking, pots and pans, and other indistinguishable sounds. Someone must have opened the front door because I heard a car driving by. And just before the door closed, I clearly saw it as it traveled in midair, the bark of a lonely dog. Boy, what a lonely bark that was. I wonder what it would be like to be there right now?. It's probably cold up there. I should've asked her. For all I know, it's not cold at all. But there was something about that bark that told me it was cold.

In my mind, I could see her standing at a table. I wonder what he ordered? Maybe it's a family, or a she. I closed the yearbook and opened it. I closed it again and opened it again. There was something exciting about opening it. It was like the beginning of a movie. I closed it again, and this time, I opened it from the very beginning and saw something I had never seen. A piece of a missing page protruding from the binding. I don't remember this. What happened here? Why is this page missing? Here, right here at the very beginning. Did I do this and can't remember? There's no way. Why would I tear out a page from my yearbook? Isn't that the point, to remember? Is this yet another deletion? Perhaps; but not instinctual, it was deliberate, with intent. As that crossed my mind, I felt myself being pulled away. As if looking through someone else's eyes, at a memory someone left behind. But by whom? Why would I feel that? How would I know what it's like to feel the remnants of someone's memory? Next came the fear. Why would I feel fear? I randomly turned many pages, stopped, and there she stood in front of her daddy's store. Looking as beautiful as ever, Joan Briganti, the love of my life.

2. MY SECOND SMILE

The first couple of days of the school year were tortures. I remember that morning in Mr. Walton's freshman math class, back in nineteen-seventy-three. I did whatever I could to sit anywhere near Joan Briganti. The fact that I managed to sit behind her was incredible. I can now enjoy her for an entire hour, and yes, I can now smell her beautiful scent for an entire hour. I didn't know what it was, but it was.

I was in the sixth grade the very first time I saw her. We had just moved to Cloverdale. The school secretary was walking me from the office to the classroom. And it was on that very first walk on that very first morning that I got my very first glimpse. I don't know why she wasn't in class like everyone else, but there she was and there I was. Watching her glide across the playground, and I mean glide. It was as though she defied gravity. There was a

11

gracefulness about her, a synchronicity with the world around her as she moved through space as her hair glistened in the morning sun. As a child, I had seen beautiful girls before, but there was more to her than beauty. I'm not sure what it was, but it was, and I liked her. One thing for sure, I was in the midst of a moment I would never forget. The secretary suddenly stopped at the classroom door and I bumped into her. "Oh, I'm sorry," she said. My antigravity girl looked my way, our eyes met, and I saw what I would refer to for the rest of my life as my first smile. Who would have known that I would find myself years later, in the midst of yet another never to be forgotten moment as I sat behind her. There was something just as magical about the way she sat, as the way she walked. I would ask myself, what is it about her that gives birth to all that I feel about her? Is this love that I'm feeling or obsession? What causes either? Her beautiful face, her wide shoulders, the curvature of her back, her little waist, her God-given hips, or all of the above? One thing for sure, thank God for hip huggers, by far the best thing that came out of the sixties.

I came out of my thought to see the classroom in mad chaos. David Johnson, a friend of mine since the sixth grade, was surrounded by kids. He used to live in the most centrally located house of all of us. So, no matter what school we attended, his house was always perfectly located. And for that reason, and a couple of others, David's house was our pit stop, our hang-out was more like it. One day back in the grade, David, and another of my friends Jerry and I walked up the side of his house and into the backyard. David stopped and looked at us.

"You guys wanna see something?" A big grin surfaced on his face.

"What?" Asked Jerry.

"Sure," I said, not thinking anything of it.

David turned around and headed for the treehouse as we had already planned, but instead of walking, he took off running. What could he be talking about, I asked myself. I mean, we used to stash car magazines and candy up there all the time. Marathon bars were our favorite, so I thought, hey, maybe he got more candy. David got right up to the tree and turned back to face us, this time with a huge smile, laughing but didn't make a sound.

"What's going on?" Asked Jerry, as he reached out and pinched David's titty.

"Ouch, cut it out," David said, pushed Jerry away, and started up the ladder.

Jerry looked at me, "what's going on?"

"Beats me."

Jerry started up the ladder. I started up the ladder. I paused halfway in, with my feet still on the ladder, and watched David as his excitement became curious to me.

"Come on, come on, get in here." David signaled me in.

I looked at Jerry questioning but said nothing.

"Don't ask me," Said Jerry.

"Come on, hurry," said David.

This had a different feel, something illegal like marijuana or beer, I thought. I got completely into the tree house. David reached over and closed the door, a blanket we had hung in the opening of the tree-house.

"Okay," he said with a devilish grin.

And with that expression, I knew something different

13

was going on. He picked up the wooden box we kept our car magazines and Marathon bars in, and moved it to the side to reveal a paper bag. He covered his mouth to keep himself from laughing. He grabbed the bag, reached in, stopped, and looked at us.

"Okay, turn around," David said.

"Why?" Asked Jerry.

"Come on, David, what's the big deal?" I said, pretending not to care.

"Turn around," David said.

"Okay," Jerry said, as if to say, whatever.

We both turned around and waited.

"Okay, turn back around," David said in a whisper.

We turned around and there it was. A huge picture of a beautiful naked blonde girl laying on a red shag carpet.

"Oh my God," Jerry said, "look at her."

I could not speak, it was by far the most amazing thing I had ever seen. The thought of a girl getting naked in front of me, I couldn't even begin to imagine, let alone in front of a camera. And in the midst of her naked beauty, I found myself thinking, boy, I bet her parents are pissed. There she was naked, naked as naked could be, right in front of a guy with a camera.

"I have got to get myself a camera," I said out loud to my surprise.

Jerry and David looked at me, questioning.

"Ah, never mind," I said and lost myself in thought, fantasy was more like it. For the next couple of hours we had a Playboy magazine Marathon Bar marathon, life was good.

I came out of that thought to me sitting in the classroom. David was surrounded by a bunch of kids.

14

They were laughing, kidding around, having a good time. David was one of those kids that had it rough at home. I would look at him with his hair sticking up in all directions, wearing the same clothes as yesterday, and would think, I don't think he took a shower. One morning, I asked him.

"Hey, what you have for breakfast?"

"Nothing", he said.

I didn't believe him. "So your mother didn't make you breakfast?"

"No." He walked off.

I followed him and persisted, "well, what did she have for breakfast?"

He stopped and turned around to face me.

"What's with the questions?"

"Just wondering man, I mean aren't you hungry? I know I am."

"Look," he said, "my mother has beer and cigarettes for breakfast every morning, okay? And just in case you're wondering about lunch and dinner? Yep, that's right."

He turned around and walked off. I tried to come up with a memory of us having lunch, or anything to eat at his house, besides Marathon Bars, but couldn't.

Anyway, the classroom was out of control except a few of us. Mark Bennett sat quietly a couple of desks in front of me. He was a kid that came out of nowhere. The story was that Mark was not the kid to piss off. A teacher in his old high school made that mistake, and as Mark told me when I asked him if the story was true.

"I burned the fucking bathrooms down," he said as if it was no big deal.

"You're kidding me, right?" I asked, not believing.

"Let me put it to you this way," he said, "if you ever go to Ukiah High School, for whatever stupid reason, take the time to enjoy their brand-new bathrooms, courtesy of yours truly."

He looked away, not smiling, not frowning, not anything. Boy, I thought, this guy is badass. As I sat there thinking of that, the classroom came to a halt as Mr., Walton opened the door and instead of walking in, he stood in the doorway, drenched in water. His last remaining hairs on the top of his head dripped onto his long sideburns and onto his shirt. He stood there and looked around as if to give everyone a chance to see him. He then slowly walked up to his desk. He looked at it, almost as if he was looking through it.

After about a minute, he grabbed his chair, spun it around, and sat down. He grabbed the desk and pulled himself right up to it, ending up with his mid chest against it. I thought for sure that he was going to say something at that point. But no, instead, his focus went from the desk to the back of the room. I then thought, am I missing something? Just in case, ever so slowly, I turned around and looked at the wall behind us and saw nothing but the wall. We all waited for him to do something, but nothing is what he did, and did it for way too long. The classroom deteriorated back into chaos. David pulled out another Magazine, the kids huddled around him. The girl behind me, Lisa, who had worn make-up since she was eight, leaned over my shoulder and whispered in my ear. "Oh my God, it looks like those guys got a bigger price than they bargained for."

"What guys?" I whispered.

"You know, Richard and those guys, they put a bucket of water on top of the bathroom door," she whispered.

16

"Why?"

"They were trying to get Neg," she giggled. "You know, Craig, they were trying to drench him just before class and I guess they got you know who."

Poor Mr. Walton, he could never get it right. He, with his bald head and long sideburns. Sideburns that no matter how long they were, they will never make up for the absence of hair on the top of his head. I swear I once saw a picture of him in a history book, from the eighteen hundreds. You know. I mean, I swear, but I'm not sure. After sitting at his desk doing nothing for way too long.

He finally reached into his back pocket and pulled out a handkerchief. He unfolded it completely and paused. He dried the top of his head, and his face, stopped and looked at us. We all looked away. I thought, this is getting weirder by the minute. Why didn't he clean up before coming to class? I couldn't believe this. He then dried his neck and under his chin. And ever so slowly, and ever so carefully, he positioned the handkerchief on the rim of the trash can to dry it. As if he was hanging it on a close line. Weird, I thought, very weird.

He reached into his desk, pulled out a comb, and combed the few remaining hairs on his head. At this point, he was looking down just past the front of his desk. At the feet of the first row of students. What is that about? He proceeded to his right sideburn. He combed it in long slow strokes over and over. Some of us looked at each other. Others looked out of the corner of their eye, afraid that they may be seen. Without needing to ask anyone, we all I'm sure asked in our minds, how long is he going to comb that same sideburn? He stopped. Right at the beginning of a stroke. It looked like he shorted out. Finally, I said to myself. But instead of starting on the left one, he froze there for a few seconds. He took a little breath. He slowly moved the comb and positioned it directly in front of his eyes. What now, I asked myself. It felt like a cliffhanger, but it wasn't. It was just a man combing his sideburns.

Why should I or any of us care? With his right hand holding the comb in front of his eyes, he reached down with his left hand lifted his handkerchief off of the trash can, and dried his comb. He placed the handkerchief back on the rim of the trash can. He slowly combed his left sideburn, once again, for way too long. He stopped again at mid stroke. I thought, maybe this isn't a willing action. For all we knew, his brain had shorted out or something. He looked at us. Everyone looked away. I, however, kept one eye on him. He placed the comb on his desk. He leaned way back as the sound of his chair squeaking filled the room as if begging for a little lubricant. He pushed up on the armrests and got up. The chair bounced back to its original position. He stood and faced us and said nothing. He turned, walked up to the chalkboard, and stood there facing the chalkboard for a few seconds. He reached out and picked up a piece of chalk, raised his hand, and gently pressed the chalk against the board. He stopped. A few seconds passed, and finally, he started working on a math problem. He stopped again and turned to face the class.

"Students, students, take your textbooks out and turn to page twenty-four," he said in a low voice.

He turned back to the chalkboard and went on with his little math problem. His voice deteriorated to a volume no one could hear what he was saying. As this was going on and on, the class deteriorated back into chaos. After a few minutes, he stopped writing and talking. He stood facing the chalkboard, once again for way too long. I shook my head thinking of how unusual this was. Maybe, just maybe, this time his brain shorted out for good, but no, no such luck. He slowly turned toward his desk, walked up to it, picked up a book, and slammed it on the desk. The class came to a halt. At that point, I was looking at a man I had never seen.

"Shut up, shut up! What do you think this is, a family picnic?" He yelled at the top of his lungs.

Lungs, I had no idea he had. An expression he hid under those long sideburns for God knows how long. We froze like deer in his headlights.

"Who the hell is this?" I said under my breath.

Mr. Walton stood tall, and for the first time, I thought proud. I don't know why I thought that, but this was definitely the face of a proud man. Maybe it was his ability to command, to bring everyone to a dead stop, that made him feel proud. Now what? Can it be that after all those stories about him being a coward, there's another man beneath that cowardly face? Maybe, this was the man that every now and then, I would catch him watching us, and I mean watching, not looking. I say this because sometimes, he would tell us to read a chapter in class, which was weird to start with. While we read, I would look up from my textbook only with my eyes, without moving my head. And to my surprise, Mr. Walton was doing exactly as I was. His pupils stuck to his upper eyelids going back and forth, as he faced down pretending to read. As if he didn't want us to know he was watching us. Like a spectator who snuck into the football game and sat under the bleachers watching. Not only the game, but listening to the people above. Listening to conversations, that in another life, I'm

19

sure he would have liked to have been a part of. But in this life, being part of the conversation would have made him one of us. And that would've denied him the pleasure of spying on his fellow humans. His fellow subjects is more like it. For all I knew, not even that. To him, I think we were all animals, bacteria is more like it. At which point, he, I'm sure, would've thought of himself as the scientist. The scientist who stood far enough from the petri dish not to get infected, but close enough to see the chaos in our little world. As if he was here to watch the show, not to be part of it. But in this case, the spectator, the scientist, has gotten too close. Not only did he get drenched with water, he was now infected. And for the first time, has become a participating member of the cast.

After slamming the book, he stood sideways, facing his desk, not the class. And there he was watching out of the corner of his left eye as everyone walked back to their desks. And there it was that little smirk, that little grin just beneath that mad expression. Which led me to believe that he, the scientist, was here to enjoy the unraveling of the human experiment. In a commanding voice, he said.

"Now turn to page twenty-four."

Everyone grabbed their books, some turned to page twenty four, others as I pretended. He turned toward the chalkboard and started to write. As if he had telepathic abilities, he stopped, turned around, and looked directly at a student. And yes, that student turned to page twenty-four. I waited for him to look at me, but for reasons I couldn't explain, he turned back to the chalkboard. He paused for a few seconds. He started writing and to my amazement, there he was again. The coward, the mumbling mathematician, once again talking under his breath. We sat there pretending to pay attention. And out of nowhere, in a loud matter of fact way, Mark Bennett said.

"Somebody pass the potato salad."

Everyone laughed. Mark said that in reference to Mr. Walton saying, what do you think this is, a family picnic? At this point, I had no choice, I too became a spectator and waited to see which Mr. Walton was going to turn around, if at all. Without turning, the mumbling mathematician calmly said.

"Mark, get out of my classroom."

Mark stayed at his desk and said, "I just asked for the potato salad," as if he was truly expecting the potato salad to be passed to him. At that exact point, this thought occurred to me. Can it be that we are witnessing the battle of two tyrants with superimposed personalities?

Mark also was quiet, calm, and relaxed, and often spoke under his breath, a non-participant of sorts. He too sometimes came across like a coward. But Mark lit the bathrooms on fire. So what's it gonna be? This I've got to see. And then, I heard Mr. Walton yell.

"Get the hell out of my classroom!" Still facing the chalkboard.

He paused for a second or two and waited for a reaction. I then thought, this must be one of his experiments. This can't possibly be a random act. He turned around to reveal the face of the mad scientist and looked right at Mark. In long quick steps, he walked right up to him. He looked down at Mark, and at lightning speed, he grabbed Mark's books off his desk, and yelled. "Stand up, stand up!"

Mark turned his head to the left and up to Mr. Walton's eyes. Without blinking and without deviating his

21

sight, he slowly stood. Not because he was being told to, but to stand eye to eye with him. Mr. Walton shoved the books in Mark's chest. Mark didn't acknowledge him. His hands remained to his sides.

"Get the hell out of my class!"

Yelled Mr. Walton. His eyes pierced into Mark's head, in search of something, something Mark wasn't about to reveal. Motionless, and without expression, was Mark's point of attack, as he stared right back at him. I felt my skin crawl as I felt the intensity of their focus. I thought, thank god, I'm close enough to get a great view of this. Mr. Walton stood firm, his nostrils got bigger and bigger with every breath as the seconds took forever. Mark slowly looked down at his books, in Mr. Walton's hands. A flinch, I thought. Did Mark just flinch? But knowing Mark, this was no flinch. A strategy was more like it, derived in the few seconds Mr. Walton mistakenly gave him. I then thought, I hope Mr. Walton knows whom he's dealing with. And then, this beauty of a thought came to me. I hope Mr. Walton has fire insurance. As if to confirm my thoughts of a strategy. I saw a slow developing grin on Mark's face as he continued to look at his books. His refusal to take them confirmed that it was all a strategy and that it was he, not Mr. Walton, who was in control. Mark slowly raised his head. He locked his stare once again on Mr. Walton's eyes, telling me, yet again, this was indeed a strategy. Now what? I almost said aloud, but thankfully kept it in my head. Mark's grin slowly got bigger. A surprise to all, but not to me. Mark, ever so slowly, raised his right foot and took a short step sideways, away from his desk.

I'm sure Mr. Walton thought I just forced him to walk around me, but I knew better. Mark took one more step and stopped. He then took another step backward and once again stopped. He kept his eyes fixed on Mr. Walton the whole time. At his own pace, he slowly stepped backward toward the door. Now and then, his eyes would dart back and forth at everyone, as if to make sure we were all taking in the show. A flare for dramatics was on display, and I was right in the middle of it, and I was loving it. This looked like a scene out of a crime series on television, I thought. But this was no television series, it was just us kids, the mad scientist, and the pyromaniac. Mark backed up against the door. The entire time, his eyes fixed on Mr. Walton, who at this point had no idea of what was going on. Mark tilted his head and calmly said. "You said family picnic. What, are we out of potato salad or something?"

I could not believe it. Brilliant, I thought, Mark nailed it. A few people laughed, while others giggled. I looked to see who was stupid enough to laugh. Instantly, I looked back to see Mr. Walton's next weapon of choice. With a commanding gesture, his arm stretched out longer than I had ever noticed, Mr. Walton pointed to the door. Mark's grin slowly faded back to a blank stare; his face almost unrecognizable. He slowly reached into his pocket. Mr. Walton's mouth began to drop. As if to make sure that everyone could see, Mark ever so slowly pulled out a lighter. He then raised the lighter to their faces, and stopped. Mr. Walton's mouth now wide open. Mark's thumb came up and dropped, striking the lighter. A huge flame shot up. This was no ordinary lighter. Nope, this was one of Mark's designs. Absolutely no doubt about that. Wow, I said to myself, look at that flame. As if capable of seeing through Mark's eyes, I saw the fear in Mr. Walton's face through the flame. He pulled his jaw up, swallowed, and tried to hide the fear that had already escaped. This told me that Mr. Walton was well aware of Mark's flaming past, but amid his dramatics had forgotten whom he was dealing with.

And for reasons I can't explain, Mark seemed to be in slow motion. As if he was in a movie. I then asked myself, is it just me, or are we all seeing it in slow motion? He, yes in slow motion, leaned toward the lighter. What the hell is going on here, I heard in my head. Instead of turning off the lighter by releasing the trigger, he inhaled, held it for a few seconds, looked around with his eyes never moving his head. His eyes came back to Mr. Walton. He exhaled, and the flame leaned toward Mr. Walton, whose head institutionally leaned back away from the flame.

Mr. Walton's face contorted into an expression of total confusion. Mark at this point couldn't help himself. His grin became a full smile. A chuckle reverberated through his teeth. He raised his hand with his palm facing down and placed it over the flame. His expression didn't change, regardless of the pain we were all sure he was feeling. He lowered the palm of his hand onto the flame and snuffed it out. Now this I was not expecting. Once again, brilliant, I thought, brilliant. I questioned myself, what else can he possibly do to intimidate Mr. Walton more? There's nothing, I mean there's absolutely nothing, this is it. And to my amazement, Mark's hand formed into the shape of a pistol, with the lighter ending up as the barrel. He pulled the trigger and laughed out loud. I could not believe it.

This was playing out like Mark had written the scene and was now acting it out.

Still facing Mr. Walton, he stepped to his left. Reached back with his right hand, grabbed the knob, and pulled the door open just enough to step into the opening. With his eyes fixed on Mr. Walton, he moved his hand from the knob to the door to keep it open as long as possible. He stepped out, released the door, and at that point, I had to question myself if the seconds paced themselves. For reasons, I couldn't explain, the door seemed to have taken forever to finally close. The next thing I knew was the click of the door echoing in the silent room. The closing of the door felt weird to me. It was as if Mark existed one second, and not the next. I don't know why I thought that, but I did.

As if my head was a separate entity, I felt it turn to see Mr. Walton, whose mouth had dropped open again. I saw the muscles move under his sideburns as he pulled his jaw up to close his mouth. He then swallowed the spit that didn't fall onto his chin and whipped the spit that did. I was absolutely sure of his next thought. I better call my insurance agent. He looked down at Mark's books still in his hands and realized he had forgotten about them. Embarrassed and surprised by his discovery, he quickly but softly, not to make a sound, placed the books on Mark's desk.

With my eyes fixed on him, Joan, my antigravity beauty, slowly turned and looked over her shoulder. I brought my eyes to hers in total disbelief. Her soft, full lips slowly stretched out from the corners of her mouth, pushing up on her cheeks. Her cheeks pushed up on her eyes turning them into a soft squint, ending in a fantastic

25

beautiful smile. I thought, to what do I owe this pleasure? All these years since my first smile, she had never paid attention to me, let alone this. She lowered her head, followed by her eyes, followed by a slight tilt of her head. Captivated and incapable of escaping, I followed her glance and to my surprise saw my hand grasping her arm. I could not believe it. I released her and was about to apologize when our eyes touched. And yes, I will forever refer to this as my second smile.

3. A BEACON TO LIFE

I once again found myself where I wasn't, back in my
garage working on my eight-track tape deck and years away
from Mr. Walton's class. There was something about the
old stereos that made me feel good. They were better
made, they were heavier. That thing was at least seven or
eight pounds, and I found that comforting. I finished
installing a new belt and re-installed the faceplate. Many
years ago, I glued Pabst Blue Ribbon Beer bottle caps on
my dashboard knobs, including the radio and my eight-
track. I grabbed the knobs one by one, buffed them out on
my shirt, and pushed them back on. I then grabbed a cloth
and buffed out the chrome on the front plate. Not that I
hadn't before, nor that it mattered, I simply couldn't get
enough of it. I sat the tape deck on my workbench and
backed away to get a better look.

"Look at all the chrome, the way chrome should be,
plenty of it," I said out loud.

I picked it up again to get a closer look. I placed it back down and realized that even the sound it made as I placed it on my workbench made me feel good. I then found myself picking it up and setting back down just to hear that sound. Yep, this was old technology and I liked it. I polished the chrome again just to make sure. There was only one thing left to do, crank it up.

I moved the battery closer. I connected the black wire of the tape deck to the ground terminal of the battery. The red wire to the positive terminal. I grabbed my old receiver off the shelf and thought, wow, this thing feels like a refrigerator. I like it. I sat the receiver on my workbench. I dusted it off and cleaned it with a damp cloth. I grabbed a clean dry cloth and cleaned it until it looked brand new. It had to look good to sound good. That's just how I saw things. I plugged it in. I backed away, looked at it and, found myself shaking my head and thinking, wow, this is beautiful. I reached out with my index finger, pushed the big aluminum On/Off button and stopped halfway in. I pulled back and felt the smooth as butter action. Why don't they build things like this anymore? I don't understand. I pushed it halfway in again and released it just to feel the action. I just couldn't help myself but to smile. I saw the tip of my finger as I reached out again. I pushed it all the way in and felt the trigger and heard a mechanical click. But it wasn't just a click. It was a low frequency click. The receiver gradually lit up in a soft green-golden glow. And I mean gradually, it was like a slow, real slow fade in.

I then found myself thinking of the time I plugged in my first stereo. I laid on my bed and looked at it to see if I had a good view. I got up and turned the stereo to face directly at my pillow. I laid back down and it was perfect. There was a comforting, reassuring feeling about that soft glow that made it easier for me to sleep. Many times in during my high school years when I couldn't sleep, I would often turn it on, turn the volume all the way down, and position myself in bed, so I could see it. Minutes later, I would feel myself slipping away as that glow found its way into my dreams.

I snapped out of that thought and there I was, looking at the long horizontal AM and FM dial. That thing was so big, it extended all the way from one end of the receiver to the other. It was like a landing strip to my music, and I loved it. My eyes moved to the huge VU meters, perfectly centered as if they were speakers. What a design. I grabbed the tuning knob. I stopped, released it, and asked myself, how big is this thing anyway? I grabbed my measuring tape. I placed it right up to the knob and wow, look at this, two inches in diameter. TWO INCHES! Now that's what I call knob. I sat the measuring tape down.

I grabbed the knob and softly spun it clockwise and saw my fingers spring outwardly, releasing the knob. It was like I had performed that very action just yesterday, but I knew better, it had been years. I leaned down to look at the knob as it turned by itself with the centrifugal force and whatever else those engineers put in there. It moved by itself. I mean, who thought of that? Who was this person or persons? How did they come up with that idea anyway? I then realized that my head and eyes were following the radio station indicator on the dial. It was as if my head was also triggered by the centrifugal force. As we came toward the end of the dial, I felt the gradual slowing of the indicator and my head as we came to a rest.

And I mean a rest, not a stop. It then came to me. They designed this to mimic the human body. These designers, these engineers, these whatever they were, were beyond incredible.

I grabbed my big speakers and I mean big, as in huge, the way speakers should be. I spread them equally apart, with me, right in the middle. I connected them to the back of the receiver. I then hooked up the wires from the back of the eight track to the back of the receiver. I walked up to a shelf on the left side of the garage, picked up a small box, brought it to the workbench, and realized the lid was taped up. Wow, that is weird. How long has it been? It bothered me to think that I couldn't remember taping it up, let alone how long it had been. I grabbed a knife out of the drawer. I cut the tape down the middle of the box. I felt my heart speeding. I cut the tape at one end of the box and the lid popped up a little. I stopped; I don't know why. I took a deep breath. Once again, I don't know why. I slowly spun the box around to cut the other end and found myself staring at it, hesitating. Why do I feel apprehension?

I pushed myself to get going. I extended my hand out and saw my hand as a tool. A tool I was in control of, but not a part of. I stopped and thought about it for a second. Something felt weird to me and I didn't like it. I pushed myself again and lowered my hand to continue with the action I had started. I saw the point of the blade come down and into the old tape. It was as if I zoomed in to an extreme close up, but how is that possible? My hand moved from right to left. The sound of the blade rubbing against the old hardened tape was loud and clear. As if my ears had also zoomed in. The lid raised as the pounding of my heart became obvious to me. The next thing I saw was both of my hands slowly reaching out. It was as if they were programmed or a predisposed action. As weird as that seemed, stranger than that was the site of my hands gently rubbing the old box. It was an endearing action, transforming my apprehension into a feeling of warmth, and tranquility. My hands slowly moved from one end of the box to the other. I felt every little bump, every little indentation as my hands moved across that landscape. A landscape I must be familiar with because I liked what I felt. My left hand carefully pulled up on the lid. Without hesitation, my right hand reached in and pulled out an eight-track tape. As if it was right there waiting for me. I stopped and stared at it. The next thing I knew, was the sinking feeling of apprehension again, but why? A noise startled me. I turned around to see three kids standing on the opposite side of the garage. They looked at me with an expression I could only surmise looked a lot like mine. I couldn't believe it. They were my neighbor's kids. Jesus, how long have they been there? Did I know they were there the whole time and forgot about them? They looked at each other.

"What is that?" One of the kids asked.

"Okay, what is he talking about?" I whispered to myself.

I decided that an action was necessary. You just can't stand here thinking and questioning. You have to do something. I clearly heard that in my head. I waved them over. The kids looked at each other. They walked up to me.

"What's in there, CDs?" the middle kid asked.

"How long have you guys been there?"

"I don't know." Said the kid.

"Why didn't you say something?"

They looked at each other.

"You told us to get back and to stay quiet." Said the youngest.

"I did?"

"Yeah." They all said at the same time.

The oldest of the kids pointed at the tape in my hand and asked again. "Is that a CD cartridge? Are there CDs in there?"

I looked at the kid and thought, he's got to be kidding, right? I ignored his question. I turned back to my tape deck and carefully pushed the tape in. It lit up with bright green and red lights. Even that was beautiful. Seventies rock-n-roll filled the space around me. Wow, I thought, now this is music. The huge VU meters on the receiver moved to the sound of the music. I felt a smile come onto my face. I felt my heart slowing as the comfort the music gave me poured out of my head onto my body. I turned around to see the kids staring at my speakers. My smile vanished as I saw their distorted little faces looking at the speakers, moving in and out to the beat of the music.

"Why are the speakers moving?" Yelled the oldest kid.

"Why? Because they do...ah, never mind. Hear that music?" They nodded. "That's the great sound of eight-track. Analog man, analog, not a CD."

"What's an eight-track?" The older kid asked,

"Dude, that sounds good." One of them said.

"That's right," I said, "it's warm, big, and fat. Hear that bass? That my friends is analog."

"What's analog?" The youngest kids asked.

"It's the best. Do you guys know who Thomas Edison is?"

They looked at each other, questioning.

"Oh Yeah, he's that dude with that band...ah." The oldest kid said.

I could not believe it. "That dude? You've got to be kidding me, right? Thomas Edison! You know." I looked deep into their eyes hoping to find a semblance of knowledge but came up empty.

"Analog, Thomas Edison, read up on it for God's sake."

One of the kids reached into the box and pulled out another tape.

"Wow, dude. There's got to be CDS in there, I'm telling ya."

"Analog, get it? Analog! A CD is digi....never mind."

I turned away from them to enjoy the music and could feel myself slipping away. "Analog, you can listen to it all day and all night, and it won't hurt your ears."

"Hurt your ears? Why would it hurt your ears?" The oldest kid asked.

"Never mind, just forget it."

I reached out and pushed the button on the tape deck to change the track, just to see if it still worked. There it was, the clunk of the tape deck as it changed tracks. Even that sounded good to me. One of the kids quickly said, "I knew it. Did you hear that? There are CDS in there. It switched to another CD."

I had no idea which of the kids said that, and didn't care. All I knew was that I found myself deep within the greatest music ever, rock-n-roll.

"Gotta love it," I said it out loud, as I continued to face away from them.

"What?" One of the kids asked.

Once again, I didn't know, nor did I care. All I knew was that I felt something I hadn't felt in years, and it felt good to feel again.

And then, there we were on the road in my nineteen sixty-eight RoadRunner. Yes, we were on the road, me and my three new friends. They weren't my high school buddies, Jerry Donnelly, David Johnson, or Anthony Villa. But as far as I was concerned, they might as well have been because we were rockin it and hot-rodding it. Just the way we used to back in the day, and nothing was going to change that.

I looked at my car from the inside, feeling it with my eyes like it was the first time. Look at my dashboard, knobs man, and I mean knobs with PABST BLUE RIBBON BEER caps on them. Yep, that's the way it was done. My eyes came to my big tackodometer that I bought and clamped onto my steering wheel column. I thought it's time to make this baby scream.

I grabbed my pistol gear shift and down shifted into second gear, not third, second, and I was in fourth gear. There was something about going from fourth gear to second that was exciting. The power, the screaming of the engine as the vibration violently tried to take my dashboard apart. I can swear that the engine wanted to be in my front seat. I saw my gauges shaking as the RPMS hit seven thousand. I looked in the rearview mirror to see the pavement unfolding behind me. The kids held on for their dear little lives. I looked at my gauges again. I grabbed third gear. The sound of the engine was almost unbearable. I shifted into fourth, I looked in the mirror to see their screaming little heads. I looked forward, and a car suddenly appeared in front of me. "Oh shit,"

I hit the brakes just enough to avoid hitting it and made sure no cars were coming in the opposite direction. I down shifted into second gear and jumped on it. We were around and beyond that car in a second. Power, now that's what I call power. I could pass anything or anyone under any condition at any time. On a curve, on a hill, or in heavy traffic, it didn't matter. That's what I thought. All I knew was that I was in total control of four hundred and twenty five horsepower. As that beautiful thought exited my head, the music slowed, sped up, and screeched to a halt.

"Oh man, damn that piece of shit eight-track, SHIT."

I pulled over and stopped. I pushed the eject button. I gently pulled out the eight-track cartridge to reveal a long dangling tail of tape. The kid in the middle, Daren, yep, I finally remembered their names. He leaned forward between the bucket seats with an expression as if Godzilla came out of my tape deck.

"Dude, what is that?" He pointed at the dangling tape.

I looked at him. "You see, no CDs."

I raised the tape to show all of them. "You see that? Analog man, that is analog."

"Can you fix it?" Asked Daren?

"Nope, not without a screwdriver."

"What do you mean?" Asked Bobby, the older of them.

"Well, if I had a small screwdriver, I could take it apart."

I turned the tape over and showed them the little screws that held the cartridge together.

"And then what?" Asked Bobby.

"And then? Ah, you know what, never mind. That's the end of the music for now."

The kids let out a big, disappointing gasp.

"Oh man, now what?" Asked Daren.

"Man, we were just getting into it." Said Bobby.

Timmy, their little brother, leaned forward, and innocently held out a tape and said, "here, put this one in."

"Where did you get that?" I asked.

"I grabbed it out of your box. It says, Peter Frampton? Comes Alive? It sounds cool."

"Good thinking," I said.

I took the tape and placed it right up to the tape deck. I looked back at them.

"Ready?" Knowing exactly what they were going to say.

All three said, "Ready"

I pushed the tape in. The music came on and took me back to a concert in nineteen-seventy-six. I looked down to see my Day On The Green concert ticket still hanging from my cigarette lighter on the dash.

"Come on, let's go." One of them said.

I looked back to see them looking at me, waiting like puppies.

"Well, let's do it." Said Timmy.

"Yep, let's do it," I said.

I turned the key in the ignition. The engine started. I released the key and felt the spring loaded mechanism in the ignition. I thought, even this is better than the new cars. It felt mechanical, and I liked it. I looked at my dashboard again and thought, boy this is beautiful and felt a little finger on my back, and I heard.

"Come on, let's go."

"Let's do it," I said.

A quick flashback of my buddies from high school passed through my head, followed by a burst of fear and then joy. Joy that was right here, to be lived right now. I heard the sound of my engine screaming as I jumped on it, followed by the tires squealing. I looked in the mirror to see their little heads fling back. I grabbed second, third, and fourth gear. I could smell the burning rubber of my tires, as I felt the wind on my face and hair from the opened window. This is the way life is supposed to be. And there in the far distance, tiny as a speck of dust on my windshield. I could see and feel the Owl Cafe, its neon glowing in the midday sun. There, there it is, I thought, I'm coming home. And as sudden as it took forever, the day had turned into night. Like a lone pilot in the sky, the vastness no longer escaped me.

"Close your eyes," I heard from I don't know where, "for this moment is yours to be had."

4. THE HUMAN AQUARIUM

With the absence of thought and memory of body and a long deep breath behind me, I opened my eyes to see the Owl Cafe before me. I pulled into the parking lot and parked in my forever spot, and once again felt someone's finger on my back. I looked in my mirror to see not one of the kids, but one of my friends from high school, Anthony Villa. He leaned forward with his head almost on my shoulder.

"What are we doing?" He asked.

Confused as I could possibly be, I tried to think but failed at the attempt to process even the simplest of thought, let alone thoughts that presented themselves.

"What's wrong?"

I heard from my right, and there, right there in my passenger seat, was Jerry Donnelly, another of my friends from high school. I felt Anthony's hand on the back of my head. He pushed my head forward.

"What are we doing here?" He asked.

Still trying to process, I saw my brother Ernie come out of the Owl and walked up to my window.

"Drive around the back," he said.

"Why?"

"Just do it."

He turned around and went back into the Owl.

"What the hell is going on here?" Asked Jerry.

"We're here to give Ernie a ride," I said.

"We are?" Asked Anthony.

"Yeah, I told you," I said.

"No, you didn't?" Said Jerry, shaking his head.

"Oh, so now I'm supposed to clear everything with you guys?"

I put my car in reverse and backed up, but I knew it wasn't over. Out of the corner of my eye, I could see Jerry staring at me. I drove around the back to see Ernie's friend, Ricardo, waving me over. I came to a stop behind the Cafe. Ricardo reached into the trash bin and pulled out a case. He walked up to me and said.

"Turn off your lights. Quick open the trunk."

"What the hell's going on?" I asked.

"Shut up, hurry."

I got out and opened the trunk. I realized that Ricardo was holding a case of beer. He placed it in the trunk. Ernie ran up and slipped another case into the trunk.

"Why don't you guys just grab the whole fridge while you're at it?" I said.

"What's the matter, want me to take you home?" Said Ernie.

"Take me home? This is my car numbnuts". I said and

thought, what an asshole.

"Jesus, what a baby," said Ricardo. He closed the trunk, looked through the rear window, and realized there were two people in the car.

"Who the hell is that?" He asked.

I ignored him, Ernie pushed me into the car. We all got in, and we drove off into a Saturday night of partying. We had beers, friends and a badass car. What more can a man ask for?

"How about some chicks?" I asked.

"We got it under control," said Lucy, who was sitting in the back seat with Anthony and Jerry.

The second I heard that, I knew we were in trouble. Ricardo reached into his shirt pocket and pulled out a map. Oh great, now we're in deep shit, I thought. Finding a party in Northern California; a place full of curvy unlit roads, was in itself a challenge. The map is another story. They were specific to the region for reasons other than the obvious. They were handwritten, sometimes with colorful drawings, and specific directions like; once you go over the fourth hill, you'll see an oak tree on your left, keep going. You will then come to a curve, right away if you're going fast, if you're going slow it will take you a little longer. Be careful, many people have crashed there - keep going. After the third curve, you'll see another oak tree - keep going a little farther. If you see a barn to the right, you've gone too far. Turn around, and go back to the pine tree and make a left turn onto the dirt road. Don't turn right, there's no road there. After an hour or so we finally drove up to a tiny little house. It was about fifteen feet wide with a little door, and a tiny little window. The music was loud and the number of cars compared to the size of the house was a bit confusing. As always, it looked promising.

"Where the hell are all these people?" Asked Ernie. "They all can't be in there."

"I don't know, man, what do you guys think? This place is kind of weird." I said.

"What's with all the questions?" Ricardo said and pushed on Ernie's seat signaling him to get out.

"Come on, let's go," barked Ricardo.

We got out and Ricardo headed for the door with the others behind him. I, on the other hand, was drawn to the little window. I walked up to it and was amazed by what I saw. I had never seen a human aquarium before, but that was exactly what it looked like. As I got closer, I could see people standing around and walking in what seemed to be thick water. But it was thick smoke which seemed to be glowing. Not only was the smoke glowing, the whole interior was glowing. The walls, the posters, even the people, their hair, clothes, teeth, and eyes. I could see long fluorescent purple light tubes, known as black lights, all over the place. I had heard of black lights before that they made everything to glow, but I had never seen them.

"I don't know man, this looks too weird to me," I said, but no one heard me. They stood behind Ricardo at the door.

Jerry leaned toward the door and said. "This sounds like hippie music."

Ricardo looked at him. "What the hell is Hippie music?"

"This," said Jerry with his eyes popping out.

"You're kidding me, right?" Said Ricardo.

"No, this is Hippie music."

"Why is this Hippie music?"

"Because it is, don't blame me, it just is,"

"I listen to this, I'm not a Hippie." Said, Ricardo.

"Okay, it's Cuban Hippie music," Said, Jerry.

"Get off my ass!" Said Ricardo, he turned and knocked on the door.

I, however, stood in front of the window looking at the human aquarium. Ricardo knocked again, but no one heard. Not that anyone would have cared.

"I don't think they can hear you," I yelled really loud.

"What?" Asked Ricardo.

I walked up to the door, turned the knob, and pushed it open. I looked in and realized that I was one step away from being inside the human aquarium. After a second or two of observation, I turned around to see Ricardo and the others standing behind me with their mouths wide open. I turned back around and yelled. "Lucy? I'm home," I turned back to the crew, "you see no one can hear us."

Ricardo pushed me and I was in the aquarium. I instantly lit up.

"Wow, look at me,"

I turned around to see them glowing. Ernie and Ricardo pointed at me laughing, their teeth so bright it was freaky. Jerry and Anthony looked around in amazement.

"Hey, Jerry," I yelled, trying to get his attention.

Jerry's wide opened mouth slowly turned into a big smile as he turned to face me and said.

"Wow, man, can you believe this shit?"

"Come on, let's mingle," I said, and found myself as the leader of the pack. We walked in, and headed in the only direction possible, toward the back. As we got to the back of the house, we once again headed in the only direction possible, down the stairs. We got to the bottom

42

of the stairs and realized the house we thought was tiny, was huge. We couldn't believe it.

"This house seems to go on forever," said Jerry.

We dropped down yet another flight of stairs into a long hallway with rooms on both sides.

"Human aquariums," I said really loud.

"What?" asked Ernie.

"Human aquariums, that's what these rooms are," I said to Ernie, wondering how he would respond.

"What the hell are you talking about?"

I turned to face them as we stood just outside of one of the rooms.

"Human aquariums," I yelled over the loud music. They stared back.

"Don't these rooms look like human aquariums?"

They looked into the room and said nothing.

"Look at it," I said, "the smoke looks like water and the people are the fish,"

"What the hell have you been smoking?" Said Ricardo.

I pointed into the room. "You see, the stoners are walking in slow motion, not because they are stoned, but because they're in water."

Ricardo looked at everyone and realized that they were all trying to figure it out. Jerry was the first one to finally see it.

"Oh yeah, look at that."

Anthony's whose mouth had remained open for quite some time, backed in trying to see it. He finally ended up with his back against the wall.

"Holy shit, you are right. Hey, you guys, back up a little."

Ernie and Ricardo also backed up against the wall.

43

Ernie squinted and stared and finally saw it.

"Oh man, look at that. Here, come here, Ricardo."

He pulled him over and pointed into the room.

"Look, look, it does look like an aquarium." Hoping Ricardo would see it.

Ricardo squinted just like Ernie and said.

"Holly molito, what the hell have you been feeding your little brother? Shit, it does look like an aquarium."

As all five of us leaned against the wall, one of the fish, a tall skinny dude with red hair, saw us looking in.

"Be careful, one of the fish just saw us," I said.

Jerry and Anthony looked at me, questioning. The man slowly walked out of the room. He stopped and looked at us. He squinted, opened his eyes really big, and squinted again. I thought, is it possible that we too look like fish? Is he also trying to see the aquarium effect? Not knowing what to say, we stare back and can only assume that we too squinted. Is it possible that we find ourselves in the middle of a squinting battle? If so, what happens next? Do we draw at the end of our squint? If so, who will be the first to draw? Never mind that, what do we draw? How does it end? Do we squint until we can squint no more? And then what? As all this was going through my head, the red-haired man tilted forward and backward like a giant redwood that was about to fall.

"Hey, you guys are jocks, aren't you?" He dropped his head to our level as if trying to get a better look. "That's cool, I used to play, man."

He straightened up tall, and raised his hand to the top of his head to show us how tall he was.

"Basketball man, badass all-league center, nineteen-sixty-nine."

Ever so slowly, he held out a joint with his other hand. Thinking slower than I ever thought possible, we stood there, yes, like zombies not knowing what to do. Where the hell is big mouth Ricardo when you need him? I looked around to see everyone frozen. I could see Ernie's brain working. On what? I had no idea.

"Oh, no man, we're fine, we've had enough," Ernie said and faked a smile.

"You're fine, what do you mean, man?" The man asked.

Ernie glanced at me as if to say, give me a hand here, and to my amazement I found myself saying. "Oh, no, thanks, we don't smoke."

Jerry threw me a look as if to say, did you just say that?

The man cupped his ear, trying to hear. "What?"

Jerry and Ernie glared at me, telling me to shut up, or to say something else. Thinking at the speed of smoke, I had no idea what they were trying to convey.

"No, thanks," I yelled, "we don't smoke."

"Hey, don't blame you man, this shit is tight. It'll drop your ass, I'm telling you."

He leaned toward us. He looked around to make sure no one was watching. As if he was going to tell us a secret.

"No shit, I'm telling ya, no shit. I never used to smoke."

He backed away and stood tall. Extended his hands out to his sides, as if to say, look at me.

"Not while I was playing, man, no siree, I'm telling ya."

He looked at Ernie, then at Jerry, me, Ricardo, and then at Anthony. I then thought, now what?

"You guys are still playing, aren't ya?"

We all nodded.

"You don't wanna do this shit while you're playing, man. Good for you."

He swayed back and forth and closed his eyes. We waited. I looked at the others, hoping to figure out what to do next. They stared back. I turned to the man to see him still with his eyes closed. I waited. He opened his eyes, tried to focus, and said.

"Hey, you guys are jocks, ha?"

At that point, I realized just how stoned this man was. Ricardo walked off and headed for the door. We smiled at the man, said goodbye and walked out, leaving the human aquarium behind.

Later on that same night, we sat in my car on top of a hill, drinking beer, talking about nothing as usual. Most of the talk around town was usually about nothing, sports, work, and who's dating who. Like I said, nothing. Conversations typically went something like this. How can it be that those two had sex? That is gonna be one ugly baby. I'm telling you. Or, we would complain to each other about the lack of girls in town.

Even television was a drag, the reception was horrid. We were lucky to get three San Francisco stations. Two would fade in and out like some kind of signal from an alien planet. A planet named, oh I don't know, San Francisco? God knows that seemed like another world to us. I remember one night staring at the television for I don't know how long, waiting for the television signal to come back. When it finally did, not only was the show I was watching over, so was the broadcast. The station had shut down for the night. A white screen with black and gray circles with lines coming out of the center pointing in all directions was on my television. Why are these circles and lines on my television? Is it possible that we're the ones broadcasting some kind of message to aliens? Hoping that they would come and rescue us oh, I don't know, from boredom. With our luck, alien zombies would show up, take over our town and no one would notice. Who knows, they may already be here.

After a while of drinking and bullshitting on top of that hill, we got out of the car. With our breath visible in the cold February night, we drank more beer and listened to more rock. It was entertainment at its best. I, as usual, got lost in my thoughts. When I came back to what I could only assume was reality, and from what I could tell, not so sure. All four, including Ernie were staring and pointing at that one signal light in town.

"There, there, it's red, man," said Ricardo.

"No, no," Ernie said, with little if any conviction.

"Where is it? Where is it?" Asked Anthony.

"Green, green man," said Jerry.

That's odd, I thought, how can that be?

One light, a bunch of dudes, and it looks like they all see it a different color? Hmm, is it possible that the human aquarium had an impact on us?

"I think it's............hell, I don't know." Ernie gave up.

So I figured, if it's not red, and it's not green, it must be yellow. It was simply a process of elimination, not that I could actually see the light, nor that I gave a shit.

"It's yellow," I yelled.

Everyone looked at me. "Yellow? How can it be yellow?" They all said at the same time.

"Well," I said and paused for a second or two, hoping they would get it.

"Yellow?" Asked Jerry.

"It was."

Jerry ignored me and instantly pointed at the light.

"Green, green man, don't give me that shit. It's green."

Anthony, came right up to me and said, "it was never yellow, was it?"

I shook my head and was about to say, wow, but why bother? Anthony went back to pointing at the light. I went back to thinking and thought, there's got to be something better to do. I opened another beer and decided to down the whole thing. With my face pointing to the stars and the beer rushing into my belly, I heard.

"Hey, slow down."

Ah, the hell with them, I thought. I'm gonna drink the whole thing.

"Hey, come on man, slow down, right here, right here." I heard.

"Right here? What?" I said.

"That's our street, you passed it up."

I came out of my seventies memory to find myself driving. I looked in the mirror to see no Jerry Donnelly, no Anthony Villa, no Ernie and no Ricardo. Instead, I saw three kids yelling at me.

"You went past our street," said Timmy.

Wow, Jesus, I thought, get it together man. I tried to calm them. "It's okay, it's okay." I then asked. "What's the one good thing about these cars?" I looked in the mirror to see them thinking.

"Can you guys tell me, what's the one good thing about these cars?" No one said a thing. "You can always turn it around."

They looked at each other, not knowing what to say. Timmy as always, a willing participant looked at his brothers and said.

"You can always turn it around." Mimicking me.

"You see, you see, here we go, get ready, U-turn coming right up."

I started my U-turn with a big, "WOW.........here we go....."

They all joined in, in unison, "WOW." as I finished my U-turn.

I looked at them and said, "you see, good as new."

5. THE SOUL OF THE OWL CAFE

We drove up to my house to see a middle-aged
overweight balding man wearing an extremely tight t-shirt.
I assumed this was their father and that this man had
never been face to face with a mirror. The t-shirt was so
tight, I could actually see the indentation of his belly
button. His nipples? Well, they were another story. They
were like two 440 magnum pistols protruding through the
thin cloth. I'm telling you, Clint Eastwood would have
been proud. In the two years I've lived here, I had never
seen the man, but I've heard him and his wife argue more
than I cared to. Most of the time I couldn't hear exactly
what they were saying, but I did know one thing, their
honeymoon had come and gone. From the sound of
things, it was somewhere beyond the event horizon. And I
can tell you something else, nothing, and I mean nothing,
is worth that much arguing. We came to a stop and he
headed our way.

"Oh, oh, Dad is coming," said Daren.

Timmy looked at Daren with fear in his eyes and asked, "Is he mad?"

"I think so," said Daren.

After hearing that, I decided the best plan was to have no plan at all. Get out and introduce myself. So I did. I got out of the car, extended my hand, and said.

"Hi, my name is...", and he walked past me. He leaned into the car and then turned back to face me and said.

"What's going on here?"

"Just giving the kids a ride."

Like two little puppies, Daren and Bobby quietly got out of the car. Timmy stayed put. Daren held up the eight-track cartridge with the tape hanging out and showed it to his dad.

"Look, Dad, no CDs."

I started to laugh but realized the man wasn't about to, so I kept my laughter inside and faked a real smile. I looked at him and thought, he must have thought that was funny, right? I could see through his attempt to stay true to the anger he didn't feel. It was as though he had loaded the shotgun, or the Magnums in this case. Pulled the trigger, the nipples, but couldn't remember why. Instead, he turned and looked at my car. Oh, yes, I thought. After all, this is a man. Tits, belly and all, at the end of the day, he, we, are still men.

"What do you think? Nice car, ha?" I asked.

Roadrunner? He asked.

"Yeah."

"Never seen it before."

"Yeah, first time out of storage in years." Okay, I told myself, I got him hooked now, so I held out the keys.

"Let's take it for a spin."

As if I owed him something for stealing his kids for about half an hour, he instantly grabbed the keys.

Darren looked at his dad. "Dad, you don't know how to drive this car."

The man looked at his boy and smiled. There I thought, now that's more like it. Daren continued his effort to save his father from what he thought was an embarrassing situation.

"Really, Dad, it's really different."

He pointed at the stick shift. "Look, it's got a pistol grip."

He ignored his son and backed up to get an overall look at my car. Placed both hands on his waist and said.

"Nice, very nice."

I realized that the voice I had heard many times, didn't match the voice that I was hearing. Somehow, his voice sounded different, but I couldn't figure it out. Then it came to me, this must be the voice when not arguing.

The song, "SHE'S A BRICK, HOUSE", started blaring out of the car. I reached in and ejected the tape. I looked at Timmy, who was still in the car and had pushed the tape in, but I said nothing. My attempt to defuse the situation wasn't over. I pulled myself back out of the car and looked at the man.

"Sorry, I went through a Disco phase back then."

He looked at me like saying, what?

"Very small phase," I said.

"Yeah, so did I. I still have my Angel Flights." (Polyester 1970s vest and pants combination.)

Unable to reject my next thought and my actions. I snuck a quick look at his belly and his protruding 44

Magnums and thought, can you imagine that in polyester? He caught my quick look and my expression and responded.

"They obviously don't fit anymore. Not that I would wear them if they did."

Timmy popped his little head out of the car and said, "Angel Flights? I think mom has that perfume."

We both laughed, Darren joined in, then Bobby, and not to be left out, Timmy quickly joined in on the laughter. The kids, not knowing why, but knowing that laughing was better than not.

"Dale," he said, "my name is Dale."

"I'm Roberto, good to meet you."

"Same here, so, taking your car for a spin offer is still on the table?"

"Let's do it."

"Let's do it," yelled Timmy.

I walked around to the other side and got in. I looked at my car from the passenger side and felt it as I've never had. It almost felt like a different car. I realized I had never been a passenger in my own car. How can that be? I found myself thinking of all those memories my friends and my brother Ernie experienced from this very seat. All those nights, the cruising, the excitement, the boredom. For years, I sat inches from where I sat at this very moment, yet, I had never seen it from this perspective. Would life be any different if only I had been the passenger now and then? Do small actions change the trajectory of our lives? And if so, how much and how would we know? Are the odds of our decisions fifty-fifty if our perspective is always from the same side of the coin?

The other side of the coin on this day will finally come to be. I tried to make myself comfortable, but couldn't.

"Man, it feels weird being on this side," I said.

Dale stretched, looked around, and said, "man this feels great. Lots of legroom."

"Dad," said Timmy, "that's a pistol grip. You have to be careful because when you pull or push on it, this car peels out."

"It does?" Asked Dale, with a fake surprised expression.

I quickly responded. "Not really, it is a little fast though, you know."

"Oh yes it does, I can still smell the burning rubber, it stinks," said Bobby.

Dale looked at them and back to me. "So you really burned them off?"

"A little," I said.

"A little? A lot, it was cool, man." Said Daren.

"Oh, yeah?" Said Dale. "You guys like peeling out?"

All three said, "yeah."

"Okay, maybe we can do a little bit of that," He then looked around, not knowing what to do.

"Where's reverse?" Dale asked.

Daren leaned over his father's shoulder and whispered, "I told you."

"Well, most cars have it on the gearshift, but this one doesn't."

"I tried to tell.....,"

I interrupted Daren. "It's alright, we've got it." I showed him with my finger. "Far right and back."

Dale and I looked at Daren, letting him know that everything was going to be alright.

"You see? It's not hard." Said Dale.

He turned the ignition and the engine revved up. Dale eased off the throttle. "Sorry, man, sorry..."

"It's all cool," I said, "don't worry."

He grabbed the gear shift and tried putting it in reverse, and we heard the sound of grinding gears.

"Oops, oh, what', what...?"

I put my hand over his and moved the gear shift into reverse. "There you are." I pulled my hand away.

"Oh, oh yeah, sorry, I sort of forgot."

"It's alright man, we're good."

After a nice ride, we ended up on top of a hill looking down on the city. We stopped earlier to get snacks for the kids, and a couple of beers for us. The kids devoured the snacks and faded into a nap. Daren, the oldest, would lift his head whenever he heard something interesting. After a few sips of beer, I showed Dale my yearbook and found myself in the middle of an interrogation.

"So, you're really going back?"

"Yeah, I think so."

"Really?"

"Yeah."

"Why?" Said Dale, "What do you think, that all your friends are gonna be there waiting for you? Just like they were back in high school?"

"Well....," Roberto started to say when Dale interrupted.

"Really? Most of those people are either gone, dead, or have changed so much you're not gonna recognize them."

I thought of that possibility and felt as though someone had punched me in the gut. I questioned why I felt what I was feeling. As if to move away from that, I responded.

"Yeah, yeah, I know, but what am I supposed to do? Forget it all?"

I paused and could see that his words and not mine had sent Dale into deep thought. It was as though he had skipped a few seconds and didn't hear what I said. After a few seconds, he looked at me and waited for me to say something. It was as if I hadn't responded to his negative rant on one of the happiest times of my life. I repeated myself.

"Am I supposed to pretend that none of it ever happened?"

Dale turned and looked toward the front of the car and caught a glimpse of himself in the rearview mirror. He looked past his reflection and, from what I could tell, into his next.

He went on. "God knows I would forget it all," he paused and shook his head slowly. "Most of the people in my past were assholes, fucked up people, if you want to call them that. Couldn't care less if I ever saw them again."

Silence and sadness filled my head, and I could only assume that it wasn't only in mine. From the looks of things, I'm not sure if Dale knew what he was truly feeling. He acted tough, but it was sadness that I saw. I, on the other hand, felt as though the people in his past were the same ones in mine and had to respond. To protect them from the onslaught coming out of this man's mouth. After all, as with all people in high school, we were just kids being kids. Innocent of the charges at hand, but somehow responding to what he said wasn't an option. He turned to me as he recognized the seriousness of his words and backpedaled a little.

"Oh, well, maybe not." He raised his eyebrows and tightened his lips.

But it was too late, his words had found a home within me. It had been a while since I had a conversation with anyone, let alone about anything as deep as this. And from what I was feeling, it was gonna be a long time till. I tried to make sense of these feelings but left it alone. After all, these were feelings forced to the surface by words spoken by this man sitting next to me. A man who, at work, I would refer to in my head as work-people. In other words, people I worked with, and I mean work and nothing else. Somehow, that allowed me the separation to exist in a hostile environment, such as the one I found myself in. But at work, unlike here, it was easy, the steps were laid out for me. It was a matter of procedure. All I had to do was follow the steps, one, always led to two, two, to three, and so on. But the drive home from work wasn't as easy. Time to be filled by random thoughts could unravel an otherwise ordinary day.

With that thought out of my head, I placed my yearbook on the dash. I looked out the side window. I waited for that moment of silence to expire. I could see on the reflection that Dale was also looking out the side window. As if time failed to pass, the seconds went on for much too long. I turned back to my old friend on the dash, my yearbook. Hoping it would help me get beyond this uneasiness, I grabbed it and held it against my belly. I felt a sensation, otherwise known as the, I gotta pee sensation, which gave me the door I was looking for.

"Time to give some of it back," I said as I rubbed my belly.

Dale took the hook, looked at me and said, "yeah, me too."

We exited the car and this thought occurred to me. I

hope he's not one of those guys who likes to stand right next to his buddies and talk while they urinate. That was something I never understood. Why do men do that? And do women do that as well? Maybe they do and I don't know. Not standing, I'm sure, unless there's really something I don't know about.

As all this was going through my head, the thought of being fearful of all urinals as a kid came to me. Especially trough urinals. Man, I hated those. I remember standing at a urinal so nervous I couldn't pee. I thought, man, if I don't pee now, they're gonna think I have a problem. There was something about standing chest high to a bunch of old dudes pissing like racehorses that I found disturbing and intimidating. The sound of piss rushing out and hitting the urinal. The splattering, the farting, the smell, oh my God the smell was horrible. There was pissing and farting everywhere. And what's with the spitting? Why do men spit before urinating or after? That was something that as a kid, I never understood. Hell, what am I thinking, I still don't. One time I was in a public bathroom by myself, so I thought. Got done peeing and thought, hey, I'm gonna give it a try. Let's see what happens. Here I go. I mustered up some spit, took a deep breath, and spat. Wow, I thought, nothing. I felt nothing.

"Oughta boy, that's the way to do it."

I heard from a man that to this day, I have no idea where he came from. With one hand on my peepee and the other on my waist, I look over my shoulder to see this man walk up and park right next to me. Why, why next to me? And why am I an oughta boy, for urinating, for spitting? My next action was to put it away. You know, it, I zipped up and got the hell out of there.

On another childhood defining experience, I stood in what I would call a packed-dude-urinal. There I stood like an animal, next to the other animals. Exposed in the middle of an act of nature. An act so natural, that one would think no thinking was required. But as always, I somehow managed to complicate matters. And as always, a solution came to me. A solution to an otherwise simple task. A step by step list of instructions I would conjure up in my head to help me get through this so-called natural act. So one day as I stood in front of a packed-dude-urinal with my in-head-instructions. I started to go through my list at the very beginning of this natural act, when I felt natural piss hitting my natural arm. I looked up at the man next to me, hoping that my look would make him move over. But instead, he looked down at me and said.

"What's the matter, can't make it trickle?"

Oh, great, that's all I need. Suddenly, I had two belly buttons. I put it back in my pants, not that it already wasn't, and walked away defeated, belittled, no pun intended. Needless to say, urinals and I don't get along. Later on, on that piss splatter on the arm night, I laid in bed and realized that I hadn't showered, or washed my arms. "Oh shit," I said, aloud, to my surprise.

"Oh shit what?" My brother Ernie asked, whom I shared a room with.

"I gotta go pee."

"Again? You just went."

"I have to go again, give me a break."

I walked into the bathroom and instantly turned on the facet, grabbed the soap, and washed my hands and arms. I dried them and said, "there, much better." I walked out and into bed.

"What you do, piss in the sink?" Asked Ernie, being the smart ass that he was. Yep, that's my brother Ernie, never a break.

I came out of those thoughts to see myself urinating and thought of how weird that was. To have water come out of a body part. I can only imagine how scary it must have been the very first time I saw water coming out of me. Boy, I wish I could remember that. Well, maybe not. I came out of that thought and looked next to me to see no Dale, good. I looked over my shoulder to see him on the opposite side of the car urinating. And then, a fart. That's right, Dale farted. Yep, nothing has changed. So what's a man to do, but to do what men do best. I got done urinating and yes, I too, farted. We got back in the car and felt relieved.

"Oh, much better," said Dale.

"I hear that. That brought back some memories,"

"Oh yeah, like what?"

"You know, farting memories," I said as I tried to keep a straight face.

"Farting memories?" He asked and laughed quietly.

"Yeah, good old farting memories. Kid farting memories to be more specific." I also laughed quietly.

"Kid farting memories, that's funny," said Dale.

"Yeah, when we were kids, farting was funnier. You know what I mean? Not that it isn't now, but it was funnier as a kid. There was something about the innocence of farting."

Dale laughed freely and looked back to see if the kids woke up and asked, "the innocence of farting?"

I had to go on. "Yeah, every fart was like the first."

"Oh my god, that's funny," said Dale

"I'll tell you what's also funny. The first time I heard a bush fart."

"A bush?" Dale asked, with a puzzled half-smile expression, wondering if he heard me correctly.

"Yeah, I remember that like it was yesterday, man. I think I was eleven, my brother and I were hunting with our dad. My dad stopped and handed my brother the rifle and said." 'You guys stay here, I'll be right back.' "He went over to the bushes just like we did a little while ago. But he actually went into the bushes. We waited and looked around, birds chirping, a slight breeze, and then." I paused.

Dale looked at me like what? I made the loud sound of a long fart. Dale instantly laughed. I stopped making the sound, and gave him an expression like saying, told you.

"You see, funny!" I said. "Man, that fart was louder than hell. Man, my brother and I died laughing. We looked toward where the fart came from and saw a bush moving. Annnnnd then another fart. I'm telling you. It looked like the bush was farting."

I paused as we both laughed quietly. I went on.

"I tell you what, the burning bush....has nothing....on the farting bush. Not a thing. Is the farting bush in the bible? I don't think so."

I paused and looked at Dale and waited for him to say something, but Dale was laughing so hard he couldn't talk.

He finally said, "in the bible?"

"Yeah man, at least an honorable mention or something, I mean why not?"

I paused so we could catch our breaths. I went on.

"My dad walked out of the bushes and saw us laughing. He walked up to us with this serious expression and in a

61

deep voice, and in Spanish, said. 'You think that's funny? It is impossible for a man to piss and not fart. No matter what. You think you are not going to fart, but you will fart. That's just the way it is, impossible.' He took the rifle from Ernie and walked off. Ernie looked at me and asked. 'Is he serious?' I said, 'I guess, I don't know'".

I stopped talking and shook my head slowly.

"What?" Asked Dale.

"Oh, you want me to go on?"

"Well, you were shaking your head like something else was going on." Said Dale

"Actually you're right. After hearing that, I tried like hell not to fart every time I pissed after that."

Dale looked at me, trying to figure out if I was kidding.

"I'm serious. I'm telling yeah. A few days later, I stood frozen in front of the toilet after pissing. Trying like hell not to fart. I held it tight, man. I'm telling you; I was going to do it."

I paused, Dale giggled.

"I slowly zipped up my pants, started to turn around, and it slipped out."

Dale covered his mouth, trying not to laugh out loud.

I went on. "Literally, the fart slipped out, man. What a disappointment."

Dale's face was beat red from chuckling quietly in an attempt not to wake up the kids. I shook my head slowly again and went on.

"I had it in the bag. You know, the non farting trophy. I had it in my hands and let it slip away. Well, actually, I farted it away. What are you gonna do? So I stood there disappointed as hell. I then said, 'Damn, he's right, it is impossible.'"

62

Dale could not stop laughing.

"And then, I heard my mother say, who I guess was walking past the bathroom." she said, 'Mijo, are you all right?'

"Yes, Mom," I said. I couldn't believe she actually heard me. 'Okay', she said, 'don't stay in there too long.'"

"No way man." Said Dale. "So you were actually trying not to fart for real?"

"Of course. I was as serious as a fart not to fart. If you don't get my drift"

We both laughed again, caught our breaths, and I continued.

"Yep, good old fashion farting memories. After a while, I just gave up, farted and enjoyed it. If it's impossible, it's impossible. What are you gonna do?"

"So, how long did it take you to figure it out?"

"Figure out what?"

"That it was possible."

"It is?"

"Yeah," he said, giggling real hard. Once again, trying not to laugh out loud.

I kept going. "Come on, what just happened after we both got done pissing, what exactly happened Dale? Ha?"

We laughed quietly and looked over our shoulder to see the kids toss and turn and woke up to see us laughing.

"Well, I think it's time to take the boys home." Said Dale. "It's getting late."

"Let's do it," I said, still laughing.

From the back seat, we heard Timmy say.

"Let's do it"

We both looked back to see Timmy smiling.

"Your kids are great, Dale, you're really lucky."

"Yeah, I am," he said with a big smile, which faded into concern and then to nothing.

I knew exactly what he was thinking. It was time to go home and face the wife. That's what he was thinking.

He turned the car on and with that sound, the smile came back.

He paused and looked at me. "You don't mind if I drive home, do ya?"

"No, go for it, I'm so lazy, I don't think I can drive."

"Right on man," he said, and we drove off.

About half an hour later, we drove up to a scene I had experienced earlier. But this time it was a middle aged slightly overweight woman standing in front of my garage. She stood with an expression I could only surmise was the expression I had heard, but not seen. It was like a helmet or a chest plate one would wear to battle.

"Oh, I hope she's not too mad," Dale said as if he was one of the kids.

Instantly, she walked toward us. This was a sign of attack, don't give them a chance to prepare, put them on the defensive. We barely came to a stop, and she leaned into Dale's window.

"Where the hell have you been?"

"Jesus, woman, let me get out of the car." Said Dale.

There, those were the voices, the voices I'd heard many times but hadn't seen. The kids woke up to the sound of fun screeching to a halt. Dale got out, I got out. I helped the kids to get out.

"Come on, we're home," I said. Even my voice sounded different.

With her hands on her waist, she looked down at Dale as she looked up at him and said, "do you have any idea how long you've been gone?"

"What's the problem? I told you I was coming over here. You saw me walk over here. What's the big deal?"

"I'll tell you what the big deal is. When you said you were coming over here, you said, I'm gonna see what that prick is doing with my kids. You did say prick, right?"

Before Dale could answer, she said. "Oh, and by the way, that was three hours ago. Three hours, Dale!"

Dale pretended not to look at a watch he didn't have. His half smile apologetic expression barely made it my way. He looked at his wife and said.

"You know what, let me introduce you to Roberto. This is Roberto." He pointed with an open hand.

"Hello," I said with a voice I couldn't recognize. Focus, you are not Dale, I heard in my head. Trying not to be rude, she sort of waved to me in a dismissive way and stormed off. She stopped and turned back to face him.

"You know, there is such a thing as pay phones, Dale."

"I didn't think about it." Hoping this would end it.

"How am I supposed to know." She started to say when Dale interrupted her.

"All right, all right already, I'm sorry."

She walked off. Dale shook his head and looked at me as if to say, can you believe this? And then out of nowhere, and to my surprise, I grabbed my crotch and mouthed.

"You need to grow some," forgetting that the kids were right there.

With his chest sunken in, and shoulders drooping, he faked a smile and looked at his kids. "Come on, let's go," and walked off without saying another word.

At that point, I knew what was about to happen, as

65

Dale did, and could do nothing but feel sorry for them. I looked at my car and was comforted by its expression, one that never changed no matter what. I clicked the remote to the garage door and walked in. I heard the argument start in the distance.

"Oh, well. It is what it is," I said aloud.

I grabbed a cigar from my workbench. I opened the garage fridge and grabbed a beer, and as the fridge closed, I looked down to see my hands. One with a beer, the other with a cigar, and felt as though I was looking at someone else's hands. The moment passed, and I asked myself, why am I looking at my hands? I felt a little out of place, sort of lost. I looked around and saw my car waiting for me and felt a smile come onto my face. I grabbed a chair, walked out and placed it facing my car. The argument got louder in the background. I reached into my car, grabbed my yearbook, and sat facing my car. I lit my cigar, opened my beer, and opened the yearbook to see the piece of the missing page. This was a showstopper. Why is this page missing? Before allowing myself to reach any conclusions, not that I could've, I turned the pages and stopped at the Owl Cafe.

Instantly, I thought of the times I had called the Owl and spoke to a waitress named Amanda. And with that, the feeling of serenity and that everything was going to be alright came on to me. I needed to touch, to feel the Owl Cafe, not only to see it. Before that thought exited my head, my hand had reached out and touched the page. It was paper, nothing but paper with an image. But there was more to it than that. How can paper have so much feeling, so much emotion? It was almost telepathic. It conveyed more than what I saw. The pages projected thought, a connection. I could only assume that it spoke all languages. I don't know why that came to mind, but it did. And now, I have to ask, is thought a language? With all that aside, it felt good to touch the page. And for that reason alone, I need to go with it, to accept what it conveyed.

"Sit here, and watch Amanda from not so far." I heard from somewhere in this head of mine.

And as I stared at the Owl Cafe, a feeling slowly came over me. It wasn't a good or a bad feeling. It was unlike anything I ever felt. I felt a separation of being. I don't know how I knew that, but I did. And for the first time, I saw the Owl from within. I felt as if I was looking at its soul. That thought had never occurred to me, to think that an image had a soul, but why not? After all, the image is the shell, the body, the exterior of an otherwise living thing. An imprint of a once living entity. And within a soul, there is breath, a heartbeat, life, the living. So why does this surprise me? And then, I heard it. Noise....noise that was coming from within the soul of the Owl Cafe. I heard a bell ring and someone said.

"Your timing really stinks, you know that?"

A voice I had heard but never seen. Instantly, I placed the face to the voice. I turned, and there she was, Amanda. She put the phone on hold, walked up to the cook line, and gave him a dirty look as she picked up her food.

"I still love you no matter what," said the cook as she walked off.

The way in which she walked had never occurred to me. One thing for sure, her walk I liked. The gracefulness of her stride, the curvature, and strength of her back, as she held all that food on a platter with one hand. It was movement I had never seen. I had always pictured her on the phone, smiling, looking around as she spoke to me, but never walking. Which is stranger when I really think about it. Often when I thought of women, I saw them walking, but not with Amanda, but from this day forward, all that will change. She walked up to a table, expertly positioned the stand she carried with her right hand, and sat her tray on the stand. A homeless man walked up to her, she turned to him and said. "Leaving already?"

The man nodded. He extended his hand and opened it to reveal a few coins.

"Oh, no, that's all right, honey. You be careful out there. Okay?"

Disappointed she wouldn't take his coins, he turned and walked toward the front door.

"Do we get free coffee?" Asked one of her customers at the table.

"Oh, he's been around for years," she said with a smile.

"So, how long do we have to come here before we get free coffee?"

"Oh, about thirty years."

"Thirty years! He hasn't been around for thirty years," said the other customer.

"Oh, I don't know about that." Said Amanda. "The older girls tell me he's been here forever. I've been here for ten, and he's been here the whole time."

"He doesn't look old enough," said the customer.

"Oh, I don't know, it's hard to tell what's going on under all that hair. Anything else I can get you?"

"Thirty years, wow! No, I think that's all for now," said the customer, not really believing her.

She walked toward the front desk, and then.....I don't

know why, and I don't know how. I found myself watching her from outside, through the front window. How can this be? I tried to make sense of it, but couldn't. I asked myself, why make sense of it? And there it was again, that warm feeling of acceptance. Walk with me, I heard from I don't know where, as warmth covered this exterior of mine. I watched her as she picked up the phone, and could see her lips say.

"Hello, hello, oh great," and hung up.

She looked down to see the coins on the front desk and smiled. She picked them up, and I clearly heard her say.

"Oh, how sweet."

Frozen in that moment, I waited as if I had a choice, as if I had the means. Silence no longer escaped me, as the inevitability of that very moment awaited. And as always, once I saw that moment behind me. I picked up my bike, took my five steps, stopped, and as always, I turned to see her glance, but was invisible to no one there.

6. THROUGH YOUNG EYES

I walked away from that, not knowing what I didn't
see, and as always, looked forward to seeing her another
day. A mile or so down the road I saw an old truck that
was exactly like the one I used to own after high school.
The same year, the same color. I thought, wow, this thing
is amazing. This can easily be my old truck. I instantly fell
into a dream or a memory, not sure what it was, but as
always I went along for the ride. The next thing I knew I
was driving my truck. Its rustic old smell penetrated my
every cell and took me where space nor time dare not let
me go. I could see and smell the Russian River to my left
as I approached the old metal bridge right here in
Forestville. It was a place that was dear to my heart but at
times tormented my brain for reasons I can't explain. But
today, on this very now? It was joy that I felt. I drove onto

the bridge, and stopped. I looked down at the water, and thought of all the wonderful memories. As kids, we used to swim under and all around this bridge. The next thing I knew was the sound of my brother Ernie calling out to me.

"How long are you gonna stand there?"

Next came the sound of Claude, saying.

"He's frozen again."

Claude lived across the highway from us. He was French and as bored as we were, so we became friends. He was older, about fourteen, and became sort of a big brother to us. I came out of my memory to what I could only assume was another. I looked around and realized that I was on the other side of the railing. I couldn't believe it. I moved my brain away from not believing and I looked down to see Ernie and Claude looking up at me. How can this be?

"What are you doing?" Yelled Ernie from below.

Confused as I could possibly be, all I could say was, "what do you mean?"

"Are you gonna jump or what?" Asked Ernie.

Claude had had enough. "He's a baby, he's scared, leave him. Come on, let's go upstream. The rapids are perfect right now," said Claude.

Ernie's frustration was visible on his face. "What is up with you?"

"What do you mean?" I yelled.

Claude shook his head, grabbed his inner tube, and took off. "Come on, let's go."

Ernie grabbed his inner tube and took off.

"Hey," I yelled. "Wait, wait, I'm jumping, wait for me."

I took a deep breath. I saw my right foot extend out. My foot was extending out to nothing. Wow, what an idea.

I then felt my left leg push out. It was like my left foot said, well, he, my right foot took off, so what choice do I have? I felt the nothing before me. It was nothing, that which I felt and realized it for the first time ever.

Next came the fear, but it was as if it was being served. It was there for me to take, or to reject. This option in reality left me no choice. It was adrenaline that which I felt next. Before today, I would've closed my eyes and hoped for the best, but this time I took what was being served and savored every second, every inch of the fall. I kept my eyes open the whole time. It was about thirty feet to the water but this time it felt like sixty and I liked it. I felt my hair leave my forehead and ears and felt the wind rush through my eyelashes. My arms wanted to be left behind, so I thought, but I was wrong. It was a million year old memory playing out in my brain resulting in actions I had no idea my arms were capable of. Was this muscle memory left behind? Stored in some obscure part of my brain, waiting to be used. It was at that precise moment that a second memory came to me in the form of emotion.

It felt like I had done this thousands of times. As if an earlier version of myself from millions of years ago had taken over and knew exactly what to do. My arms became wings, rudders, or something. I could use them to steer my fall. They were moving in all sorts of directions making sure that I was perfectly vertical. My upper body wanted to lean forward, my brain went to work. My arms made the quick correction and kept me from leaning forward. I then realized that my eyes were perfectly focused on the water. They were proximity sensors, calculating the distance that passed me and knowing exactly that which was before me.

My eyes were scanning, approximating, sending data to my brain that it used to control my body parts to precisely hit the spot my eyes choose for me.

My toes suddenly pointed. I hit the water, it was more like I split the water. I felt its pressure against my skin as it rushed up past my legs, body, and face. I felt my toes hit the sand. The bottom of my feet felt it next. I pushed up with my legs as hard as I could. My arms and hands were already above my head. My first stroke was with both hands, my second with my right, followed by my left. I then saw a Salamander right next to me. I couldn't believe it. It matched my every action as we crawled up through the water. Three strokes and my face felt the sunshine just above the water. Next came the spray of my exhale reflecting the sunlight in all directions. I then felt the peacefulness of the moment, once again as if I had done this thousands of times before.

"Good one." Said Claude. He looked at Ernie. "Did you see that?"

Ernie shook his head as if to say, whatever, but had to acknowledge my jump.

"Um, not bad."

"That was pretty damn good," Said, Claude

I swam out as fast as I could. Claude placed his hand on the top of my head and pushed me forward away from the water.

"Now that was a jump. Good job." He said.

"Thanks"

I grabbed my innertube and we headed to the rapids. I was ten years old, my brother was eleven, and as I said earlier Claude, was fourteen. His family had moved to Forestville from France a few years ago. They spoke

French around the house and he had a sister that was beautiful and sexy. And Yes, I thought that at ten years old. His mom and dad were as cool as cool could be. His dad smoked a pipe and they seemed to read books all the time. Being around them felt like being in a movie or something. By far some of the friendliest, coolest people to be around.

We headed upstream where the river narrowed. The rapids were perfect in the early spring while the water was still raging but not muddy as it was during the winter. The rules for good inner tubing were simple. Rule number one, hold on to your inner tube. Rule number two, if you lose your tube, you better swim fast and go with it, or you'll be out of fun in a quick way. Not only that, if you didn't have enough money to buy another, you were out of luck for the whole summer. So we held on no matter what. Technique was important. The idea was to start just before the beginning of the rapids where the water was somewhat calm. The problem was that in those areas, the sand at the bottom was always shifting. So we would step into the water, plant our foot in the sand, and move it around to get a firm footing. Claude being older and stronger would always go first. He took a couple of steps into the water and shifted his feet around.

"How is the sand?" I asked, hoping he would give me good important information that would help me when it was my turn.

He took one more step and he was gone.

"It's perfect," he yelled.

"Gee thanks," I said.

Ernie stepped in, he shifted his feet around, and just as I was about to ask, how is it, he was gone. Now it was my turn. I put my arm through the hole of my innertube and held it against my body to make sure I wouldn't lose it. I took my first step in. I shifted my feet around feeling the sand give under my feet until it was good and solid. I took a few more, felt the sand give away, and froze.

"Yahoo, it's hauling ass man!" Yelled Claude.

"Hurry, it's perfect," Ernie yelled.

Now that was the sound of fun. I took one more step and the water was just above my knees. I positioned the tube to my butt, and squatted down to where the water was just below the tube. If the tube dipped into the water with my feet still in the sand, it'll spin me around and I'll go downstream backward. So I dropped into the water and lifted my feet at the same time and I was on my way. We ran the rapids until the cold water forced us out. Claude dropped his inner tube on the sand. I laid mine to his right, and Ernie placed his to Claude's left. We laid on the inner-tubes and felt the warm spring sun hit our cold bodies. It felt terrific. Claude shoved my head away from him and said. "Good job man, you kicked ass today."

After a while we were bored.

"Hey, can we go upstream? Maybe there's something cool up there." I said.

Claude jumped up. "Let's do it."

We got up.

"What about our innertubes?" I asked.

"Let's hide them in the bushes." Said Ernie.

"Good idea," said Claude.

"Oh man, this is gonna be cool," I said.

A new feeling of excitement came over us. We picked up our innertubes and headed for the bushes. Even hiding them was exciting. It was like we knew something no one else did. We hid them, backed away, and looked at the bushes.

"Looks good." Said Ernie.

"Yep, let's go!" Said Claude. He ended the word go, really loud.

I couldn't wait. Claude took off running. Ernie took off and I was right behind them. It was exciting to get away from the same spot we had been at so many times. I always wondered what was beyond the rocky cliffs as the river narrowed and I was about to find out.

"So this is an adventure, right?" I asked.

We all stopped. Claude looked at me and then at Ernie. He smiled as we all looked at each other and said.

"Yep, this is an adventure,"

I could see Ernie's brain ticking. His smile got bigger.

"Man this is cool." Said Ernie.

"Right on, let's do this. Let's go on an adventure." Said Claude.

We took off walking side by side at a fast pace. There was something about walking side by side on the sand and rocks that made me feel like I was in a movie. It was like we were walking across the desert in search of a lost city or something. I could feel and hear the sand and rocks as they shifted and rubbed against each other under my sockless tennis shoes. Everything seemed different, louder, closer to my eyes. It was like everything was magnified. The day had a brand new feel and I liked it. We walked for about half a mile and I had to look back. It was as if I wanted to make sure the bridge was still there. It was, but it was small. It felt weird to me. To see it smaller was odd. I saw the distance between us and the bridge and not just the bridge. It was like my brain was measuring. I was fully aware of the distance, and I became aware that I was aware. The sound of Ernie and Claude walking away brought me out of that observation. I turned around and caught up with them.

"What were you looking at?" Asked Claude.

"The bridge."

"The bridge?" Asked Claude as he wrinkled his forehead.

Ernie looked at me. "It's just right there," he said, "we were just there, I don't get it."

Claude looked at me and sort of laughed. "Yeah, what the hell?"

Ernie shook his head. "What a weirdo."

Claude and Ernie looked at each other and laughed. At that precise moment, it became obvious to me that I knew something they didn't. Or that I had noticed something they hadn't. I had to say something. I stopped, I turned around, and pointed.

"You see, it looks smaller."

They looked at me, questioning, but not knowing what to say.

"The bridge got smaller as we walked away," I added.

"Well no shit. What? You want it to get bigger?" Said Ernie.

"No, I mean..." Claude interrupted me.

"Ernie is right. You are a weirdo."

He placed his hand on my head and pushed it back. Like saying, get out of here, and he took off running.

"Come on, let's make the bridge really tiny."

"WEIRDO!" Yelled Ernie and took off.

I ran after them, but couldn't let it go.

"Weirdo? You're the weirdo, you kill mosquitoes with farts."

Claude stopped and bent over laughing. Ernie turned around and stopped me with his hands and pushed me back.

"Liar, I do not," Ernie yelled at me.

"Wait a minute," said Claude, "you actually killed Mosquitoes with farts?"

"That's right," I said, "one night….."

"No, no he's lying." Yelled Ernie.

"No, I'm not. He was on his bed and…."

"You're a weirdo," yelled Ernie, "and a liar."

"Oh, my god, that can't be true." Said Claude.

"It is, it is true," I quickly added. "He killed a mosquito with a fart."

"No, I didn't." Yelled Ernie and looked at Claude to make his case.

"I'd be bragging if I was you." Said Claude. "That is badass man."

Ernie looked at me. "You hear that? I'm badass." He pointed at my face, almost poking my eye. "You're a weirdo and I am badass."

He grabbed my nipple and twisted.

"Ow, ow, cut it out. You shit farthead." I pushed him, I turned away, and placed my hand on my nipple as I bent over in pain. "Ow, man that hurt"

"What a baby. You're a weirdo and a baby!" Said Ernie.

"Okay, stop, stop!" Yelled Claude as he tried to stop laughing. "So what happened? I gotta hear this man."

He leaned toward me. I looked at Ernie who was suddenly full of pride. My story had backfired. No pun intended.

"So what happened?" Asked Claude.

I was about to start my story when Ernie jumped in. "So I was laying there on my bed…"

"Hey, hey, I'm the one that saw it. You just fart like you always do."

Claude dropped his head and shook it as if he couldn't believe it.

I went on. "So he was on his bed in his pajamas, I was in my bed. I saw this mosquito flying over by where he was. And it was flying right next to his butt."

Claude laughed a little. "And then what?"

"So I sat up and I was gonna say, hey be careful there's…" I made the sound of a roaring fart.

"He ripped one. It was a huge fart and boom the mosquito flung over and went down."

Claude and Ernie laughed really hard. It felt good to see them laugh at my story. I too, laughed but controlled myself to finish the story.

"I told him, I said hey, you just killed a mosquito with your fart. He said, 'No way.' I was yeah man you did. He said, 'no I didn't.' So I went over and looked for it and…"

"So wait a minute," said Claude. "You looked for the mosquito?"

"Yeah, and I found it. It was dead. He wasn't moving. He killed it with his fart I'm telling you."

"That is so funny." Said Claude as he continued to laugh.

Our laughter finally faded.

"Okay, let's go." Said Claude, "come on."

We took off and my nipple pain was back. About half a mile later we saw something big ahead.

"What is that?" Asked Claude.

"I don't know. It looks like a car." Said Ernie.

"Hey, wait. There's another one right over there." I said.

We took off running. We got right up to one of them.

"Man, look at this," said, Claude

"Why is there a car right here in the river?" I asked.

"I don't know." He said. "Maybe it got caught up in the water during a storm or something."

"Do you think somebody died?" I asked.

"I don't know." He said.

Hey, what if there's someone inside?" Said Ernie.

"Like dead inside?" I asked.

"Oh, that would be cool." Said Claude. We looked at him, like, what? "I mean, cool but not cool because somebody died. But I don't think so. This car has been out here for years I'm sure."

"What if there's a skeleton inside?" I asked.

We looked at each other.

"No way," said Claude. "I mean look at this thing, it's rusted and everything."

He walked around to the side of the car. He looked in it like it was no big deal.

"Nothing," he said, "nothing but sand and rocks."

The driver's door was gone. The seats were also gone. Ernie got in and sat on the sand as if he was driving and grabbed the steering wheel.

"Man, this thing is cool. Look at all this chrome. It looks almost new." Said Ernie.

"Yeah, that's weird." Said Claude.

"Hey, there's another one over there." I said and pointed to a car in the far distance."

We took off, We ran around a bunch of trees, bamboo, and bushes. I saw a big puddle of water right next to the trees. I stopped and couldn't believe how deep it was.

"Hey, what are you doing?" Asked Claude.

"I looked in the water. "Hey, there's fish in there."

"Really?"

They came back.

"Wow, you're right. Look at that," said, Claude.

"Holy moly, those are big fish. Look." Ernie pointed.

"They are big. Right there, can you believe it?" Said Claude.

"How did they end up here?" I asked.

Claude looked from the puddle to the river. "I guess they got stuck there."

"What do you mean?" Ernie asked.

"I've seen this before, on National Geographic. When a river gets smaller, some fish get stuck. They get separated from the river and get stuck like right here." He pointed at the fish.

"So what's gonna happen to them?" I asked, feeling sorry for the fish.

"They're gonna die. When the water dries up, they'll die." Said Claude.

"They're gonna die? When the water dries up they'll die?" Before anyone answered me, I said, "maybe we can help them."

"We'll help them alright," said Ernie. "Let's come back and fish them out."

Claude and Ernie got a devilish grin.

"I was just gonna say that." Said Claude.

"Fish them?" I asked.

"Yeah, we can come back later, or tomorrow with fishing poles." Said Ernie.

"Cool man, we're going fishing." Said Claude.

"You're gonna eat them?" I asked.

"Yeah, why not. What do you think Tuna is?" Asked Claude.

"Right on." Ernie.

I was stuck on the fish being stuck and couldn't get over that. I thought of how horrible it would be to get separated from the other fish in the river. To get stuck right there and the river is just right over there.

"Do you think the fish know the river is right there?" I asked Claude and pointed at the river.

"No, they're stupid, they don't know anything."

"How do you know that?" I asked.

"I just do," said Claude.

I felt sorry for them. I then had a vision of the fish crawling out of the water and toward the river. One of them stood up and said.

"Hey, look at me."

The other fish looked up and one by one they all stood and walked right up to the river and stopped. One of them looked back at the puddle and said.

"Look at that, this whole time we were right there."

They all looked back and nodded.

One of them said, "you're right. It's just right there. We should've done this a long time ago."

One of the ladyfish said, "I tried to tell you but you think you know it all."

"I don't remember you......"

"Hey, Roberto, hey." Said, Claude

I came out of my little fantasy and realized they had walked away, and I didn't know it.

Claude waved me over. "Come on, let's go. Let's go see another car."

We took off and once again I had to look back at the fish. Ernie caught me looking.

"What happened? Did it get smaller?"

I gave him a dirty look. We took off. We came around the other side of the trees. We stopped as we saw something we had never seen before.

"What the hell." Said Claude.

On the other side of a creek that fed into the river, were a bunch of cars lined up against the bank of the river and the creek. There were at least a hundred cars or more. It was like someone picked them up and stood them side by side like dominoes. Most had no hoods and none had windshields. Some had fenders, others didn't and most had doors missing. We looked at each other in disbelief.

"What do you think this is?" Ernie asked.

"I don't know," said Claude

Claude and Ernie looked around. I looked around but had no idea why. Claude's face got serious. Ernie's face got serious. My face got serious. Claude pulled his head back as if he was asking himself a question. Ernie pulled his head back as if he was asking himself a question. I actually asked a question.

"What's going on?"

"Shh," Ernie said.

I looked at him like what the hell. He put his finger to his lips.

Claude's expression had turned into a deep frown without me noticing it at first. What now?

"This is weird. Cool, but weird." Said Claude.

"What do you think?" Asked Ernie.

"I don't know." Said Claude.

I felt butterflies in my stomach. The feel of the day had changed and I didn't like it.

"Come on, let's go find out," said Claude. "Let's stay in the bushes as much as we can. And be quiet," he looked at me and raised his eyebrows.

We started walking.

"Why do we have to be quiet?" I asked.

"We just do." Said Claude.

"So what do you guys think this is?" I asked.

"I don't know. Some kind of place where old cars are thrown away I guess. I don't know." Said Claude.

"People throw away old cars?" I asked.

"Yeah, if they're no good you have to do something with them."

"Yeah, what else are you gonna do with it?" Said Ernie as if he knew what was going on.

Claude stopped and did another quick look around and squatted down. Ernie squatted, I squatted, but once again had no idea why.

Claude whispered. "Okay, here's our plan."

"We have a plan?" I asked.

"Ssh, shut up, and listen up." Said Ernie.

"Okay, here's the plan," said Claude.

"We're gonna stay in the bushes as far as we can."

He pointed at the bushes next to the creek. Ernie and I looked. Claude went on.

"We go all the way to where the creek is shallow and narrow and then we cross the creek." He paused. "Now this is important. We quickly get between the cars so no one will see us."

"Do you think there's people out here? I didn't see anybody." I said.

"There might be. Don't want to find out, that's for sure."

Claude paused and looked at me. I looked at him but had no idea why. I waited. He waited.

"What?" I asked.

"Do you want to see people out here?"

I couldn't tell if he was serious or not, so I just looked at him and said nothing.

"Okay, are you guys ready to go? Let's get to it," said Claude.

He was crouched and sort of stood. Ernie matched him. I sort of matched him, but didn't want to. We made our way toward the cars as we stayed in the bushes. The sound of twigs rustling was clear and loud to me. The feeling of leaves and debris shifting under my feet became evident to me. It was once again as if everything was magnified. Ernie accidentally broke a twig. Claude looked at him like, what the hell. Ernie made an oops face. Claude turned back around. Ernie looked at me as if he was Claude looking at him, but he was looking at me and he wasn't Claude, and I did not break a twig. Apparently, Ernie was stuck, mimicking everything Claude did, but this was going too far.

"What's your problem?" I said in a clear voice.

Claude instantly turned around and hushed me. I had had enough.

"There's no one here. What is going on with you guys."

I stood tall and looked around showing them that no one was here but us. I felt like the fish that finally realized the river was just right there. I wanted to walk right up to the water just like the fish. The next thing I knew, there I was, not at the water's edge, but crossing the creek. I got to the other side and leaned against one of the cars. I waved to them. They dropped into the bushes. I was like,

what is wrong with them? What a bunch of babies.
Claude's head came up from the bushes with his finger to
his lips hushing me. He pointed repeatedly toward my
right. He brought both hands up and gestured as if he was
pushing me back. I saw movement out of the corner of my
eye. I wanted to look but instead instantly got between the
cars and hid. I had no idea what I was hiding from, but I
was. I replayed Claude's gestures in my head. I backed up
and dropped down and into a car.

My heart pounded in my head as the sound of my
breathing reverberated off the metal car I was in. I leaned
forward just enough to look for Claude and saw him drop
into the bushes again. What the hell? I knew that couldn't
be good. I waited. I don't know what for, but I did. Hold
it, hold on, I told myself. Is that the sound of steps? No, it
can't be. If so, those are huge steps. I mean they are huge
steps. Is this possible? I heard one foot come down and
hit the gravel. The gravel gave under the enormous weight.
I heard the rear foot come up, and then a gap. What the
hell? I heard it come down and hit the gravel. Another
gap, what is this? A shadow slowly moved into my line of
sight. But what kind of shadow is this? It was a head. But
whose head is this? And why is this head so big? And why
is it moving so slow? Next came his long neck. And then
came this body of shadow that covered the entire car next
to me and the one I was in. That's it, I'm dead.

He, it, whatever it was, walked in slow motion. I was
gonna ask myself why, but what's the point? I felt like I
was in a movie. I waited for him to turn around and shoot
me. Throw a knife at me hitting me in the jugular. A
flamethrower, a bazooka, a hand grenade, something. I
was ready for my death at the hands of a monster. He

stopped, turned around, and I heard the absence of my breathing. The inescapable sound of my heart was nowhere to be found. Am I dead already? Is this what it's like to die? You just die, and suddenly you're on the other side. Not breathing, no heart pounding, not anything? After all, I am dead, so why would I be breathing? Why would my heart be pounding? But the fear I felt. This mean that I'm alive? If so, shouldn't I be breathing?

He took one step toward me, and he was right there in front of me. I heard the sound of his hand as he placed it on the car. It was loud. It was big. This man was humongous. His breathing was long and deep. It was like the breathing of an elephant. I don't know how I knew that, but I did. I swear I could hear his heart pounding. It was like a huge drum. The gaps between each beat were like a pause one would take to think about your next beat. But I knew that wasn't the case. No thinking was required for the heart to beat. These were the heartbeats of a huge animal. An animal called a man. His shadow and his figure came together as he bent down to look inside the very car I was in. His huge face came down into my line of sight. If I wasn't dead, I was about to.

"Hello," he said in such a deep voice, it almost sounded like another language.

"What are you doing in there?"

He sounded like a tape recorder that someone had slowed down with their hand. But this was no tape recorder, and I was not ready for my death. Let's do battle. A fight to the death. I heard in my head. But here I was looking at a giant that was calm, relaxed, almost cool. This I was not expecting, now what?

"You like this car?" He asked.

87

Is this happening? Am I going crazy? Am I making this up in my head?

"I'll sell it to you cheap, zero dollars. But that's for today only." He said and laughed. "Ho, ho, ho, ho."

His laugh sounded like a giant Santa. The sound of my rapid breathing and speeding heartbeat were back. The huge man smiled. Look at the size of those teeth was my next thought.

"It's okay, you can come out if you like. Or, you can stay in there all night. But it gets cold out here."

What is this man gonna do next? Sing me a lullaby or something? Wait a minute. He's trying to get me to come out. What am I thinking? Hey, what about Claude and Ernie? Maybe they can save me. I could see them in my head rushing through the creek. Water splashing up over their heads with every quick step as their feet plunged into the water at speeds so quickly the giant couldn't possibly do anything about it. They would make it across the creek and stab the giant in the heart with a huge spear. As I finished that thought, beyond this man's shoulder, I saw two figures running in the opposite direction. So much for that. I felt my heart sink further into my chest.

"That's okay, I have all night," he said.

He backed away and leaned against the next car. He crossed his legs and leaned way back as if he was relaxing. What is this? Is he gonna wait me out?

"I saw your friends across the creek. I don't think they're coming to help you." He said.

He squatted down and leaned toward me. This is it, fight or die. He extended his hand out. It was the size of my whole chest.

"Hi, my is….."

The next thing I knew, I was lying on a couch or some kind of bench car seat. I'm in a building? What the hell? I sat up and there, right there in front of me was a woman sitting reading a magazine. Maybe I'm not dead. She lowered the magazine and smiled.

"Well, how was your nap?"

I couldn't begin to answer. All I knew was that nothing and I mean nothing was as I thought it would be in the event anything like this would ever happen to me. Where's the dungeon, the ropes, the chains?

"He's awake!" Yelled the woman.

Oh, no, maybe the dungeon and the chains come later. I looked around to see I was in a barn or warehouse, or something. It was a big building. There was a phone on a plank of wood on top of three fifty-five gallon barrels. A calendar on the wall behind it. But this was no ordinary calendar. This calendar had naked women on it. Oh, this was a Playboy calendar. The lady saw me looking at it.

"I know, pretty aren't they?"

Now that was weird. A woman saying that naked women were pretty? Never heard that before.

"Well, are you coming or not?" Yelled the woman.

A door behind the counter, right next to the calendar opened. The giant walked in. My Dad walked in. Yes, that was my Dad. Boy, I bet he's mad. Wait a minute, how is this possible? It was weird seeing my Dad not only right here, but right next to a calendar with naked women. He saw me looking at him and then my eyes went to the calendar. He looked at the calendar and smiled. I then realized that he was carrying a car part. What? He walked right up to me and his smile got bigger. Oh, maybe he's not mad I thought. He placed his hand on my head and asked.

"Are you okay?"

I nodded. The giant also smiled and there it was again, the ho, ho, ho, of his big laughter. My Dad turned around and walked up to him. What's gonna happen next, are they gonna break into song or something? But no, instead, my dad placed the car part on the counter. I still wasn't sure of what was going on. All I knew was that my dad was glad that I was okay and that was a win for me. He pulled out his wallet and I guess he paid for the car part? Yes, that's what's going on here. He just bought a car part. I then thought, wait a minute. I was thinking I was gonna die. That maybe I was already dead. And my dad bought a car part?

"Gracias, Rick," said my Dad. "For the car part anyway. I don't know about that one."

He pointed at me. And there it was yet one more time, the laughter of the giant. Next came the sound of my dad and lady laughing. So what am I to do? I looked at everyone and I too laughed. There I was in a building with a giant, my dad, who just bought a car part, and a lady who thinks that naked ladies are pretty. What the hell?

7. THOUGHTS THAT WILL NOT PASS

I came out of that memory and looked around to see that I was still on the old metal bridge sitting in my truck. Question is, what now is this? I looked down, and my question was answered. There was no Ernie and there was no Claude. I looked downstream to where the river was wide and slow-moving with shrubbery right up to the water's edge. Some trees extended out and over the river. Oh boy, do I have memories of those days. There was a big tree at the edge of the river that fell into the water during the winter. Part of the tree stuck up out of the water during the summer. It was by far one of our favorite spots. We would climb up to the highest point and dive into the water. From the highest branches, we could see fish and turtles in and around the branches that ended up in the water. One day a cloud of smoke came around the bend.

"Why is there smoke on the water?" Ernie asked.

"I don't know," said Claude.

Next came the smell of Marijuana. And then came the sound of hippies having fun. We had no idea what Marijuana was, what it did, or why they smoked it. One thing for sure, by far some of the friendliest people you could encounter.

"What a great life you guys are living." One of them said to us.

The entire group smiled and gave us peace signs. We gave the peace signs right back thinking we were cool. And then, my heart stopped.

"Hey, they're naked," I said.

"No, shit," said Claude.

"Wow!" Said Ernie.

"Do they know that we can see them?" I asked.

"What are you, stupid?" Claude said, never taking his eyes off them.

"Yeah, what are you, stupid?" Ernie repeated.

Next came a moment I would never forget. There she was looking at me and there I was looking at her. At that precise moment, the difference in age was nonexistent. As far as I could tell she was exactly my age and smiling directly at me. I smiled right back and then came the wave of my lifetime. Before I could think about it, my hand raised and there I was waving to a naked beautiful girl. How is this possible? No one is going to believe me. She not only embedded her image in my brain, but she also solidified my reason for existing. She was by far the most beautiful girl I had ever seen. It was the first time Ernie and I had ever seen naked people. For sure the first time we had seen naked girls. For Claude, maybe not the first time, but his eyes were glued to the body of flesh floating down the river.

I came out of my deep thought to me standing out of my truck. I couldn't remember getting out of it, and to be honest, it bothered me a little. But here I stood, out of my truck looking at the water below. I could see boulders, tree trunks and other debris the water had dragged down from up north. Yet everything within the water's edge was green. I thought of the irony in place. Of how destructive water is, and life-giving at the same time and in many ways as strong as it is weak. Look at that, I heard in my head. Everything in its path will shape it. Every boulder, every little rock, tree, even the wind will shape it. It drops to fill every little dip and will rise at every little bump. Forced to turn left or right, yet, with the purpose of time, it will move everything in its path.

With that observation, I felt a sudden shift in mood and lost myself farther into the gorge of thought. It felt physical as if the energy of thought was twisting my brain. Forcing me to a negative state of mind. Is this depression? If so, why? I looked down to see my hands grasping the handrail. There was something about holding on to the rail that made me question if the bridge had anything to do with what I was feeling. As that question came to mind, I felt a slight vibration from the rail to my hands and up my arms. I released it and looked around thinking that a car had driven onto the bridge, but there was no car. So where did that vibration come from? Did the bridge just try to communicate with me? Is it trying to tell me something?

"What am I thinking?" I heard myself say.

Things don't tell people anything, they are things. So why am I feeling this depression? Did something bad

93

happen here that I can't remember? Or was it my observation of water? My dissecting of water is more like it. Why can't I leave things as they are? Why must I take everything apart? I told myself to look around and leave things as they were, see and enjoy. But as I did, something held on to me. There's got to be something here that's causing this. I felt feelings, emotions without reason. But must there always be a reason? Can't something happen without reason? Is that even possible? I pulled myself out of that, and looked around for my reason. Maybe it's not one thing, but all that surrounds me. The time, the place, the way things are, where they are. But things alone can't do this to a human. How about a memory? But my memories of this place are good, nothing bad so why do feel as I do? Wait a minute. Maybe, I've walked into someone else's memory. Is that even possible? Can a memory be left behind, without a picture, without writing it on paper or on these metal beams? Not sure, but I stood there, I felt emotions, it was fear at first, anguish came next, followed by loneliness, a terrible loneliness caused by memories that were not mine. Why must these thoughts flood my head? I don't like it.

"Jesus," I said to myself, "let it go."

So, I looked around as if to erase my thoughts or to change their willful direction. Maybe, that's the secret. To look around without the chance to think. Look and look away before the next thought. Could it be that simple? In an attempt to try my theory, I looked around, and if I felt something, I turned to something else. I did this over and over. But as always, a question came to mind. What about the thoughts I didn't have? That's a thought I shouldn't have had. I looked away to erase that thought and realized that a thought was needed not to have a thought. Now that's a problem. Not so easy after all. There it is, another thought. So once again I looked around and focused on not focusing. I told myself not to stay on any one thing. How does one do that? To never allow oneself to have a thought, only an observation. A distinction difficult to make, but I must. So I did. And after a while, and ever so slowly it snuck up on me. I felt joy and wasn't sure of what I felt. How can that be? A thrust of fear went through me as that realization came to mind. Can you imagine? Not knowing that one is feeling joy? What is the reward? What is the reason for living?

A part of me told me to look around, so I did. To take what was and leave what wasn't, without thought, without judgment. As if my eyes and ears were simply portals for consumption, a socket, a means of input to the images and sounds to be left on the brain as a reflection. As a mirror, incapable of judging, always reflecting truth. And for once I saw life as a fleeting moment. I felt joy and felt it without distortion, without deception, only honesty, and I liked what I felt.

I looked at the water below and saw the beauty in its fluidity, in its synchronicity with all that surrounded it. I looked at the destruction it left behind and saw the beauty in the life that resulted. I looked at the path the water carved and saw the beauty in its ability to find the path of least resistance. I looked at everything within the grasp of my eyes, within the reach of my ears, opened the vault to my brain, and placed that moment in its place. For this was a memory to be had not to be left behind.

I got in my truck and crossed the gateway to my next moment. As I took it all in, I felt as though my truck was driving me. Is this what it's like to be one with all? If so, it felt great. We came out of a curve and saw a cow with a cowbell as she led the herd of black Angus across the road and onto a field with a white house and barn on the far side. I looked at the house and felt like I had been there. Before allowing my thoughts to escape, I told myself to look away, but it was too late. I felt an emotion, and then, I didn't know how or why, but inside that house was where I stood. I was standing behind a woman as she stood in front of the stove dressed in traditional 1800s attire. Five children sat at the kitchen table just to the left of me. I heard a door open. She turned to face it, but her face I couldn't see. It was there, but it wasn't. It was as if her face could've belonged to anyone, yet no one. She walked up to the man in the doorway whose face I also couldn't see. She kissed him, turned back around, and there she was. The face of a woman I could've sworn I knew, but for the life of me, I could not remember from where, when, or how. It suddenly hit me. She looked like my anti-gravity girl. The children called out for their father. She walked back to the stove. He walked to the table, knelt, hugged, and kissed the children. He stood and hugged the woman from behind as she continued to cook. A car honked and snapped me back to where I was, sitting in my truck as the woman in that kitchen stood in the field looking directly at me. It was not only the same woman; it was Joan Briganti, my anti-gravity girl. And even though I knew it was her, she felt different, strange. The honking car drove around me, passed between us, and she was gone.

"What the hell?" I said it out loud.

I got out of my truck and ran into the field looking for her, but she was gone. I stood there thinking. I asked myself what just happened? Wait a minute, how can I ask myself what just happened? Things either happen, or they don't. Thoughts are one thing, reality is another, and there was no doubt as to whether this happened or not. This happened right in front of me, not in my head. Not wanting to leave that moment behind, I got back in my truck and sat there for a few seconds trying not to think of what not to think. I finally drove off. Seconds later, out of the corner of my eye in my rearview mirror, I saw a man walking behind me. I hit the brakes, and he also stopped. I looked away not wanting to see him. I have no idea why. I sat there looking at my feet, the only place to look where I couldn't see around me. One foot on the brake the other on the clutch. I heard it in my head and then I said it out loud.

"My left foot on the clutch, my right foot on the brake."

The sound of me breathing through my nose gave me a sense of self awareness I wasn't prepared for. What is wrong with me? There was a man in my mirror and I was afraid to look at him. It was a reflection of a man not the man. Why am I afraid to look at him? What if the mirror is a reflection of my thoughts? What if all that is there, is the reflection and not the man? Why would I think that? That thought I did not like. At that point there was only one thing to do because looking at my feet was no longer an option. As if the eyes of the mirror could deceive me, as if I hadn't already, I had to see it through my own. I turned around and there he was the man I saw in that kitchen. The pounding in my chest started as I realized not only was it he, who stood in the kitchen, it was I who stood behind me. As if being at two places at once, I found myself staring out the back window while watching myself staring at myself in the truck.

"Why is this happening? Why is this happening?"

I heard myself say. I snapped out of whatever that was and awoke surrounded by my bedroom walls.

"I'm in my bedroom? What?" I asked and felt the yearbook on my chest as I laid in my bed.

I sat up breathing rapidly, looked around, and felt out of place, or out of sync, I'm not even sure but something felt wrong. As if I belonged somewhere else, or here, but not now. Is that even possible, to be where one is at the wrong time? And if so, why, and how would I know? I have been in this bedroom hundreds of times, nothing has changed. These are objects all around me, without brains, without hearts or souls. Dead wood, dead metals, dead organic matter, at one stage or another of decomposing. Formed into objects to satisfy people's needs and desires. With the yearbook still clenched to my chest and still sitting on my bed I looked down at the floor as if to confirm it was still there. I don't know why I did that and didn't want to know. I spun around, got up, and walked out of my bedroom.

I walked into the kitchen and placed the yearbook on the counter. I opened it and saw the piece of the missing page. Instantly I was back in my dream, in the farmhouse with Joan Briganti. I pulled myself out of that and tried to make sense of my dream, but couldn't begin to. But then I had to ask. Is it always a dream because it happened while we sleep?

On the way home from work the next day, I thought about my dream again. It seemed too real and felt like I had lived it. How would I know the inside of that farmhouse? But then again, what does the inside of that house really look like? As a child, I had seen that same house from that very spot on that same road. I always wondered who lived there, and what would it be like to live on that farm. But it's not like I walked into that house. How would I know if what I saw in my dream resembled the inside of that house? I don't why, but I truly believe that I have been in that house. I know that kitchen, the stove, the cabinets. I know what it's like to look out of that kitchen window. As that thought entered my head, it felt like previous memories of a past life still existed in my head. Am I the same person of long ago? What if I'm two separate entities? Roberto is in that kitchen looking out the window and the now Roberto looking at that house from the road. Am I seeing the world through past or present eyes? That thought jolted me right back to this reality. Me, sitting on this so-called freeway. I looked around to see that none of us so-called commuters were free to go our free way. I took my foot off the brake, I eased up and accelerated for about fifty feet, and stopped. Here we are, thousands of us encapsulated in the cocoon of our demise. Something we call an automobile. But was it really an automobile? With that, came the realization that there was nothing auto about this mobile. It was just a car.

Just like my dream was just a dream. But then I had to ask, where did the information for my dream come from? The color on the walls for example. A color I have never seen. No one paints their house that color, but I see it in my head. How about the table? I know for a fact I've sat at that table. It was an uncomfortable table. It was too low for me. I did not like that table, but the kids love it. What about the kids? Whose kids are they? I mean we're they? Are they dead now? From what I saw, that had to have been seventy, eighty, or even a hundred years ago. Is Joan Briganti their mother, and am I their father? And if so, shouldn't both of us be dead? Alive only in my dreams. Now I have to ask, if she's in my dream, am I in hers? But she's a dream, how could I be a dream's dream? And there I go again.

It feels as though my life has become an endless stream of dreams. An endless road of thoughts that never seems to end. And in the last year or so, the difference between a dream and a thought, almost irrelevant. But why, and why so much dreaming? I don't remember dreaming like this before. And why have my dreams become more vivid as they've become more frequent? Not only do I dream more, but I also find myself endlessly thinking about my dreams. I see people in my dreams I've never seen before, let alone met. Yet, they seem beyond friendly, more like dear friends, but I have no idea who they are. In some cases, I recognize their soul, but not the shell, their physical self. Other times I recognize the body, but not the soul, but I know not who they are. Questions and theories flood my head resulting in confusion to all ends.

And now I find myself reading up on dreams; searching for some kind of truth to the questions I have. Some people say that dreams are an extension of our everyday life. When we experience something, it affects us, and we dream about it. That's all dreams are, an extension of our day, a time to reflect. But as I dream more, and remember more, I find myself questioning that concept. I'm not sure that I understand it all, but I think it's the other way around. I, most of the time, used to forget my dreams, but as I said, that hasn't been the case lately. Perfect detail within my dreams has become the norm. Not only do I remember more, I find it possible to stop within a dream, take a look around, and question, the very essence of my existence within whatever this is. Is it possible that dreams come from a consciousness in a transitional state of evolution? A consciousness truly unfamiliar to us. Triggered by genetic memories from the forever changing plains of distant lives. Only to relive them over and over again until we get it right resulting in our next mutation. I say this because things I have never seen, look familiar to me. Places I have never been, feel as though I have. Smells will trigger unexpected emotions from the depths of my soul, I have no idea as to where they come from or why. And now and then, I'll recognize a perfect stranger knowing we have never met, as if we were transitional souls wrongly placed in bodies meant for another time.

8. MAN-SON

As I was thinking of that, I realized that I was driving into my garage, my questions at that point, irrelevant. I walked into the kitchen and instantly saw a man sitting in my backyard in one of my lounge chairs. That had to be Dale, still wearing the same clothes as yesterday. I walked out to see him surrounded by beer bottles with his head hanging between his legs. I stood in front of him to no reaction. I thought, poor son of a bitch, it must have been a bad one.

"I could have taken the day off," I said in a matter of fact way. I waited. He slowly lifted his head but said nothing.

"Not a good day ha?"

He dropped his head again. "I'm sick of it. I am so sick of it," he said, shaking his head.

I pulled up a chair, sat down, and grabbed myself a beer.

"Yeah, I know how you feel," I said, exhaled, and waited for a reaction.

He said. "Do you really know how I feel? Come on man, you've got it made. You have your freedom. I can't even get drunk in my own backyard. The bitch is out of control man."

I thought about what he said, and then I said, "I couldn't get drunk in my own backyard?"

I paused for a second and said, "pretty funny," and laughed.

Dale looked away not believing that I was laughing. "What's so funny?"

"I couldn't get drunk in my own backyard? You're kidding me right?"

Disappointed that his new friend wasn't jumping out of his skin to support him, Dale shook his head and looked away.

"You're a man for God's sake. It's not that you couldn't. It's that you wouldn't."

With more backbone, and with an expression like he had taken a bite of some real nasty, he then said.

"Oh, come on. You have no one to answer to. I have kids, and a monster of a bitchy wife."

"Yeah, you are right about that. I saw the way she treated you."

"Yeah, pretty embarrassing."

"And yesterday wasn't the first time I've heard you two."

He hung his head down between his legs and then said. "What else is new?"

I decided to let things simmer a bit, and said nothing for a minute or two.

I then said, "you know what Dale? You are a man though." I looked around.

"Now I know we just met and all, and I know you've had a few beers, but man, ball up God damn it. Don't be a puss."

I had no idea where that came from, but it was too late, the words were out.

"What the fuck man," said Dale.

I laughed and said. "Look at you. You look like a little boy sneaking around drinking his daddy's beer. Come on man. It's your backyard, it's your beer, and sure as shit, she's your wife."

"Is this supposed to make me feel better?"

"Am I supposed to make you feel better? I didn't know that. You want to feel better? Scratch your balls. That oughta make you feel better."

Not believing what he heard, he dropped his mouth wide open and said, "I don't fucken believe this," and looked away.

I got a bit annoyed. I got up and walked around a little. I was disgusted by this man who had everything any man could want but didn't have the balls to control a situation otherwise commonplace for a man. Instead, he sat on his balls in my backyard on my patio chair. Waiting for someone to appease him, for a little pity, a hug. Waiting for something that wasn't about to happen. I looked back down at him and saw a pathetic little boy looking up at me, waiting for a sign, any sign of support. I could see why and how his wife was able to control him. This was a percentage of a man. This was a decomposing man. With that thought cultivating in this brain of mine, the thoughts and dreams or whatever that was of earlier came rushing back. And with that, my own shortfalls came knocking at my door. Wanting to pull myself away from that, I grabbed a cigar from my shirt pocket. I looked at my cigar, and I tried to remember when I started smoking, but couldn't. Oh, what the hell, I said to myself, quit thinking so much. I reached into my pocket again and pulled out another cigar and held it out to him.

"Here, have a cigar." Hoping to reel him in. He shook his head and looked away. I too looked away and decided to let things breathe for a while. But Dale's pathetic situation had managed to bring back emotions without reason. Emotions from what I thought was a distant past. But then again, for all I knew there were plenty of reasons, and perhaps not from a so distant past. I say this because now and then, micro flashbacks of people and places would surface just like in my dreams. But these were not dreams, they felt like memories. I felt like I was right back on that metal bridge confronted by lingering memories that someone left behind. I then heard myself say.

"Come on Dale, you decided to come over here, instead of dealing with her."

I waited for him to say something, but I heard nothing. So I went on.

"Decisions, we all make them. Some, we regret, as a matter of fact, most. Have you ever made a life-changing decision and not know it?"

"What the fuck are you talking about?" He said, irritated.

A question from him. This was the opening I was looking for. I positioned the chair right in front of him, sat, and looked right at him.

"Okay, a little advice. You have what most people

105

want. Don't fuck it up. Okay, so she's a little bitchy."

"A little?" He interrupted me. "What the hell are you talking about?"

"I'm serious Dale. Everything we do from day to day will affect the next event in our life."

He tried to figure out what I was saying, but couldn't.

"It's like a chain reaction. You pull, she follows, or she resists." I could see that I wasn't connecting.

"This is some deep shit man. I just wanted to get drunk."

You've gotta be shitting me I thought and placed my hand on his shoulder.

"You think this is about getting drunk?" I said. "Is that what you think? Even as we sit here Dale. This conversation you and I are having may lead to your life changing, or mine. Don't take it lightly. If something doesn't feel right; ask yourself why?"

He shook and dropped his head between his legs again. I watched as his head went back and forth. He dropped his head even lower. I heard his breathing deepen, but couldn't tell what was going on. And to my amazement, right beneath him, I saw tears on the pavement. His pain was one of constant torture, and this was his exhale.

"Nothing ever feels right anymore. Nothing man! It's one big fucking struggle from day to day. Fuck!" Dale said as he looked down.

He paused for a while. I thought about saying something, something to make him feel better, when I heard him say.

"I've tried to make her happy. I've tried, I'm telling you, man. No matter what I do it's always wrong. She's like a giant ball cracker."

He looked around as he wiped his tears and went on.

"After a while, I just gave up - I just gave up man. Jesus, from day to day I have no idea what I'm coming home to. It's like Russian Roulette or something. You know? I just want to come home and feel good, man. That's all, I just want to feel good, that's it."

"Well, you wanna feel better? Scratch your balls and play the banjo, now that oughta do the trick."

I have no idea why I said what I said, but I did.

He hesitated, but couldn't hold back the laughter. Seeing him laugh through his tears brought joy to me. At that point, I knew I had found a friend. There, that wasn't so hard, I heard in my head. Not sure where that voice came from, but I heard it.

After laughing, Dale said. "You son of a bitch. Now, that was funny. At least you made me laugh that time."

With that, we let things flow for a while, but I wasn't done, I had to drive the point home.

"You know Dale, it's all in the decisions. If you don't make them she will. Next thing you know, she's wearing the pants, and you're wearing..."

"Ah, fuck you, man. Look, stick to the funny stuff, will you?" He said almost begging.

"I'm serious. Start making decisions, right now."

"Like what?"

"I don't know, anything. You know. How about, wait a minute. What's the one thing you've always wanted."

His eyes searched from side to side and said, "I just want to feel good."

"No, I mean something physical, something tangible, a thing that you want. That will make you feel better, you know."

107

"Like what?"

"Let's make it simple, so you can start making decisions. It doesn't have to be anything big, something small."

Dale searched his head for a while. I watched him, hoping to get an easy answer.

"I want your car."

"My car?" Now that was a surprise.

He saw my reaction and said. "Well, not your car, but one like it. I felt so good in your car man."

He looked around as if to search for that feeling again, and said.

"Son of a bitch. I felt like a man. You know?" He teared up a little.

"So go out and buy one," I said. He looked at me, as if to say, you've got to be kidding, and instantly started processing my idea. After staring at me for much too long, there was only one thing to say.

"Why are you looking at me like that? Go out and buy one, the hell with the bitch"

His expression changed, telling me he had already accepted the idea, but just simply wanted to hear it from me.

"Where am I gonna get a 68 Roadrunner?"

"Now that's a stupid question, don't you think? I mean think about it. You asked, where am I gonna get a 68 Roadrunner?

My question did exactly what it was supposed to, to confuse him.

"What? What do you mean?"

"In the only place, you can buy a Roadrunner, the Roadrunner store, for God's sake," we both laughed.

A few hours later, I was following Dale who was driving not a 1968 Roadrunner, but his 1970 R/T Challenger. At every turn, I had the pleasure of its profile followed by the great sound of the engine revving as it pulled away. I then realized that I had never seen my car pull away. We drove into my driveway, not his, which seemed kind of weird. I got out of my car and rushed to his passenger side door, opened it, and got in. I looked at the perfect black interior. I looked up and touched the headliner, the dash, the knobs.

"Now that's what I'm talking about," I said, as Dale followed my hand.

"Is this bad-ass or what?" He said.

Then, to my surprise, these words came out of my mouth. "All wifey now needs is a slap in the ass and roll in the hay."

And with that, the great moment came to an end. Dale's expression vanished.

"What's the matter?" I said, wanting to take back what I said.

He looked out his window and mumbled, "Well, that's gonna be a little harder."

Knowing the answer to my question, I had to ask. "Why?"

"I don't know man." Still looking out his window.

"You don't know what? I'm telling ya. That is exactly what she needs. That is what you both need." I paused for a couple of seconds. The silence ushered me forward.

"Something tells me it's been so long you're both plugged up. That's it, we're gonna have to call a plumber."

He continued to look out the window ignoring my attempt at humor. He finally looked at me and said.

"I'm serious, we're not into each other anymore."

"No shit."

He reached out and touched the dashboard, "not only that, just wait till she sees this."

"Oh, come on!"

"Come on nothing. She's probably gonna chew your ass off too,"

"What the hell do I have to do with this?"

"What you, what do you mean?" His forehead distorted with a deep frown.

"You know what? Never mind, I take my question back. She gives me any shit, and I'll have to slap her in the ass. Remember that."

"Fine with me," he said with a sense of relief.

"Boy, you're a puss. You're gonna need a lot of work."

Movement caught Dale's eye, he looked at his house to see his wife looking out a window.

"Oh boy, here we go," he said.

I could see his fear, and felt his apprehension. The little boy of a few hours ago was back. At that point, his fear had become mine, and asked myself what the hell was I thinking? Why did I put myself in this position? This ability to connect with people; not such a good idea, now that I think about it. Distance was my point of no attack which had worked for years, but now, near, is where I found myself, much too near. I have changed the course of someone's life, now what? I thought I said but didn't. It was just another thought. The sound of the engine starting sort of snapped me back, but not all the way. Something kept holding on to me.

"Hey, hey! Are you okay?" Said Dale as I saw myself through his eyes, and didn't like what I saw.

"Yeah, yeah, I'm fine," I said, not quite sure of what had happened.

"What were you thinking?"

"When?"

"Right there." He pointed with his eyes.

"What do you mean right there?"

"I mean right there, what were you thinking when I said right there."

"I don't know, nothing, just...just things, you know."

I looked out the window and decided to let things pause. I could see on the reflection that Dale was also in deep thought. I was about to say something, anything, to move things away from me when he said.

"I'm sorry man. You're right, don't worry about it. I'll deal with her."

"You'll deal with her?"

"Yeah, you're right, you have nothing to do with this."

"Well..."

"No man, I mean it. I'll handle the wife."

His attempt to put me at ease was admirable but fell short. A sudden need to get out of the car overcame me. I got out and he drove off.

9. WHO'S THE PARASITE
WHO'S THE HOST?

Nights were often hard for me. I didn't know why. On some nights it was one thing, on other nights it was something else. One thing I could always count on was the fear that came before a bad night. I'm not sure if it was predisposed, or premonition. There was a cause and effect in my situation that made it difficult to know which came first. Not that it made a difference, in the end, it was all the same, fear. Later that same day when Dale bought his car, I was fighting the idea of going to bed when I heard a knock on my garage side door. I walked into the garage to see what was going on when I heard Dale's voice through the side door.

"It's me, man, it's me, let me in."

I opened the door. He walked past me without saying a thing. He grabbed a chair, sat, and looked at the floor. I guess it didn't go well I thought. I grabbed a chair and I too sat but wasn't about to say anything. I wanted the course of the conversation to seek its own path. I waited and waited for Dale to say something, but nothing. This is what I get for being a big shot. Now I have to say something, something profound, like.

"That bad huh?"

"Yeah, that bad," he said as he rubbed both knees with his hands.

"Man, I could see you two on a date. Two kids having fun driving around in that Challenger, you know?"

I waited. He said nothing, I said nothing. I stood and paced back and forth. I thought about it. I had to come up with something. An idea, an angle to deal with this situation. It then came to me, another great idea. As if my hand had a brain of its own, my hand extended out and landed on his shoulder. I heard myself say.

"You need a vacation, my friend."

Dale's expression remained void. But then, there was movement. Very slow movement. His expression melted into confusion.

"What? What are you talking about?"

"You see, you don't get it. This is perfect. She doesn't want to participate, and apparently, the idea of going on a date with you is nowhere within the realm of her imagination, or her reality for that matter. So...."

Dale stopped me with a look as if I meant to insult him or something. Or, maybe the idea of him repulsing her had never occurred to him. I went on.

"Don't take it personally, just saying, you know."

"Don't take it personally? How else am I supposed to....." I interrupted him.

"No, no, don't take it......" I stopped short of finishing my redundant sentence. I looked away as my next great idea came to mind. I looked at him.

"I'll tell you what we need, we need a couple of girls to go...."

I stopped as I heard the sound of the word girls. I pushed myself to finish my thought, but Dale stepped in with his next question.

"A couple of girls?"

"Yeah, a couple, you know, two, I'm sure we can find a couple of girls who want to participate. You know, that want to go on vacation with us."

After a few seconds of silence, Dale's confusion went into overdrive.

"Two girls? Vacation? Are you serious? What the hell are you talking about?"

"Well."

I waited. I don't know why. I was hoping he would catch on, or up, or something. I'm not sure, but I should have known by now that I wasn't about to get anything from him, so I went on.

"I mean, we don't really have to get the girls, but we can make her think that we did."

His eyes moved from side to side as his mouth slowly opened. He looked at me questioning, wanting to know where the story was going. So what am I to do but to go on?

"You know, we can nudge her in that direction. You know your wife."

"So, are we really gonna go on vacation?"

"Well, yeah, why not? Let's give her a reason, a real reason to get a little jealous."

He looked around searching for something, anything.

"You don't get it, do you? You're gonna have to take notes. I'm not gonna teach this shit twice. Now pay attention. It's called decision time. She doesn't want to participate, and apparently, she didn't think too highly of our purchase, and she's already pissed off, right?"

Dale nodded. "Yeah."

"How pissed off?"

"Reallllly pissed off!"

"In that case, it's vacation time, hell, how much more pissed off can she possibly get?"

The next day flew by. I drove up to my house and saw Dale's wife, Christina waiting near my garage. I clicked the remote. The garage door rolled up. I rolled down my window to say hello but could tell by her expression I would be wasting my breath. Instead, I faked a smile to myself. I drove in thinking that my mind must be playing tricks on me. Hoping that this was all my imagination. That there was some chance in hell she wasn't there. I looked in my rear-view mirror to see my hopes vanish by the reflection of this woman. At that point, I had to accept that she was here. Coming right at me and could tell by her walk, she was not only here, but here to do battle. I got out of my car. The next thing I knew; were eyes bulging, lips flapping, and spit was flying.

"What the hell do you think you're doing?" She asked in a loud voice.

"What do you mean?" I said, knowing exactly what she meant, and thought this woman is on fire.

"What do I mean? Are you serious?" She asked.

Not only was she on fire, she was throwing herself right at me. I could feel her breath on my face and could

115

tell as I searched deep into her bulging eyes, that I was about to take her entire being straight on. She meant war.

I heard myself say, "ah, yeah, I am serious."

"Look, I don't need some man-idiot like you meddling in my family affairs. Do you understand me?"

She pointed her finger right in my face. She must be mistaken, I thought. Maybe she thinks she's talking to Dale or something. I regrouped and launched forward.

"Family affairs? Is that what you call it? That one-trick pony you made for yourself."

"What?" She exhaled and dropped her head slightly. As if changing the trajectory of her head was going to change what obviously came out of my mouth and into her ears. Apparently, an explanation was in order, so I explained.

"Yeah, you might have heard of him, you know, Dale. That man-son of yours."

"Man-son-? What the hell is that?"

"Oh come on, as if you don't know. If you wanted another son, maybe you should've had another. Ever thought of that?"

"Look," she said, "let's get one thing perfectly straight here, this is none of your business. And as far as that car goes, keep your stupid shit-head ideas to yourself, do you understand me? I don't need him coming home with another boy-toy."

"You see that? You see? You said boy-toy, not man-toy, but boy-toy, and you're not gonna blame me for that?

"Well, who the hell else am I gonna blame?"

She looked at my car, placed her hand on it, leaned on it, and gave me a cocky sarcastic look. Like saying, hey look what I'm leaning on.

"I'm telling you; the car thing was not my idea."

I asked myself. Why am I explaining myself to this woman?

"Not your idea? Do you honestly want me to believe that?"

She placed both hands on the fender, and lifted herself just high enough to sit on my car, and once again gave me that same cocky sarcastic look.

"Okay, okay you're right, I did have a little to do with that. I reminded him about those things that hang between a man's legs, you know his balls, man-balls, not boy-balls, man-balls. For some reason, gee I have no idea why, he forgot all about them. But you're not gonna blame me for anything else."

"Really?" She said, rolling her eyes.

"Ah, yeah, really! I'm not responsible for man-son, I'm not the one that chipped away at him for the last whatever amount of years. Chip, chip, chip, slowly but surely until you turned him into that ball-less piece of mush, that little man-son of yours, or whatever it is you call him."

Before allowing her to respond, I positioned myself squarely in front of her.

"What do you call him anyway? When he's fucking you real good what exactly do you call him?"

I paused just enough to let it sink in. "Oh, wait a minute, you don't fuck anymore."

I felt my words leaving my tongue. I could see them projecting through the air as they struck their target, and saw her expression undermined by the truth of my words. Unable to look at me, she turned away. She hesitated for a second and walked off. I decided I wasn't done. I grabbed her by the arm and pulled her back.

"Get away from me you asshole," she said and pulled away, but I held on.

I got right in her face, "what's the matter ha?"

I paused and could see by her demeanor she knew I wasn't expecting an answer.

"I'll tell you what the matter is. You forgot what it's like to have a man, a real man."

I pulled her right up to me, and wrapped my left arm around her waist. She resisted, only to feel my impulses overtake me. I tightened my grip. Her fear revealed itself with the pounding of her chest against mine. Her struggle fueled the rage within me. I could see in her eyes what she wasn't saying. I wrapped both arms around her, encapsulating her with my vicious hug. I could hear and feel her struggle as her breath touched the side of my face and neck. And to my amazement, as her breath became mine, our struggle had become one.

"There, there, you go. Remember that? Ha? Remember what this was like? A man. That's what I am, a man," I whispered in her ear.

I eased my grasp and pulled back enough to see her beautiful face. If eyes could touch, and if moments could be owned, this moment would be mine. I could not take my eyes off of her, nor hers off of mine. Light as a feather, I picked her up and sat her on my workbench and found ourselves incapable of escaping what felt like a forever moment. Our faces were almost touching, I could feel her breath on my lips and I knew she could feel mine. And out of nowhere and into the moment, time presented itself. I felt as though I could reach out and touch it, grasp it with my hand of mind, and set the speed in which it passed.

In slow motion, we found ourselves and could smell her heat radiating against my body and face. But the struggle within me raged on as the joy within madness confused me even further. A part of me wanted to back away and be done with this. But I wasn't about to go anywhere because this is where some part of me wants me to be. The thought of fighting this beautiful creature came back into my head and baffled me even further, and excited me at the same time. Confusion was my only state of mind, and found myself once again, saying what wasn't in my head.

"Remember when Dale used to pick you up like this? Ha? Remember those days?"

How can I be saying what I'm saying while feeling what I'm feeling? I wanted the voice that was coming out of me to stay in my head, as the urge to kiss her took over. But the words kept coming.

"Remember when he was a man and not that ball-less piece of shit you turned him into?"

I backed away and watched her fall to the floor.

"Now get your ass out of my garage."

I heard from what I could only assume was this person within me.

Not believing what had happened, I looked at her on the floor. And just before her attempt to recover, she looked up with an emptiness I was all too familiar with. Confusion filled her eyes followed by anger. With the speed of a lioness, but in slow motion to me, and as if our moment never happened, she got up and headed for the door. She stopped and turned to face me.

"So that's what you think of your new friend ha? So you think he's a ball-less piece of shit? Well, we'll see how he feels about that?" She walked off.

I heard myself laughing and said. "You don't know men, do you?" She stopped. I went on. "Do you honestly think I haven't told him that? What planet are you on?"

Still facing away from me, she looked around searching for something. She reached out, grabbed a beer bottle off a shelf, turned around, and pulled back to throw it at me. Instantly I pointed at her.

"Don't you even think about it. Put it down! Put it down!"

To my amazement, she put the bottle down, turned, and walked out. And apparently, I wasn't done.

"Oh, and by the way, don't worry about your man-son. I'll bring him back in one piece. Some cute girl may wear him out, but he'll be in one piece."

She stopped, turned to face me, and marched right back into my face. The spit was once again flying, eyes bulging.

"You piece of shit, who the hell do you think you are anyway?"

"Wow, look at you," I said, "all hot and bothered, cheeks nice and red. Hm, hm, hm!"

"Fuck you!"

"Oh, you'd like that wouldn't you?"

"You think...."

I interrupted her. "I already know the answer to that."

"You must think...," I interrupted her again.

"You see, I told Dale, you know, your man-son. What your little wifey needs is a slap in the ass and a roll in the hay."

I looked around, "or the garage for that matter."

120

She swung at me. I caught her wrist. I got right in her face, almost kissing her. This time, I felt nothing but anger.

"You see, you don't know men. You think you do, but you don't. You don't even know your own husband."

I waited for her reaction but felt as though that moment had skipped me. I found myself within the walls of silence, seeking deep into her eyes of madness. Her lower lip quivered. How long have I been looking at her? I heard in my head. Why is there so much silence? Not sure if I said it or kept it in my head. I felt her tears falling on my hand. Tears? Why tears? What kind of tears are these? As if trying to answer my questions. I looked at my hand and realized the grasp of my strength and knew I was causing other than emotional pain. I released her. In silence, she walked away.

As if trying to run away from myself, I walked out of the garage and into the kitchen. I grabbed a beer out of the fridge. I leaned against the counter and tried to make sense of what had happened. Never mind what I was feeling. Disgust, that's what I was feeling, total and utter disgust with myself.

"What the hell am I doing?" This time I heard it.

The questions in my head kept coming. What happened? What was that? Where did that come from? Why did I respond that way? I don't even know this woman. And what's with this anger? What the hell is going on here? Are these so-called deep fears, deep anger or feelings that come out of nowhere? Is this what they mean by an out-of-body experience? Did I just have one? I've had conversations with people who couldn't explain their feelings. Or how they reacted to something. Some people felt like someone else was inside them. But I didn't believe it. But now, I have to ask, is there? Is there a part of me, of us, we don't know about? A part of me that just surfaced after all this time? What? Wait a minute. Wait a minute. Are you kidding me? A part of me? There's no part of me. It's me, I am me, not some part. I told myself to stop thinking, to stop trying to explain everything.

I then heard the sound of my lungs breathing, and the sound of my heart beating as I argued with myself. It was like a soundtrack to my inner voice. But why would my inner voice have a soundtrack? Is this so-called soundtrack my other inner voice? Is this possible? It was the sound of being alive, that's all. We breathe because we are alive. I heard it, the sound of my breath again, followed by my heart. And there it is again, a breath, a beat, a breath, a beat. I found myself not only hearing it but listening to it. It was like a soundtrack. It evoked a response, as it should. I heard, I felt, I thought. There it was my response, my thoughts. I then felt the in and out movement of my chest again. I waited for the beat, I felt it. I waited for the sound, it was late. The sound of my heart was late. How is that possible and why would that happen? I felt it again and there it was again, an echo to my heart.

As if it was at a distance, reflecting off the walls and back to me. As if it was trying to make me aware that it was coming at me and not from me. But why and what is this soundtrack trying to tell me? That I'm out of sync with myself? Is that it? But when was the last time I thought of it as such? Never!

This makes no sense because the body is an extension of the brain. They are one. My brain tells my heart to beat. It's got to be something else. Something outside this body, outside this mind, that's telling me something is wrong. That's why I heard it out of sync. As that thought left this head of mine, the answer became all too clear. It was my soul reaching out to me. I don't know why I knew that, but I did. And now I have to ask which part of me is asking my next question? What if there's more than the mind, the body, and the soul? And how would I know? What if there is something wrong going on with me? Something hovering inside. Why hovering? It's more like lingering. But why even that? Isn't it more like hiding? If that is the case, I now have to ask, how can I have something, or a part of me within me and not know it? Is this what people feel when they do something tragic? Like those people you see on the news that kill someone.

"What a bunch of shit,"

I heard the sound of my voice bounce off the walls with a slight delay. But this time it was the presence of mind and space that came to me. The distance that existed between me and the walls called out to me. Why would that happen? Can distance be a thing? How can it call out to me? I looked around trying to find answers to questions I didn't know I had and shouldn't have. I then found myself looking at my feet. I became aware of the distance between my head and my feet. There it is again, distance calling.

Next, came the sound of a heartbeat, but this time, there was no doubt about the delay. It was as if my soul, or that other part of me, was next to me and I could hear the sound of its existence. My next instinct was to look. But I stopped myself. I tried desperately to keep myself from looking. The seconds passed and there it was the feeling of my neck twisting as I turned to my right. I saw...nothing. I blushed as I looked around to make sure no one saw me. There it was again. The feeling of the third. What if there is something to what I am feeling? To what I'm thinking. What if there's a truth so distant, that one must question its existence and whose truth it is. A deep-rooted truth to that which lies within me. Within us. Something so deep and so distant, that it sits there silently waiting. Like a parasite, a monster, a third, waiting for the perfect moment to surface. Do its damage to whatever and whomever, not only to the people around it, as I did, but the person it resides in, as it did. Only to rear itself back into the host and deny it ever existed. Is that what I'm doing right now, denying? And what about everyone else? Does this mean we all have this thing, this monster inside? Or just some of us. And if so, what is it? What causes it? Do we create this it, or does it create us? And now I have to ask, who's the host, and who's the parasite?

10. IT'S VACATION TIME

Dale sat in his brand-new old car waiting for me. I walked up to the Challenger, opened the door, and got in. I felt uneasy about the argument I had with Dale's wife the night before. I saw him smiling, but I continued to wonder if his wife told him about the argument, and if so, how much. Dale saw me looking at him with a questioning expression and said.

"Yes sir, you're looking at the smile of a happy man. I got some great sex last night."

"Did you really?"

"Hell yeah. Like I haven't had in years. I tell you what buddy, you oughta get into more arguments with her. Can we arrange that?"

We both laughed, easing some of the tension, but I still wondered how much she had told him. Dale reached for the ignition, turned the car on and we took off. There was a great feeling that one gets when going on a road trip that I was looking forward to. But that feeling had escaped me for reasons evident only to me. I decided to deal with the tension.

"So she told you about it, ha?"

"Hell yeah, thanks, man."

"No problem. I'm here to help. A slap on the ass and a roll in the hay. The hell with an apple a day."

As soon as the words left my mouth, I regret saying them. But Dale laughed so I figured, hey, why not? I too laughed. In an attempt to continue with my idea, Dale said. "That's right, an apple, an apple, how does that go again?"

"A slap on the ass and a roll in the hay. The hell with an apple a day. I think we oughta make that our own public service announcement. What do you think?"

Dale nodded in agreement, I continued, "you know, so we can teach the young guys how to deal with life, you know, wife issues."

"I think we should", Dale said as he laughed loudly and once again made an attempt. "A roll in the hay, and a slap in the ass....ah shit," we both laughed. Dale tried again.

"A slap on the ass and a roll in the hay. The hell with an apple a day."

I corrected him, "The hell with an apple a day. A slap on the ass and a roll in the hay. Hell, now I'm confused."

Dale gave it yet another attempt.

"A slap on the ass rolling in the hay. As she's rolling in the hay." We both laughed, he went on, "hey, how about that? Not bad, ha? Hey, maybe we should change it a little."

126

I caught my breath after laughing. "Oh man, that is funny. Sure, why not, we can always improvise."

Our laughter faded and there was a moment of silence. I decided this was a good time to ask.

"So how much of the argument did she tell you?"

"All of it."

"All of it?"

"Yeah, why?"

"Just curious."

Dale got a devilish grin as he started laughing, but this time his laugh was somewhat reserved, and turned to me.

"You son of a bitch."

"What?"

"You know what? When we got done. I see her white pants on the floor with grease from your workbench. I was like shiiiit, man he wasn't bull-shitten."

My tension eased up as I heard that and laughed. "I told you."

"I know, but I didn't think you were gonna actually do it."

I looked around and then back to him, "she left me no choice."

Dale shook his head, "I told you, she's a tough one."

"That she is."

Dale continued to slowly shake his head and in a very low voice, as if he was talking to himself, he said.

"Now I know that when Roberto says something, he is serious, serious, man."

He reached out with an open hand. I flinched, not sure of what was going on. He frowned and said.

"Man, you sure are tense this morning. What's up with you? Come on, let's shake on it. You know, for the apple thing, the slap on the ass thing."

I reached out and shook his hand and said,

"I'm sorry man. Yeah, you know, I didn't sleep well last night. Unlike you, of course, you hound dog you."

Dale grinned from ear to ear. I also grinned almost as if to say, I'm proud of you. I looked out my window to see my reflection with the terrain passing by in the background. And just like that, the image of the man before me brought me back to the reality, not before me. I turned away from the window and looked at the winding road ahead. The sound of the engine sent me way back to the days when all a man wanted was the sound of that engine purring and the smell and touch of your woman next to you. A tiny grin came onto my face. It almost felt like it wasn't mine.

Dale looked at me, smiled, and asked, "what's that little grind about?"

I looked at the stick shift and then at Dale.

"Come on, let's make this baby scream."

Dale frowned, I pointed to the stick shift and said. "Come on, grab second. I wanna hear it scream."

Dale looked down at the stick shift, "Second?"

"That's right, second."

"But I'm in fourth gear."

"And?"

Dale looked around thinking. "Okay, here we go."

"Okay, here we go?" I asked.

"What?"

"You don't have to announce it. Just do it. Go for it, quick! Grab second."

He slowed down as we came into a curve, he grabbed the stick shift, grabbed second gear, and slammed the throttle to the floor. The engine screamed like a mountain lion, I yelled, "third, third!"

He grabbed third and his instincts took over. We came out of the curve, and he grabbed fourth gear and eased up as we came to another curve. I laughed and enjoyed the ride.

"That is, it, that is it! You see? That's what I'm talking about. We are men, men God damn it. Well, we are dogs too, but men, and men have to take control. You know what I'm saying?"

"You mean we are Dogmen?"

"That, my friend, is right. Dogmen, and women like it when we take control. Just like you took control of your car right here right now. Control baby."

"Well," Dale said and stopped for a second. "I tell you what though. She was in control last night. And I'll tell you something else. I didn't mind that."

I looked at him like saying, I can't believe I just heard that. He made a face and said, "What?"

"That's different. That's a different kind of control. We can't do shit about that. We are genetically incapable. They wiggle their ass and we're like baby, baby. Okay, I give up. That's the dog part in us. Nothing we can do about that."

"That's for damn sure!" Dale said and nodded in agreement.

The sound of the engine calmed everything down and we both took a breather. I looked out the window and there it was again, the reflection of the man not in the room. I felt an uneasiness come over me again as the reflection questioned me. I sighed. Dale heard me but said nothing. About a minute later, the length of silence ushered Dale to say something.

"Sure got quiet here."

I turned to him, smiled without reason, and said, "yeah

it sure did." I looked around again as my thoughts sunk me way back. "Isn't that amazing though, Dale? If we don't do something that we used to do all the time, if we stop doing it, whatever that may be, we forget it. We lose it." I pause for a second or two.

"It's like, it was another person. That Dale, or that Roberto...was...another person in another life. You know what I mean? It's like, whose life was that or who's life is this?"

Dale pretended to know what I meant.

"Yeah, yeah I know what you mean."

I went on. "You can't lose yourself; you know? You're the only one you have."

I paused for a few seconds as I felt unexplained emotions. I shook them off and said.

"You have got to get the old Dale back!"

I could see Dale thinking. His eyes went back and forth. As if he was going to ask something but couldn't figure out how.

He decided to go for it.

"So, what about you? Have you ever lost yourself? Or a part of you?"

I looked at him questioningly.

He went on. "You know like you said."

I waited. He went on.

"You know, just a little while ago. You said I couldn't lose myself."

My expression went from one of questioning to one of not believing.

"Jesus Christ!" I yelled.

Dale pulled his head back. "What?"

I went on. "Listen to us. What the hell is this? We

sound like a bunch of women. Damn, pullover I'm gonna puke. Pull over I'm gonna puke I'm telling you."

We both laughed, Dale wasn't exactly sure why but he laughed anyway. The conversation faded to the sound of the engine purring which gave us a feeling of relaxation. After a few minutes, Dale couldn't stand the silence.

"Well?"

"Well, what?"

"Well, have you?"

"Oh, you still want me to answer that?"

"Yeah, come on man. You know a lot of my shit."

"Well, there's a lot of shit there."

"Come on!" Dale begged.

"Well, there is."

"How about women?" Dale went on. "The whole time since you moved there, I haven't seen a woman over there. What's going on?"

I looked out the window again and thought of how to answer him without answering. I asked myself; do I have a choice? How do I answer something I don't know? How do I answer without admitting that I don't know? Dale looked at me thinking I would at any moment say something, but I kept on thinking of what not to say.

"Hey, hey!" Dale said.

I continued with my thoughts as if no one was around.

"Hey, hey buddy. What's up?" Dale asked.

"Hey, are you all right?"

I came out of my thought to see Dale looking at me. "What, what? Oh, yeah, yeah, I'm fine, I'm fine."

I faked a tiny little smirk and turned toward the window again. "You know Dale, no matter what, you are lucky to have her, imperfections and all you are lucky to have her."

I felt his questioning expression. I turned to see it. "I know, I know. A little confusing isn't it?" I looked away. "You are lucky to have her."

"What are you......." Dale started to say.

I interrupted him, "I know, so much for the hard ass right."

"So what do you mean?"

"Nothing. Just, you know, you never know."

"You never know what?"

"Life.....you never know life."

I waited for him to say something but heard nothing, so I went on. "How does that go, some days you win some, some days you lose some. Problem with life, some days you feel like you're winning....not knowing you're losing. Bit of a problem, life is tricky that way."

I paused; I have no idea why. Maybe to process my thoughts, not quite sure. I went on. "Just when you think you have it figured out, all shit breaks loose. And I mean loose."

"So....did you lose someone or what?

"No... well, we all lose someone at some point, and everyone at another."

The intensity of my words surprised me. I looked at him wishing my words were a bit prettier, softer, or something. But Dale was too busy processing, so it didn't matter. I went on. "It's the shit of life. That's all it is, the shit of life, you know? It would be nice though wouldn't it?"

"What, what would be nice?" Asked Dale.

"Knowing.....knowing when....ah never mind. You know what? I used to play guitar a long time ago. Let's talk about that."

"You did?"

"Yeah, we even had a band. Me and Anthony Villa. In the fifth grade. Can you believe it?"

"Wow, that is cool."

"At first it was just two of us and then Frank....ah, God I don't remember his last name. He was our bass player, but he didn't have a bass."

"What do you mean?"

"We were the only band in the world with a bass player without a bass."

"He didn't have a bass?"

"Nope."

"So what made him a bass player?"

"That he said he was a bass player."

Dale laughed and made a face like, what?

"Yeah, right?" I said. "Who would've thought of questioning that?"

"Oh my God, that's funny." Said Dale.

"Poor Frank, his dad wouldn't let him buy a bass. And it was his own money."

"Are you serious?"

"Yep, as serious as his dad was an asshole. I'm tellin ya."

"That is for damn sure." Said Dale, I went on.

"I coulda been a contender, I coulda been somebody....."

"Marlon Brando, On the Waterfront." Said Dale.

"That's right man."

"So you feel you guys coulda been contenders? Were you guys that good?"

"We had a bass player without a bass, Dale, what do you think?"

We both laughed.

"That's funnier than shit." Said Dale and looked at me wanting more of the story.

"The band broke up. The bass player without a bass stopped playing his none-bass. Anthony stopped playing his drums. It was sad. But I went on playing for years. That's something I miss. I don't know what happened. I just stopped playing and...."

I stopped, looked away, and thought about Anthony, and Frank, and felt a change in mood. I looked at Dale and said.

"I, ah, I..." I sighed, looked away, and pretended not to pretend to have lost my train of thought. Or that I didn't know what to say, but neither was true. I knew exactly what it was. It was sad.

"You know to change the subject just a little. One day in, ah, let me see, I think I was a sophomore. Anyway, so this friend of mine, Mills, walked up to me in the hallway. He used to think he was that guy in the show, Then Came Bronson. You know, that old show on television back in the seventies?"

"Oh, yeah, I remember that."

"So anyway, he walked up to me wearing his black beanie pulled down to just above his eyebrows. With his guitar strapped to his back. He stopped like two feet away and looked at me. I'm talking to someone so I'm just whatever, and I keep talking and I hear. 'You wanna buy my guitar?' I couldn't believe it. He said it like it was no big deal. I mean this was his guitar. So I said, what? 'You wanna buy my guitar?' And hands me his guitar. So I said are you serious? He just looked at me and said nothing. So, I play a few chords, tune it up a bit and I say sure, how much? 'Twenty dollars.' I'm like no fucking way. I then hear, 'Twelve dollars and fifty cents.'"

Dale laughed and said, "Twelve dollars and fifty cents?"

"My question exactly. How the hell did he come up with that? He could've said fifteen dollars or fourteen dollars, but no, twelve dollars and fifty cents. Jees so I'm like, sure. Man, I was excited. For all those years I had a guitar my mother bought for my brother Ernie when I was ten years old. What a piece of shit that thing was. So, I pull out my wallet and hand him twelve dollars. I dug into my pocket. I stopped and looked at him. He looked at me like, what? I said, 'do you really need fifty cents?' Without even thinking about it, he calmly said, 'yes.' I pulled out a bunch of change and started dropping pennies, dimes, and nickels. I mean here's a guy whom I've known since we were in the sixth grade. You know what I mean? We used to give each other candy bars, magazines, trade records, and everything. But he had to have the fifty cents."

I looked at Dale wanting to hear him say, what a douche. Instead, I heard, "wow."

"Yep, wow. But anyway, he was a good guy. I remember dropping the last nickel. His hand closed like a trap door and he took off."

I stopped talking as the events of that day came pouring in, and I felt the excitement of having a new guitar.

"Man, I got home after school and I installed new strings that I had for god knows how long. I plugged my new guitar into my little amp and man that thing sounded like a real guitar not some stupid toy. You know what I mean?"

"I bet," said Dale.

"I was happy as shit. A week went by and there I was in the hallway and Mills walked up to me and held out......yes, twelve dollars and fifty cents. I look at his hand. I was like what the hell? He said, 'here, I want my guitar back.' What the...what are you talking about? 'I want my guitar.' So I said, you sold me your guitar, it's my guitar now. 'Well, I changed my mind.' Ah, I don't think so. He was actually thinking that he could use my money, to..."

I paused, looked at Dale, and waited.

"To what?" Dale finally asked.

"To buy weed. Can you believe it?"

"Oh man," said Dale.

"Yeah, and how did I know that? Well, I found out later that one of my friend's older brother was selling these little baggies of weed for guess how much?"

"Twelve........" Said Dale and laughed.

"That's right. So, I said to him. How was the weed? 'Weed? What weed?' I was like come on Mills. You know what I mean. I already put new string on......my guitar. What do you think I am a pawnshop? He pulled his hand back. Turned around and walked off. Man, I felt like shit. I felt sorry for him. But what are you gonna do, right?"

"Man, that is some funny shit." Said Dale.

"And you know what?"

"What?"

"I don't even know where that guitar is right now. How can that be? I don't know where that guitar is right now. I don't remember."

"Well, you know how that is," said Dale, "we grow up and forget our kid shit. Because that's all it was, shit. We used to think it was important, but most of it was just shit."

"Yeah, but that guitar was so important to me. I wrote a lot of songs with that thing."

"You used to write songs?"

"Yeah, I couldn't afford guitar lessons. In my house, I had to pay for every little thing. Not like my friends whose parents paid for their guitars, their guitar lessons, and everything else. So I would make up my own songs. It was cheaper, you know. I didn't see it as writing songs. I saw it as cheaper. You know what I mean?"

"That is pretty cool man."

"Yeah, I guess, but I think you're right. It was just kid shit. I probably gave that guitar away or who knows what. I miss those days though. But as you said, we grow up."

"Yep, we sure do."

"Grown up shit. That's what we have now. Shit like work and shit like bills and shit and more shit."

I placed my right hand with my palm facing up in front of me. I did the same with my left hand.

"Kid shit. Right here on the left." I raised my left hand over my head, "much funner." I said.

"Either way, it's still shit." Said Dale and made a face as if he actually smelled shit.

"The shit of life. Hey, we should make that a public announcement. Watch out for the shit of life. Quick, run, it's the shit of life." I said and we both laughed. I turned toward the window again and paused for a few seconds.

"I just stopped playing. I look back now and it doesn't even feel like me. It doesn't...feel like my life."

I looked at Dale. "It's like, maybe that was someone I used to know. You know what I mean? But I'm not even sure of that. It's like, that was an intruder...and this is me. Or that was me and I'm the intruder, not quite sure."

"Wow, that's weird man. Are you serious?"

"Yeah, you don't feel like that? You know when you look back at your life. When you were young."

"I ah....I don't think about it."

"You don't think about it?"

Dale shook his head.

"At all?" I asked and kept my mouth open. As if keeping my mouth open would emphasize the word all.

"I guess not. I mean I try not to."

I looked at him not believing. Dale shrugged as if to say, I don't know what to tell you.

"That's not right. That...is...not..right." I said in a low voice. I have no idea why I went into that low voice, but I did.

Dale questioned his own words and said. "Well, I guess, sometimes I do. I do think about it sometimes."

He looked at me nodding, as if nodding would make me agree with him, or believe him, but it didn't so I kept going.

"Like I said, there's only one Dale, one!" I held up my index finger. Dale went into deep thought. I kept going.

"That's why I hold on to my car. It's me. It reminds me of who I was, who I am. You know?" I looked at Dale and gave him a short pause to process.

"Totally. You're right. You are right." Said Dale, "I now get in my new car, and it changes my whole day. I feel better, I feel like a man."

Dale made a face, went into a weird character, and changed his voice. "I once again scratch my balls, and I feel good about it."

We laughed. "I'm glad you said that man. Shit, I was getting ready to puke again."

"Here it is," said Dale and pointed to the hotel.

We pulled into valet parking. As soon as we got out, I pointed over Dale's head. Dale turned to look. I took off running and yelled.

"It's the shit of life, run!" I ran into the hotel lobby and waited for Dale to catch up.

A few minutes later we walked into our room and instantly decided to go for a swim. We walked into the pool area wearing our shorts and saw two women in the Jacuzzi. Dale's eyes almost popped out of his head and said.

"Well looky here. Last night I got the best sex in years and now looky here. Is it my birthday or what?"

I smiled from ear to ear, "if it isn't yours? It must be mine; wow look at them."

We walked around the opposite side of the pool to get a better look. We made a complete lap and stopped at the Jacuzzi.

Dale full of confidence due to his great sexual experience the night before, said. "How's the water?"

One of the women looked at us and tilted her head as if to study us. She completed her observation and said. "You boys sure took the long way here."

The two women looked at each other and laughed. Dale decided once again to be the point man and responded.

"Well wouldn't want to miss any of it, so we decided to take the scenic route, and boy was it scenic."

I looked at him with an expression of disbelief. Dale ignored me and asked, "so, how's that water?"

The same lady by the name of Darlene responded. "Very hot, just the way we like it."

The other lady sort of laughed and said. "Very, very

hot, you may want to take another lap." They looked at each other and laughed loudly this time. We looked at each other and thought, wow, good-looking and funny.

Dale once again took the lead. "Another lap? Ah, come on don't be like that. Can we join you?"

Darlene looked up. Her eyes went back and forth as if to think about it. She placed her index finger under her chin. "Sure, if you take another lap."

Dale frowned, not believing. "Another lap?"

Dale looked at me. I decided to stay out of it. Dale looked at Darlene. "Not serious, right?"

"Oh come on, we enjoyed it so much." She drew a big circle in mid-air with her finger and added.

"Come on, please, one more lap. Pretend you're supermodels. Nice long strides, just for us. One more lap? Please."

"How do you say no to that," said Dale and took off.

"Are you serious?" I asked.

Dale looked over his shoulder. "What part of two beautiful women asking us to do a lap for them don't you understand?"

I looked at the ladies as they both pointed to Dale. As if to say, get going. So, I took off and caught up with him. Now and then we looked at them, smiled, and waved.

"We like it, we like it," said Darlene, "that's right." added Brenda.

We came to the home stretch, Dale really strutted his stuff leaving me behind. He got to the Jacuzzi and the girls cheered.

"Now that's being a good sport," said Darlene.

"Thank you, thank you," said Dale as he bowed. "I have to admit it did feel a little weird."

"And weird we liked," said Brenda.

"Can we join you now?" Asked Dale.

"Yes, of course."

"Great," Dale stepped into the Jacuzzi.

I pulled over a chair and sat next to the Jacuzzi. The girls couldn't believe it.

"What's the matter? Scared of a couple of mature girls?" Asked Brenda.

"Hey, hey, mature yourself," said Darlene.

Dale quickly said. "He's a clean freak. He thinks the water is not clean enough for him. I, however, think it's just dirty enough."

They all laugh.

Dale continued, "As a matter of fact. I think we need to dirty it up so more." He looked at me. "Get in here you baby."

I shook my head and said, "nope, no human soup for me. No thanks, I'll just sit here and watch."

"So," said Brenda, "you're the watching type ha?".

"Not quite." I looked at Dale and pointed with my chin. "By the way, the dirty one over there is, Dale, I'm Roberto."

"Roberto, well," said Brenda and looked at Darlene.

"We should've known. Come to think of it, I don't think I've ever Jacuzzied with a Roberto before." She looked at me hoping for a response.

Darlene also looked at me, "they're the clean ones, that turn out to be, the dirty ones."

The girls laughed. Darlene whispered in Brenda's ear. "Oh my God!" Said Brenda.

Dale and I looked at each other questioning.

"Hmm, hmm, hmm, Mr. Clean," whispered Darlene and backed away from Brenda's ear to see her response.

Brenda's eyes moved back and forth as she thought about what she heard. She tightened her lips and kept her mouth closed, "well, I could use a little of that."

"Yes, you could. Right about now as a matter of fact." Said, Darlene.

"Shh," Brenda said with her finger to her lips.

Dale looked at me as if to ask, what's going on? He looked at them and said, "ah, hello? Elvis has not left the building. We're still here. What are you two whispering about?"

"Don't ask. You don't want to know, believe me." I said.

Darlene quickly said, "That's right, too dirty for you, Mr. Clean."

Dale looked back and forth from the girls to me, trying to figure it out. He raised his hand as if to stop everything and said. "Okay, okay, let me start over, so, as you know, I'm Dale, he's Roberto, and you are?" He looked at Darlene.

"Darlene, clean Darlene."

Brenda pushed her away and said. "Get out of here clean Darlene."

She looked at Dale. "I'm Brenda, just Brenda. Not dirty, not clean, or anything, just Brenda."

"Just Brenda, that's a funny name. I can't imagine going through life with a name like Just Dale." Said Dale.

"Better than dirty Dale." Said Brenda. We all laughed.

"Dirty Dale, I like it. It sounds like a western." I said and we all laughed again.

Brenda looked at me with a sad face. "Come on, get in. You're making us feel uncomfortable."

Darlene tapped Brenda under the water. Brenda gave her a quick, what was that for? She finally caught on to what Darlene was trying to tell her and said.

"Never mind. Stay out there, we wouldn't want you to come in here and filter our water with your pureness, your cleanliness."

The girls laughed and clink their wine glasses. Dale also laughed and asked. "So, what kind of wine are you drinking?"

"Chardonnay, good girl wine," Darlene said.

"Yes, good girl wine." Added Brenda, reached into the water, and pulled out a bottle of tequila. They laughed.

"As a matter of fact, my dear." Brenda uncapped the bottle, "allow me to good girl wine you, my dear."

"Wow," I said, not believing.

"Now that's what I'm talking about." Said, Dale and looked at me. "You see? You see, what I mean. I could never do that with my wife."

The girls looked around like, did you hear that? "Boy, you are a smooth one." Said Brenda.

"Why is that?" Dale looked around.

My eyes darted back and forth and made the quick decision to put an end to the mystery. "Oh well, I guess you were gonna find out sooner or later."

"Find out what?" Asked Dale.

"That you're married." Said, Darlene.

"Married, who said I was married?"

"You did. Jesus, we're the drunk ones, but then again maybe not."

"Oh, I meant x-wife." Said Dale, like no biggie.

Darlene shook her head slowly. "Too late buddy, you blew it. And now that we're all being honest."

"Honest! I'm not married."

"Whatever." She brushed him aside with a hand gesture and continued. "Brenda over here? Also married. So there you go."

Brenda wrinkled her forehead as she searched her brain, not believing. "Oh, great."

"Who cares?" Said, Darlene. "You're probably gonna be married to him for the rest of your life. Misery and all. So what's the big deal?"

Brenda looked at Dale. "What are friends for ha?" She looked at me with an expression as if to say, yeah, you. She looked at Darlene. "Anything else you want to tell them?" Brenda took a swig of tequila and once again looked at Darlene and mouthed, "thanks."

Brenda looked at me. "Okay, here, you guys need a shot. Here, Mr. Clean." She held out the bottle. I looked at the bottle and hesitated.

"Oh my god, are you serious? Come on, don't worry about it. It's tequila, Jesus! Any germs on this bottle are dead. Dead, get it. They can't do anything to you." Said, Brenda, and looked at Darlene as if to ask for help. Darlene faked a smile but said nothing. Brenda then turned to me and added. "Dead! Get it? Dead!"

Darlene tilted her head toward Brenda, her eyes followed. "Somehow, I don't think that's gonna make a difference. Dead germs touching his lip? I don't think so."

"It's not that," I said. "Warm tequila? Chilled I understand, but..."

Brenda, already annoyed, couldn't believe what she was hearing. Her left eyebrow raised as if it was on autopilot. "Oh, poor baby, I'm sorry. What was I thinking? Let me call for a special delivery for ...."

"Never mind," I interrupted her. "Here, give it here." I

grabbed the bottle, took a swig, and handed it to Dale.

Dale took a swig. "Wow, now that's what I call a shot." He handed the bottle to Brenda and asked.

"So, you're married?"

I looked at Dale and asked myself, what is he thinking? "Really? You really want to go there?"

"What?" Asked, Dale and looked around as if to ask what's the big deal. "I thought we were all being honest here?"

Before Brenda could answer, Darlene quickly added. "Yeah, she's married and miserable."

Brenda made a face of utter disappointment. "Yeah, married and....married. What can I say?"

Darlene, who had heard it all before, decided she had enough. "She's married and tired of him. Tired, tired, tired of him. That's what she says all the time, but she won't leave him. That's my girl."

I tried to figure out what was going on, and to my surprise heard myself say to, Brenda.

"So, what are you tired of? I mean now that she brought it up."

Brenda responded calmly. "Of my husband. He's always doing the same thing. Watching the game, cleaning his car, rearranging the garage, scratchen his ass. You know, the kind of things that all you men do."

She looked at Dale and then at me and said. "As you guys do I'm sure. You know, I mean you are men and with men it's one endless ball and ass scratchen, right?"

Dale and I looked at each other realizing we were attacked. I frowned at the turn of events. I gestured to Dale telling him to leave it alone, not to say anything.

Darlene turned her attention to Dale. "Let me ask you

something." She looked at Brenda as if to say, here we go, are you ready for this? Brenda made a face like saying, go for it.

Darlene turned back to Dale. "When you come home after a hard day's work. And your wife is all dolled up for you. You know, to give you a little love for your hard work and all? Do you still get a hard-on?"

"After a hard day's work? Are you kidding me? I'm lucky if I can aim straight and piss in the toilet. What are you talking about?"

I laughed thinking that was one of the funniest things Dale has ever said. The girls looked at me as if to ask, what's so funny?

I said. "What? You didn't think that was funny? Come on...."

Dale raised his open hand and stopped me. He went on.

"What are you talking about? I mean really. Do you know what it's like to feed three kids, plus your wife and yourself? And keep a roof over our heads?"

He looked around hoping to get some impute but got nothing. He grabbed the bottle from Brenda and took a double swig. He looked down at the water as his head began to move from side to side.

"Work, work, work. Same old shit. Day in and day out." He looked at the girls. "Do you honestly think that I'm not tired of doing the very same things you're talking about?"

He looked at me as if to ask, isn't that right? I cautiously nodded in agreement. He looked at the girls and waited for them to say something.

"What, you're not gonna say anything?"

Darlene tightened her lips, tilted her head, and gave him an I don't know what to tell you expression. I couldn't believe the turn the conversation had taken. I thought of how I was looking forward to this trip, and now? This was all too familiar, and it brought back feelings I had no idea where they came from.

"Oh, no not this again." I said, and laid back on the lounge chair, and closed my eyes hoping to make all go away.

"What? What do you mean not again?" Asked Dale.

"Yeah, what do you mean, not again?" Asked Brenda.

"Go on, take a nap Mr. Clean," said Darlene. "Hey, you should've cleaned that lounge chair before you laid on it, don't you think? Think of all those people who laid on that same chair. You are laying on that skin covered lounge chair Mr. Clean. Think about it. Human dirty skin cells right there."

"Jesus Christ, don't freak him out," said Brenda. "Let him sleep. Hey, wait a minute. Maybe Mr. Clean thinks we're boring and that's why he's sleeping."

"Why are you lying down Roberto?" Asked, Dale, and stood up to look at me.

I kept my eyes closed, but I knew he stood. I could hear the water falling off of him as his body came out of the water. I inhaled some of this so-called vacation air and there it was the sky to my closed eyes. Not quite sure if it was blue, gray, or what. To be honest, I didn't want to know. I stretched my head way back and felt the plastic straps give under the weight of my head. Don't know why I noticed but I did.

"Hey, hey, Roberto." Said Dale. He looked at the girls. I don't know how I knew that but I did.

"Okay, this is getting a little insulting. What's going on here?" Asked Darlene.

"I think we're boring, aren't we Mr. Clean? Is that what's going on here?" Asked Brenda.

"Hey, Roberto, are you falling asleep?" Asked Dale.

I could feel Dale looking at me. I then heard it just before he said it. "I don't believe this. You're embarrassing me, man. What's wrong with you?"

I tightened my closed eyes hoping this wasn't happening.

"Oh, I just saw him move, he's not sleeping." Said Dale.

Here we are on vacation with two gorgeous women in a Jacuzzi, and what are we talking about? Bullshit, nothing but good old-fashioned bullshit. All the stuff we came here to get away from. I closed my already closed eyes yet again and faded into what I could only assume was a deep sleep. I laid there for what I thought was a minute or so and felt as if something had changed. I felt a transition of sorts. As if time had jumped over me as I laid there. I realized that my nothing had gone on for a period of time of which I had no idea.

Wait a minute, the silence, where did the silence go? I heard nothing, and there's a big difference between nothing and silence. This is the absence of all. I almost opened my eyes again. There it was again that feeling of transitioning; in and out of something, or out and into something. Not sure what that was, but it was. Is this another one of those out of place, out of sequence moments? In the past, I had questioned if this was possible, but couldn't tell if it was or not. This time I'm gonna ride out. After all, if it's out of sequence, it's out of sequence. What am I to do? When I'm ready, I'll open my eyes, and as dreadful as that conversation was, I'll just pretend not to pretend.

I opened my already opened eyes to find myself right back in my kitchen. I knew where I was but when is another story? I felt a sudden stream of apprehension, fear, and god knows what else. I looked around and questioned all that happened and all that didn't. Was that a memory, a dream, or a thought? Did Dale and I actually go on vacation? No, we didn't. We were planning on going, but we didn't. But why not? Wait a minute. How would I have a memory of a vacation that we didn't go on? Was I projecting? Thinking of what it would have been like to go on vacation? Why would I do that? What if we did go and I forgot? But why would I forget?

"Oh man, I need a beer." I heard myself say it out loud. I started toward the fridge and realized I already had a beer in my hand.

"What the hell?" I once again heard it out loud.

I stepped back to lean against the counter, and there, against the counter is where I already was. I questioned myself. Did I have a predisposed memory of something that was about to happen? Or was it an action already taken? Did I have a flashback of something I hadn't lived? Or it already lived it and I repeated it? I tried to make sense of what I felt. Oh, yes, disgust, that's what I'm feeling, total and utter disgust with myself, but why? Oh, yes, I now know where, and now I know when I am. After the argument with Dale's wife Christina. One thing for sure, the argument with Christina happened. There is no forgetting that. I can still smell her and I feel her heat against my body and face. And here is where I've been.

Have I been here in my kitchen the whole time? How is that possible? I looked at my hand to see her tears still hanging on to the skin of my hand. An overwhelming feeling of anxiety came over me.

"I have to get out of my head."

I heard it out loud as my voice bounced off of the walls that contained me where I didn't want to be. I looked around begging for an exit and saw the Owl Cafe looking at me. There it was, my yearbook on the counter greeting me, ushering me to my next destiny.

11. WE AIN'T BEEN ANYWHERE WE AIN'T BEEN BEFORE

I walked up to my yearbook, looked at it and my hand reached for the phone on the wall. Why not? Let's get out of this place. I dialed the number to the Owl Cafe; I heard it ring. It was ringing some four hundred miles away and I could hear it ring right here. Wow, that is weird when you think about it. Am I hearing it ring on the other end? Why would you ring the phone four hundred miles away only to send the sound back to me? Or, is the phone company making it sound like it's ringing on the other end when it's ringing right here in Southern California? Wait a minute, why even do that? Maybe it's my phone right here in my hand that's making that far away phone ringing sound. Oh, never mind, what's the difference? It felt like it was ringing four hundred miles away, and that's what matters. What if somebody answers? What am I gonna say? I started to hang up when I heard a lady say.

151

"Hello, Owl Cafe. Can I help you?"

I felt panic and heard myself breathing rapidly.

"Hello! Hello, FREAK!" She hung up.

I heard the click, followed by the silence. In this case, there was no doubt as to where the silence came from, it was right here. Not made up by the phone company and definitely not from that distant place some four hundred miles away. It was right here within the perimeter of this absence. I held the phone to my ear as I waited. I don't know why. As if holding on to it would keep me at the Owl Cafe a bit longer. I could feel my heartbeat in a tiny space between the phone and my ear. It felt like my heartbeat was sparking from my ear to the handset. Like a radar to my now; it kept me where I was, and not where I wanted to be. My world became smaller, and most definitely more evident. After all, not all can be escaped.

I looked slightly to my left and saw my arm attached to my body. I saw my hand attached to my arm, and my hand grasping the phone, as it pushed it against my ear. They felt like separate entities. As if that thing trapped inside my skull grew them as extensions to communicate with the outside world. Wow, that's weird now that I think about it. My brain grew extensions because it was trapped? I don't know about that. I saw my hand still grasping the phone as my arm moved my hand away from my head and toward the wall. My arm was moving my hand. I heard the sound of the phone as it came to rest on the wall set. Uneasiness was now the feeling at hand as fear made its way to the surface from the depths of this body of mine. I looked for my escape, grabbed the yearbook, and walked into my bedroom.

I could see daylight behind the shade on the window. But what kind of sunlight? Was it morning sunlight? Was it midday sunlight, or late afternoon? One thing for sure, the fear I felt was most definitely late night. But the fear was different this time. It was like earlier when I thought I heard myself breathing next to me. As if the fear was a separate entity. Right here within these walls.

Unable to control my instincts, I looked around not wanting to see the fear. Definitely; not wanting to confront it. As I panned the room, I felt a tiny vibration coming from my left hand. I looked down and there it was, my escape calling me, my yearbook. I sat on my bed and opened it to see the protruding piece of the missing page. This was not the escape I was looking for. I turned the pages to my anti-gravity girl. And there she was looking as beautiful as ever, finally my escape.

I spun around, laid in bed, and consumed her beauty as her image projected itself off the page and into the portal to my brain. A few minutes later I felt myself slipping away. And then, from the depths of what I could only assume was this brain of mine, there it was, the sound of my old truck. I opened my eyes and in the far distance beyond my yearbook, coming toward me was that beautiful old truck of mine.

Confused but pleased, I could do nothing but to wait. I opened my eyes again and found myself driving, and in the midst of that rustic old smell that could only belong to my truck. I looked out the side window and in the far distance was the house and the barn I had seen before. As if to frame it with the window of my truck, I stopped. From the realm of a distant memory, a painting of that exact moment revealed itself onto the canvas of my brain. The

cracks on the paint revealed its age. The faded paint and
the hand strokes, reminiscent of its creator. It was like an
old friend from who knows where and how long ago. All I
could do was look into the eyes of that friend. With every
second my friend came closer to convey what I could not
see. I could feel that painting wrapped itself around me. In
the midst of a deep breath of that wonderful smell, there I
was, right back in that kitchen again. In the stillness of
sound, I floated just above the floor. As if my vision could
travel, everything moved toward me as I spun around to
look at everything.

The intensity of this reality, almost too much to bear,
impossible to comprehend. Every little thing was visible to
me. Like the wings of a motionless fly lying on its side on
the window sill. A grain of salt inauspiciously on its own.
Not only did nothing escape me, everything sought me.
Minute detail was the only choice at hand. I could read the
smallest of print on cans and bottles of spices through the
partly opened cabinet door. A bubble in oil confused me,
how can this be? Knowing this was not only rare but
seldom seen my vision zoomed in. Trapped within the
glass vessel's walls and not in oil was the secret the bubble
tried to keep from me.

I could smell and taste the food that she was cooking.
She, Joan Briganti, whose reflection on the window I
would have to accept as hers as I stood behind her. I
questioned, am I the man in my dream? I then realized that
she was frozen. No movement whatsoever. I spun around
to see the children sitting at the table, still, as the walls
around them. Knocking was the first sound I heard. I spun
around to face the sound and outside the kitchen sink
window, with his knuckles to the glass, stood a white hair

elderly man in denim overalls. I heard knocking again, this time from another direction. I spun around and there I was back in my truck, and there he stood, next to the hood of my truck, the man that was outside the kitchen window.

"Man, that must be a real good one," he said in a loud voice with a thick southern accent.

In disbelief, and as if knowing he was going to walk up to me, I could do nothing, but to wait for him to complete the moment. He did and stood outside my driver's side window.

"Jesus, what is her name?"

I had no idea who this man was, nor what he was talking about, or how he got here. He pressed on.

"You know, the girl, the girl in your dream."

The girl in my dream? I said in my head. How does he know that? So he was in my dream. And now he's here? No, that can't be.

"You're looking at me like I'm walking on..."

He backed away to show me his feet. And said.

"Look, I ain't walking on water or floating or anything. You see, my feet are firmly on the ground there young man."

I thought of me floating in that kitchen. Is it possible that he also knows that? He leaned toward me and smiled from ear to ear.

"What, she doesn't have a name?

"I'm sorry....." I started to say.

"What are you sorry about?"

"Ah..."

"You can't be sorry if you done nothing and said nothing."

He looked toward the back of my truck and then toward the front. As if to show me both sides of his face.

155

But why, and why do I think that? He looked at me again.

"Okay, just so you don't think I'm crazy or anything. Was there a girl in your dream?" He squinted as he focused into my eyes.

"There was, wasn't there?"

I looked around thinking of how I was going to explain this. He laughed.

"Sorry about that. Didn't mean to spook you there. I figured a girl was the only thing capable of inducing that expression. If you know what I mean. And from what I'm seeing. You, young man, and all of humanity is and will always be capable of what I'm seeing confusion. So don't take it personally, yes, confused, you are my friend."

As I tried to process what he said. I realized that I wasn't about to, so I said.

"You're right, ah, I must have taken a wrong turn back there and I guess I am confused and lost."

He shook his head and twisted his body from side to side to emphasize his body language of disappointment.

"No, no young man, you see, most people figure out they're lost about seven or eight turns back from where you are. Not too many people come this far to get lost."

He stopped and waited for me to say something, but I had nothing to say.

"When I said confused, I meant confused, not lost. To search for something doesn't mean you're lost."

He leaned toward me as he pierced into my eyes. As if trying to take the thoughts of the unwilling.

"Okay, let me make it a little easier for you. What is the reason for you being here? Ha? Now that's pretty simple, ain't it?"

"Ah....." He interrupted me.

"You see, you've come too far to be lost. You are here for a reason."

"What do you mean?"

He laughed. "Here." He looked down and pointed with both hands at his feet.

I leaned out the window and looked at his feet. He went on.

"Here, right here, you must be here for a reason."

I said the only thing that came to mind.

"I.....guess....I am."

He burst out laughing again and said, "yeah, yeah, I do believe you are. We all are my son."

He looked past me and saw the yearbook on the seat.

"Is that it?" I said nothing. "That is it, ain't it?"

I looked at the yearbook, and took a deep breath, answering his question.

"Come on, young man, get out of that truck before we lose you. Something tells me your journey is a long one."

I wasn't sure if I opened the door, or if he did, all I knew was the door was open. He turned around and walked toward the edge of the road. I waited for a few seconds and watched him as he looked down at the valley below. I got out and walked to the edge of the road. I looked down and across the valley and couldn't believe that I was seeing the white house and barn in the far distance. I once again asked myself a question I could not answer. How can this be? In silence I stood, in silence we both stood. After a minute or so, out of the corner of my eye, I realized that he was watching me. He slowly turned toward the valley until he got to the house and barn and simply stared at it. His head began to move up and down slowly as he went further into his thoughts. A few seconds later he said, "yep, been here since before I was born."

I looked at him questioningly. He continued to look at the house. Since before I was born? I said to myself, but questioned if I kept it in my head or said it out loud.

After a few seconds, he looked at me and said, "in a dream."

He once again looked at the house. Before he was born? This time I was sure I kept it in my head. Without taking his eyes off the house, he said.

"We dream before we are born, you know," he paused. "Yep, been here since before I was born. And something tells me even before that."

I smiled, not knowing why.

"I believe we ain't been anywhere, we ain't been before."

I once again, did the only thing I could, nothing. What could I possibly say after hearing that? I realized there was pleasure to my nothing so therefore I said nothing.

"Well, go on," he said.

I looked at him questioningly.

"Go on, get your book. You've got my curiosity going now."

I walked back to my truck; reached in and grabbed the yearbook as he walked up to the hood. I closed the door. I turned toward him as he reached back and pulled out a handkerchief from his rear pocket. There was a peacefulness to his motions that captivated and relaxed me. They were familiar, yet obscure actions, like a memory I was yet to have. Or had and forgotten, but wasn't sure if I had it to forget. As if the distance between us hadn't existed, I couldn't remember walking up to him, but I must have because next to him is where I stood. And there it is again, distance calling out to me. I placed the yearbook on the hood. I could feel his presence radiating next to me. I opened the yearbook.

"Wait a minute there young man, let me see that."

He reached out, closed it, and looked at the cover for a few seconds. His hand slowly reached out and rubbed the engraved year on the cover with his fingers.

"Ninety-seventy-two, long ago, not so long ago when you really think about it. It could go either way. If you don't think about it. If you know what I mean."

I found myself sort of laughing within, thinking of how right he was.

"Yes siree, now go right ahead."

Without thinking, I opened my yearbook to the ACE Hardware store. The old farmer leaned down to get a closer look. His hand slowly reached out and softly touched the picture with his fingers as my Anti-gravity girl looked back at the man before her.

"Look at her. She is a beauty, ain't she?"

"Yeah, she sure is."

"Now she is one of the other reasons for your journey. That, I now know."

He looked at me as I stared at the picture and felt as though I heard myself say his words. I looked at him to make sure that it was he and not I who said the words when I saw him say.

"But something tells me there's more. Now, ain't I right?"

All I could do was breathe. We both turned to the picture of undeniable beauty as we ushered forward the seconds that waited. Seconds to be filled with the joy she had taken upon herself to share with us. Our expression turned to one of fulfillment, driven by the taste of our eyes. His head began to move from side to side and said.

"Look at her. Hmm, hmm, hmm. Yep, I remember the days when I was young just like you. You don't get any older in here you know?"

He pointed to his chest. "Now I know I look old and everything." He looked down at himself. "But inside? I feel it all the same." He looked at me. "If it wasn't for these old bones? This old flesh? I'd be young again!"

He laughed. I joined in on the laughter.

"Let's start from the beginning there, young man."

I turned back to the first page, instantly we both saw the piece of the missing page. I felt a tremendous urge to move away from it, but something held me back.

"Well, well, well, what do we have here?"

I looked at him and felt as though he already knew. There was something about his actions, the movement of his mouth and eyes that felt like an afterthought. It was as if they were thinking words, written thoughts on the paper of his mind to be read by those who looked into his eyes. He reached out and rubbed his fingers on the protruding piece of page.

"I do believe this...is...the other reason for you being here. Now ain't I right?"

Before I could answer, and with his eyes on mine, he reached out with the other hand and took the yearbook from my hands. Wait a minute, I don't remember taking it off the hood.

He raised the opened yearbook and held it with the pages facing me as if to show me what I already knew. He closed it and opened it. But this time it was the empty pages at the end of the book that looked back at me.

"Search for what you already know, and deceit will find you. The answer lies within your truth there young man. It's not that hard."

"What? What are you talking about?" I pulled the book away from him.

"What's the matter? Afraid of what you may find?"

I heard him say, with his mouth perfectly still.

"You do find yourself at the end of the journey, young man. There's nothing else to find. You can't turn back now. It's already now. Life awaits!"

Before I knew it, my precious yearbook was back in his hands. As if tempting me to follow him. With a rock steady stare, he slowly backed away. I could do nothing but to watch and to ask, why is he doing this, what is he trying to do? There I was right back in my head. And through my eyes, I saw me say the words as if I was him.

"Why, why are you standing there? The silence of fear can't help you now. Life awaits!"

Movement escaped me no matter how hard I tried. Seconds perfectly still, minutes nowhere to be found, and knowing he already knew, he walked back to me, knowing he hadn't walked away.

"Let's put an end to this, shall we? Let me help you."

He reached out and grabbed the yearbook that I thought was in his hands. He opened it to the blank pages and raised it to show to me as if I hadn't known. These were blank pages, unwritten thoughts by those of us who wouldn't dare. He grabbed one of the pages, toured it off, and flung it over his head.

"You want the truth gone?"

He grabbed another blank page, tore it off, and flung it over his head again.

"How about the people in your dreams? You know, the ones, the ones you want to ignore, but they don't want to ignore you. Remember? Dreams from the forever changing planes in a transitional state of evolution? A fancy way of saying, I can't stop dreaming about my past. Who you trying to fool anyhow? Who are these people? Ah, never mind that. Why are they in your dreams and not in your life? Now there's a question for ya."

"How does he...."

I started to say, but I stopped. He grabbed another page and ripped it off. The sound of ripping paper catapulted me out of that nightmare and into my next. Me, leaning against the headboard of my bed. Without any confusion about where I was, and knowing that I hadn't slept. I turned to the exact location of the yearbook on the floor. I knew exactly how it got there. I spun out of bed and onto the floor. I walked up to it and dropped to my knees. I looked at it. I waited for my feeling of comfort, my feeling of familiarity, but felt nothing. I grabbed it, and for the first time felt nothing.

"Nothing? How can this be?" I said it out loud.

I closed my eyes and waited for my memories to play out as they had before, but it was the elderly man who came to mind. Who is this man anyway? Why is he in my head? Is he the one taking my feelings of familiarity, and warmth, away from me? I brushed that aside and tried to visualize the pictures that I had cherished for so long, but it was as if they had never existed. Not a thought, not a vision, not a single feeling.

"How is this possible? I don't believe this. Come on, come on, give me something," I said out loud. I looked around for reasons, and couldn't begin to explain how or why I saw myself from above. It was as if I was begging my yearbook. There was a patheticness about it that was difficult to escape. I had to deal with it.

"Am I talking to a book? What is wrong with me? Am I expecting it to talk back?"

I heard the sound of my voice and didn't like it. And now, I'm talking to myself. Why? These are thoughts, not conversations. Is it possible that I'm decaying into madness? I looked down at this thing called my body and saw it for what it was. An object like the objects around me, decaying, yes, that's what they are and that's what I am. What did I call Dale, a decomposing man? Yes, that's what I said, and that's what I am, a decomposing man.

What a terrible thing to say to someone. But wait a minute. Did I say it, or did I think it? Hopefully, I didn't say it. What am I going to do now? Sit here on the floor and talk to this thing? I looked around as if expecting my surroundings to somehow help me decide. But the objects around me gave me nothing. As that thought exited my head, embarrassment came rushing in. I, a living organism, sat there waiting for a dead organism to respond.

"Very good Mr. Decision maker." I clearly heard myself.

Oh yes, now I remember that conversation with Dale. Boy, who am I fooling now? Word per word, I heard the conversation in my head and was overwhelmed by my hypocrisy. I can't even face the truth that's right inside this book. Wait, what am I talking about? There's no truth here. It's only a piece of a missing page. The rest are blank

163

pages at the end of the book. So what am I trying to do? To justify my inability to make a decision? A decision about what?

"Decisions," what did I say to Dale? "Some, we regret, as a matter of fact, most." I heard myself say it.

Now comes my next question, will I regret it? I should be asking, do I regret not making the decision? The decision to deal with this missing page.

"You want the truth gone?" I heard the elderly man say.

How would I know the outcome of a decision not made? But then again, I guess if I don't make a decision, that is a decision made. An action not taken, is an action. How do you get away from that? I guess as I sit here doing nothing, I am doing something. No matter how I don't look at it, I look at it. How long have I been looking at that piece of the missing pages anyway? When did I first notice it? And why am I now carrying this yearbook everywhere I go? When did this start? And why does it feel familiar to me? As if I've done this many times before. Am I replaying this scene, this episode over and over? Wait a minute. Shouldn't I be asking, Am I reliving this over and over?

"How and why would that be?" This time, I heard it out loud.

I came out of that to find myself standing in the kitchen with my precious yearbook on the counter. From my perspective, it looked like I was spreading the wings of a bird. I don't know why that came to mind. I don't understand why I have visions like that. But then again, what is there to understand, except everything? All I knew at that point, is that the piece of the missing page was protruding straight up. My head filled with questions, thoughts, and feelings I couldn't begin to process. I realized that I was watching me watch me. This person; this thing, this whatever it is I am, was holding my yearbook open. And there I go again, talking about me as if I was someone else. Why? And why ask why? The more I go into deeper thought, the more I want to know. The more I know, the less I know. And there lies the conundrum, my vicious circle. And all of this because of a missing page?

I turned the pages to my anti-gravity girl in front of the ACE Hardware store. And without effort, I did for a change what I had done once, maybe twice before. Not to process her beauty. I enjoyed her without question. And for a few seconds or two, I felt my mind relaxing. As if the wrinkles on my brain were being ironed out. But not for long for it was a futile attempt at an action taken by a man incapable of accepting as-is. My next image unfolded from a part of my brain I knew existed but had not visited from this perspective. It was like looking in from the outside and seeing me looking right back at me standing outside. A part of me had opened its door and I now have no choice. The image was of the elderly man in denim overalls. He turned the pages of my yearbook one by one until he got to the first blank page at the end of the yearbook.

He stopped and looked at it for a few seconds. He then turned the pages back to the missing page at the beginning. He again turned the pages one by one to the first blank page at the end and stopped. He looked at it for a few seconds and did this over and over. He started to go back to the beginning and stopped midpoint. He turned his head and looked at me. I froze as if I wasn't. With his eyes on mine, he turned the pages back to the blank page at the end. With his eyes still fixed on me, he reached out and felt the blank page with his fingers. As if he was feeling the page with my anti-gravity girl, but this was a blank page. I looked away from the image in my head to see me holding the yearbook. At that precise moment, I knew I was looking through his eyes and not mine. And there it was again, that feeling of separation. And then, an afterthought came next. My hand was already on the first blank page, moving from right to left feeling what wasn't there. It felt like the images in my head were dictating my physical actions. Is this a replay of some kind? Is that what's going on? And if so, why? I then realized that my physical world, my physical actions had merged with the moving images in my head. They became one. As if my hand had a mind of its own, it slowly moved toward the lower right-hand corner of the page. I stopped it and was about to move my hand back, when I heard the farmer in his southern accent.

"No one comes this far to get lost. Life awaits, you can't turn back now."

I looked around to see where his voice came from, but he was nowhere to be found. I looked toward the kitchen window just in case he was outside only to see what I already knew. I walked up to the window anyway just to make sure. I looked out to see where I had always been. I'm not in the farmhouse. I'm in my kitchen, right here at home.

"Search for what you already know, and deceit will find you, young man. Don't think about what isn't, think about what is."

I not only heard him, I listened to his message. I'm here at home, right here in my kitchen. I looked down to see my feet exactly where they had always been. Not only had I remained in that same spot, I, did not walk up to the window. Not only that, my hand had never left the blank page. So why did I look for the old man? I don't understand. Did I look for him, or did I think of looking for him? Were my actions taken?

"Stop asking questions, Jesus. Take a breather." I heard myself say.

I stopped thinking and took that breather. There it was, the sound of my lungs breathing. There it was, my heart beating. I stood there listening to the sound of the living. A peacefulness, an acceptance, a silence never to escape came next. I looked down to see my hand at the lower right-hand corner of the page. I felt it. And as real as it wasn't, I felt the indentation to someone's thoughts, of someone's memory left behind. I am feeling someone's thoughts, absent of their physical body. Absent of their voice, absent of their writing.

But I didn't need their writing. To see is hope for the intent. To touch is to feel the very essence of their thoughts. It was a connection more real than anything I've ever felt. It was telepathic, direct without obstruction. No pictures, no images, no writing, yet I felt their need to convey, the honesty of their void which I too felt, but had no reason or idea as to why. A tremendous need to escape came over me. I pulled my hand off the page, turned around, and started to walk away.

"You can't turn back now. Life awaits, life awaits!" I heard him say.

After hearing that, I turned back around to face the yearbook. I felt the grasp of his hand on my shoulder, reassuring me that it was time. I opened the cabinet drawer, reached in, and grabbed a pencil. It felt like an echo again. As if I had done this before. I knew exactly where the pencil was. I know this is my house, but I never find anything, let alone a pencil. But there it was, in my hand. I positioned the lead of the pencil on its side, on the indentations that spoke to me.

I once again felt the strength of his grasp on my shoulder. And to my surprise, I turned around and threw the pencil. I saw it in slow motion, end to end rotating in midair. I saw it hit the wall, lead first as it exploded with the impact of my strength. Still in slow motion, I saw its kinetic energy at work as it hurled it off the wall, and onto the floor. I waited for it to stop moving. And there he was again.

"Now that's more like it. You see you don't need a pencil, the truth lies within you."

I exhaled a breath taken long ago. I don't know how I knew that, but I did. I placed my fingers on the indentations. I felt his hand leave my shoulder. I then felt that little spark between my fingers and the page, as it revealed what I must have already known.

Rest in Peace.
My loving Joan Briganti, my one, my destiny, my one love. Missing You!

The floor hit my knees. Refusing to believe, I saw the floor rush away. I grabbed my car keys, grabbed the yearbook, and ran out of the kitchen and into the garage. I got in my car, clicked the remote to the garage door. I backed out and stopped. I looked down at myself but had no idea why. I could feel the movement of my chest to the rhythm of my rapid breathing. But instead of hearing the sound of my breathing, I heard the sound of rain hitting the roof of my car. My next revelation came from a moment I could only assume was from my now. Not from my past, and definitely, not a recycled thought. This did not feel like an echo. A burst of fear came next, followed by the sound of my voice asking.

"What am I doing? Where am I going?"

I looked over my shoulder and saw the falling rain that seemed as though it existed only in the luminance of the streetlight. To have such a thought, felt weird to me. Once again, not an echo. I refocused to see Dale's house through the sparkling rain in the background across the street. The questions started to line up in my head. As if my hand wasn't mine, it pulled my gear shift out of reverse into first and I took off.

12. A DIMENSION THAT HAD
ESCAPED ME

Slipping in and out of what I could only assume was some state of consciousness, I have come to the realization that I have no recollection of how I got here. Nor why I find myself staring at a black and white picture of the Owl Cafe. I then realized that I was looking at my yearbook as it sat on the steering wheel of my car. To what do I owe this pleasure, or am I still in some state of whatever this is?

To find oneself in a familiar place I have never been, felt strange, to return to a place I have never been, felt like the stranger within. I have gotten so used to him, that recognizing myself is often the norm. I don't know why, or how I know that, but I do. As if staring through the lens of a narrowed brain, and as if the anchor to the world had vanished. From this point forward, only the truth will be my lifeline to what lies ahead of this portal to my brain. Everything is real, yet everything is not, it's not that it isn't, it's just that it is.

I looked up and beyond the black and white picture to see a color picture of the Owl Cafe right in front of me. And then, a conclusion to the realization of the otherwise obvious. As in real life, and all things before me, a dimension that had escaped me, the third, right here in front of me. Not a yearbook, not a picture, not on paper, this my dear friend, is the real, I heard from I don't know where.

And then, a memory of the journey that led me not to where I was. I say that because nowadays, it has become a process of elimination. I remember driving in a night of endless possibilities, nowhere would my thoughts not take me. After many hours, I looked out the side window and everything around me was perfectly still. How can this be? My speedometer said eighty-five miles per hour, yet everything I see, I should not, seconds, minutes from where I am right now, yet I do.

Not sure of what was going on, many thoughts filled my head. One of many, is that my thoughts lingered on for much too long regardless of my efforts to move them along. How can one's brain get stuck? Or is it that my thoughts are simply matching the speed of what's going on around me? The physical world. The still, going nowhere world, where the forces at hand dictate to the limitations of that, not in my world. Is this truly what is happening? After all, it is the brain that dictates to the body. Action is an afterthought, the effect to the cause, the process to the means. Is it possible that there is some kind of separation of thought and action, and that's why I'm questioning the speed of what's going on around me? Is it possible that I'm in a snapshot of a past event? I looked out the side window and saw the stripes on the pavement, waiting exactly where they were dropped off. As if to give me a point of reference as to where the seconds expired, where thought is, and where past and future should be. Is there some kind of break in the sequence of events? Is this a thought out of place? If so, linear thought does exist. Strange when you think about it, but does linear thought really exist? How would I know? After all, the sequence in which all happens constitutes lineage. Question is, at what point? Are these distant thoughts that I have left behind? And if so, why now and not then, and is this the first, second, or third? Is this a thought not had?

"A thought not had?" I heard myself say it out loud. How would I know? Can you imagine, all the thoughts not had? All the actions not taken. Distances not traveled, seconds not left behind, destinies I will not find. Nowhere, will I go where I have not. Is it possible that I am in a reality of my own making? And if so, isn't one reality questioning the other? If that is indeed the case, am I not questioning two realities, the now, the then, from where I do not stand? And if so, am I the third one, they observer looking on? As that exited my head, I knew the answer to my questions and didn't like what I concluded. At this point, with all that has not been left behind, only one conclusion was possible. Asking the questions, is indeed I, the third one in the room. From this point forward, nothing, and I mean nothing will escape me, or I, it, for the inevitability that lies somewhere between here and I, I have come to know all too well. Mute at this point I will not know.

13. EMPTINESS

As the rain intensified on a cold February night, Margaret, a retired high school teacher, drove into town in search of a homeless man. Earlier that day, she saw him walking along the highway and couldn't get him out of her mind. The sound of the rain on her nineteen sixty-six Volkswagen van throws her into deep thought of a conversation she had earlier with her friend Susan who's retiring next year.

"Two years Susan, two years of absolute boredom. Why do people call it retirement? It's more like imprisonment by default. You really need to think about this."

A smile came onto Susan's face thinking her friend was being a little melodramatic. Margaret saw her smile and decided she had to drive her point home.

"I'm serious Susan, I'm telling you, all day long I find myself thinking, what have I done to deserve this? And why do so many quests for the day they'll find themselves behind the bars of retirement? I don't understand."

Margaret snapped herself out of thought and reminded herself that she was driving. But the memories of the days she left behind kept coming. It was wonderful watching the children grow. Every day was different, forever changing. And now, the only thing that seems to change are these forever longer days. She wrinkled her forehead as continues with that very thought and heard herself say.

"I don't remember the days being this long or the nights for that matter. What the hell is going on here anyway?"

She came over the hill from the north side of town on Highway 101 to see the lights of Cloverdale ahead. She had lived in this little northern California town her entire adult life. And now, even the lights looked different, prettier, she thought. How can it be that the only gift to her imprisonment is the many things that had escaped me, while I was teaching, regardless of their undeniable presence? And to think that out of all the glorious things that life has to give, a homeless man is a gift this town has come to know all too well, much to my surprise.

She couldn't believe it the very first time she noticed him. An avalanche of questions invaded her as she watched him from across the street. How can this be? Why didn't I see him before? Where does this man sleep? What does he eat? Who is he? Why wasn't I told? She came out of her thought to see the only stop light in town and stopped.

"Why is the stupid light red?" She heard herself say as

174

the rain pounding on her windshield brought forth her next thought. What is this poor man to do on a night like this? I'll tell you what. To be at the mercy of whatever comes his way, that's what. I can't believe it; this man is going to freeze out here. And to think that I turned the temperature down on my heater at home. I thought it was too warm, too warm! I can't believe it.

She looked around for the man as she came into town on Main Street. She found herself once again seeing for the first time what has always been in front of her. A deserted town. Not a single car driving on Main Street, not a single car parked on Main Street.

"This is odd." She said to herself and continued with her thoughts.

Silence, nothing but silence with the exception of the sound or the rain, and the only living thing in this town, me. How can a place be so different in a matter of hours? When was the last time I was in town this late anyway? Years, and years, that's how long ago. What is happening? There it is again. That stupid question keeps popping into my head. What is going on? Maybe I can write a country song about this or something. I mean look at this place. Can you imagine if aliens from outer space landed in the middle of town? What would they think? I know what I would think, let's get the hell out of this place. Not only that, they would probably think, why is that lady in that van just sitting there. What is she doing? Well, come to think of it, they wouldn't even know what a van is, would they? They would most likely ask, why is that lady in that metal box? A metal box that's going nowhere. Of course, the next question would be, does that light have anything to do with her sitting there? And if so, how can a light have so much power over an intelligent life form? Better than that, what is she doing out here on a night like this? I'll tell you what I'm doing you little Martian. Wait a minute, what if the aliens were from Jupiter? What do you call an alien from Jupiter anyway? She realized the ridiculousness of her thoughts and referred back to asking herself. What am I doing here? She looked up and said.

"I'm looking for the man that has caused this little event, that's what."

The questions kept coming. What exactly is this anyway? Is this guilt I'm feeling? Is guilt one of those things that has been in front of me and didn't know it? Didn't feel it? Is it possible for a person my age not to feel guilt? Is that why I'm out here? Because of the guilt that overwhelmed me as I saw my hand push that little lever to low heat. So now, I have to ask, am I doing this for him, or am I doing this for me? She continued with her self interrogation. Yes, I do believe this is guilt, and I guess guilt comes with a voice? It must, because I now hear the voice of guilt, imagine that. That voice can't be mine. Why? Because it keeps asking, what's going on? Not only that, it's relentless. If it was mine, I would've turned it off. Yeah, dream on. But if it isn't mine, then whose? Mars? Who knows, if it is from Mars, that little green alien has brought me the gift of guilt. Thank you very much. He has looked at me straight in the eye and that little alien's voice is now asking.

"What gives you the right to all the comforts of life?" She heard her voice loud and clear. "Nothing, that's what."

Hey, wait a minute. If he's from Mars, the red planet,

why is he green? Oh, never mind, Mars, Jupiter, red or green, what's the difference? Wait a minute. He may be talking to me right now, red, green, get it? Red light, green light? She looked at the stoplight and said.

"Why is this light red?"

She went on with her thoughts. Is this light punishing me? Because I am doing this for me and not for this poor homeless man? I'm giving myself the satisfaction of attempting, but not committing. This way I can say, well I tried. What can I say? I drove all the way into town for him. All three miles, in the rain. And I couldn't find him. So now I get to go home and get into that warm bed.

"Oh I hate myself. What's with this stupid light?"

She looked around to see not a single car in sight but saw a pile of something in front of the old dilapidated theater to her left.

"Oh my god, that must be him."

She looked at the light, "the hell with it," and turned left toward the theater. She pulled up to the theater and saw a pile of something against the boarded-up doors. She parked and got out. She opened the side door of her van, grabbed the blanket and the thermos and walked up to the pile.

"Hello? Hello! I have a blanket, and food for you."

She cautiously removed a few of the newspapers and a dirty blanket and saw a pair of feet. She looked toward the opposite end and pulled off the blanket. She saw a pile of hair almost completely covering his face, and saw his breath in the cold February night. He partly opened his eyes.

"Oh, thank god you're alive. You must be freezing."

She knelt next to him and laid the blanket on him. She opened the thermos and poured soup into the lid. She grabbed the spoon and as she dipped the spoon into the soup, memories of going fishing with her dad came pouring in. She moved away from that and focused on the task at hand.

"Here, you have to eat something."

She extended her arm out to feed him and realized she couldn't feed him if he was lying down. She sat the lid down.

"Here, sit up."

She grabbed him by the arm, pulled him up, and spun him around enough to lean him against the wall.

"There, that ought to do it."

The man looked down the entire time. She grabbed the blanket and once again placed it on him and carefully positioned the blanket around his neck. She picked up the soup, scooped up a spoonful, and raised it against his shivering mouth and against his clattering teeth spilling soup on his beard.

"Oh no, here, let me."

She reached into her coat pocket, pulled out a napkin, and wiped the soup from his beard and mouth.

"Here, let's try it again."

Oblivious to her surroundings, a police car drove up and shined a spotlight on them. She saw the face behind the hair and felt as though she may know him. He quickly looked away but it was too late. She felt his pleading heart and soul with her now conscious heart. It was a split second that would last her a lifetime. Questions flooded her mind. Can it be that I know this man, or are these paternal emotions? Emotions she had denied herself for a career that came and went. And now, her empty heart was in search of something. Thrown into deep thought and nowhere near to where she was, she heard a man say.

"Hi, Margaret"

Startled, she backed away, dropped the soup, and spoon, and looked up.

"Are you okay?" He asked.

The policeman reached out to help her.

"You startled me, for god's sake. You should've said something before hovering over me like that."

"I thought you saw me drive up."

"I did, but....."

"I can't believe you're out here all by yourself. In the middle of the night Margaret. You have to be careful, come on."

"Oh, he's harmless."

"Here, let me help you up."

He reached down again to help her up.

"No, no that's all right I'm fine. I need to feed this poor man."

"You need to feed him? You know Margaret, they're not as harmless as most people think. You have to be careful."

"I know, it's just that, I couldn't stop thinking, you know? It's so cold out here, it's so unfair."

He looked at the homeless man and made a face as if to say, whatever.

"I don't know about unfair. Most of these guys are druggies you know. Drunks, losers."

She thought of how easy it would be to walk away after hearing that. The homeless man looked at the policeman with a questioning expression. He then looked at Margaret and back down. The impact of that expression solidified what she had recently come to know. That she had been absent for far too long. She looked at Paul, the policeman, who just a few years ago was one of her students.

"Drunks, losers? Oh, come on Paul. Don't be like that. Some of us simply aren't as lucky. You have a good father and a wonderful mother."

She turned back to the man sitting on the cold concrete leaning against the wall with his eyes fixed on the floor.

"God knows what circumstances led this poor man to..." She stopped as she felt water hitting her head and looked up to see rain dripping through the ceiling of the theater entrance. She shook her head, looked at Paul, and said, "to this, to this, can you imagine, Paul?"

She almost waited for Paul to answer, but instead, she looked around and tried to imagine being out here all night. Paul watched her and realized the intensity of Margaret's reaction. He asked himself, what is going on with her? Why is she looking around like that? He looked in the same direction in an attempt to see what she was seeing, but he saw nothing but a cold rainy night. He shook his head and said.

"Oh, I can pretty much tell you what led him to this, but I don't think you want to hear it."

"Just think, this was somebody's little boy. Just like your little boy is to you, Paul."

Paul thought of that very possibility but quickly rejected that premise and said.

"Yeah, yeah, what can I say, except...NOT! He'll be alright. You need to go home, Margaret."

As he turned toward his car he noticed the clean blanket and stopped to look at it.

"You brought him a blanket? Boy, wish my wife was half as nice."

Margaret continued with her observation.

"This, this is terrible. I can't believe that...we would let a human suffer out here like this. There must be something we can do."

"These bums don't want to be helped. Leave the food and blanket, and go home. He's used to this, he'll be alright I'm telling yea."

Still on her knees, Margaret looked at Paul and back down at the man.

"I don't know...."

"You don't know what? He's been out here for years Margaret. I mean come on! You know that."

He shook his head. "I gotta get going."

He walked off. Margaret looked at him as if to confirm he was actually leaving.

"Paul?"

Paul opened the door to his patrol car. "Yeah."

"What happened to you?"

"What do you mean?"

She turned back to the homeless man. "What happened?"

Annoyed by the question, Paul hesitated.

"Ah, can you narrow it down a little bit?"

He waited but heard nothing which annoyed him more. He took another look around and felt the rain on his head and face.

"What happened can take me a week, Margaret. It's cold out here."

Margaret wouldn't or couldn't hear him. She continued to look at the man and ask. "What happened? I don't understand."

"What?" Paul asked, not wanting to know.

"Never mind," she almost didn't finish the word mind. Paul got into the patrol car. She looked to see him in the car. She asked herself, is he really leaving? She heard the car go into drive.

"Oh my god."

She looked at the homeless man as if to ask, can you believe this? Next came the sound of the patrol car as he took off. She looked to see the tail lights reflecting off the rainy street and the sidewalk. And for the first time, noticed the brighter reflection of the center line on the street. She brought herself out of that and couldn't believe that Paul, one of her favorite former students, just left her in the middle of the night with this poor man. Not knowing is one thing, but knowing and walking away is another. A visual of her standing in front of the class with Paul looking at her plays in her head. She asked herself what could I have done differently? Have I failed, Paul? Where did I go wrong? How about the rest of my students? Did I give them the tools to feel what I'm feeling right now? Empathy, empathy...is that too much to ask? And then, an avalanche of her life rushed through her head like an old history film of the world. But instead of the world, this film was of her. She stands in front of a panel of judges as they watch her life projected onto the wall. As the years unravel to her standing outside that theater, the film breaks, and the tail of film slaps the projector over and over. And then, a thought within a thought, this can't be the end. She looks around in search of answers, but no matter which direction she looks, all she sees are empty frames projecting on the walls. Fear rushes through her body as she asks herself, is this my now life? A broken film? Blank frames projected onto empty space. She came out of her inner thought within a thought to hear herself say.

"Is that all there is?"

She turns around to see the panel of judges looking past her and asks, "what are they looking at?" She turns back around to see the empty projection on the wall as the sound of the film slapping the projector gets louder and longer. She sees that the reel is not empty. She points.

"Look, there's more, there's more".

The judges continue to look past her at the empty frames on the wall. One of them stands, looks directly at her, and asks, "well, was it all worth it?"

The question frightens her out of her thought to find herself right back in front of the theater. The sound of the rain now louder than ever. She looked up at the theater sign, past a broken piece of neon tube overflowing with water dangling by a long thin wire. In a whisper, she heard the judge in her head.

"Was it worth it?"

"God, I hope so." She said it out loud, but it was a whisper the street heard. Still looking past the broken neon, she turned slightly to the left to see thousands of raindrops falling through the streetlight. In the far distance, brilliant tiny lights shimmering like diamonds clasped on to the hillside. She looked around again to see the old dark theater and couldn't help but make the comparison of where she stood and the shiny diamonds on the hill. Thoughts of the theater of long ago came rushing in.

The theater all lit up, vibrant, people buying tickets. Her mind sunk way back into the pit of forgotten thoughts. A distant memory played out. It was like a scene from a movie she had seen long ago but had forgotten, or a scene from a previous life not had.

A mother and her son drive up in an old station wagon

and park in front of the theater. The passenger door flies open. A young boy gets out, slams the door shut, and takes off running toward the theater. Hoping to slow him down, his mother yells, "hey".

The boy stops and hesitantly looks back at his mother. She says, "come here."

The boy makes a face like saying, oh no, and walks back to the car. She moves over to the passenger side. She reaches out through the open window, grabs his face with both hands and kisses him on his left cheek. The sound of her loud kiss makes him look around to see if anyone is watching. He tries to pull away, but she holds on.

"Come on, just one more kiss." The boy looks around again, sees no one, and hesitantly says, "okay."

She tickles him with one hand and pulls him toward her with the other. She gives him another loud kiss. They both laugh. He leans in and hugs her. He lets go of her and starts to turn around, but she holds onto his arm. He finally pulls away. He runs up to the ticket booth. She watches her beautiful boy buy his ticket. Happy as he could be, he turns to see his mother smiling. He waves, turns around, and walks in.

Margaret came out of her thoughts, looked around and couldn't believe that she had not only stood, but had walked up to the curb. The thought of time passing without her knowledge disturbed her. To have walked up to the curb and not remembering doing so, even more disturbing. But the reason for being where she was came back to her. She turned back around to look at the homeless man, but instead saw the empty space where he once sat.

"Oh, my God, where did he go?"

She looked around for him, and just like the broken film, empty space revealed itself like never before. Emptiness all around, she heard in her head and thought about that very idea and how weird it seemed. But why? Is there a meaning to what I'm feeling? I mean, I've seen empty space before, but never saw it as such. I've seen films break many times, but never saw the empty frames as empty frames. I thought of it as a broken film. Come to think of it, I didn't even think about it. If we search for something and can't find it, we see it as not found. If we see no one, we see it as no one is here. Or, we don't think about it. We don't see it as empty space. Seeing the empty space would mean that we see the nothing. So why am I seeing the nothing, the void? What is this? What's going on with me? I seem to be a virgin to all kinds of things nowadays. I don't understand. She came out of her thought and looked back as if to verify that he, the homeless man was indeed gone and saw the blanket and thermos on the ground.

"I don't believe it, how can it..." She stopped herself not only from completing the sentence, but from saying it out loud. She once again looked around to see an empty street in an empty town. She then saw herself from the third perspective. Standing there all by herself almost in total darkness in the rain like some homeless crazy lady. An old woman, standing in front of an old dead theater. She felt a sense of panic and heard herself say.

"My God this must be what he's feeling."

She once again turned toward the theater to see her blanket and thermos. She walked back, looked down at them, and saw them as living things. As if they were looking up at her. As if to ask, "what are we doing here?"

Paul and the homeless man had rejected her. That made her feel pathetic. And now that she's looking down

185

at her blanket and thermos, downright ridiculous. But her old self came back online. Oh well, worse has happened to me, so what is one to do but to go on. She picked up the blanket, folded it and placed it against the wall next to his pile of stuff. She picked up the thermos, put the lid back on, picked up the spoon, and also placed them against the wall. She turned toward the street to face the big world of rejection. But a smile had found itself onto her face as she saw the one thing that never seemed to disappoint. The one thing that never seemed to change no matter what. And for that reason and for many more, by far one of her favorite things, her beautiful van.

With that image in her head, things weren't all bad. So I saw empty space as empty space. What's the big deal? One thing for sure, not a virgin to empty space, and definitely not a virgin to rejection. I did away with that one a long time ago. So what is one to do but to focus on the good in life. And yes, good I will take any day, any night, rain or shine, cars on the street or no cars on the street. So here I am, the lonely crazy lady, in front of no one. In front of nothing in the midst of emptiness, but with a clear and present smile for this is my beautiful van. She walked back to her van and opened the door. She paused as if to punctuate the moment. She looked up at the theater tower and tried to remember when the theater had closed, but couldn't. Feelings of insecurity came over her and asked herself, am I making a mistake trying to save this man? The rain crawling down her face brought her out of that and once again looked around to take it all in. For this time, she said it out loud to herself.

"I will be absent to nothing, I will be absent to no one, and in the moment I'll always be, as the moment before me. And yes, thoughts, feelings, and all, even emptiness I will take with, for I will be insignificant no more."

14. DUSK TO DAWN – DAWN TO DUSK

After Paul and the homeless man rejected her, Margaret got home, cleaned up, and got into bed. An endless array of thoughts about the homeless man, and her now life, captured her every waking moment. The next day, she got up, had a quick breakfast and far too many cups of coffee, and went on her way. Her search was once again on. This time, rejection was not an option. A new day is upon us she told herself and failure? An unattainable outcome to be had by others. A new beginning is at hand and this day my dear homeless friend is your second birthday.

More resolute than ever, her commitment to help him now stronger with every passing hour as the sun began to settle after a day of searching. It's time to go home, she heard from one of her inner selves. Her other, other voice told her to ignore that, and to turn right onto yet another narrow dirt road. After countless twists and turns the sound of Highway 101, almost too far to hear. She made a few more turns and saw something lying on the left side of the road. She drove up to it and saw her blanket lying there. Motionless, lifeless she said to herself and questioned, why would I think that? Is this another emptiness moment like last night? Where I saw everything differently? I then have to ask.......never mind. This means one thing, he's somewhere near, that's all this means. That poor man probably has no idea he dropped it. Her other voice says to her, maybe a part of him wants help and this is his way of.....

"Oh, my god, that must be it." She said out loud.

She parked, got out, and picked up her blanket. She dusted it off, folded it, and tucked it under her arm. She saw a trail that led down the hill. She thought he must be somewhere down there. She heard Paul's voice in her head, "you know Margaret, they're not as harmless as most people think". She brushed it aside and took a few steps into the woods, realized how dense the bushes were, and stopped. She walked back and put the blanket in the van, locked it, walked into the woods, and stopped again. She turned around and looked at her van as if to make sure it was still there. As if it was a friend that would be there waiting for her. Ever since she bought her van, she can't seem to walk away from it without turning back to make sure it's still there. It was joy she felt but had no idea why. She thought of a time at a truck stop in Arizona many years ago. She got out of her van, took a few steps, stopped, and turned around to look at it. And just beyond her van, she saw a truck driver do exactly the same. He, too, saw her. They smiled at each other and went on their way, knowing exactly how they felt about their friend on wheels.

She came out of that thought and sighed as she saw the deep blue sky to the east. She thought of how beautiful it was and how all this beauty meant that the end to her day was near. She looked west to see the sun on its way down. The dawn to dusk, she thought. The teacher in her, thought of the two words and how weird it was to use them alternatively. Dawn to dusk, dusk to dawn, and that it was appropriate to use them as such. I am witnessing the beginning of the night and the end of the day, she heard in her head as she smiled.

She told herself to look around in true detail. To take it all in as she did last night when she stood alone in the midst of emptiness. But today, emptiness is nowhere to be found. For it is beauty, nothing but absolute beauty that lies within the reach of my eyes. She took it all in, folded her picture of mind, and saved it in its special place. For this very moment, I will take with, no matter where I go. And with that, excitement filled her every cell, and started down the hill.

A minute or so later, she heard voices and stopped to listen. But heard nothing and thought that her imagination must be getting the best of her. A few steps later, a voice came out of nowhere. She stopped. This time, there was no doubt because whoever was talking, kept talking. Most people at this point would have been scared, but Margaret felt a bolt of energy. She listened and locked in on the direction of the voice. She squatted below the bushes to look through them. She saw what seemed to be an old abandoned small building of some kind. Ivy and bushes had overtaken it so it was hard to tell what it was. One thing for sure, mother nature was hard at work taking it back. Surrounded by nature herself, she heard herself say, "maybe, just maybe, she's taking me back as well."

That little thought and what it meant, brought a little fear to her. She told herself to focus. Are those voices, or a single voice? She listened for a few more seconds. She tried separating the voices but couldn't. The voices stopped. Her curiosity now impossible to control, she took a few more steps and the voice started. She stopped. She looked for an easier way to get to the building, but everything was overgrown. She made her way around fallen trees, poison oak, blackberry bushes, and plants she had no idea existed. The sound of the voices got louder as she got closer. Now and then she would stop and listen. But she couldn't tell what was being said. She finally made it past a huge wall of shrubs and vines and there it was. She couldn't believe that the building was completely overtaken by nature.

With her now rewired brain, she couldn't help herself and the questions raged on. What is this place? Is this a house, a cabin? How did this man find this place? What brought him here? Did he grow up in this town among us? Is it possible that this man at one point was one of our peers? A contributing member of our little society? And somehow faded into this? Am I right about this? You don't wake up one day and find yourself in this place? You have to evolve into this. Maybe he woke up one day in some alternate state of mind and he has no idea, so to him, there's no evolving. What if at one point in our lives, it happens to all of us? Wait a minute, what if it happens to all of us at the same time, and we're all in a different reality every morning? How would we know? What if now and then something goes wrong and one of us, or a few gets left behind? Wait another minute, what if he's the only one to jump ahead and we all got left behind? What if he is the norm, and we're all running around thinking we're sophisticated deep thinkers? In his reality, he's looking at us thinking, what a bunch of morons, crazies. I mean who am I to say? For all I know he's a genius and has access to parts of the brain we can't even begin to understand. Maybe he has the ability to access future memories, and he has seen the outcome of the human experiment.

After seeing that, he said you're on you own, I'm out of here. With all that in his mind, I'm sure he must have said, might as well hang out, relax, and let people feed me. He has achieved total happiness and here I am trying to take it away from him. I mean look at this. He lives out here where it's quiet, beautiful, he has free food, and free housing. Where do we sign up? But it's dangerous out here. What about in case of a serious accident? No one would know for days, if ever. Hey, wait a minute. What if mental state is an accident? Or a series of accidents that resulted in who we are? And here we are the so-called sophisticated deep thinkers taking credit for intelligence. When all along we're an accident waiting to happen. Wait yet another minute. Whom am I kidding? Am I trying to talk myself out of this? Is that what I'm doing? Am I too close to the fire, or should I say, to him, so now I want to run?

She told herself to stop thinking. She looked around to see her so-called dusk to dawn pretty much on its way out. To find herself almost in total darkness way out here. This made her think she might have already woken up in a different reality. I mean look at where I am. Some would argue that point. If I'm thinking it, I'm sure others would. But there's no one here but me and this man, who has no idea that I'm here. What if he looked out and saw me here? Wouldn't he think I'm the crazy one? After all, it is I who is out of place. How does that go? A plant out of place is a weed. Well, right now, I am the weed. Which leads to this again. What if there's nothing wrong with this man? What if I'm the one with the problem? If I'm the only one to perceive a problem, I am the problem, right? I mean no one in town thinks this man has a problem, yet here I am. Trying to solve a problem, that may not even be a problem. The way I'm thinking right now, even I would have an issue with me. And that, she found funny and laughed quietly, her smile louder than her laugh.

"Oh my god, I've got to get going," she whispered to herself.

She made her way through more vines, more bushes, and saw a partly open door. But completely overtaken by shrubbery. The voices continued as if she was invisible and completely silent, but she knew better. So what's going on here? He could be watching me right now and I don't know it. She looked around to make sure that wasn't the case. Wow, she told herself, even in this low light, this place is like a garden of Eden. But in this garden, Adam is talking to himself. She smiled as she suppressed her little laugh. Just a few more steps and she'll be there. She lifted a huge vine with her left hand, but couldn't quite lift it high enough to walk under. She got down on her hands and knees, crawled under and finally made it to the door.

She sat there for a few seconds and thought of where she found herself. How different one spot is from another and how different one moment is from another. How can it be that people are doing normal things right now? Like having dinner, going to a baseball game, or whatever? While this man survives way out here all by himself, in his norm. So much for being connected.

She placed her left hand on the door and her right on the wall. She leaned in, and her skin crawled as the voice made its way toward her. A slight vibration advanced through the darkness, past her, and out the small opening. I was like an entity that ran past her and into the wild. She pulled herself back out as she visualized his voice running through the wilderness. She heard Paul in her head. "You have to be careful Margaret." The homeless voice stopped.

As if he was capable of hearing her thoughts. The natural reaction would've been to back away, but to Margaret, that wasn't an option. She hesitated for a quick second. Collected herself, and leaned into the small opening. She saw total and complete darkness. She tried to slow her breathing. After a few seconds, her breathing finally calmed. Her eyes adjusted to the low light and zoomed in. It was as if her vision could travel, clawing through the darkness with the ability to stop, and look around. As that realization crossed her mind, she questioned herself, what is going on here? Is this another of my firsts? Her other inner self told herself to go on. And right there, what felt like within her reach, still as the darkness around him, against the far corner of the room, stood the once invisible man. How is this possible? How can one not see one second and seconds later see everything? There he was and there she was looking at him. The question is, is he looking at her? And if so, the questions he must have. But straight ahead is where his vision went.

And out of nowhere came this thought, is this the same man? Her heart now pounding, her breathing louder than ever, if only I could stop breathing. If only I could be invisible, this fear I would not feel. As if transitioning from one emotion to another, next came the feeling of what she could only assume was the feeling of one. She wasn't sure of what was going on, but this, she told herself, I have never felt. It was as if she was in his head, within the walls of this poor man's life. She felt his walls of pain, his walls of anguish, his walls of fear. And with those walls came an enormous weight. But what kind of weight is this? She asked herself. Is it regret? Is that what I'm feeling? Am I feeling his regret? If so, how can someone have so much regret? And then came calmness, a feeling of safety, a reassurance telling her this was the same man.

She felt as if they spoke. How can this be? She asked herself. Maybe the thoughts of earlier were right. He may have access to parts of his brain we don't. I guess I do as well; because I truly feel as if we spoke the unspeakable language of thought. She felt his beauty next. How can I feel his beauty? Not only that, how would I know what his beauty is? Kindness was his next projection, followed by a profound deep loneliness. Amid a short deep breath, she came out of that to feel her eyes tearing up. Why am I so emotional about this man? Are these his feelings or mine? And why am I feeling and thinking so differently nowadays? Is this an alternate state of mind? Or, something much simpler? She slowly pulled her head out of the opening and looked behind her to make sure she was alone.

"Hello, Ms. Himes."

The voice came out of the opening, past her, and into the wild like earlier. Her brain now in a tumble, she told herself, Margaret Himes, that is my name. That is me. How can he.......her skin almost crawled, but her confusion didn't allow it. It was as if her brain couldn't communicate with her body to express fear. Her body was none responsive. Am I damaged? Is that what's going on? But the logic in her brain asked, why express fear if there's no one and no reason to fear?

Maybe that's it. This advanced state of mind is telling me, why waste my breath expressing fear? That must mean something, right? There must be some logic to this confusion, to the madness I managed to put myself in. But there is no madness here. Just a man talking, right? I mean, if I decide there is no madness, there is none. The ability to choose, to accept, or deny is where I am. Am I choosing to feel nothing? There it is again, nothing. Am I choosing my reality? Could it be that simple? As if she left and came back to use the seconds she hadn't spent. She asked herself, how long was I thinking? All that thought in such little time. How is that possible? And all that thought only to fuel my curiosity? Because now as in a second ago, I can't begin to look away. And that is most definitely not a choice.

He waited for her to finish her thoughts. And then, the sound of his voice came crawling through the opening again. His words unrecognizable, mumbling, saying something, but who knows what. She leaned back in. Her vision zoomed in like before. And there he was, still standing against the corner, but this time his head hung low. And then came that feeling of familiarity. That same feeling she got back at the theater when Paul shined the

195

light on them. She told herself, I remember it well. I felt as if I knew him. When the light hit his face, instead of looking away, his eyes came to me as spoken words. But I felt more than words because he bypassed the spoken word. He transmitted thought, emotion. This man has a memory of me and I of him. Question is, why does this memory escape me? That's a scary thought. To have something recorded in my head and I can't retrieve it. Why would that happen? Are we unfinished? Are we a work in progress? Here I am again going off the deep end. She pulled herself back out and felt ridiculous. As if she was a few feet away looking at herself. There she was on her knees leaning into a partly opened door into a completely dark room. But it wasn't her looking at herself. It was a body, a face but no face, an entity, that existed in her head from time to time.

She realized that, didn't question it, and accepted it as the norm. She didn't know why, but she did. The it, I'm sure would ask, what is that woman doing here? Doesn't she have something better to do? What is wrong with her? As if arguing with herself, she had to ask, is there something wrong with me? I mean look at me. I'm out here god knows where on my hands and knees in the middle of this overgrown jungle. Trying to do what exactly? Not only that, I heard a perfect stranger say my name. Someone who I've never met. Yet, here I am cool as a cucumber, trying to justify the spoken words by someone whom I've never met.

Trying to convince myself that I might have met this man. Why would a logical woman like me allow herself to enter that arena? An arena where everything is possible. But then again, everything is possible, at one point or another. If we do have genetic memories, then not a problem. Who knows where, or when we could've met? Millions of years ago on the Serengeti, or in a cave? How romantic of me. I mean think about it, Miss logical. He said, Hello Miss Himes. Millions of years ago? I don't think so. What would have been my name a million years ago anyway? Probably a grunt or something. On another day, I would've thought my thoughts were crazy. Today, I don't know why, but not so crazy, well a little. And now I have to crawl out of this. Crawl, on my hands and knees. Right about now it does feel like a million years ago. What if...I walked up toward the road, and there was no road. And therefore, no van. Oh, my god. What if...I looked down the valley toward town, and there was no town. Now that would be crazy. When was the last time I crawled anyway? I have no idea. Why does that seem weird? Well, I guess it should, I mean really.

She looks around and whispers, "I have got to get out of here."

On her hands and knees and totally surrounded by bushes and ivy, she came to the conclusion that there was no room to turn around. I'll just pretend I'm in my van and put it in reverse. She started crawling backward and asked herself, is this how my van feels when I'm backing up? She stopped and evaluated her actions and her thoughts of the feelings her van may have. Maybe, just maybe, mental disease is contagious. I may have gotten too close to him. She sort of laughed and said, "I hope not."

She put those thoughts aside and without hesitation as if she was her van, she crawled backwards through the bushes and ivy. She made it through, spun around, and crawled like a baby. She stopped, and looked around again.

"Oh my god, what am I doing, there's plenty of room to stand. What am I doing? What am I doing?"

She stood, looked back, and realized she could've stood a few feet back. And....there it was again, the feeling of the ridiculous. She sort of whipped the leaves and dirt off her pants and decided not to look around and to stop thinking. Just because it's in my head doesn't mean I have to process it. A few steps later the sound of her mumbling man made its way to her. She stopped to listen. This time she was able to discern some of his conversation.

"After a hard day's work? I'm lucky if I can aim straight and piss in the toilet."

Forgetting not to think, and not to process, she said to herself, out loud. "What is he saying? Something about aiming straight into the toilet?" She turned her ear in his direction.

"What are you talking about? I mean really. Do you know what it's like to feed three kids, plus your wife and yourself? And keep a roof over your head?"

"He's talking about kids and a wife. Oh my god, they probably have no idea where he is." She once again said it out loud. She took a few more steps, stopped and listened again.

"The same old shit. I'm just tired. And sick of it. Sick, sick, sick. Just like you said, one endless ball and ass scratchen. So here we are on vacation."

"That poor man. He thinks he's on vacation." This time, she heard her voice, out loud. She went on with her out loud thinking. "I'm talking to myself out loud. Whatever he has, it must be contiguous?"

The voice went on. "I told her, please don't, I begged her, please don't go."

Forgetting to breathe, Margaret swallowed, sighed, and listened to the clear voice in the quiet of her dusk.

"I told her, please don't, I begged her, please don't go."

The anguish of his words, too close to home. Memories of the times some pompous idiot rejected her came back to her. Lowlifes she thought. She caught herself inflicted memory, and told herself to stop. I have no idea what this man is talking about and here I go thinking about things that have nothing to do with this.

She headed up the hill. She got into her beautiful van and sat there in silence. She once again thought of how different one moment is from another. Now, not as before, I have the permanent imprint of his voice saying my name. And of him begging someone not to go. How sad is that? Is this the head loop that will keep me awake all night? What if this man was born this way? What if the only difference between him and the rest of us, is that he verbalizes his thoughts? As I just did. If everyone heard my stuck loops in my head, and my rant about the idiots in my past, wouldn't they think I was nuts? Are these imperfections or something else? For all I know, he did have an accident and damaged his brain. Or, he did jump ahead of the pack, ahead of us, as I thought earlier.

Instead of jump, I should be saying evolving. Maybe, mother nature's wiring got messed up. She accidentally skipped a mutation and didn't make it all the way. And now he's stuck in a state of transition. If so, a transition to what? A better self, or a worse self? How would we know? Margaret brought herself out of that thought, reached out, inserted the key into the ignition, and stopped with her hand grasping the key. There was something about this moment that told her it was a life-changing moment and once again lost herself in thought.

After all, I have found him. In that process, I have
questioned my sanity and the sanity of life itself. I have
questioned whether it was choice, accident, mutation, or
perspective. I think he's nuts, he may think I'm nuts.
Denying all that we reject would justify where we find
ourselves, who we are, and who we are not. Too much for
some to accept, therefore diverging into the only possible
existence in an otherwise uncompromising world where
people reject, accept, or deny. A world where humanity
has digressed into a swirl of options justified by those who
look away. This is a decision not to be made, but to be
had.

15. CLOVERDALE REUNION

A homeless Roberto pushed his bike on a stretch of
road in Cloverdale in norther California. He stopped
before First Street at the Russian River and stood there for
a minute or two as his brain went into a tumble. There was
something about bridges that bothered him. They were
abnormal structures that confused him. They connected
two pieces of land that nature didn't want together.
Crossing the bridge meant going against the forces of
nature. In this case, it was water that had divided the land.
He would stand before a bridge for hours, losing himself
to relentless questions and thoughts that led no further
than where he stood.

He saw himself in one of his thoughts in a car, a
Roadrunner somewhere in San Francisco. He looked out
the window to see the huge buildings in the distance. He
looked at his gas gauge and decided it was time for gas, got

off the freeway, and into a gas station. He got out and stretched realizing he had been on the road longer than he thought. He looked around and took a deep breath of Northern California air. He thought of how nice it was to not have to chew your air before inhaling and had a little laugh. A nice cold orange juice would be nice right about now he thought. He walked into the gas station and headed for the fridge. He grabbed an orange juice, turned around, and almost bumped into a man.

"Hey, how are you doing?" The man asked.

Roberto tried to remember who this man was, but couldn't and said the only thing he could, and that was nothing

"Remember me?" The man asked.

Roberto's eyes stuttered as he tried to process.

"I'm....not sure."

"Yeah, we went to school together." He put his arms out like saying look at me.

Roberto searched his memory. The man went on.

"Yeah, my name is Dan, Dan Fisher, Arlington Heights man."

Roberto heard Arlington Heights and thought, what is the man talking about?

"Arlington Heights?" Asked Roberto.

"Yeah man, yeah, Arlington Heights High, remember? Your name is, God I can't remember. Wait, wait, don't tell me, it's....it's."

Homeless Roberto came out of his deep episode and found himself in the middle of the bridge. He looked at the water below. The sound of the water seemed loud. A car suddenly passed behind him. Confusion rushed in. He asked himself out loud, "why did the sound of the water get louder and then faded?"

He looked toward the sound just in time to see the car make it across the bridge. He looked at the water and then at the car and tried to make sense of it but couldn't. There was something about the car making it across the bridge that told him to get going. A few steps later the sound of the water got his attention again and stopped. He listened. This time, he thought the sound of the water was white noise. What's making that noise? Is it coming from the refrigerators? He snapped out of that and into the gas station.

"Arlington Heights man, I'm telling ya." Said the man.

Roberto couldn't handle it and walked around him. The man grabbed him by the arm.

"Really? You don't remember?"

Roberto looked at the man's hand grasping his arm. The man released his arm.

"Sorry man, sorry. Ah, really man, you don't remember me?"

Roberto turned and looked straight at him. "You're confusing me with someone else. Don't know what to tell ya." He walked off.

The man couldn't believe it and couldn't let it go. "How can that be?"

Roberto walked up to the cashier. As he sat his juice on the counter, the man walked up to him. Confusion began to take over him as his breathing intensified. The sound of water got louder. Homeless Roberto snapped out of the gas station to him standing on the road. He looked around and couldn't believe it. He saw a car go past him. He turned to look at the water, but there was no water. He was beyond the bridge. Someone said, "Are you getting gas?"

He looked around for the person talking but instead of seeing a person, he saw the vineyards next to the road.

"Sir, sir, are you getting gas?" Said the cashier.

The sound of her voice brought him back to the gas station and felt the pounding in his chest.

"No, no, this is it." Said Roberto.

She looked at his car next to the pumps and made a questioning expression as if to ask, are you sure and said.

"Okay, that will be two dollars and fifty cents."

He pulled out his wallet. Dan watched him. As Roberto opened his wallet. Dan took a step toward him and looked at his wallet. Roberto pulled his wallet against his chest and asked.

"What are you doing?"

"Nothing," said the man and stepped back. "It's just...I don't believe this."

The cashier gave them an expression as if to ask, what is going on? He pulled out three dollars, sat them on the counter, and walked off.

"Hey, hold on, let me get your change."

"Keep it." Roberto walked out.

She looked at Dan and tilted her head.

Dan quickly said, "I swear I know that man."

"And?" She raised her eyebrows.

"He said he doesn't know me."

The cashier's eyes went back and forth and shook her head. "Have I heard that before?"

"No, I mean it, I really do know him. I went to high school with him."

"And yeah, I too mean it, have I heard that before."

Roberto looked over his shoulder as he walked toward

his car. Dan watched him through the window. The sound of Roberto's footsteps and the freeway got louder with every step. He got up to his car door. He looked at it and froze. The sound of a car passing by brought him out of that to him standing on the side of the road next to the vineyards. He looked around for the man.

"What the hell?" He heard himself say.

The sound of the freeway and cars honking brought him back to the gas station. He looked over his shoulder to see a car drive up to a pump. The feeling of wanting to escape overpowered him. He quickly got into his car, turned it on, and drove off. A feeling of safety as if he was getting away, came over him. He turned right onto the street. The traffic light turned red. He stopped. He looked down to see his left leg shaking out of control as panic overtook him. He asked himself, why? Why am I feeling this? Who is this man? Why would anyone I don't know think that I do? He looked in his rearview mirror to see Dan run out of the store and toward the gas pumps. Roberto's hands began to shake. More questions invaded his brain. He heard himself say.

"Is this man following me? Arlington Heights? Why anybody.....?"

He stopped talking as his brain told him the traffic light was still red and to look at his speedometer. He looked at it and saw it on zero. He looked around for cops and didn't see a single cop in sight. He took off. Dan ran up to his car, got in, and asked his wife, "you see that car?"

He pointed to Roberto's Roadrunner. His wife leaned toward the windshield and said, "yeah."

"Do you remember who drove that car?"

She looked at him, "the Dukes of Hazard?"

The RoadRunner screamed as Roberto drove up the on ramp.

Dan rolled his eyes. "No! I mean someone we used to know."

"Someone we used to know?"

"Yeah."

She made a face trying to figure it out. "I, I don't know. Give me a hint."

"Remember that guy that used to race his car?"

She looked up thinking.

"You know, there were three or four of them and a girl. Remember that girl? Ah, she had the Mustang. They used to go out."

"Oh, yeah, um, what was her name? She was cute. She always hung out with those guys."

"Yeah, yeah, that's her." Dan smiled.

"Ah, Roberto?"

Dan lit up, "that's it."

He pointed at the on-ramp as if Roberto was still there. "That was him."

She looked toward the on-ramp. "Still driving the same car?"

"Yeah," Dan said with an expression as if to say, what's wrong with that?"

She made a face not believing him. "In San Francisco?"

"Yeah. He blew me off, man. Can you believe it? He said he didn't know me."

"Well, maybe he doesn't. Or, he doesn't remember you. It's not like you guys hung out or anything."

"Well, actually we did, a couple of times."

"You did?"

206

"Yeah, we hung out at parties a few times."

"Where was I?"

"I don't know, I mean, I don't remember everything."
Dan had a flashback of him sneaking out without her.

"Maybe it's not the same guy." She said.

"Oh come on, same car, same guy."

"Ah, same car, not the same guy?"

Roberto looked at his speedometer to see it at eighty miles per hour. His heart pounding, his hands shook. He tried opening his orange juice and spilled most of it on his lap. Confusion engulfed him as he dialed back his brain in search of anything that may bring some resemblance of this man. Instead, he looked around to see himself pushing his bike on the highway, surrounded by vineyards with the sun setting on the horizon. He looked at himself in search of the spilled orange juice and instead saw the orange tint of the setting sun covering his entire homeless body.

He asked, "why so much orange?"

He looked straight ahead to see the sun sitting on the road. He couldn't believe it.

"Why is the sun touching the highway? Why is it doing that?" He said it out loud.

The passage of time escaped him as the sun dipped behind the horizon. "What happened? Where did the sun go?"

Questions and more questions took over him. Unable to process, paralysis took over him. Unbeknownst to Roberto, a class reunion was taking place in the Victorian house right next to him. People were eating, drinking, and dancing to seventies music. A banner hung from the balcony. "Class of 1976 Reunion". One of the men, Henry, looked over the hedge. He saw Roberto standing on the side of the road with his hands grasping the handlebars of his bike. Henry asked himself, what is this man doing standing there? Not sure if the man was moving, he leaned over the hedge to get a closer look. A memory plays out in Henry's head. It was nineteen seventy-six. Henry and his friend Tom, had a homeless man buy them beer, on the night before going off to college. As if standing at the intersection of now and then, Henry asked himself, how can this be? That was thirty-five-years ago and he was old back then. How is it that he's alive today? A smile came onto his face as the walls of doubt disappeared. Henry looked back at the party and yelled.

"Hey, hey look at this guy."

A few people walked up to the hedge. Henry pointed at Roberto.

"Remember him?" He looked around hoping they would recognize him. "Remember? He used to buy us beer."

Mike, who used to hang out with Henry, tried to process the image of a long ago forgotten man.

"You've got to be kidding." Said Mike.

Tom, with his mouth wide open, said. "No way man. That can't be him."

"Yeah, that's him. Remember Tom?" Asked Henry, Tom looked at him questioningly. Henry added.

"Remember graduation night? He bought us beer."

Tom's distorted expression told Henry that he didn't remember. Linda Southern, who used to be a cheerleader, ran up to the hedge to find out what the commotion was about. She tried to look over the hedge but wasn't tall enough. She grabbed a chair and stood on it as everyone pointed at Roberto.

"Who is that?" Linda Asked.

Henry quickly answered. "That's the guy that used to buy us beer man. Remember?"

"The guy that used to buy us beer?" Linda repeated under her breath. But she couldn't remember any of the guys that bought them beer, let alone one specific guy.

Henry looked at her. "Yeah, remember?"

Linda's face distorted trying to remember.

"Remember! The homeless guy. He was always really nice." Henry looked at Dave, another of their buddies who was also trying to remember.

Linda finally got a glimpse of a memory. "Oh, my God. I remember. Do you think that's the same guy?"

Dave looked at Roberto and then at Linda and said. "I don't know. I think so, maybe."

He looked around for reassurance. "Hey guys, remember that bum that used to buy us beer? Way back when?"

More people stood and looked over the hedge. Melinda, another of their cheerleaders, looked at Roberto. Her nose wrinkled as a memory came to her.

"Holy shit, I can't believe this."

Jerry, one of their hard-ass friends, had no idea nor did he care if that was the same guy. He leaned way over the hedge and yelled. "Hey, hey, remember us?"

Henry looked at Jerry and started yelling. "You used to buy us beer, man. Hey man."

Dave looked around and settled on Tom.

"What was his name? Do you remember?

"I...I don't remember."

"I don't think that's the same guy." Said Linda and looked around. "Hey, get Debbie. She's been here all these years, she'll know. Debbie, Debbie!" Yelled Linda.

Roberto stood frozen and heard absolutely nothing.

Debbie walked up to them. "What's going on?"

They all point over the hedge.

"Take a look at that guy." Said Linda.

Debbie got on her toes and looked over the hedge. "Okay, I now looked at him. Now what?"

Linda smiled as she looked at Debbie. Debbie returned the look with a little confusion. Linda covered her mouth trying not to laugh.

"What's so funny?" Asked Debbie.

Linda looked at Jerry and said, "isn't she funny?"

Jerry ignored Linda and asked Debbie.

"Is that the same guy that used to buy us beer?"

"I buy my own beer now you idiots. How the hell am I supposed to know?"

Henry stepped toward Debbie and said.

"Well, you've been here all these years."

"And?" Said Debbie and paused waiting for an answer.

"And jeesh," said Jerry, "what's up with you? We're just asking a question."

"Ah, no.....you're asking a stupid question."

There was a moment of total silence. Dave looked around in frustration.

"Jesus, still bitchy after all these years."

Linda laughed and hugged Debbie. "Don't you just love her though? She's still our bitchy Debbie."

She kissed Debbie on the cheek. Debbie smiled and put out her arms like saying, take it or leave it. She looked at the group and said.

"Well, what do you want from me? I mean really."

Henry felt the excitement drain out of him but held on to little hope. "Has there been a bum in town all these years?"

Debbie sighed and cocked her head. "Okay, if it makes you feel better, yes."

Tom who stood behind Debbie said. "All towns have a bum, I mean come on man."

Everyone looked at him.

Tom went on. "How do we know that's the same guy, I mean really?"

Henry looked around as he tried to remember his name. "Oh, I know his name, I know it. Ah, ah, damn I had it right here." He pointed to his head.

Everyone tried to remember. Henry's face lit up, "George, that's it, it was George, it's George." He looked over the hedge. "Hey, George. Hey!"

"That's it!" Said Dave and he too looked over the hedge. "Hey, George!"

Roberto saw movement to his right but remained perfectly still. Dave held up his beer toward Roberto. "Hey man, wanna a beer?"

"You guys cut it out." Yelled Melinda.

"Yeah man, how bout a shot." Said, Henry.

Roberto turned his eyes toward the movement, but his face remained fixed. People pointed at him. Their mouths moved. Their silent yells he could see as they held up beers and drinks.

Debbie looked around not believing. "Oh, really smart. I can tell you guys grew up."

"Come on George, have a beer." Yelled Mike.

A bunch of people yelled and offered Roberto beer. Debbie decided it was time to step in.

"All right everybody, leave him alone, leave him alone." She yelled.

"Jesus, you think we were back in high school." Said Melinda.

Roberto's ears popped and everyone's hollering and yelling rushed into his head. He took off as fast as he could.

"Hey, where are you going?" Most of them asked.

"Come on George, join us."- Collectively.

"Hey, come back, we need beer." A few others yelled.

His head was pounding and found it difficult to breathe. The sound got louder instead of fading. He looked back to see if they were following. He tripped and fell on his bike. He untangled himself, picked up his bike, and took off. He turned right at the fork. He looked for a place to hide. He saw a barn and a small shed next to the house where the reunion was being held. He ran to the back of the shed. Dropped his bike, squatted down, and leaned against the shed. He stayed there for a few minutes and settled down. He could hear the loud music and people talking on the other side of the fence. After a while, he crawled to the fence. He looked between the pickets to see them talking, dancing, and drinking. Something intrigued him about these people. He wasn't sure what it was, but he couldn't stop watching them. He then thought, wait a minute, they like the same music I do. The music rejuvenated him. I love this music, he heard in his head. But something else was calling out to him, but he couldn't quite pinpoint it. He went back to his bike and pulled out his yearbook. He went back to the fence and opened it. He turned to the senior pictures as if he knew exactly where that page was. He positioned himself and the yearbook so the light from the other lit up the pictures.

"Here we go, here we go."

He heard the sound of his clear voice. He turned away

and thought about how different his voice sounded. He heard the sound of his breathing. He closed his eyes and told himself to settle down.

"Debbie! Debbie MacCann, come here." He heard from the other side.

He positioned the yearbook so he could see the names. He pointed to the names. His heart was once again pounding. What the hell is wrong with me? He heard from his inner voice, which sounded even weirder to him. He lowered the yearbook and thought about his inner voice. He told himself not to, to just let it go. He raised the yearbook again and his eyes went to work.

"Debbie MacCann, there she is." He whispered.

He looked through the fence and saw a lady talking to another lady. He looked at their name tags. His brain zoomed in and saw Debbie MacCann and Linda Southern. He searched for Linda and found a picture of both of them together as cheerleaders. I was like time traveling, he thought. One second they're young, the next, not so young, but they looked good, he thought. He liked what he saw. As the night went on, Roberto heard names, and excitement kept coming every time he found them in the yearbook. He could not believe it. How in the world could this be happening? He could not stop watching them and listening to them. After a couple of hours, the sound from the other side faded and so did he, into a deep sleep.

Three of the guys that thought he was George, walked up to the side of the shed and relieved themselves. They got done and started to walk away when Tom said, "hey, hey, what is that?"

They stopped and listened. "That sounds like snoring dude," said Dave.

213

"Maybe someone passed out," said Henry.

"Let's go see," said Tom.

They walked to the back of the shed and saw Roberto sleeping next to the fence.

"Oh, man, look at this," said Henry.

Dave walked right up to Roberto and looked down at him. "Check it out, man."

Tom leaned down to get a closer look. "Dude, I told you that wasn't him. This guy is too young. Look at him."

"Oh, come on," said Henry and walked up to Roberto. "That is him. And I mean George dude!"

"Wake him up, man." Said Dave.

Tom pulled out a cigarette lighter and lowered it right next to Roberto's face. "You see, this guy is too young, I'm telling you."

Tom grabbed a stick and poked Roberto in the ribs. "Hey, hey, George, wake up, wake up man. We need some beer man." Tom tapped him on the head. Roberto instantly grabbed the stick and took it from him. They jumped back.

"Oh, shit." Said Tom.

"Holy fuck, shit did you see that?" Asked Henry and laughed at Tom. Dave also laughed.

Startled by Roberto, Tom kept his eyes on him. Roberto kept the stick raised between him and Tom to protect himself.

Dave placed his index finger to his lips and said. "Sssh," he looked at Roberto. "It's all right. We're not going to hurt you, relax."

"So hey, wanna buy us beer?" Asked Henry.

"Shut up, that's not the same George," Tom said to, Henry.

"Yeah, it is. Ha, George?" Said, Henry.

Dave smiled at Roberto happy to see him and said. "It's drunk-George man. Our bum is alive and he took your stick dude." They laughed.

"Yeah, man. He took your fucking stick." Henry said to Tom. He looked at Roberto, "what are you, a ninja bum?"

They laugh even louder.

"Jesus, you scared the shit out of us man. Whoever you are." Said Tom.

Henry looked at Tom and made a face. "Shut up man. This is, Drunk-George. Whether you like it or not."

Roberto remained silent. He couldn't believe that the three men in front of him looked familiar to him. But why and how is that possible?

Dave, who was drunker than he thought, leaned down and almost fell on Roberto. He put his hand against the fence and regained composure. "Oops, sorry there George."

Tom shook his head. "Good job there buddy, way to go."

Dave laughed a little and said, "come on George. Say something. Why won't you talk to us? Ha, how come? Come on man. Say one little something for us."

Tom grabbed Dave and pulled him away from Roberto. "It's not George God Damn it. I'm telling you."

Tom took the stick from Roberto and threw it aside. He grabbed him by the shirt and shook him. "Tell them. Go on, tell them. What's your name? You fucking bum."

Henry and Dave grabbed Tom and pulled him off of Roberto.

"Wow, wow, hold on, man, let him go, let him go, man!" They both yelled.

Dave placed his hands on Tom's chest and pushed him back. "Take it easy man."

Roberto finally recognized them and softly said. "Tom!"

All three froze. Tom looked at him. He pushed Dave and Henry away and walked up to Roberto.

"What? What did you say?"

Roberto said. "Tom."

Henry sort of laughed but wasn't sure if he heard him correctly. "Oh, shit, oh, shit. What did he say?"

Dave shook his head slowly as he looked at Roberto. He looked at Tom. "Told you, man. I told you, hell yeah. It's Drunk-George dude."

Tom's expression of disbelief changed to one of anger and yelled. "Bull-shit. He heard someone say my name earlier."

Roberto raised his hand and pointed at Henry. "Henry," he looked at Dave. "Dave."

Henry always thought it was Drunk George. But was as surprised as Tom and Dave to actually hear it.

"Holy shit. It is him. It truly is him, man."

Tom relaxed. He looked at Dave and Henry. "Oh, my God. Can it be? Can it possibly be? I don't believe it."

Tom's expression once again changed from one of awe to one of deep thought and confusion. He looked at Roberto.

"No way, this can't be. What am I thinking? This can't be the same guy."

He grabbed Roberto. Henry grabbed Tom from behind, and pulled him off and yelled. "Hey, hey what are you doing?"

"What is your problem?" Asked Dave.

Tom extracted himself from Henry's grip. He dropped to his knees. He grabbed Roberto and positioned his face between the pickets.

Henry and Dave both yell at Tom. "Hey, hey, take it easy." "Jesus Tom go easy on him," yelled, Dave.

Tom leaned into Roberto's face and shouted, "looked through the fence. Look through the fence damn it."

Henry started to pull Tom off, Tom turned to face him. "Don't you fucken touch me!" He looked at Dave. "Don't even think about it."

They both froze and let things play out. Tom turned back to Roberto and once again leaned right into his face. He looked through the pickets and searched for a couple of seconds. He looked at Roberto and said. "Okay, who's the girl in the orange dress?"

Roberto tried to focus but couldn't identify the face. Tom shook him trying to make him answer.

"Come on! Come on! Who is she? Remember? You used to buy both of us beer. She knew exactly where to find you whenever we needed beer."

Roberto remained silent. Tom went on. "You see. You see. It's bullshit. That's all it is, bull fucking shit."

"Really?" Asked Henry and reached toward Tom to pull him off, Tom swung his hands away. Henry realized that Tom was out of control. "Man, I don't believe you. Why are you all pissed off man?"

"Because I hate liars, that's why I'm pissed off."

"What is he lying about? I mean really, if he did hear our names earlier, how would he remember? Did he write them down or what?"

"Margo." Said Roberto.

Henry and Dave once again froze. Dave placed his hand over his mouth. He then raised both hands and placed them on top of his head and slowly spun around. He stopped to face Tom and said, "oh, shit! There it is, man. There it is, it's him. You heard it. You fucking heard it."

Henry stood tall and said to Tom. "I knew it, I fucking knew it. Release him. Fucking release, him"

Dave, who was still bent over laughing, stood up. Spun around and looked at Tom.

"Fuckin'ay man. He fucked you up...again. Ninja George took your stick and then fucked you up again."

Henry kept looking at Roberto with a blink-less stare. "Our Drunk George is alive, right here with us man."

Roberto looked through the fence again. "Sheri."

"What the fuck?" Said Tom.

All three looked through the fence.

"Well, I'll be God Damn." Said Tom.

Henry raised his hands way above his head as if he just scored a touchdown. Kept them up for a few seconds and lowered them. He grabbed his hair and pulled up. "Oh, my God."

Tom grabbed Roberto by his jacket, spun him around, and pulled him to his feet. He backed away and looked at him from head to toe. He placed both hands in front of him. Roberto flinched.

"It's okay, it's alright man." Said Tom. He grabbed him by the shoulders, pulled him in, and wrapped his arms around him. "I'm sorry man, I'm sorry man I really am."

All three gave him a group hug. Tom backed up and looked at him. "Come on George, let's go have some beers."

"Right on." Said Dave, "this time we're gonna get you some beers. How about that buddy?"

Henry took it all in with a huge smile. As if frozen in a sphere of time, Tom could not take his eyes off of Roberto. He felt tears of joy and regretted his actions. He looked at Henry and said, "I'm sorry man, I'm so sorry, I don't...."

Henry put his hand on his shoulder. "It's okay, it's okay man, we're good, we are damn good."

The next thing Roberto knew was a huge smile cemented on his face and his ass on a comfortable chair. Something he hadn't felt in who knows how long. As if not believing it, he reached up and felt his smile with his fingertips. A quick flashback of him smiling with someone rushed through his head but couldn't see the face. His smile vanished.

Tom saw his expression. "Are you okay?"

Roberto slowly turned toward him as his smile came back.

"That's more like it," said Tom.

"Is he hungry?" Asked one of the girls.

"Bums are always hungry." Said Jerry, a few people laughed. Tom gave Jerry a dirty look.

Henry also gave him a dirty look. "Don't call him bum. His name is George, George! Get it?"

Jerry made a face as if to say, whatever, and walked off.

"Come on, come on!" Said Dave said. "Let's get him some food, fooood for god's sake."

A couple of girls took off to get him food. Tom held out a cigar.

"Here, let's do what men do best. Let's smoke a cigar, you and me. Come on George."

Roberto heard, "what men do best," and deep inside

219

his head an echo rang out. "I mean you are men and with guys it's one endless ball and ass scratchen, right?"

He snapped out of that and saw the cigar Tom held out for him. Another memory rushed through. He sat in a garage smoking a cigar with a yearbook on his lap.

"What's the matter?" Asked Tom.

"Maybe he doesn't smoke." Said Melinda.

"He knows it's not good for you." Added Kathy.

"Oh, give me a break." Tom gave them a look.

Roberto came out of his flashback. He saw the cigar right in front of him. He hesitated, looked around as if to see where he was, and saw nothing but friendly faces, and his smile came back.

"That's it, that's it." Said Tom, and looked around like saying, told you. Tom placed the cigar in Roberto's hand.

"That's my boy." Said Tom.

He pulled a lighter from his pocket. Roberto slowly placed the cigar in his mouth. Tom flicked the lighter, raised it to the cigar, and watched Roberto puff on it like an expert. Tom pulled the lighter away and watched him with absolute joy. Roberto pulled the cigar away from his mouth. He looked at it and made an expression as if to say, not bad. Tom reached out and squeezed Roberto's shoulder.

"Life is good. Ha, George?"

Henry watched from a distance and thought of how different things were from just a few minutes ago.

Roberto smoked, smiled, and scanned the faces. In his clear mind, nothing would escape him. He matched most of the faces in his now, to the faces in the forever yearbook in his head. A quick flash of fear rushed through him. His inner voice asked, where's my bike? He looked around thinking he said it out loud. No one responded which told him he kept it in his head. He looked at the fence a few feet away. The thought of being on the other side confused him. It felt like two separate worlds. He asked himself, how can it be that I was on the other side, alone? And now, here I am with all these friendly people. Smoking a cigar with a man who a few minutes ago was yelling at me. Was that a few minutes ago? It feels like hours, maybe days. He tried to organize his thoughts, but couldn't. He processed that which he could, and rejected that which he could not. All along he puffed on his cigar and kept up his smile. He thought of his precious yearbook. The urge to look at it, almost unbearable. The thought of seeing all these faces that he had seen in his yearbook confused him, and brought joy.

"Here you go, George." Linda placed a dish of food on his lap. "I hope you like ribs."

Everyone waited for his response. He looked down at the plate and a huge smile came on to him. Everyone laughed. He grabbed the fork and dug in. Enjoy this moment, he heard from a place deep within his head. A place that in the past brought him pain. But tonight, it was joy he felt. Everything is good, he heard that voice again. He chewed, smiled, chewed, and smiled more. A woman inside an open window on the second floor caught his eye. She too, he recognized, Cathy is her name. Her conversation with someone on the phone, once beyond his reach, was now well within his grasp.

"So, how's the weather in good old Southern California?" Asked Cathy. She paused.

"Really, that's great. Hey, you know what? Remember that guy that used to buy everyone beer?" She paused.

"Yeah, yeah that guy. You're not gonna believe this."

He came back out of that window to a feeling of acceptance, a feeling of belonging among friends. This was his yearbook in the flesh. He had made the leap between fantasy and reality as he had hoped so many times before, and didn't even know it. For these were the friends he had come to know all too well.

16. ENERGY-SUCKING VAMPIRES

Margaret stood in the waiting room of the Cloverdale Police Department. She was looking at pictures on the wall of two policemen who lost their lives in the line of duty. She read the plaque below one of the pictures and lost herself in thought. Paul walked in and stopped a few steps from her. As a teacher, she had always told them it was better to read than not. He waited, watched her, and wondered what was going on in that head. Her biggest surprise was not remembering the death of one of these men. It happened a few years ago and she had no idea.

She questioned how, or why our state of presence was so different from one person to another, or from one stage of our lives to another. What causes that? Was it age, or an event in our lives that changed us? That caused us to open our eyes, or close them for the sake of survival? Or, something as simple as not caring is more like it. She went on to ask herself, what was my state of mind for me not to care? What does it take for one to be present, to be in the moment? How does one achieve that kind of conscience? Where one doesn't have to force oneself to pay attention to that which is in front of us? That must be wonderful, serene, self, to be one. I guess, because at this point in my life, I may never know. It's not like I hit puberty yesterday, so what's taking me so long?

"Hi, Margaret." Said Paul.

She turned around and found herself out of breath. "Oh, hi Paul."

"What were you thinking?"

"Oh, I don't think you want to know." She turned back to the picture.

"Oh, I beg to differ."

"Okay, if you must. I was thinking that I didn't hit puberty yesterday."

"You're right, I don't wan....."

"Told ya," she said without taking her eyes off the picture.

"So looking at this guy's picture made you think that?"

"How long have you been there Paul?"

"Oh, about ten minutes."

She looked at him not believing and looked back at the picture.

"Not really, just walked in. You're out of breath. What's going on?"

"How do you know I'm out of breath?"

"I can hear you and see your breathing. Not that complicated."

"Yeah, I guess you're right. I forget to breathe sometimes. You know, when I go into deep thought. You probably do as well, you just don't realize it."

There was a pause which surprised her. She looked at him almost as if to make sure he was still there. She turned back to the picture.

"This wasn't that long ago. How tragic is this?"

Paul thought about the policeman that Margaret was so intent on justifying her not knowing of his tragic death.

"Yeah, that's for sure." Paul finally said.

"What took you so long?"

"What do you mean?"

"Not that complicated, remember?"

He frowned, still not knowing what she meant. She went on.

"My question, Paul....wasn't so compli..." He interrupted her.

"You're right, it's just that I remember this guy."

He pointed at the picture.

"You do? You were still in school when this happened."

"Yep, I was....and yep, he pulled me over a couple of times."

"What do you mean?"

"He pulled me over when I had my Camaro."

"He did?"

"Yeah, sure did, a few times as a matter of fact." He pointed to the writing on the plaque below the picture.

"They forgot to write on there that he was an asshole."

She turned completely around to face him.

"Paul!"

"What?"

"The poor man was shot. He's dead."

He cocked his head, "yeah..and..he was probably shot by someone he was an asshole to."

225

"Paul, I don't believe you."

"Well, I don't know what to tell you. Except that everyone around here also thought he was a, you know what."

"Yeah but...." Paul interrupted her.

"Oh, come on Margaret, just because the guy is dead doesn't mean he wasn't an asshole."

Margaret didn't know how to respond. He grabbed his belt with both hands and swayed back and forth as if to say, okay so now what?

"So, what can I help you with?"

Her expression was one of disappointment with Paul.

"Come on Margaret. You mean to tell me you don't have a single person in that deep brain of yours that was an asshole while living and continued being one as dead?"

"Well....maybe one."

He gave her a look.

"Okay, two." She shrugged and looked at the picture, as if to say, sorry, and looked at Paul. She hesitated for a few seconds.

"Ah, remember the homeless man?"

"Yeah."

"What do you know about him?"

"Not much, why?"

"As you know, I've been sort of feeding him, and..."

"What happened?"

"Nothing."

"Come on what happened? We can go out and get him right now."

She uncrossed her arms and said. "Nothing happened Paul, this man has done nothing."

"So what's going on?"

"Ah, he knows my name."

Paul searched his head for something he might've missed. "He knows your name?"

"Yes."

"Margaret...I too know your name. What's the big deal."

She ignored him and asked. "Do you have any idea who he is?"

"No, but let's get back to him knowing your name."

"Well, I've never told him my name."

"Well," said Paul, mimicking her. "Are you sure?"

She made a face.

"Sorry," said Paul, "he must've heard us the other night, remember? I..said, hello Margaret."

"No Paul, not Margaret. He said, Ms. Himes. Hello, Ms. Himes. As if he knew me."

"Hm, he must know you from somewhere. Maybe he read about you in the newspaper or something?"

"Newspaper? Which one? The Wall Street Journal?"

Paul gave her a look.

"Sorry, just kidding." She waited for him to say something. He waited for her to go on.

"Ah, can you help me find out who he is?"

"I guess, but why?"

"I just want to know. Well, I also want to know how he knows my name, but I can figure that one out later."

He faked a smile and tilted his head as if to say, really? He said, "we....we can figure it out, Margaret?"

"Sure I mean if you have the time."

"Come on, I have the time right now. Let's see what we can find."

He opened the door. They walked into the hallway and

227

into an office. Paul pointed to the chair in front of the desk. Margaret sat as Paul walked behind the desk and sat. Margaret looked around, taking in the decor in his office.

"This is nice Paul."

Paul nodded and said. "I'll make it a point to tell my wife."

"Oh, so she did this?"

"Yes, without a doubt. Okay, we're gonna look for any missing persons, dating back..how far back do you want to go?"

He logged onto his computer. Margaret looked up thinking and said, "I don't know. What do you think?"

"Hmm, hey wait a minute. Maybe he was one of your students?"

"No, I thought about that. I checked the yearbooks, and he's not in any of them."

"And you know this how? He could be in front of his mother and she wouldn't recognize him."

"Believe me, I would."

His left eyebrow raised, questioning her, and said. "If you say so. Okay, how far back? How long has he been in town anyway?"

To admit that she noticed him for the first time just a few weeks ago would embarrass her. So she looked up and around as if she was thinking about his question. Paul recognized what he would refer to as, the bull shitting expression, and said.

"You know Margaret, ah not that complicated. What were you thinking?"

"What do you mean?"

"When you were looking around. What were you thinking?" He pointed with his chin.

"Nothing."

She tried to figure out how much she had revealed by trying not to reveal.

Paul asked, "nothing? Well, that took a while. Are we gonna go round in circles here?" He pointed toward the waiting room. "You know, how we did earlier in the waiting room."

She frowned questioning.

"You know..." He stopped himself and shook his head to reset. "Never mind, how far back do you want to go?"

"Ah, well, I retired two years ago and he was already here."

She looked directly into his eyes trying to convey truth. Paul's head went up and down slowly.

"Hmm, let me see, let me see, I graduated eight years ago and he was already here."

He looked at her questioning, hoping to get some feedback but got nothing. "Oh, my God. He's been here......" He looked away thinking. "Is he the same guy all these years?"

"I don't know. I mean....." Margaret's voice faded.

He wrinkled his forehead, and started typing on the computer.

"Let's go back ten years and see what happens."

"Okay."

Paul raised his hand above his head with his index finger pointing down and stopped. Margaret looked at his finger. She then looked at him questioningly.

He made a face and said. "It's funner this way."

"You mean more fun."

"That too."

He dropped his finger on the enter key. The computer made a sound and went to work.

He looked at her, "you see what I mean?"

A little smile came onto her face as her eyes feasted on the little boy she used to know. She got a little teary eye.

Paul saw her tearing up and asked, "what, what happened?"

She shook her head as her smile grew and pointed at him.

"That's the boy I used to know."

"Boy?"

"I mean that in a good way Paul. Don't ever lose that."

They both smiled and waited for the computer to do its thing. Margaret looked around. Paul reached into his desk and pulled out a file. He opened it and looked through it. Out of the corner of his eye, he saw her looking at him. He looked at her questioning.

"You know Paul, it's really nice to have been your teacher, and to see you here."

"What do you mean?"

"I mean, all grown up and a policeman. Your mother must be proud."

He felt a little uncomfortable, looked down at his file, and said, "I guess."

"You guess! Oh, I'm sure she is. I know I am."

He frowned at her.

"Well, you know, being your teacher and all."

He smiled and thought about it. There was a long pause. She placed her hands on her lap and looked around with her eyes. And then she said.

"Of course, I wish you would've been a better student, but....."

He stopped her with a look.

"Oh, I mean you were a good student, but you know?"

"I know what?"

"Your grades, your grades could've been a little better."

Paul felt like he was back in high school and decided not to respond. Instead, he tilted his head, like saying, really? Next came his expression of absolute boredom. Oblivious to his expression, she went on saying something. God knows what because Paul had checked out. It was just like being back in her class. Her words all mesh together indistinguishable from each other.

Margaret finally saw his expression and stopped talking. This time it was she who felt like she was back in school. She spiraled into a mishmash of memories, questions, thoughts, and whatever her brain managed to process. She came out of that to find herself staring at Paul. She couldn't remember why, but this felt like a good old-fashioned stare down. Paul, steady as a rock, stared right back with his boredom expression. She questioned in her mind, what is he doing?

What is he trying to say? Oh, I get it. He's trying to insult my teaching. And all this because I said his grades could've been better? What a baby. He's trying to get back at me by saying I was a boring teacher, but I know better. He has got to be acting. He's doing this to annoy me. How long is he going to keep this up? She started to question herself. Was I really that boring? Or maybe this was his natural state of mind to my teaching? What if, what if I induced this? I don't think so. He's got to be putting this on. She pointed at him with her chin and asked.

"That was your go-to expression, wasn't it?"

He pretended to yawn, stretched his arms, and turned slightly away from her. He hung his head and said.

"I don't know about my go-to expression. I mean it's not like I had to go to it. I mean once you started talking, this was it, it all just....."

Her eyebrows raised; her eyes bulged. She leaned toward him, keeping him from finishing his sentence. In total disbelief, she said, "are you saying....."

The computer beeped. He looked at the monitor and said, "saved by the bell, literally." He looked at her, "just like high school."

He slowly turned his head toward the monitor, but kept his eyes on her. His eyes turned to the monitor. She started to say something, but he raised his hand and stopped her without taking his eyes off of the monitor.

He said. "Rounds over, once the bell rings, it's over."

Her brain replayed many of her experiences in front of the class and asked herself if Paul was right. And with that question, many others rushed in. How many students felt as Paul did? Was I that boring? Do you mean to tell me that all those times I thought they were looking at me with wonder? They were actually thinking, when is she going to shut up? Is she long-winded or what? What about those times I saw their expression at something profound I said? Maybe those were, man am I hungry expressions. Or, I can't wait to get the hell out of here. What have I done? The sound of Paul's voice brought out her mental slide.

"Oh, boy."

"What?"

"Let's see what we've got here."

He turned the monitor to show her the list of names that seemed to go on forever.

He sighed and said. "Considering my grades weren't all that good and everything, knock yourself out."

He got up and pointed to his seat, telling her to take over.

"Well, what do I do?"

Paul crossed his arms. "Oh, so now you need a little help from bad grade Paul? Is that it?"

"Paul, I didn't say you had bad..."

He brushed her off with his hand and sat down. He turned the monitor back to face him. She moved over to get a better view.

He grabbed the mouse and said. "Scroll down, here, like this. You see? You can look at all these." He pointed with his finger. "Any that had pictures will have the picture. If you don't see a picture, it's because it doesn't have one."

She turned from the monitor to Paul with a robotic blank expression and said. "Thanks...."

"I mean..." Paul started to say.

"I understand." Said, Margaret.

A feeling came over him. He asked himself, did I take it a little too far with my boredom thing? Was I disrespectful?

"I got it, Paul! I really do."

They exchanged a quick look. He got up. He walked up to the door, grabbed the handle, and stopped as he heard her say.

"Just so you know. I didn't say your grades were bad. And for the record, you were always one of my favorites."

He walked out and the door closed. She felt a tremendous emptiness, as she thought about what he said. But her other voice came to save her.

Wait a minute, I'm to blame for all this? There were times I knew they were bored, what am I thinking? She remembered looking at all those blank faces and thinking, oh no, not again. Not another day with these prepubescent, energy-sucking vampires. It's a good thing that's all they sucked otherwise I'd be dead. This low energy thing was always indicative of the rest of her day, dull, boring, and uninspiring. There was something about the human psyche that puzzled her. She remembered thinking, they were like sheep following each other off the cliff. But in this case, these sheep didn't have the energy to jump.

They would all sit there staring in the same direction, at me. With their brains chewing on a sliver of my energy. And I mean a sliver because at times that's all they left me. Jumping off the cliff would have been more exciting, but this? Give me a break. How can it be that all students, on the same day, acted as if they didn't have breakfast? As if they all read the same book, at the time, and they were all on the same page. How can that be? It couldn't have been all my fault, right? I mean, I too am human and need inspiration. They too needed to give a little. Those selfish little booger eating, energy sucking vampires. She inhaled a deep breath as a feeling of being right came over her. A tiny smile came on to her as she exhaled that deep breath.

17. CAUGHT IN A LOOP

Roberto walked up to Cloverdale High School with the heart and soul of a seventeen-year-old boy. He was excited and couldn't wait. As he got closer, his present eyes saw it for what it was and thought, I was expecting it to be much bigger, taller. He walked up the stairs and up to the double glass doors and stopped. He looked down at the brass handle on the right door. He reached out and stopped just short of the handle. A memory of him pushing that same handle came up and stopped. It was as if the memory was waiting for him. The image in his head of that exact moment hovered there waiting. He pulled his hand back. He questioned, what just happened? Is something telling me not to go in? His other voice said, go on, life awaits! He pushed the door open, walked in, and the memory played out and came together with his now actions. He stopped. His memory went on without him and disappeared into thin air.

"What the hell?" He heard himself say it.

He looked down to see himself already inside the building. The sound of the door closing behind him snapped him out of that to the smell of this beloved place. A feeling that everything was going to be alright came upon him. He looked at the shiny wooden floors and thought of how beautiful they were. He took a few more steps and stopped. He shifted his body weight from one foot to the other, feeling the give of the wood floor. It had spring, like a rubber floor with the beauty of wood. He thought of how good it felt as his eyes called out to him to look around.

"I can't believe I'm here."

He panned the room with its high ceilings and beige walls. The counter is right there he thought, but the trophy case to the right called out to him. He almost turned toward it but forced himself not to. He walked up to the counter; looked down at it and his hands reached out. He touched it and felt it with both hands.

"I haven't seen this in years." He whispered to himself.

He saw a little bell to his right. He rang the bell. A few seconds later, a thirty-something-year-old lady walked up.

"Hi, my name is Jill, how can I help you?"

"Ah, yes, ah," he placed the yearbook on the counter.

"This yearbook is from the previous year that I became a freshman here."

She looked at it. "May I see it?"

"Sure"

She spun the yearbook around.

"So I'm back in town, and I was wondering if you had any yearbooks from when I was in school that I can buy? I can't find mine."

She opened the yearbook turned a couple of pages and said. "Oh wow, look at this." She thumbed through more pages.

"Oh, wow. Look at that. Are you in here?"

"Oh, I'm not in this one. I started my freshman year in 1973."

"Oh, I'm sorry, you did say that."

She looked past him and out the front windows. "Oh my god, there she goes."

He turned to see a Volkswagen van at the stop sign.

"I love her van. She is so cool."

He looked at her questioning.

"Ms. Himes. Do you remember her?"

Roberto felt his heart speeding and couldn't quite understand the question.

"Oh, I'm sorry. I don't even know if she was here when." She paused, "you know what?" She thumbed through a few pages. "Let me see...."

Ah, a little annoyed, Roberto said, "can you ask someone about my yearbook? I'm in a hurry."

"Oh, I'm sorry. Yes, yes, of course. So, you want to look at a yearbook from when you went to school here, right?"

Roberto told himself to focus. There was something about being questioned that confused him. "Ah, yes. Well, I want to buy one. Maybe they had some left over?"

"Okay, well, we...they...may have some...but."

She leaned toward him and whispered. "You know they're very strict around here with this sort of thing."

She looked around to make sure no one was around.

"I've been here for about a year. And ah, I guess their storage building burned down a few years back."

She looked around again and motioned him to lean in closer. She whispered.

"I guess one of their brilliant students burned it down. Can you imagine that?"

She pulled out a piece of paper and placed it on the counter.

"Can you imagine?" She shook her head.

Roberto looked at the paper.

"Oh, can you write your name down for me?"

"What? Why do you need my name?"

"I have to make sure you attended school here before I can show you anything. As if you were gonna lie about going to school here, I mean really."

She made a face as she shook her head. He wrote his name down. She grabbed the paper and walked off. She looked over her shoulder to catch him looking at her. She smiled and said.

"I'll be right back."

He gave her a little smile. She walked through the door. He then heard the sound of the absence of thought. Is that even possible, he asked himself. A quick flashback of him standing on a bridge asking that same question came back to him. He tried to remember where that bridge was but couldn't, and with that he answered the question. I guess not. He stood in silence in a place he hadn't seen since he was a child. He looked around. How is it possible that I stood right here, so many years ago? How is it possible that I now breathe the same air? That I walked this very floor. That I see now, what I used to see so long ago. This silence for sure I don't remember. But it's summer, so what am I expecting? Everyone is on summer vacation, so it should be silent. I like it. This silence is

238

what makes it possible to accept all that's before me. It's like a blank sheet of paper waiting to be written.

He stepped away from the counter and heard the squeak of the old wooden floor. The sound reverberating off the walls gave him the presence of being, of distance of space. As if his ears measured the distance between him and the walls. The same walls that made this space so loud during school. He asked himself, what is it that makes ambiance? Is it the walls? How about the objects that occupied the space within the structure? They give the space character, giving it ambiance. He stopped thinking to get a better observation. Has it changed in any way? All that I feel tells me, no. So what is it about this ambiance of space that intrigues me yet puzzles me? Silence once again occupied his brain, and with that, came the answer, the human. The human must experience the space for it to have ambiance, and therefore, it exists. The memory of the phone call he made to the Owl Cafe a couple of years ago played out in his head. He remembered thinking of how weird it was to hear the sound of another place. And now, here I find myself in that other place, and now I not only hear the sound, I see the sound of that other place.

He quietly said to himself, "it feels like time travel, wow this is weird, but cool".

He looked to his right and saw a trophy case. He walked up to it. There they were, some of the people in his yearbook, right there inside that case. One of his childhood buddies, Larry Walsh was looking right at him from within that case. Roberto smiled and thought of a time he went to Larry's house in nineteen-seventy-six. A memory that could only be triggered by where he stood. Roberto knocked on the front door. The door opened, Mr. and Mrs. Walsh stood at the door.

"Hi, is Larry home?" Asked Roberto.

"Hi, Roberto, come on in." Mr. Walsh said.

Roberto walked in and past them. He turned to look at them thinking they were going to say something, but they didn't. Instead, there was a long uncomfortable pause.

"Is Larry home?" Asked Roberto.

Mr. Walsh pointed with an open hand and said, "here, this way."

They led him to the dining room. Mr. Walsh pointed to the left side of the table.

"Here, sit down Roberto."

"Would you like some lemonade?" Mrs. Walsh asked.

"Ah no, thank you, I'm fine." Said, Roberto.

He sat down. Mr. Walsh sat across from him as Mrs. Walsh watched and said.

"I'll get us some water."

"So, how's everything?" Mr. Walsh asked.

"Fine."

There were a few long seconds of silence. Roberto felt a little uncomfortable.

Mr. Walsh went on. "Ah, Larry is....he hasn't been home for a couple of days."

"Where is he? I've been trying to call him and....."

"I know, I'm sorry about that." Mr. Walsh said and looked away, embarrassed about not answering the phone. Roberto turned his attention to Mrs. Walsh who poured water out of something he'd never seen in real life, a glass pitcher.

"Thank you." Said Roberto.

Mr. Walsh looked at his wife as she filled his glass and one for herself. They looked at each other and faked a little smile. Mr. Walsh turned to Roberto.

"Ah, we want to ask you something."

Mrs. Walsh sat down looked directly into Roberto's eyes and asked.

"Do you know if Larry does drugs? We want you to please tell us. We don't know what to do."

Mr. Walsh looked at her as if to say, slow down. Roberto frowned at the question. His eyes darted back and forth and said.

"Drugs? What makes you think he's doing drugs?"

Mrs. Walsh started to say something but was stopped by her husband. He gently grabbed her arm. They exchanged a glance. Mr. Walsh continued. "He.....he hasn't been the same."

He closed his mouth as he completed the word "same" and tightened his lips. His nostrils moved in and out. Mrs. Walsh teared up. Mr. Walsh comforted her. He went on. "Have you noticed anything different?"

Roberto hesitated. "Well......."

"Look, we think he's doing drugs. He acts differently."

Larry's fifteen-year-old brother Martin, walked into the room.

"Hey Roberto, what's going on?"

"Hey, what are you doing?"

His parents gave him a look, Martin walked out of the room without answering and disappeared into the hallway. Mr. Walsh watched him walk away as if to make sure he was gone.

"Anyway," said Mr. Walsh, "we don't know what to do. I think he's doing drugs or something. Has anything, anything happened that....." Roberto interjected.

"He hasn't been to practice for a while."

241

"He hasn't?" Mr. and Mrs. Walsh.

"No....that's why I was...." Roberto stopped.

Mr. Walsh got up, walked out of the room and into the hallway. A couple of seconds later, a door slammed shut. Roberto took a drink of water and looked around knowing Mrs. Walsh was looking at him.

Mrs. Walsh leaned toward him. "I'm sorry. We don't know what to do anymore."

Mr. Walsh's yelling rang out in the background. Roberto ignored her question. He looked around to see a clean, meticulous house. Everything exactly where it should be. It looked like one of those houses on television or a magazine. He noticed the curtains that covered the entire rear wall of the living room. Mrs. Walsh studied him and saw his young mind working.

"That is a big window." Said Roberto.

Mrs. Walsh looked at the curtains. Mr. Walsh walked in to see them looking at the rear wall and sat.

"Sorry about that," said Mr. Walsh.

"That's okay." Said Roberto, but meant not to say anything.

Mr. Walsh sighed, paused for a few seconds, and asked, "how long has he missed practice?"

Roberto didn't know what to say. He thought if I do say something, am I going to get Larry in trouble? I should've stayed home. They're waiting for me to say something.

"Ah, well, he started missing now and then."

As soon as the last word left his mouth, he knew another question would follow.

"How long ago was that?" Mr. Walsh asked.

"Ah, he used to practice every day. Even after team

practice, we would practice together. He wanted to get better. And so, we would play one on one. He was getting good."

Mr. Walsh's lips tighten. He looked at his wife and then at the table as if searching for a target for his stare. His left hand rubbed the tablecloth as his nose expanded with every deep breath.

"How long ago Roberto?"

"How long ago what?"

"When did he start missing practice?"

A simple question, he told himself and heard his grandfather in his mind. A simple question gets a simple answer, remember that.

"He started to miss a day here and there."

"How long ago was that?"

"Ah, three weeks, or more, maybe?"

Mr. Walsh shook his head thinking that he couldn't believe what he was hearing. He turned his head toward the living room and down at the floor. He got up and walked into the hallway. The sound of the door slamming louder than the first time. Roberto looked at the big curtains again. Mrs. Walsh looked at the curtains and wondered why he was so intrigued by them, but didn't ask. Instead, as if turning the page, she asked.

"How's your family?"

"My family? Fine."

"Good, good."

There was a minute of silence as Roberto thought, I've got to see that window. Mr. Walsh walked in. He stood behind his chair and placed his hands on the back of the chair. He looked down for a few seconds. He grabbed the

243

back of the chair with both hands as if he was going to lift it. He released the chair, walked around it, and sat. He looked right into Roberto's eyes and asked.

"Three weeks?"

Roberto hesitated, and couldn't believe the position he found himself in.

"Yes, I guess."

Mr. Walsh tapped the table with his index finger as he looked at Roberto. Roberto's eyes darted back and forth from Mrs. Walsh to Mr. Walsh.

"Roberto, we need to know.....is he...? I mean do you know?"

Roberto was about to say something when he heard someone walking toward them in the hallway. Martin walked past them without saying a word. Mr. Walsh couldn't believe what he was seeing and followed him through the door and the front window. He shook his head and then looked at Roberto.

As if saying, how's the weather? Roberto casually said, "I would look in his room if I were you."

Totally surprised, Mr. Walsh and his wife looked at each other. "What do you mean?" Mr. Walsh asked me.

Roberto couldn't believe that he had to explain this. "I mean look in his room to see what's in there."

There, that ought to do it, he thought. Instead, heard Mr. Walsh say.

"He has a lock on his door."

The thought of having a lock on your bedroom door had never occurred to Roberto. And then he heard.

"He said he wanted his privacy."

Roberto grew up with six siblings, he heard, privacy and thought, what the hell is that? He did a quick look

244

around as he asked himself, who are these people? He then said.

"If I told my father that I wanted my privacy? Things would get ugly."

They looked at each other, questioning having no idea what Roberto meant. Mr. Walsh asked.

"What do you mean ugly?"

Roberto leaned toward them not believing and finally asked. "Do you have a key?"

The looked at each other and back at Roberto and said, "we don't have a key."

He tried not to shrug, but it was too late.

"You don't have a......" Roberto stopped himself.

His face distorted, attempting to understand what was going on. Mr. Walsh looked at his wife as if to say, help me out here. At this point, Roberto knew who he was dealing with. His feeling of being interrogated left him and said.

"Just go in there, I would. Go through his drawers and everything."

Mrs. Walsh tried to process the idea but instead felt uncomfortable. She got up and walked into the kitchen. Roberto watched her walk up to the sink. She placed her hands on the kitchen counter and looked out the window. Roberto leaned toward Mr Walsh conveying he was about to whisper. He then gave Mrs. Walsh a quick look and back to Mr. Walsh. This was his way of telling her, you may not want to hear this. Mr. Walsh leaned toward him and thought finally, I am about to get useful information.

"Do you have a screwdriver?" Roberto asked. He waited. His eyes darted back and forth as the seconds took way too long. Can it be, Roberto asked himself, that he doesn't have a screwdriver? Mr. Walsh sighed, turned away, and shook his head. I don't believe this, Roberto thought. Mr. Walsh got up, walked into the kitchen, and stopped. What the hell is he doing? Roberto asked himself. Mr. Walsh looked up as if looking at god and back down at the counter. He opened a drawer and grabbed a knife. He showed it to Roberto. Roberto nodded. As if nothing was going on, Mrs. Walsh looked out the window. Roberto pointed toward the hallway with his head. He took off toward Larry's room. Mr. Walsh followed. Roberto walked up to the bedroom door and stopped.

He looked at Mr. Walsh to see doubt in his eyes. Roberto took the knife from him. He forced it between the doorstop and the door jam. He grabbed the knob and pushed with his shoulder on the door. He pushed harder, the door opened. Mr. Walsh couldn't believe how easy that was. Roberto stepped into the bedroom and turned back to see Mr. Walsh standing just outside the door. Roberto pointed to the bottom drawer of the dresser. Mr. Walsh finally walked in, looked at the drawer, and hesitated.

"Right there, it's all yours." Roberto had to say it.

He walked around him and headed for the front door. To his surprise, Mrs. Walsh waited at the door. She looked at him wanting to say something but said nothing. She opened the door, Roberto sort of smiled, and walked out.

"Ah, sir, sir!" Roberto heard. He snapped out of that to see Larry's picture in the trophy case.

"Hello, sir!" Said Jill.

He turned to see her leaning over the counter toward him.

"Oh, I'm sorry," he said and walked back to the counter. "I'm sorry, I sort of lost myself there with all these memories."

246

"That's okay, ah, I'm afraid we, well, they don't have any record of you attending school here."

As this was going on, two middle-aged women walked into an office. They sat and looked at a black and white monitor with live video of the front counter. Mrs. Johnson, one of the ladies leaned toward the monitor to get a better look and said.

"He didn't go to school here."

Mrs. Neuvo, the other lady, watched with dreamy eyes and quickly responded. "I think he did, he's so handsome."

Back at the counter, Roberto focused on Jill and said. "That's impossible."

He turned around, and pointed to the picture of Larry Walsh in the trophy case.

"You see that guy right there? Larry, Larry Walsh, I went to school with him. His parents asked me once if he was doing drugs and......."

Jill interrupted him. "Oh, oh, don't get me wrong. You see......"

She looked around to make sure no one was listening. She leaned way over the counter, and whispered, "these people aren't exactly the brightest stars in the sky if you know what I mean?"

The ladies in the office froze, their venom spewed as they heard what she said. They looked at each other.

"Well, that little bitch. Did you hear that?" Mrs. Johnson said.

They looked at the monitor to see Jill looking around again and said.

"They all kind of look alike. I think everybody is everybody's cousin if you know what I mean?"

She cupped her mouth to direct her voice right at him.

"It's probably a good thing you got away. You don't look anything like......."

Jill heard the door open behind her. She looked over her shoulder. Mrs. Johnson came through the door and headed toward her with an expression that told her she was in trouble. She walked up to the counter. Looked into Jill's eyes and paused long enough to see her swallow.

"I'll help him," said Mrs. Johnson. "You get yourself to the back and do something."

She took off. Mrs. Johnson watched her for a few seconds. She looked at Roberto.

"How can I help you?"

Jill stopped at the door and looked at Roberto.

Mrs. Johnson continued. "Apparently, you went to school here?"

With Mrs. Johnson's back to her, Jill raised and extended her left arm, as if she was holding a stick or something. She placed her right hand to her midsection and pretended to play the banjo. Her head tilted from left to right over and over, like saying, guess what I'm doing? Roberto tried not to look, but his eyes darted back and forth from Mrs. Johnson to Jill. Mrs. Johnson noticed his eyes and looked back to see what was going on. Jill stopped pretending to play the banjo and made a face, like saying, oh well, and walked out. Roberto lost his train of thought and had to regroup.

"Ah, I went to school here from nineteen seventy three to nineteen seventy six."

Mrs. Johnson looked at the yearbook on the counter.

"This is from the year before I started here." He said.

"Hm, I checked our records, Mr. Tenna, is it?"

"Yes."

"Has your name changed, perhaps your mother remarried and....."

"No, no, I've had the same name my whole life."

"Well, I'm afraid we have no record of you attending school here."

Roberto's heart raced. "How can that be?"

"I'm not sure. I've been here, going on forty years now. Believe me, if it happens in Cloverdale, I know about it. Everybody knows everybody's business. That's just how it is around here."

She waited for him to say something but instead, Jill's words rang out in her head. "I think everybody is everybody's cousin if you know what I mean?" Her blood boiled and looked away trying to hide her expression. Roberto's desperation revealed itself not only to his face and body but to Mrs. Johnson. She looked away thinking she may have missed something but then thought, there's no way. She looked at him to see a disparate man digging into his memory. She felt sorry for him. She looked around trying to give him time. She then thought, maybe he didn't get his picture taken.

"Did you get your picture taken Mr. Tenna?"

She waited, not sure if he heard her.

"Ah, well, let me ask you, who was your freshman math teacher?"

Roberto clearly heard the question, but confusion had captured him. He looked around as if to search for evidence of him being here. He grabbed his yearbook and slowly backed away.

"Mr. Tenna? Mr. Tenna! Who was your freshman math teacher?"

Roberto backed away as flashbacks of Mr. Walton, the

mumbling mathematician played in his head. He heard Mr. Walton yell, "get out, get out of my class!"

Roberto looked down and shook his head trying to get the memory to stop. He looked up and there she was, right there behind the counter was Mrs. Johnson, in black and white just like in the pictures in his yearbook. He looked around and realized that she was the only thing in black and white. He asked himself, how can this be? Mrs. Johnson repeated the question over and over.

"Who was your freshman math teacher? Who was your freshman math teacher, Mr. Tenna?"

The door behind her opened. A black and white Mr. Walton stood at the doorway, completely frozen. His hair soaked, water dripping onto his right eye, down his face, and sideburn. He looked fake, like a robot. He stepped in, stopped, turned around to face the door, and closed it. He spun back around, looked at Roberto, and cocked his head like saying, guess who? He smirked and walked up to the counter. Mrs. Johnson and Mr. Walton looked at each other and smiled like two robots. Mr. Walton turned to Roberto and yelled, "get out, get out of my class!"

They looked at each other again, and in unison yelled, "who was your freshman math teacher, Mr. Tenna?" They burst out in laughter. They stopped laughing and yelled, "get out, get out of my class!"

Alternating each other's lines, they continued, "who was your freshman math teacher, Mr. Tenna?" "Get out, get out of my class!" over and over.

Roberto's heart pounding, he backed away, ending up against the front door. The yelling stopped. The real Mrs. Johnson couldn't believe what she was seeing.

"Are you all right Mr. Tenna? I can check again if you want me to?"

250

Roberto tried to step back. His foot bumped up against the door. He turned around. He looked down at the door handle and saw it in black and white. He looked past the door handle to see his shoes and pants in full color. Everything else was in black and white. A memory triggered and saw himself in his garage looking at his yearbook. He came out of his memory to see everything in black and white. He looked back at the counter and now, Mark Bennett stood between Mr. Walton and Mrs. Johnson. He raised his hand as if he was holding a gun. He pointed at Mr. Walton. Mark's body turned to face Roberto but kept his gun aimed at Mr. Walton.

He said, "should I shoot him, should I shoot him?"

He turned the gun at Roberto, and pulled the trigger and all three fell into a chaotic episode of laughter. They stopped laughing.

"Somebody pass the potato salad." Said Mark.

All three burst into laughter. Roberto turned around and looked at the door. He started to open but the laughter stopped. He turned back around and Mark and Mr. Walton were gone. Mrs. Johnson's lips moved, but silence was his only state of mind. Before he realized it, he was outside running down the stairs. His ears popped and heard himself say.

"Why am I here?" He heard it over and over. "Why am I here? Why am I here?"

Another voice in his head asked, "why am I hearing this? Where is this coming from?"

Convinced he was being chased, he turned around to see the front of Cloverdale High School growing with every backward step he took, towering over him like a skyscraper. He tripped and fell on his back. The sound and pounding of his heart echoed in his head. He got up, took another step, tripped, and fell on his bike again.

251

"Whose bike is this?" Roberto asked as confusion engulfed his everywhere.

"Where am I?" He heard himself say.

"Why are you here?" This time he wasn't sure where that voice came from.

"What is this place?" He truly wanted to know.

"Cloverdale High School? Why am I here? I don't understand." His voice was loud and clear.

He untangled himself from his bike, stood, and looked beyond the front glass doors of Cloverdale High School and asked. "Who are those ladies? Why are they looking at me?"

Behind the glass doors, a now mid-fifties Mrs. Johnson and Mrs. Nuevo watched him as he looked at them. Roberto closed his eyes, grabbed his head with both hands, and bent down almost to the ground.

"Not again, not again."

The loud ringing in his head almost pierced his skull, he fell to the ground again.

"Oh my god, oh my god."

He rolled over onto his back, opened his eyes to a blank blue canvas, and felt a calming sensation. The ringing in his head faded. The pounding of his heart calmed. A long ago forgotten feeling of comfort and familiarity engulfed his every cell. He sat up, looked around, and tried to remember why and how he got to where he was. He looked at his bike and finally, something he recognized. He got up, took one more look around. He picked up his bike and walked away from the only two people who had known him throughout the years.

"Poor man, remember the first time he came in?" Mrs. Johnson.

"Yes, yes, I do, he was so handsome. Just think, that used to be someone's little boy. The pride they must have felt the day he was born."

Mrs. Johnson looked at her, "I believe you said something like that all those years ago."

"Did I?"

"I think so," said Mrs. Johnson and tried to remember how long ago that was and asked. "That was about fifteen years ago, wasn't it?"

Mrs. Nuevo's face distorted at the thought of how long ago that was. "Has it been that long?"

"Yes, at least. Pretty scary isn't it?"

"I don't understand, why would he think he went to school here when he didn't?"

"I, I don't know. I mean you and I have had this conversation almost every time he shows up over the years." Mrs. Johnson said.

And as always, Mrs. Nuevo kept going.

"Yeah, I know, but we still don't know why. I mean why wouldn't he go back to where he actually went to school?"

To Roberto, there was no question as to where he went to school. Fifteen year ago, he came to Cloverdale in search of answers. But the answers he found were to a world where he didn't exist. To a world that rejected him. Every few weeks he would fall into one of his looping schizophrenic episodes. He would return to Cloverdale High School as if it was the first time. Forever attempting to change the outcome to events he could never accept. It was after one of these episodes that Margaret saw him in the shack, and he called her by her name: "Hello Mis. Himes". He had seen her picture in his precious yearbook. And throughout the years, he had not only seen her around town but had actual conversations with her in his head. To him, she was a familiar stranger whom he had never met.

18. MUTE EARS

Paul and Margaret walked out of the police station.
They did a missing person search that resulted in nothing.
He thought about their heated exchange earlier about all
things, his grades. That conversation made him feel like he
was still in high school. It was as though the act of
discussion, hearing it out loud, penetrated the walls of
time. He had always respected her and had always worked
hard to get better grades. Hearing her say his grades could
have been better, wasn't such a bad thing. As in the past,
this will make him work harder. Why did he get so upset
with her? The thought of pretending she was a boring
teacher to insult her worried him. I should be over this by
now, he told himself.

All those immature emotions are still in me. I reacted
like the child I used to be and in some ways will always be.
After all, here was a woman who wanted only good for me

and others. A woman who was trying to help this homeless man, and I got mad over something so petty. He regretted it and told himself to keep that in mind.

"Well, maybe we'll come up with something. Was he at the theater again?" Asked Paul.

"No....ah.." She kept herself from finishing the sentence.

Paul gave her a firm expression. "Give it up, come on, let's don't do this all right?"

"Okay, okay, I've...I've been watching him...." She stopped at the sight of Paul frowning deeply and leaned toward her. She went on.

"I don't know what to tell you, I keep running into him, Paul. Everywhere I go, there he is."

He rolled his eyes, "are you sure it's not the other way around?"

"What do you mean?"

"Everywhere he goes, there you are."

"Are you saying that I..."

Paul raised his hand to stop her. He reminded himself to be respectful. "I'm just kidding," He smiled.

But it was too late, her expression changed to one of self-examination, and thought he may have a point. Am I a stalker and don't know it? After all, it was I on my hands and knees out there in the woods. Crawling under bushes to get a glimpse of him. Paul waited for her to say something as she looked away in thought. He told himself yet again, be respectful, after all, she did say I was one of her favorite students.

"Oh, who cares?" She decided to put it all out there. "I keep seeing him a couple of miles north of town on the highway. There's this dirt road not too far from where I see him. I figured he may be down there. You know I...."

Paul interrupted her. "I don't believe you."

"I know, I know, but I'm retired, Paul. I need something to do. Honest, I'm not a stalker."

"A stalker? Who said you were a stalker?"

Her eyes went back and forth in search of a way out. "No one, it's just what you said earlier about me being everywhere he is and not the other way around."

"Well, I didn't mean to imply that. But you know Margaret, when people retire and get bored, they volunteer at the library or something. They don't go in search of homeless weirdos."

She saw a true expression of concern on Paul, which made her pause. Her next thought was, wait till he hears where I've been. He watched her. She looked around and decided once again, oh what the hell.

"So anyway, I went down there and ah, I see this old house or shack, and I heard a couple of people talking. So I figured he must be talking to someone...so..."

He interrupted her. "So, let me get this straight. You heard not one weirdo, but two or three weirdos. And you thought, hey, I have a great idea, let's go see what's going on."

The memory of her father saying something similar when she was a teenager played out in her head. As if her father was saying it, Paul's words went in one ear and out the other. She came out of that thought to see Paul looking down at her and for the first time realized how tall he was. She looked away. Paul, once again thought that he didn't want to be disrespectful. He let things pause for a while.

She thought of how different it was to think about her experience compared to talking to someone about it. There was something about hearing it out loud that made her think Paul may have a point.

After all, it was I who was out there in the middle of nowhere. By the time I made it out of there, it was dark and the temperature, low enough to be dangerous. If something terrible had happened to me, god knows how long it would've taken to find me, to find my body. Is this the next vicious cycle in my head? The alternate ending to an otherwise good outcome. Which brought to mind how the events of that day hadn't left her for a single second. He watched her, and couldn't wait to hear the rest of the story. From the length of her deep thought, it must be a hell of a story he thought. She exhaled a deep long breath. He thought she must have taken that breath yesterday because he didn't remember her taking that deep breath.

"So...." She stopped to self-edit for the sake of avoiding his fatherly response. She once again thought, oh the hell with it.

"So anyway, when I got closer, I looked through a partly open front door. And there he was. And I mean, there he was. Talking all by himself, to himself."

She gave Paul an expression as if to ask, can you believe it? She looked away and thought of how damaged the poor man was.

He shook his head, waited the amount of time he thought would be respectful, and said what needed to be said.

"That is what crazy people do Margaret."

She looked at him.

He went on, "they talk to themselves."

He asked himself, do I want to hear this? But his

257

concern for her kept him right where he was. He thought, hey let's lighten things up a little.

"So what did you do next? Have a beer with him? Smoked a doobie, what?"

She was so engaged in replaying the events of that day, she heard nothing and continued to look away. Paul noted her lack of response. He asked himself if he had overstepped his boundaries with his smart-ass remarks.

Margaret went on as if he had said nothing. "It was the first time I'd heard his voice. I thought I knew what he would sound like, but..."

She stopped thinking he was going to say something, but instead, she saw that Paul was curious to see where this was going. She went on.

"We, as social animals, think or presume to know what someone should sound like. Without even thinking about it. It's all those human to human interactions in our past that make this possible. It's a predisposed assumption as to what a face should sound like. And most of the time we're right."

She stopped and looked down as his image played out in her head. She slowly looked up at him and went on.

"There is something about our faces that gives it away, but in this case...."

She shook her head. Paul's curiosity at this point got the best of him and triggered a memory.

"Where exactly is this again?"

Finally, Margaret thought, and quickly responded.

"Over the hill on the north side of town. A couple of miles or so down the other side."

"Before, or past the creek?"

"Past, why?"

"Hm, you know what? A few months ago, I was working on a project. I was going back looking at unsolved cases. Do you remember that car that was found a long time ago over there by where you're saying?"

"I don't know, maybe, I think so."

"Yeah, that was about thirteen, fourteen, maybe fifteen years ago. And they never found the driver."

She looked at him like really? Paul felt a sudden bolt of excitement and said. "I tell you what. Let me see what I come up with. I'll call you later."

Margaret looked at him and once again thought of how grown up he was and how the roles had switched. She felt like the teenager that always had to be told to be careful.

"I recognize that look." Said Paul. "I'm walking away." He walked off.

"Thank you, Paul."

"You're welcome." He turned back around. "I'd tell you to be careful, but I know mute ears when I see them."

19. HE'S A WEIRDO

After they told Roberto on his first visit to Cloverdale High School that they had no record of him attending, Roberto unraveled. By the time Mrs. Johnson asked him, who was his freshman math teacher, it was too late. The door had opened to an alternate world. He saw everything in black and white within a world of true color. It was the epicenter of two worlds colliding, catapulting him into a reality of his own making.

He ran out of the building, fell down the stairs, and onto his back. Mrs. Johnson and Mrs. Nuevo ran out to help him. He saw them as if they were attacking. Paranoia engulfed his every cell. He got up and walked backward to keep his sight on Mrs. Johnson, Mrs. Nuevo as the school building got taller and taller with every step. They, including the building, had become his enemy, the interrupter of his world. He turned around and took off running. He made it off the school grounds and down the street. He got into his car, locked the doors, and slid down his seat, hiding from the two women chasing him. The sound of his heart was so loud, he thought it couldn't possibly be coming from him. He asked himself, how can this be? It must be coming from outside, from something much larger than me. Maybe I left the radio on. He reached for the radio, turned the knob, and couldn't believe he did that. What am I thinking, he thought. The car is not even on. How can the radio be on? He felt his chest and told himself out loud.

"It's my heart, it's the beat of my own heart beating so loud it's echoing in my head. This is the sound of me."

The thought of Mr. Walton finding him rushed through his head. More panic came on to him.

"Where are my keys? Where are my keys?"

He reached into his pocket and nothing. He looked at the ignition and nothing. He looked down between his legs and there they were. He grabbed them, turned the car on, and took off. He made a right turn onto Main Street. He looked in the rearview mirror to see Cloverdale High getting smaller. He looked at the yearbook next to him on the passenger seat. He opened it with one hand and flipped through the pages. He saw the Ace Hardware store coming on his left.

He looked at it as he drove past it. He made a u-turn and parked in front of it. He grabbed his yearbook, got out, and faced the store. His car door remained open. He placed the yearbook on the roof of his car. He looked at the black and white picture of the Ace Hardware store with his anti-gravity girl standing in front of it. He then looked at the store in front of him.

261

"Now you can't tell me this isn't it? I wonder if she's here?" He said aloud.

His hearing muffled slightly. A distant ring presented itself. It got louder as he compared the picture to the store. He looked around to see where the ringing was coming from.

"Why did I do that?" Roberto said as he continued to look around. "It's in my head. But do I know that for sure?"

He looked at the yearbook again, grabbed it, and walked around his car. The ringing got louder as he walked toward the store.

"Why is this happening?" He heard himself say out loud.

He stopped; the ringing leveled.

"Is the ringing coming from the store?" He thought about his question and felt ridiculous. He looked around trying to clear his head. He saw his car door wide open.

"What the hell? Who opened my door?"

He walked back, closed the car door, and looked around for the person that opened the door.

"Son of bitches." He said as he stood there for a few seconds.

He realized that the ringing in his head had faded. He headed for the store. The ringing got louder again as his hearing muffled. It was as if the outside world was being shut down. He stopped, looked at that picture, and then at the store. Defiant, he marched up to the front glass door. His reflection looked back at him. "Who the hell?"

The ringing in his head now almost unbearable. His hearing was completely mute. The sound of the world around him was completely silent. He reached out and touched the glass door as if to touch his image on the reflection.

"Is that really me? Wait a minute. Maybe the lady at school didn't recognize me. How could she, I look so different."

The people in the store saw him talking to himself with an expression of complete confusion.

"Maybe you didn't get your picture taken." He heard Mrs. Johnson say.

He turned around expecting to see her, but she wasn't there. He turned back to the door.

"We have no record of you attending school here. Mr. Tenna. Mr. Tenna!" He heard from behind. He turned back around and no one was there. He turned back to the store and instantly heard.

"Mr. Tenna, are you all right?"

This time he felt anger. He turned back around and no one was there.

"Get out, get out, get out of here, go!" Mr. Walton yelled.

He turned back to the door to see his image speaking in Mr. Walton's voice.

"Was I your freshman math teacher? Ha? Was I?"

The people in the store back away.

Roberto's reflection reached out through the glass and almost grabbed his yearbook. He swung at his reflection. He missed, spun around, and fell ending up with his face against the glass. As so many times before, his mind zoomed in on a plaque on the inside of the glass and read what he already knew.

"In Loving Memory of our Daughter Joan Briganti."

That was all his mind allowed him to read. His hearing muting on and off over and over. The ringing in his head pulsing, getting louder with every pulse. He screamed trying to get out of his head. The people inside couldn't

263

believe what they were seeing. A couple of them rushed
toward him to help. But to Roberto, it was Mrs. Johnson,
Mr. Walton, and Mark Bennett coming at him. He backed
away on his hands and knees. He got up. The door
opened. He backed away with his eyes bulging out of his
head.

"Sir, are you alright?" One of them asked.

"Sir, can we help you?" Someone else asked.

Roberto backed away and heard what wasn't being said.

"Sir, sir, who was your freshman math teacher?"

"You didn't go to school here."

"It's a good thing you got away, you don't look
anything like them"

"Get away, get away," yelled Roberto, as he kept
backing up.

"You can't turn back now. Life awaits." Roberto heard
the southern older man in denim overalls.

Now against his car, he pulled the passenger door
open, got in, locked the door, moved over to the driver's
side, and took off. He looked in the rear-view mirror to
see Mrs. Johnson, Mrs. Nuevo, Mr. Walton, and Mark
running after him. A few hours later, Roberto had no
recollection of driving to where he was. He sat in his car
across the street from the Owl Cafe. Questions rushed in
but he rejected them. He placed the yearbook on the
steering wheel. He looked at a black and white picture of
the Owl Cafe and then at the Owl Cafe across the street.
He asked himself, how long have I been here? The thought
of Amanda being across the street came to him. He got
out and ran across the street. His hearing once again began
to muffle. As he got closer to the Owl, his hearing began
to short out, on and off. He got to the front door and
stopped. He said to himself, I don't really have to go in,

do I? I could very easily walk away and everything will be fine. He took a deep breath and held it for a few seconds. He exhaled and opened the door to the sight and sound of a once distant place. A girl in her mid-twenties at the front counter looked up as the door opened. Roberto stood holding the door open for a few seconds.

"Hi, will it be only you?" She asked.

Roberto couldn't say anything.

"Can I help you?"

His eyes went beyond her in search of Amanda.

"Sir, can I help you?"

He looked at her and said, "ah..." He slowly walked up to her, looked at her name tag, and saw Cindy.

"That's me, Cindy." She said smiling, almost laughing.

Roberto finally asked. "Ah....is Amanda working?"

Before she could answer, Roberto looked past her into the dining area.

"Amanda?" She asked.

"Yes, Amanda." He brought his intense eyes back to her. "I would like to be seated in her section." He looked past her again.

Cindy followed his glance to see what he was looking at. "Ah, we don't have an Amanda here."

"Are you sure?"

"Yes, there's only seven of us here." She looked over her shoulder and yelled. "Judy!"

"Yeah." Judy yelled back.

"Do you know of anyone that works here named Amanda?"

"No, who's asking?" Said the thirty five year old with long black hair. She looked at Roberto. She quickly walked up.

"Oh, hi, I'm Judy." She said flirting.

Cindy and Judy? Roberto questioned in his head. There was something about those two names together that triggered an unattached emotion. He snapped himself out of that to find his eyes darting back and forth from Judy to Cindy.

"Ah, so there's no Amanda here?" Asked Roberto.

"No, but I tell you what. I'll be Amanda if you want me to." Said Judy.

Cindy pushed her away and said, "Be serious, Jesus."

"I am serious."

Cindy laughed, "oh my god." She looked at Roberto. "I'm sorry, she's always like this. There is no Amanda here."

"Hey, don't apologize for....." A bell rang. Judy stopped, and looked at the cook. "Boy, your timing stinks," She looked at Roberto. "I'll be right back, don't leave," she walked off. A few steps later she turned around and walked backward and smiled at him.

Roberto and Cindy looked at each other. There was an uncomfortable moment of silence as Cindy held on to what she thought was a real smile. He looked past her toward the dining room again. His hearing began to muffle.

"Ah, would you like to be seated anyway?"

Roberto's head began to slowly move from side to side. "Ah, no, I'm fine."

He once again looked past her hoping to see another waitress but saw only Judy at the cook line. Confusion, anxiety, and shortness of breath came onto him as the reality of the moment began to formulate.

"She's a clown, don't take her seriously."

He looked at her, saw her mouth moving but heard nothing. He looked past her again.

266

Cindy went on. "But, she's a lot of fun to work with, you know? She's actually....."

She stopped talking as the emptiness of his expression made its way to her. She zoomed in on his eyes as the sound of his rapid breathing became obvious. She asked herself, what is he looking at? She looked behind her to see what she already knew. She turned back around to see him backing up. She thought, is there something wrong with him?

"Are you leaving sir?" she asked.

"Sir, are you alright?" Is what Roberto heard. He turned around to see his reflection on the glass door. Hesitated for a second, opened the door, and walked out.

Judy ran up to Cindy.

"What happened, did you run him off?" Asked Cindy

"Run him off? No!"

Roberto walked as fast as he could, stopped, and froze as he heard a distant but familiar voice.

"Can you hold on? Don't hang up." He heard Amanda say.

Cindy tried to explain to Judy what happened.

"He kept looking back there," She pointed toward the dining room. "And he...got a strange look on...." She stopped herself and looked out the window to see Roberto looking down as if he was seeing something.

"There, there you see? Don't you think that's weird?" asked Cindy.

"The man is looking down. What is so weird about that?"

"Well, not only that, he looked confused or something."

"Confused? If there's anyone confused around here honey it's you. I mean really." Said Judy.

Roberto's refusal to accept what wasn't, gave him no option.

"Can you hold on? Don't hang up, I'll be right back." He heard and saw Amanda say. As if he was on the phone with her. He snapped out of that to see himself standing in an empty parking lot.

Amanda's voice asked him, "where is it that you're supposed to be?"

He looked back at the Owl Cafe to see it closed, lights off, and no one inside. Cindy and Judy stood inside looking at him.

"There, there, you see that? That's what I'm talking about." Cindy said.

"Hey, hey, you know what?" Said the cook as he looked past them.

Judy and Cindy looked at him. "You know what, what?" Said Judy mimicking him.

"What that guy want?" Asked the cook.

"He want nothing." Said Judy once again mimicking him. Cindy gave her a look.

"He was looking for me. Ms. Right." Said Judy.

Cindy gave her another look as if to say, yeah right, and pushed her away. She looked at the cook.

"He was looking for Amanda. He said she works here."

"Yeah, yeah that's it. He asked the same thing yesterday." Said the cook.

Cindy made a face, not believing, and said. "Are you sure?"

"What, you think I make this stuff up? He's a weirdo."

20. YOU MAY RETURN TO A PLACE YOU'VE NEVER BEEN

Roberto woke up in the middle of the night sitting in his car with the yearbook once again on the steering wheel. He then looked across the street to see the Owl Cafe, its neon glowing as beautifully as ever. He looked down at the black and white picture of Cloverdale Liquor on the yearbook and a smile came on to him. He placed the yearbook on the seat next to him. He turned the car on and made a right onto Main Street in the opposite direction of the Owl Cafe. A minute later in the far distance he saw the neon of Cloverdale Liquor and could almost hear it calling him to its destiny. Nothing will escape me, or I, it, he heard in his head as the reflection of the streetlights on his shiny hood moved toward him, onto the windshield, and over his head. "This is absolutely beautiful." This time he said it out loud.

He leaned over his steering wheel, and looked up through the reflection of the streetlight to see the real streetlight as both images came together and over his head they went. He shook his head as the idea of both images coming together triggered questions. He told himself that tonight was a time for joy not to be unraveled by the beauty of the physics of light. He slowed down as he drove up to Cloverdale liquor store.

"Wow! Look at that." He said as he saw the brilliant neon colors of the Cloverdale Liquor sign on his hood. He pulled over and looked up at the sign. A memory started to play out, but the image of the real sign snapped him out of it. He looked around as if to ask, what was that? But the image on his hood brought him back to where he was. He eased up on the clutch and turned into the alley that divided the liquor and the furniture store next door. He stopped in between the two buildings and looked around. It felt like a tunnel. He was surrounded by brick walls as the sound of his engine reverberated off the walls.

Another memory played out. He sat in his RoadRunner as Joan Brigantti sat in her Mustang directly behind him in that same brick alley. Joan would always go first. Her Mustang idled like a pony at the starting line. It had a deep resonance that made it impossible not to make it scream. She plunged her foot to the metal and there it was, her Mustang screaming like a mountain lion. As her engine settled down, the Roadrunner would scream out, filling every square inch of that brick reverberating space. It was the sound of power, the sound of excitement, and by far one of their favorite things to do.

He came out of that memory and looked around again and couldn't believe it was as beautiful as it was so many years ago. He asked himself, how would I know this isn't nineteen-seventy-six? I wouldn't, this is exactly as it was back then. A huge smile came onto his face. He eased up on the clutch and drove into the parking lot behind the building. As he turned to the right, a long ago memory and his now actions became one. Without thinking and as if he had done this very action yesterday, he parked in the exact spot where he had parked, all those years ago. He looked to his left to the exact spot where the yearbook picture of the two Georges was taken.

"This has not changed at all."

He heard his voice out loud. He reached for the yearbook. Opened it and turned to the picture of drunk George standing next to the other George. Roberto's head began to move from side to side, accepting all that was and all that wasn't.

"This is incredible?"

As if coming out of a dream, or a thought, or whatever that was, he realized that he was frozen. He looked down at himself and asked, for how long and why would I do that? And now I have to ask, did I actually stop moving or is it that I think that I stopped moving? Then again, what is the difference? He looked at the spot where the picture of the two Georges was taken, and leaned way back to get an overall look. The frame of his car window had framed that spot as if it was a picture. It looks two-dimensional, he thought. He raised the yearbook and positioned it to the right of the window.

"Wow, wow, wow, look at this. Two pictures at the same time of the exact spot but many years apart."

He lowered the yearbook and turned to his right. He looked up at the neon sign. And there it was, protruding

271

from the right corner of the building. The streetlight they had argued about many times all those years ago. To Roberto, it looked like a streetlight attached to a building. He thought it looked weird.

"That is the very same light, I can't believe it's still there." He heard his voice within the confines of his car and thought it sounded a little different.

There was something about saying it out loud that bothered him. It was as if he heard the Roberto of yesterday and not the now Roberto. He asked himself, is my voice still the same? Is Pat Daily's voice the same? How about Cathy's voice or Anthony's voice? This was a memory of three friends that had snuck up on him and wasn't prepared for it. He waited for joy, but instead, a quick flash of fear jolted him. The thought of not knowing where they were at that very moment came to him. He asked himself, how is it possible to have been so close to them, yet not know where they are right now?

"It's not a streetlight if it's not on the street." He clearly heard Cathy say. She made a face like saying, come on really?

Anthony said, "it's a combination building streetlight, okay?"

Pat couldn't care less, "who gives a shit? It's a fucking light come on."

Instantly the night of nineteen seventy six played out. He heard Pat say, "you call this Rock n Roll?"

He ejected the tape and pushed in SteppenWolf.

Roberto snapped out of his memory to catch a glimpse of himself smiling in his rearview mirror. He looked down to see himself holding an eight-track tape. From a place only the words would know, "you better not be putting on some of that disco shit."

He wasn't sure who said it but he heard it. He pushed the tape in and the song, Born on The Bayou filled the space around him. And this time, joy was once again right there next to him. He closed his eyes, leaned way back, and heard all three of them say, "now this is music." Amid a forever moment, a voice from long ago sang along with the tape. The voice stopped. Loud knocking jolted Roberto back to where he wasn't.

"Hey, not bad ha Roberto?" The voice said.

Startled, but present, Roberto had no choice, but to see that which was before him.

"How can this be?" Roberto had to ask.

"Hey man, what's going on man?" The voice asked.

Roberto stared and thought, is that really George?

"Come on, Roberto! Why you looking at me like that for? Come on, roll down the window man."

As if to confirm where he was, Roberto looked beyond the hood of his car. And yes, there it is, the brick wall he was sure he had parked in front of. He saw the neon sign attached to that wall, and the streetlight they had argued about. They were things of long ago that are not living. Things that are not walking, talking, or breathing. Right there, stationary as they should be. But the living? Talking to me? How can that be? He looked at his dashboard to see his Day on The Green concert ticket. He reached out and touched it. Wait a minute he said. This was a concert we had not been to before that night in nineteen seventy-six. But this is not that night, so here it is as it should be. So, what's going on here? He looked out the window again and this time saw his own reflection on the window but heard.

"Jesus Christ Roberto, you'd think you saw a ghost or something man. Come on roll down the window." Said

George and hung his head not believing. He waited a few seconds and said. "So what? Are we gonna look at each other through the window all night or what?"

Born on the Bayou, ended, Bad Moon Rising, came on.

"Hey, hey, I been practicing this one, watch, watch."

Roberto hesitantly, little by little started rolling down the window. George started singing. With every turn, the sound of his singing became louder, his unforgettable smell unavoidable, his image more revealing of the undeniable truth just outside the window. George stopped singing as the clear image of Roberto became visible. He leaned in and looked past Roberto.

"Hey, where's Cathy man?"

"George?" Ask Roberto.

"What's the matter? What's the matter, man?"

"Jesus," said Roberto, "you look exactly the same."

"The same? The same what?"

He looked into Roberto's eyes and waited for him to respond, but heard nothing. He looked around the inside of the car. He backed up. Roberto's eyes fixated on the image he couldn't believe was there.

"Why are you looking at me like that?" Asked George.

His mouth remained open after finishing the word, that. He waited for an answer. He backed up a little more and looked at Roberto's car from end to end.

"Hey, where's your dad's truck? Ha? Hey, how is your dad anyway?"

He stepped forward, leaned into the car again, and looked around.

"Where the hell is Pat? Ha? Hey, how about Anthony, where is he? Hey, are you guys still in the band? Ha?"

Roberto's inability to answer irritated the man that wasn't supposed to be here.

"What's the matter, man? What's the matter?"

Now that's a good question, thought Roberto.

"Hey, hey, I know, you want me to buy you beer?" Said George as he tried to fall back into the routine.

"Ah, ah....." Roberto said.

"Ah, ah? Is that it? Is that all you got?" George asked with a face caught between demanding and confusion.

George took a long drink of his beer. He wiped his mouth with his sleeve and his face became that of the old George trying to please. "It's okay, it's cool man."

George turned around, took a couple of steps, stopped and came back.

"Oh, oh, hey...." Said George, and made a gesture with his hand like wiping away all that was said.

"Don't worry man. I'll get it. I'll get it. Don't you worry. You can catch me later. Here, hold on to mine. I'll be right back man."

He handed Roberto his beer and walked away. He stopped, hesitated for a few seconds, and came back. He swallowed the excess saliva, wiped his mouth, and cleared his throat. He leaned in and whispered.

"Be careful, there's cops around."

He pointed all around. He pulled his head back, stood up tall, looked over the car, and whispered.

"The coast is clear man."

He walked off and once again stopped. He laughed and turned to look at him. "You little punk."

Roberto smiled not knowing why. There was something about being called a little punk that made him feel good. George pointed at him, turned around, and walked into the alley. Roberto looked at the beer in his hand and thought, what am I gonna do with this? He looked around for cops to make sure the coast was clear. He looked behind the passenger seat and placed the beer on the floor behind it. He grabbed a small towel from the back seat and carefully placed it around the beer so it wouldn't tip over.

He leaned back and tried to relax. He shook his head as if to reset the moment. The sound of him inhaling and exhaling the air around him became evident to him. He closed his eyes and visualized the air going into his nose, into his lungs, and back out. Is this new air that I'm breathing? He asked himself. If so, what makes it new? Or is it old air and if so, where has this air been? Have I breathed this air before? Wait a minute, whose breath am I breathing? And as always, the questions lined up. But there was something different this time. He actually saw the list of questions in his head come alive, and getting longer. The questions distorted and forged into people. Each with their own list of questions in their own brain. And in that brain, yet another tiny brain with their list and on and on. The endless line of people and tiny brains now in front of a popular restaurant. He asked himself, where am I? He looked up at the sign but was unable to read it. It was some kind of code or something.

He turned around to ask the person behind him if he could read the sign and saw a questioning expression on his face. Roberto looked at the person behind that person to see everyone with that same expression. I can't ask a question, a question. What's wrong with me? But these are people. Yeah, people with nothing but questions. He

looked around and beyond the person behind him to see
the line extended all the way down the block and around
the corner. The thought of answering all those questions
exhausted him. He asked himself, why all these questions
and why in the form of people? He opened his eyes and
there he was right back in his car.

"What the hell?"

He told himself, listen to the music. A few seconds
later, the music stopped. He reached out to restart the
tape, but there was no tape in the player.

"What am I doing?" He said aloud and pulled his hand
back. He felt embarrassed. He looked around to make sure
no one saw him. The feeling of being trapped in his car
came over him.

"Is this claustrophobia that I'm feeling?"

He heard his voice as if it was coming from outside the
car. His eyes looked around but his head didn't move. It
was as if his eyes were making decisions on their own. He
felt his eyes moving. He became aware of the fact that he
was feeling his eyes moving and that freaked him out. He
grabbed the door handle and pulled on it with great force.
He pushed the door open with his shoulder. The door
swung all the way out and swung back. He stopped it with
his left hand, held it open, and got out. He stood tall, with
his neck stretched way up. It was as if he was presenting
himself to himself. He looked all the way around
questioning all that he saw. He asked himself, is it possible
to ask yourself, when is this? That is crazy, that's the kind
of thing you ask when you're watching a movie or reading
an article or a book.

"I'm standing right here, right now. What the hell?"

He said it out loud. He looked over his shoulder to see

the alley between the two buildings. It was like a trigger, a call to action, he felt it, knew it, and didn't ask the question that had to be asked. Where the hell is George? He took off toward the liquor store. He stopped and looked back at his car. That good feeling he always felt when doing so, escaped him. He started to ask himself why but shook it off and walked into the alley. The sound of his steps reverberating off the walls brought forth the presence of space and time. As it always did when actions taken made their way back to him. And for reasons he couldn't explain, these reverberations were different. They felt like long ago lost reflections, trapped within the confines of this brick space. This thought brought him to a halt. It was his mind that which he felt next. What is this that I am feeling? Is it a reflection of my own mind? Is this the presence of mind left behind? That must be it. That's why it feels different. Is that even possible? To feel something with a long ago mind? The next thing he knew was him exiting the alley. He turned left to the front of the liquor store. He stopped, and looked at the front of the store. How is it possible that it has remained unchanged?

He walked up to the door, his hand extended, grabbed the door handle, and pulled it open. He felt a small delay. It was as if a second or two held on a bit too long. He felt it and thought, maybe I shouldn't be going into this building. That felt weird. He brushed that aside, walked in, and stopped. He waited for an emotion. A response to him looking around to see the old store of his childhood, but felt nothing. He brushed that aside and looked for George.

"Can I help you?" Asked the cashier.

"Did you see George come in here? He was on his way over here a little while ago"

"George, who's George? No one's come in for a while."

Roberto looked past the cashier at an elderly man sitting behind him against the wall. He squinted as he looked at Roberto.

Roberto looked at the cashier. "So no one came in here a few minutes ago?"

"Nope, it's been really slow tonight."

"Hm, that's kind of weird." Said Roberto and did another quick look around. "Oh well...I guess he went somewhere else."

He stood there for a few seconds too long.

"Can I get you something?" Asked the cashier.

"Ah, no, thank you."

Roberto raised his eyebrows, faked a smile, and instantly asked himself why, why smile? He headed for the door.

A reflection made its way to him, but it was instant without delay. His eye caught it on the front window. He stopped to see the cashier say something to the elderly man. The cashier realized he was being watched and stopped talking. He looked at Roberto with a questioning expression. Roberto frowned, wanting to ask what was being said, but a flashback of a cashier asking him if he was getting gas rushed through his head. The feeling of wanting to escape came next. He pushed the door wide open and quickly walked out. He looked through the window to see the elderly man stand and watched him walk away. Roberto thought, why would he look at me? Why would he watch me walk away? Do I know that man? Maybe I look like someone he knows or something. He walked through the alley, but this time there were no reverberations and no hesitation. He walked up to his car. He turned around and stood there for a minute.

"Where the hell is he? Jesus Christ!" He leaned against his car and waited.

"What the hell is wrong with me? It can't possibly be George."

He looked around just to make sure. He looked down and thought for a few seconds.

"Wait a minute, wait one doggone minute."

He reached into his pocket, grabbed the keys, opened his car, and got in. He reached for the beer behind the passenger seat and there's nothing there.

"How can this be?"

He refused to accept it. He reached past the passenger seat. Dipped his hand between the door and the seat. Found the lever, pulled on it and the passenger seat released. He pushed it forward. He looked behind it and saw absolutely nothing.

"What the hell is happening here?"

Refusing what his eyes didn't see, he leaned behind the seat to get a better look, and once again, no beer. He felt under the seat.

"Just in case," he heard himself say and found nothing.

Out of the corner of his eye, he saw the small towel on the back seat. He turned to it.

"God damn, I don't believe this."

He turned back around to face the front of the car and took a long pause. The sound of his rapid breathing came to him.

"Why am I out of breath?"

He looked around again not knowing why. There was

something about looking around that bought him time but then asked, time for what? He thought about George singing just outside his window. How the window somehow made it easier for him to question, to accept, or deny. It was almost like looking at a picture or watching a movie, but then, he rolled down the window, and reality came calling on a friend. George was not only singing, his smell made its way to him. Not only that, George had handed him his beer.

"Wait a minute," he said to himself. "Maybe, I put the beer behind my seat. No, I'm sure I placed it behind the passenger seat. I remember placing the towel around...."

He stopped talking. He looked at the towel on the rear seat once again as frustration over whelmed him and asked.

"Maybe I didn't place the towel...."

He stopped again. He got out. Spun around to face his car. He asked. "What if the beer is not there? What then?"

He did a quick look around. "I can't believe that I'm actually thinking that George was right here."

He pointed to the ground with both hands, "right here."

He knelt next to his car. His right hand slowly reached out. He grabbed the seat lever, pulled and the seat released. A slight dizziness came over him. He heard the sound of his rapid breathing. He pushed the seat forward. He reached into the car and stopped. As if his eyes were questioning his brain, he heard, what is it about this picture you don't understand? The word picture repeated itself many times.

"What the hell?"

With his hand hovering and still on his knees, a deafening silence came calling on a friend. Knowing already what he didn't want to know, he reached in, hoping, just in case, but only to confirm what wasn't there. Like the short quick breaths, one would take before your tears, Roberto took his, but on this relentless night, his tears were nowhere to be found. He pulled his hand back, and ever so slowly stood. He closed his eyes, tilted his head back, and as always, rain or shine, the sound of rain brought him joy. And as always, rain or shine, he felt the rain upon his face. And as always, he opened his eyes to see the picture of where he stood, in the opened yearbook in his hands. He closed the yearbook and tucked it under his arm. Picked up his bike, and as he had done so many times before, he turned around to see the night pretend no more. And as he had done so many times before, he slowly raised his hand to wave to no one there, but on this relentless night, he could wave no more.

21. TOO SMART FOR YOUR BRITCHES

Margaret was in the police station waiting for Paul. She told herself not to look at the pictures on the wall of the two deceased policemen. And now that it crossed her mind, don't these men deserve a few minutes of my time? Unbeknownst to her, Paul entered the waiting room and saw her looking at the pictures. He told himself to be respectful and forced himself to wait. Her thoughts continued to their destination. If their relatives were right here, they would want me to look at them, to read about them, right? To feel if nothing else, just a fraction of what they feel. So why am I trying to ignore them?

"Hello there Margaret." Paul finally interrupted her.

"Oh, hi, Paul, and thank you."

"For what?"

"You don't want to know."

"I'll take your word for it this time considering what you said the last time."

"Oh, really. What did I say?" Asked, Margaret.

"You don't want to know," Paul said, tightened his lips, and did a quick little nod punctuating his sentence.

"Really? What exactly did I say to warrant that expression?"

Paul thought if he should respond and went for it. "Ah, hmm, let me think, something about you not hitting puberty yesterday?"

She looked up trying to remember. "Oh, yes-- unfortunately I didn't."

"Okay," said Paul, "let's not talk about that."

"Happy not to." Said, Margaret.

Paul gave her a look that ended in a little smile. He ushered her toward the door with his left hand and said.

"Come....on....in." As he opened the door.

"Thank you."

"You're welcome."

As she entered the hallway, Paul stepped around her and led the way. She watched his perky step. He opened the door to his office.

"Come....on.....in," Paul said, sounding like a game show host.

She looked at his relentless smile as she walked past him into the office. He closed the door and saw her staring, smiling, and frowning at the same time.

"What's wrong?" Paul asked.

"Whatever you're drinking? I'll have two."

"What do you mean?"

"Never mind."

He slid a chair across the office and up to the desk. He looked at her. His smile got bigger. He waited for her to sit, but instead, Margaret found herself not knowing how to respond to him. Paul padded the chair as if it had a cushion that needed fluffing and said.

"Sit righhhht here."

Margaret's smile began to fade at the unusual courtesy and said, "thank you, Paul."

She kept her eye on him as he went around the desk and sat. He turned the monitor to show her a map.

She frowned and asked. "What are all those Xs?"

He pointed to a spot on the map. "Is this where you saw him?"

She leaned into the monitor. "Is that the creek right there?" She pointed.

"Yes, that's the creek."

"Well, in that case, yes, right about there, is where I saw him."

"You know Margaret, I can't believe you went down there. That's some pretty dense shrubbery right there. But you know what? Good for you, that means you're pretty tough."

Margaret couldn't believe what she was hearing. He looked at the monitor and pointed to several Xs.

"These are unsolved crimes or incidents. We keep track of them in this map. You'd be surprised how often crimes are geographically connected."

"What a great idea." Said, Margaret.

"For example: Let's take a look at this one right here."

He clicked on the x near the shack. A report came up.

"So, there it is. That's the crash I told you about." He stopped to think. "Fifteen years ago. Can you believe it?" He looked at her. Margaret was in disbelief but for all the wrong reasons.

"This map is amazing." She said, not hearing what he said. She looked up to see his smirk. "I know that little smirk. What's going on?"

Paul's head began to slowly move up and down as he processed her compliment, of which she had no idea.

"Well, when I created this map last year...." She interrupted him.

"You created this map?" Her eyebrows raised way up.

"Yes....I went back to our records and found anything that was pending, and I imputed these incidents into my map."

She turned from the map to him in amazement and back to the map. Her hand slowly raised from her lap and moved across the space between her body and the monitor hovering like a helicopter in midair. Her index finger slowly became a pointer.

"This map is your idea?"

"Yep, this map is my idea." He placed a single sheet of paper in front of her. "So, as you can see," he pointed to a spot on the page.

Margaret leaned down to get a better look.

"The driver was never found. He was from Southern California. A place called Arlington Heights."

He backed away from the desk and looked at her. As if to ask, what do you think? Hoping to hear, good job, but instead heard.

"Are you sure this map is your idea?" She saw his smile vanish. His nostrils moved to his sudden rapid breathing.

"You know Margaret, that's insulting."

"No, no, I mean, what a great idea." She tilted her head as she ended the word idea.

"Yeah, right."

"Yeah right what? What do you mean? I mean it. It is a great idea."

She looked around in an attempt to correct her behavior. She looked at the monitor and then at the paper he placed in front of her.

"Did anyone report him missing?"

He pointed to a specific spot on the report. "Nope."

His finger moved to another spot on the report.

"Next of kin - Unknown. No one to report him missing, apparently."

"How sad is that?" Said, Margaret.

They looked at each other. Paul nodded in agreement.

Margaret couldn't wait to know. "What is his name?"

He pointed to a spot on the monitor.

"Roberto Tenna."

"Roberto Tenna? Do we have a picture?"

"No, I don't know why. Well, it's probably because the case is so old. We didn't even have computers fifteen years ago."

He looked away thinking about not having computers fifteen years ago.

"What about his driver's license picture?" Asked Margaret.

"No driver's license on file. I'm not sure why, but if his license had expired, especially for a long time, the new system probably wouldn't have picked it up. I mean, I guess. A picture wouldn't help us any."

Margaret looked at him questioningly.

"Because we have no idea what this guy really looks like."

"Oh, you mean because....yeah I guess you're right. So, how do we know this is him?"

"Well, at this point, we don't. The whole report will be here later today."

She gave him another questioning look.

"It's in storage."

"Oh."

He looked away thinking and then back to her. "You know what? If we had one of his prints." He paused. He looked away and quickly looked back to her.

"Do you still give him food in that thermos?"

"Yes, yes, I do, why?"

"Do you have one with you? A fresh one? You know, one that you picked up recently?"

"Yes, I just picked one up earlier."

"So, you picked it up from the theater?"

"No, he hardly goes to the theater anymore."

"Well, I should be able to lift a print I hope, and I'll run it later." Said Paul.

"Okay," Margaret said and looked around thinking of how great it will be to know who this man is.

Paul looked at his map on the computer. He thought how a few days ago, he was willing to walk away from all of this. And actually, did when he saw Margaret and the homeless man at the theater. And now, not only has he been able to put his map idea to work, but this is by far the only interesting thing in his police work. He came out of that thought to see Margaret, in a zombie-like state. Her eyes frozen on the computer monitor, but not seeing what was on it. As if she was looking through it. He wondered what she was thinking. She looked at him.

"You know Paul, for the first time in many years, I feel like a passenger. A change that for whatever reason, I'm okay with. Not sure why that is, or if that's a good thing for that matter."

Paul started to say something, Margaret interrupted him as if anticipating his question, and said.

"I know, I know...it's good to let go sometimes. To let someone else take control from time to time. I mean I wouldn't have thought of that."

"Thought of what?"

"The fingerprint....and the map."

"It's what I do, Margaret." He said in a matter of fact way.

He watched her as she looked away and went back into thought. A burning feeling brought to her attention that her attempt at an apology left something to be desired. He opened his mouth to say something when Margaret interrupted him again.

"You know Paul. I didn't mean to insult you earlier. You do know that, right?"

Paul said nothing, dropped his index finger on his desk, and tapped it repeatedly. She looked at his hand. He stopped.

She added. "It's just that it's so high-tech you know, that's the part that I didn't understand."

"Get over it." He gave her a smirk.

She raised her hands as if to say, I tried. A day later, Paul sat at his desk looking at the report after running the prints on the thermos. There was a knock on the door.

"Come in."

The door opened. A female cadet wearing a neatly ironed uniform, with her hair up in a bun, escorted Margaret to his office.

"Come in, come in."

Margaret walked in and looked down at the report.

"Sit down." Said Paul.

He looked past Margaret at the cadet still at the door, with a look of excitement.

"Thank you, Linda, that'll be all." The cadet smiled and closed the door.

"I have good news."

"What's that?"

"He is that guy."

"So he's been here for fifteen years?"

Paul nodded and said, "Can you believe it? He has been here since I was in the sixth grade. My God!"

Margaret tried to visualize Paul as a sixth grader playing with his friends. Paul went on and brought her out of that thought.

"I know, I mean, I'm still trying to wrap my head around that. I mean...who would have thought? Actually, I'm embarrassed to admit that I didn't even think about him...till that night at the theater." He paused hoping Margaret would say something.

"I also know something else." He cocked his head and raised his eyebrows.

Margaret couldn't wait as a deep frown developed and said, "What?"

"This guy was in a mental institution and..."

"A mental institution?" She interrupted him.

"Yes, you see what I mean?"

"You see what I mean, what?" Said, Margaret, as her eyes darted back and forth.

"I told you this guy could be dangerous. Remember?"

"Well, if he is so dangerous, why would they release him? I mean obviously, this man was of no threat to anyone. I mean look at him."

"Ah, well," he stopped to make her ask.

"What, what?"

"They didn't release him." He leaned toward her.

"He escaped. He disappeared, nada."

Her frown deepened and decided not to say anything.

"And, I guess no one from the institution reported him missing," said Paul. "Technically, he didn't do anything illegal. He had no previous record of any kind, so they let it go. And, I guess, and I do emphasize, I guess, that's why he didn't come up on our missing person's search."

He waited for her to say something, but got no response. He went on. "Now you know the true definition of falling through the cracks."

"Well, I guess that's good. I mean at least he's not...a criminal."

"Margaret?" Paul said, sounding fatherly again.

"Yes Paul"

"We have no idea what this guy is capable of. Okay? I mean think about it. We have absolutely no idea what this guy has been doing for fifteen years." He stopped, and thought, there, that ought to put end to that.

"Actually, we do know. He has been eating out of the trash cans for fifteen years." She made a face as that visual went through his head.

She went on. "And, you guys, and by you guys I mean you policeman, would have known if he had done something criminal and...." Paul stopped her with a look.

"Look, people do all kinds of shit that we don't know about, okay? Just because we're the police doesn't mean we know it all."

"Ain't that the truth?" She looked away.

"Are you done? Margaret?"

Margaret sighed.

"I mean really." Added Paul and shook his head.

He looked at the report. His index finger landed on the page and moved around in search of something. He stopped. "Hey, maybe we can talk to the doctor that treated him. He is right....there it is, right here, Dr. Culpa."

Margaret looked at the report. Paul slid his finger to another spot and stopped.

"Here is the facility's phone number. Maybe he's still around, who knows?"

He picked up the phone and dialed the number.

"Hi, can I speak with Dr. Culpa please?" Paul listened.

"Oh, really, do you have his contact information? I'm with the Cloverdale Police Department and we need some information on one of his patients." He listened.

"That would be perfect." He gave her Cloverdale Pd's phone number.

"I'm looking forward to it, thank you. You're welcome." He hung up.

"What's going on?" Margaret asked.

"He doesn't work there anymore, but they're going to give him our phone number, so hopefully he'll call back."

"Let's hope so," said Margaret. "Maybe he's retired."

"Most likely, it has been fifteen years." Said Paul.

She thought about the passage of time and how hard it was to be thought of as someone who was retired. The retirement life was something she hadn't given much thought to. Doing whatever she wanted, whenever she wanted, was a concept beyond her comprehension. Margaret was like an old teenager on steroids. She had the knowledge of a forever seeker of truth, the need to help and to teach others, coupled with the relentless feeling that all was never enough. Little did she know that her life as a teacher would never allow her that lifestyle and would forever keep her on her path of a forever teacher.

22. BIGFOOT IS REAL
You stupid idiot

It was nineteen seventy-four. Mark Bennett, Cathy Crittendon, Roberto, and a few others, were hanging out in the hallways of Cloverdale High School. The double doors burst open to the sight of Bob Mills as he walked in and stopped to make sure everyone saw him. The neck of his guitar protruded up over his shoulder as it hung from his back with the strap across his chest. His long hair hung halfway down his back. He grabbed his huge headphones hanging from his neck, raised them over his black beanie, and perfectly positioned them over his ears. The hallway was now in dead silence, everyone wondered what the hell was going on. Mills reached up to the huge eight-track tape deck hanging from his neck. That thing was the size of a refrigerator. Everyone's eyes followed. This was Mills at his best. He slowly pushed the tape in. The lights on the eight-track lit up. The song, Feel Like Making Love, by

Bad Company exploded in his headphones catapulting his ego into the arena of rock legends. He strolled down the hallway like a scene from a Hollywood movie.

"What the hell? I knew he was crazy, but....did you know about this?" Roberto asked Mark.

"Hell no! I don't even know what that is."

Cathy could do nothing but wrinkle her nose as she always did whenever she smelled something cheesy. "What the hell is he doing?" She asked.

"Who the hell knows." Said Mark.

"Is he listening to Music?" Asked Roberto.

"If he is, it's shit music! I guarantee it. What a freak." Said Pat.

"Oh, my God." Was all Steve could say.

"How is he powering that eight-track?" Asked Roberto.

"Bat shit if you ask me." Said Mark.

Cathy, who didn't like Mills, said, "he thinks he's so cool."

Everyone looked at each other as they tried to figure out Mills's contraption. The music from his headphones got louder as he approached them.

"What a stupid fucking idea." Said Mark.

"I like it. I don't know how he did that, but I like it." Said Roberto.

Mills looked out of the corner of his eye to see them looking at him as he strolled past them. Mill's brain exploded into a fantasy right out of the Hollywood Magazines. In his mind, every girl in that hallway wanted him. He made a U-turn, this time he danced his way back to them. Their jaw-dropping expressions solidified his rock-star fantasy. He saw Cathy's what the fuck expression, and thought, she must really want me. She is the lucky one, he told himself. He turned directly to her.

294

He sang the lyrics right at her. Cathy heard his out of key voice with the music from his headphones in the far background. Mills heard himself in perfect pitch. Cathy's eyes glazed over in total confusion. Her body froze as her emotions responded in a way she couldn't begin to explain.

Mills moved in closer, raised his arms over his head, and rubbed up against her throbbing to the beat of the music. Cathy felt her heart speeding, her body overheating for reasons she hoped no one would know. Mills heard the loud music; Cathy heard his out of key voice. Mills was in total control. He touched her nose with his, and thought, she's all mine. He sang to her, "feel like making love to you," totally out of key.

His sexuality shot out of his eyes and into hers. Cathy, now incapable of looking away. Mills took a quick look around to see them all in a trance. He blew her a kiss, spun around, and danced away, in search of his next victim.

"What the fuck?" Said Pat.

"Oh, my God." Said Cathy and touched her face to feel her temperature raging.

Roberto looked at her, "I think he had you."

Cathy punched him on the shoulder, "Are you serious?"

"I saw it too," said Mark. "He had you man, he really had you."

"Not a chance." Said Cathy, "He's so gross."

In the far distance, Mills had his next victim against the wall.

Roberto looked at Mark. "Love that idea, man."

"What the hell are you talking about? Cat shit if you ask me."

Mike Davidson and his brother Joe walked up to Mark.

"So, what about this ghost town we've been hearing about?" Asked Mike.

"What about it?"

"Where is it?"

"You'll never know."

"Why not?"

Joe leaned into Mark, "Because it doesn't exist."

"Not in that pea brain of yours that's for sure. Not enough room, man." Said, Mark and sort of laughed, so did Roberto.

Joe took a step toward Mark. "You know and I know it's bullshit."

Mark smiled, "yeah man, we made it up." he turned away ignoring Joe and Mike.

Mike tilted his head as he looked at the back of Mark's head. "Come on Mark, where is it?"

Mark looked at Mike. "Wait, didn't your brother just say it didn't exist, that it was bullshit?"

"What do you want to know for anyway?" Asked Roberto.

"We want to see it. Why else?" Mike said, with a softer expression.

"You're crazy man." Said Mark.

Why? Why are we crazy? Asked Joe.

"Because it's scary as shit, that's why," said Roberto.

Joe laughed, "scary as shit, come on man."

"What's so scary about it?" Asked Mike.

Mark's expression turned serious, "because it's haunted, that's what."

"Bullshit. Is this like your Bigfoot story?" Asked Joe as he pulled his head back.

Mark turned directly at him with a deep frown,

"bullshit story? You don't believe in Bigfoot?"

Joe smirked and looked at the others like saying, can you believe this, "ah, no!" He raised his eyebrows.

"What the fuck stupid kind of idiot are you? Bigfoot is real man." Said, Mark and walked off.

"Okay, okay, Bigfoot is real. Come on man," said Joe.

Mark stopped and turned back.

Cathy looked at Joe, questioning.

"What?" Asked Joe.

"Look, we went on that trip." She hesitated. Everyone waited. "And it was weird man."

Toby, who also went on the Bigfoot excursion said. "Weird, spooky, and scary, oh my God?."

"What was so scary?" Mike asked with a sour face.

"She's right." Cathy said, "I don't know if it was Bigfoot, but whatever that was, man...when we heard that scream.....we all jumped into the truck, and I mean inside the cab of the truck. All of us, there were like ten of us and we all jumped in. No one wanted to be left out." Cathy played out the event in her head.

Mike waited. He looked around and back to Cathy.

"Well....?"

Cathy came out of her memory. "Well what, what?"

"What happened then?" Joe asked.

Cathy and Toby looked at Joe like, weren't you listening?

"That's it, the scream?" Asked Mike and looked at Joe like saying, can you believe this?

"Yeah, that's it, the scream, the screeching loud almost forever scream that...." Cathy stopped. She looked past Mike as the events played out in her head again.

Joe, Mike, everyone watched as fear came onto her face.

"It was so weird." She quietly said as she continued to look past them. "Like nothing we've ever heard before."

She turned to look at the group and settled on Toby and Judy who were standing next to each other. They both nodded in agreement.

Cathy went on. "It was like something was screaming for their life, but, but who knows what and...."

Toby couldn't wait and jumped in. "And it was so loud and, oh my god, it sounded like, I don't know, but it hurt my ears, and it echoed throughout, everywhere, I mean, my God."

She stopped, shook her head, and refocused her vision. As if she was coming out of the experience. Everyone stared at her. "I mean, am I right?" Cathy and Judy nodded in agreement.

Judy added. "I was so scared, I froze, and then started shaking so bad, I couldn't even talk."

Mike couldn't wait to hear the rest of the story.

Cathy went on. "And, and all of a sudden, everything stopped."

"What do you mean?" Asked Mike.

"Well, first," she paused, swallowed and went on. "We heard the loud screeching scream." She made a face as if she heard it again.

"My God, we all looked around....confused. We didn't know what to do. We looked at each other, and my god, we were almost fighting each other to get into the cab. We were like a mob or something. I was like, it turned us into animals"

She looked at the group to see them waiting for more. "The screeching scream went on and on, like forever." She paused.

"It finally stopped and," she looked past Joe and Mike again as if she was right back in the woods. Her eyes were big, her mouth slightly opened.

"And everything, and I mean everything, the birds, the wind, everything....stopped"

Cathy continued to look past them as if she was looking at something. Joe did a quick look over his shoulder just to make sure and quickly turned back to her.

"There was complete silence," Whispered Cathy.

"What?" Joe asked.

"There was complete silence.....out in the woods."

Her focus came back to Joe to see him searching her eyes. She asked him. "Do you know how weird that is? I mean, have you never heard complete silence out in the woods? Evvvverr?"

Joe replayed the scene in his head. Mark also relived the memory, but in his version, things were a little different. A couple of weeks before this, Mark and Roberto told a bunch of their friends they had seen Bigfoot, and as Mark said it.

"It scared the shit out of us. He had to have been at least eight feet tall."

At first, they didn't believe him, but Mark's ability to tell a great story left them no option. Mark and Roberto finally had enough participants to go on their Bigfoot adventure. A few days later, they all got into Mark's four-wheel-drive Dodge Power-wagon pick-up. Or, as Mark called it, Power Wagon. This was a truck not to be taken lightly. It was more like a monster truck, lifted high with huge tires. This truck could go over large rocks, logs, whatever was in its way, including a river. It had a front bumper that extended out a couple of feet past the hood.

The bumper had what they called, a full guard. I was two feet tall made out of two inch diameter pipe. It wrapped around the front corner of the truck for extra protection. You could ram through the brush, fallen trees, or whatever.

During deer hunting season, Mark, and his dad used it to strap dead deer on it. It was like a trophy case. There's nothing like a Power-Wagon coming at you on the highway with dead deer staring right at you. The bumper had a winch strong enough to lift that truck out of any situation. River, creek, gully, ravine, or good old-fashioned mud. This truck had two gas tanks and a huge auxiliary propane tank. If you ran out of gasoline, you flipped a switch on the dash and this truck could run on propane for days. And of course, there was the triple stack rifle rack against the back window. On top was a thirty, thirty Winchester rifle. Second, was a thirty aught six Mauser. At the bottom, strategically placed, always within reach, was a twelve-gauge shotgun loaded with double aught buckshot. Of course.

They all got into the back of the "Power-wagon" and drove north out of town on Highway 101 for about seven miles. Mark turned left onto a dirt road. They drove around a hill and alongside the Russian River. About a mile later, Mark turned onto another dirt road, through a bunch of trees, and right up to the river and stopped. Mark and Roberto got out.

"Okay," said Mark, "we're gonna drive across the River so hold on."

"How deep is it?" Someone asked.

"Just deep enough," Mark said with a little grin.

Judy and Cathy caught his grin and didn't like what

they saw. Mark leaned toward them and said, what, without saying it. At that moment, an expression was all it took. The girls said nothing.

They got back in. Mark reached for the ignition and stopped. "Oh man, we forgot to lock the front axle."

"Shit!" Said Roberto.

They jumped out. Each walked to their perspective front tire; leaned down and twisted the hub locking the axle. They got back in.

"Okay, here we go." Yelled Mark.

"Wait a minute." Said, Cathy, stood and leaned around the driver's side toward Mark's window.

"What if it's too deep?"

"Don't worry, this thing is like a submarine, we're FINE! Sit down for shit's sake."

Pat, who was sitting in the back, stood as he saw something upstream. "Hey, hold on, hold on, what is that?" He pointed.

Everyone looked. Mark knew exactly what he was asking about. The one thing he was trying to keep from them. He opened his door, got out, but remained standing on the side-step of the truck. He looked at Pat, and then in the direction he was pointing, and said, "that - is a bridge."

"A bridge? What the hell kind of bridge is that?" Asked Pat.

Mark gave him a look. "That is what you would call a hanging bridge. For pedestrians. What's with the questions?"

Pat ignored him.

"What's a hanging bridge?" Asked, Toby.

Mark extended his arm out toward the bridge. His index finger popped out as if he was shooting it.

"That, that right there is a hanging bridge. Now come on, we have to get going."

"Wait a minute. What do you mean hanging?" Judy asked.

Mark stepped off and walked back to face the group.

"Jeez, what do you think this is, a tour at a state park or something? What am I, you tour guide?"

Everyone looked at him and waited. Judy tilted her head, asking him to explain.

"Okay, man, what a bunch of babies." Said Mark.

Roberto got out and walked back to the group to help Mark. Mark gave him a look, nodded, and mouthed, "I got this."

Roberto gave him a look as if to ask, are you sure?

"Okay," said Mark, he looked at Judy and then at the bridge and pointed.

"You see how there's two thick cables coming from the other side of the river?" Everyone looked.

Pat leaned toward the bridge. "Oh yeah, I see that." He looked at everyone as if to ask, can you see that?

Everyone saw the two thick cables. "Oh, yeah, I see that," several people said.

Mark went on. "Now I know you can't see them on our side of the river because of the trees. But those two cables extend from the other side of the river to this side behind those trees. And, if you look really close, you can see smaller cables hanging from the big cables that hold the boards that you walk on. All those cables hanging, make it a hanging bridge." Mark punctuated, "hanging bridge" with a long downward nod.

"I think that makes it a suspension bridge; I mean..." Judy was saying as Mark cut her off.

"Bacon and eggs, eggs and bacon. What's the difference Judy, I mean really?"

He looked at the bridge and extended both arms out with his palms facing up as if he was presenting the bridge. In a loud firm voice, he said, "look at it, it's hanging." Mark looked at her, twisted his head slightly, and raised his eyebrows.

"Why are you mad?" Asked Judy.

"Do I sound mad?"

Judy frowned, looked at Toby and Cathy who looked at Mark and nodded, telling Mark that Judy was right. Mark looked down. Regrouped and looked at them.

"I'm sorry, you're right. I didn't mean to come across like that. It's just that, you know, it's getting late." He looked up at the sun and back to the group.

"The last thing and I mean the last thing - you wanna do - in the dark?" He paused, "is to come face to face with Bigfoot. In the dark, believe me."

"Hey, what is that?" Someone asked.

Everyone looked at Anthony to see him pointing downstream. They turned to see a metal box hanging from a cable that also extended from one side of the river to the other. Mark's face flushed and looked down not believing what was going on. Roberto saw Mark's disappointment and took over.

"Well," he looked at Judy. "I hate to tell you Judy, but that's," he paused, "a hanging car. That's what they call it around here anyway." Roberto made a face trying to get under her skin.

"Why is everything hanging around here?" Someone asked.

303

Judy made a face. "That is a cable car, that's what that is, I mean you have heard of a cable car, right?"

She turned from Roberto to Mark who was still looking down. She waited. Mark felt her glare and finally looked at her and said. "So why is that not a suspension car Judy? I mean you know. Just asking."

"Really Mark?" Judy raised her eyebrows and twisted her head slightly to mimic his earlier expression.

Mark sort of smiled as if to say, whatever. He looked at everyone.

"Are we done here?" He waited. "What? No more questions?"

He wiped his mouth as if he had something on it, but there was nothing there. It was just something he did to get under their skin.

"Okay, let's get the hell out of here and across this river before the hippos get here."

"Hippos? What is he talking about?" Someone asked.

"I thought hippos were in Africa?" Someone else asked.

Mark caught a few questioning glares as he walked up to his door. "Not anymore." He got in and added. "Some escaped from a zoo a few months back." He yelled and closed the door.

"God knows where they are by now," said Roberto and closed his door.

Everyone in the back heard and felt the truck start up. They looked at each other hoping to hear someone say, he's kidding. But instead heard, "is he kidding?"

"Well, we are here looking for Bigfoot, so, who knows?" Said Pat.

Mark grabbed the four-wheel drive gearshift and pulled it all the way back setting it to low gear ratio. He eased off the clutch, and drove right up to the water's edge and stopped.

"Ready?" Asked Mark.

No one said a thing.

Mark looked at Roberto. "What a bunch of wusses." He drove into the river. "Steady as a rock," Mark yelled, "and don't stand up, I don't want to lose anyone."

Roberto added, "let us know if you see any hippos," They both laughed as the water got deeper.

Everyone in the back looked around. The rushing water hitting the side of the truck amplified the sound making it louder. Water began to seep in through the rear tailgate.

"Oh my God," said Cathy and Toby. Panic ensued on their faces. They looked at each other questioning.

The entire length of the hanging bridge was now visible as they made it to the midpoint. Anthony looked up to see yet another set of cables on the other side of the bridge. "Wow, look at that." Said Anthony and pointed. A few looked up, said nothing, and instantly looked back down at the rushing water.

"More hanging cables? What's with this place?" Someone asked.

"It looks like there was another bridge there, maybe?" Anthony said.

"What do you think happened to it?" Asked Pat.

"Probably got torn down by the river." He looked at Pat, "you know in a flood, I guess."

The front driver's side tire drove over a boulder. The truck went up and violently dropped as the bolder shot out from under the tire. They looked at each other. The rear tire went over the same boulder. The tire slid off and dropped jolting everyone. The fear was evident on their faces. Most felt regret, and couldn't believe that a few minutes ago, they were back in the school parking lot. Playing around having fun and looking forward to this very trip. And now? Here they were, crossing the river like they were on a safari in the farthest regions of the world. Insecurity was sitting in as Mark and Roberto had hoped. They came to the other side of the river and onto the dirt road. They drove up to a gate and stopped.

"What do you mean you forgot the key?" Yelled Mark making sure everyone heard him.

Cathy stood and looked over the cab. Anthony also stood and looked over the cab.

"Holly shit; it has a chain and lock on it." Said Anthony and looked at everyone to see their reaction.

Cathy leaned over the driver's side toward Mark's window. "You don't have the key?"

Mark got out and stood on the sidestep of the truck. "Roberto forgot the key. Can you believe it?" He leaned into the truck and said to Roberto. "What the hell is wrong with you man?"

Mark pulled his head out of the cab and looked at everyone. "We got this."

"What? I don't....." Said Cathy.

"Who needs a key when we have a truck like this one?" Mark said.

He got back into the truck. He backed up and revved up the engine.

"What the hell is going on?" Anthony Asked.

"Hold on, we're gonna have to ram through it." Said Mark and saw Roberto trying not to laugh.

Anthony and Cathy sat down, everyone held on. Earlier that day, Mark, Roberto, and Mills positioned a chain around the gate as if it was locked. But instead held it together with a wire.

"Okay, ready?" Yelled Mark.

"Wait!" Yelled, Judy.

"Can't help you there Judy!" Mark yelled.

He took off. The front guard rammed through the gate. The gate swung all the way out and back almost hitting Pat on the arm as he held on to the side of the truck.

"Fuck, did you see that?" Pat Yelled.

"Oh, my god, that almost got you." Said Anthony.

"We're in the clear." Yelled Mark.

Judy grabbed Pat's arm and looked at it to make sure he was alright. She rolled her eyes. "What an idiot." She yelled loud enough so Mark could hear her.

They drove on the dusty road alongside a creek that fed into the river. They drove under the railroad trestle. Mark stopped and got out. He stood on the sidestep again. He looked up at the trestle.

"You see that?"

They all looked up.

"That my friends is a railroad trestle." He looked at Judy and pointed at her. "No, it's not hanging, it's not a suspended something or other. We know that."

Judy gave him a look.

Mark went on with his story. "One day many years ago, a railroad worker was repairing part of the track on that trestle right there. When suddenly, a train came around that curve."

He pointed to the railroad curve to the left.

"Needless to say he's no longer with us."

"Oh my god." Several people said.

Mark got back in the truck.

"Why is he telling us this?" Anthony asked and looked around hoping someone would know.

Judy couldn't believe they all bought that story. "Oh my god, what an idiot."

Mark got back out. "And for those of you who don't believe that story. Go to the cemetery on First Street and look up a grave with the name, Railroad Jack."

"Railroad Jack?" A few people repeated.

Mark looked directly at them. "I'm serious. His name was Jack, and he died right there." He pointed up.

"On the railroad, so you know. Railroad Jack, God bless his soul."

Pushing the envelope was half the fun for Mark. He got back in and drove off. To make sure they stayed on edge, he purposely   drove off the road and into a steep gully. The front of the truck dropped, the back of the truck lifted like a teeter totter. Down into the gully, they went. The sound of people gasping and yelling was music to Mark's ears.

"Oh, my God, what are you doing?" Someone yelled.

"Relax, relax, everything is fine," Mark said in a matter of fact way. "What a bunch of city pussies. Can you believe these people?" He looked at Roberto.

"That was pretty steep Mark," said Roberto, who also was surprised by his detour.

They drove across the creek at the bottom of the gully and up the other side. They drove onto the road again and up a long gradual hill. This was working out exactly as they had planned. Earlier that day, they drove out a couple of miles into the woods. They found a spot that was perfect for the Bigfoot reveal. The road came to a dead-end, with no way out and no way to turn around. They got out. The terrain was steep. To the left was a cliff that dropped off into the hole of hell. To the right, an embankment that shot almost straight up. It gave them the feeling of no escape. This was the perfect spot to scare the shit out of their friends. Roberto pointed to the right and to the highest spot above the road and looked at Mills who was going to stay behind. This was one of the reasons why Mark was so impatient earlier. He knew Mills had already been there for a couple of hours.

"There, I think that's a good spot for you," Roberto said to Mills.

Mark laughed quietly as a devilish grin appeared on his face. "Man, I can't wait."

Mills climbed up the embankment and hid behind a tree. "Can you see me?"

"No, that's perfect." Said Mark.

"Man, they're gonna shit their pants." Said Mills.

"Hey Mills," Mark called out.

Mills came out from behind the tree. "Hey, what?"

Mark walked to the end of the road, turned around, and looked at Mills.

"Wait until we get to right here." Mark pointed down with both hands. "I'll accidentally kill the truck."

Mills focused.

Mark went on. "I'll try to start it a couple of times, then do your scream."

"Wait," said Roberto. "Before you scream, I'll get out and I'll say something to scare them even more. And then hit them with the scream."

"What are you gonna say?" Asked Mills.

"I don't know, I'll think of something."

"Okay....I'll be ready."

Mark looked at Mills and then at Roberto and yelled, "perfect!"

After a while, Roberto became the tour guide. He opened the rear window behind the gun rack so they could hear him, but that wasn't enough. He leaned way out the side window and looked back to tell them something to edge them on. To prime them, as Mark would say.

"It was right here where we first heard something."

A half mile later, he leaned out again, "we came around this curve right here and there he was in bushes."

He pointed ahead and to the left. Mark hit the brakes.

Roberto went on, "we stopped, he looked at us."

"Who?" Someone asked from the back.

Roberto couldn't believe it. He climbed out of the window. Sat on the window ledge and looked back to see who said it. Everyone pointed at Judy. Judy pulled her head back.

Roberto leaned toward her. "Bigfoot, who do you think, Peter Frampton?"

"I like Peter Frampton." Said Toby.

Roberto dropped his head as he turned to her. Toby looked at Judy who ignored her.

He shook his head, "so anyway," said Roberto as he rolled his eyes. "Mark and I looked at each other. We looked back, and he was gone."

Roberto snapped his thumb. "Just like that. One second he was there, the next he was gone." He paused and slid back into the truck. He quickly climbed back out. "So keep an eye peeled, that son of a bitch is quick."

They came to the end of the road and stopped. Mark popped the clutch, the truck did a hop, and died. He flipped a switch just under the dash that killed the power to the engine. He tried starting it and nothing.

"God damn this thing," said Mark.

310

"What happened?" Said Roberto, loud enough so everyone could hear him.

Mark tried starting the truck over and over. Roberto got out. He walked to the back and said. "Oh man not again."

"Terrific," said Judy. "Why didn't I see this one coming?"

"The truck is not starting?" Toby asked.

"Should've known." Said Pat.

"What, what's going on?" Asked Kelly.

Roberto looked around as if he was searching for something. His breathing intensified.

"What? What do you mean not again?" Someone asked.

"What are you looking for?" Anthony asked.

"Not Peter Frampton, that's for sure." Roberto quickly turned his head as if he heard something. His breathing got louder. "There's something about this spot."

"Something? This, what?" Asked Cathy with her eyes peeled.

He looked at her. "I don't know man." He looked over his shoulder, Cathy looked in the same direction and saw nothing.

"Must be some kind of magnetic anomaly or something because......" Cathy interrupted him.

"Magnetic ano...what? That sounds like something on Star Trek, are you sure..."

Mills let out the loudest primal scream through the bullhorn that anyone had ever heard. Everyone froze. Next came their silent screams and into the cab they all piled in. The scream kept going and going.

23. GHOST TOWN
Yesterday People

Mark came out of reliving his memory and found himself back in the hallway, to see everyone focused on Cathy as she told the same story from her perspective.

"Oh, that's nothing," said Mark.

Mike looked at Mark. "I don't understand this. You go on this Bigfoot thing, the hanging bridge and everything, then to the ghost town and we don't even hear about it till later? Why weren't we told?"

"Why weren't you told?" Mark looked around. "Are you hearing this?"

Mike frowned, not understanding. Mark pointed at him and at Joe. "Ah, because of this."

"Because of what?" Mike asked.

Mark pointed at them. "The what, is you guys."

"I don't believe this shit..." Mike started to say.

Mark interrupted him. "My point exactly."

"What? What are you saying?" Mike asked.

"You guys don't believe anything." Said Mark.

Joe stepped in. "Oh, come on, you have to admit that story was hard to bel...." Mark cut him off.

"Oh, so you get to choose which story is true? Is that it?"

Joe quickly interjected. "No, no,I mean..."

Mark cut him off again. "What's the fun in that Joe? Ha? So we verify things for you, make sure it's all in the up and up, and then you want to go? I mean really, what...is...the....fun in that?"

"Come on Mark. You have to admit that...." Mark interrupted Joe.

"Whatever man," and walked off.

Joe went on. "Okay, okay, Bigfoot is real man. We believe it. It's just....." Mike stopped him with a look.

"I believe it. Honestly." Said Joe and looked at Roberto begging him to get Mark to come back.

"Mark" Yelled Roberto.

Mark stopped. "What?"

"Come on, they believe it. Give them a break, man."

Mark turned around, came back, and got right in Joe's face.

"No, no you don't. You don't get to decide which story is true Joe, we do. You see, we went out there. We!"

He looked at the group and waved his hand over everyone.

"And you know why we went out there? Because we believed. You, in the other hand, a fucking crocodile can bite you in the ass, and you're like."

Mark went into a baby character. "No, no it didn't."

Mark came out of character.

"Meanwhile, the crocodile drags your ass into the water."

A few laughed, others thought about being dragged into the water by a crocodile.

Mark looked around trying to regroup. "So, what was I saying?"

Mike looked at Joe and mouthed, "relax, relax."

"Okay, you're right, I'm sorry man you know, it's just that sometimes...." Joe stopped as he got yet another look from Mike.

Mark hesitated for a few seconds, just enough to make him suffer. "Okay, tell you what. I guess I can tell you a thing or two, but that's it."

Joe and Mike exchanged a look. "So how did you guys find it anyway?" Asked Joe.

"Well, we were hiking one day, and we saw this.."

"Who's we?" Joe interrupted.

Mark froze. He looked at the group. He pointed at Joe and made an expression as if to say, this is what I'm talking about.

"Never mind, sorry," Joe quickly responded.

"So anyway, we were hiking and made our way up this long ass hill. And as we walked down the other side, I saw this reflection coming from down below. I stopped and pointed at it. Roberto was like, 'what the hell is that?' And I said, I don't know."

Mark saw Mike frowning. He gave him a look as if to say, don't even think about it. Mike looked around like, what? Mark went on. "So we were gonna go see what it was right away. But this wasn't a little reflection, this thing was really bright."

Roberto took over. "We thought maybe it was one of those water tanks on a tower like in the old days. Or maybe a tin roof or something. But we couldn't really tell because it was so bright that you couldn't look at it, you know what I mean?"

Roberto looked at Mark who went on with the story. "We thought, if it is a water tank, or a tin roof, like a barn, it must be a ranch you know with a house. So we said hell with it."

Roberto took over. "So we kept going, but as we walked, the reflection started to dim. We could actually look at it without this thing blinding us. And we saw something that looked like a building. But it was hard to tell."

Mark went on. "So, we kept walking and the reflection totally disappeared. We stopped and really looked, and I'll be damn."

"We saw buildings." He shook his head as if he couldn't believe it. He went on. "Well, it was more like parts, because they were in the trees. You know how when you see a ranch, there's a clearing with the house and barn and stuff?"

People nodded.

"Nothing like that. There were trees everywhere and I mean everywhere. Little parts of buildings were visible like here." Mark pointed to a spot in front of him. "Another part there." He pointed to another spot to the left. "We thought, man this is some cool shit, you know. So, we made our way down this really steep hill and into the middle of all these giant trees."

Mark looked up as if he was looking up at a tree. Everyone watched him and wondered, what is he doing?

"We were in the thick of it." He stopped for dramatic effect.

"We keep going down this really steep hill and all of a sudden. Dirt," he paused, "bark," he paused, "pine needles and debris start sliding down the hill with us."

"What do you mean?" Asked Joe.

"As we were stepping down the steep hill, we were pushing all this debris. You know what I mean? It kept building and getting bigger and bigger and the next thing we knew, it was all sliding down the hill with us."

"Are you serious?" Toby asked.

"Yeah man. It was like our piece of earth was coming along for the ride. Can you imagine?" Mark smiled.

"Oh my God." A few people said.

"And it's not like you can hit the brakes, because we had an avalanche of dirt sliding down the hill, right along with us. The only way to stop was to grab a branch or a bush or ram up against a tree. That's it or at the bottom of the hill."

"Wow, that sounds cool." Someone said.

"It was kind of scary at first because we were hauling ass. But when we made it to the bottom? We were like this is some cool shit man."

Roberto took over. "So I said, let's do it again. We went back up....and hauled ass back down the hill. Man, it was a blast."

"How many times did you do it?" Asked Pat.

"Three times," said Roberto, "It was so much fun, we almost forgot about the reflection."

Roberto and Mark smiled as the feeling of sliding down the hill came back to them.

"Maybe we can go back, and we can all do it?" Said Roberto.

"That would be cool," Joe and others said.

"I want to go," said Toby, "yeah, me too," others said.

Roberto went on. "So after that, we had to climb up another hill and down the other side into this ravine."

Mark took over. "For a while, we thought we were lost, because we couldn't see any of the buildings that we saw from the hill. It was like that saying how does it go? You are too close to the trees to see the trees."

Mark stopped, quickly looked around. He knew he screwed up but didn't know how. He caught a look from Cindy who rolled her eyes. Judy made a face. Others looked at each other questioning.

He went on. "So we worked our way through all these thick bushes and shit, under these huge oak trees. Finally, we saw something through the brush that we thought was a tiny little shack. It was kinda far, so we weren't really sure."

Mark stopped talking. He looked around from side to side, he extended his head forward. He leaned toward the group. He squinted as if he was trying to focus.

"We were like.....are you sure that's a building?"

Mark stood up straight. "You know what it was?" Mark waited.

"What?" Someone asked.

"A crapper dumper." Said Mark as he dropped his head.

"A cracker what?" Asked Judy.

Most of the guys laughed. Pat looked at her and asked. "A cracker what?"

Judy looked right back at him and waited for an explanation.

"A crapppppper dumper. A shitter!" Pat said really loud.

Judy, Cindy, and Toby pretended to laugh. Pat could tell they had no idea.

"Really?" Pat asked.

The girls waited.

"An outhouse! Jees," said Pat.

"Oh my god." The girls said.

"Leave God out of this." Said Mark and scratched his head. "Like I said, a crapper dumper." He shook his head. "Didn't think I was gonna have to explain that one."

He placed the palm of his left hand firmly on his forehead and kept it there for a few seconds. Everyone wondered, what is he doing? He slowly swept his palm up, stretching his forehead and opening his eyes really big. His hand moved onto his hair and stopped for a couple of seconds. He continued to push up, stretching his forehead even more. He then swept his hand back over his hair as if he was combing it tightly. He finished his act with his eyes almost popping out of his head and said, "whoa," he looked down. Judy and the other girls looked at each other.

"Judy?" Said Mark in a soft calm voice, still looking down.

"What?"

"Pay attention, Judy. Please." He kept looking down. "This is important information."

"I am, I thought you said cra..., what do you mean important inf....?"

Cathy gave her a look saying, really?

Mark, who had kept looking at the floor, slowly raised his head and looked at the group. "Now that we got that out of the way."

Judy frowned and looked around to see them looking at her. She made a face like saying, whatever?

Mark went on. "We finally made it into a little clearing."

He extended out his arms and opened them as far as he could, as if to say, look at all this open space. He went on.

"Man, it felt good to have open space. So that's when we saw the buildings way behind some trees."

He gestured with his hand to emphasize, way back.

"Some looked like cabins or little houses."

He looked at Judy as if to ask, do you have any questions? She raised her left eyebrow but kept the same expression.

Roberto took over, "We came in from the back, so it was hard to tell if we were looking at an actual town. As we got farther in," he paused and stretched his neck up as if he was looking over something. "We realized," he looked at Mark who nodded. "We realized that we may be in an actual, and I mean an actual old abandoned like...ghost town, or something."

"Wow, holy shit, really?" The group responded.

Roberto went on. "You know how in the movies you see these old western towns?" They all nodded. "It was like that."

"Shiiiiiit!" Said Joe.

"Fuckin aye," said Pat.

Mark wrinkled his nose, "can you believe this shit?"

Roberto added, "but overgrown with bushes, trees, and ivy everywhere," He raised his hands and moved them all around. "All over the buildings. So we keep walking and looking around at everything. Man, this was amazing and.."

Mark interrupted him. "And we see these two bigger buildings. One on each side of the dirt street. Both were

319

two stories and a few other smaller buildings. The one big building to the left, had swinging doors you know like in the saloons in the movies?" A few people nodded.

"The upstairs was a hotel called Dante. Whatever the hell that means"

Judy started to say, "it means.." Marks stopped her with the palm of his hand. "It's okay, Judy, we got it."

"It had a balcony and we could see four or five doors." Mark stopped and looked away. He softly said.

"It was like one of those episodes in the show, The Twilight Zone. It didn't seem real. We walked up to the double doors and looked in. But it was hard to tell what kind of building it was because there was all kinds of shit in there. Trash, furniture thrown around all over the place. Tables and chairs on their sides and stoves and all kinds of shelves and restaurant kind of stuff. Bushes growing in through the broken windows. There was a door that was open in the back covered with bushes and shit. But you could still see out back."

Mark paused, turned his whole body to the right, looked down, and slowly turned his body to the left as he kept his eyes on the floor. He slowly shook his head. He pointed at the floor and made a long straight line with his finger. "Grass growing through them."

He looked at the group. They all tried to visualize what he was saying. "There was grass, fucking grass, ivy, and weeds growing through the cracks in the wood floor man." He paused, "plants, real living plants growing through the floor. When was the last time you saw that?" No one said a thing. "Exactly."

He waited. He sighed, "this....was some weird shit."

Roberto laughed quietly, not because of the story, but at Mark's ability to tell a story.

320

Roberto went on. "We were just looking around you know. He went that way and I went another way and then it hit me. I stopped and looked all the way around. I was like is this really happening? Here we were in the middle of this big room with stuff from the thirties and forties. It was so hard to believe that we were in this place. You know?" Roberto stopped to let everyone think.

Mark took over. "I was right up to it and didn't even realize it." He stopped, pulled his head back and did a quick look around as if he was back in that building. "I was almost leaning on the bar, and I didn't even know it. I said, holy shit. I said look at this. Come here, come on man look at this. I start pulling crap off it, and..."

Roberto interrupted. "I walked over as fast as I could and I said, is that what I think it is?"

"It sure as hell is," said Mark.

Roberto looked at Mark to see him smiling. Mark went on, "we - had – walked - in, and I mean we were in an actual saloon. Wow, man can you believe this? This place was just like in the movies. We went behind the bar, there were all kinds of old whiskey bottles, and corks lying around." He shook his head a little. "Can you imagine what this place was like back then?"

"What about the bathhouse across the street with the creek under it? Remember?" Roberto asked.

Mark tightened his lips as he slowly nodded.

"A bathhouse with a creek under it?" Asked Anthony who had just walked up a few seconds ago.

Roberto went on as Mark gathered his thoughts. "Yeah, there's a creek on one side of the street and they built a bathhouse on top of it. Across the street from the saloon."

"Are you shitting me?" Someone asked.

"What do you mean?" Asked Anthony.

Roberto raised his hands in front of him with his palms facing up. "Imagine a creek running between my hands. Okay? Well, one part of the building sets on my right hand, and it extended all the way across to my left hand. With the creek under it. So, the bathhouse is on top – of - the creek. Can you believe it?"

"So the bathhouse is like a bridge?" Asked Judy.

Mark ignored her and went on with the story. "When we first walked up to the building we were totally confused. We couldn't tell what it was. The door was wide open, so we slowly walked in. There was some kind of, I think it was a waiting area. There were a bunch of old dirty cushions lying around all over the place. And there were burnt candles on the floor, and all over the place and I mean a bunch of candles. Smoke marks all over the wall and on the ceiling. We thought, what the hell?"

"Yeah," Said Roberto, "we were like maybe we shouldn't be here."

"Was this place trashed?" Someone asked.

"Oh yeah, there were newspapers and crap everywhere and you know like shit everywhere." Roberto stopped to let everyone visualize.

He went on. "So then we walked farther back, to the left, and up a few steps, maybe three or four steps, and into a big room."

He paused and looked around as if he was back in that room.

"And what do you know? More baths and more showers I mean everywhere in this place. Burned candles around the baths and these pool like things, whatever they were."

322

"Probably some kind of sex ritual, I'm telling you." Said Mark.

"Sex - what?" asked Toby.

Mark ignored her. Roberto went on. "You know that place freaked me out, I didn't like it. I couldn't wait to get out of there."

"Why were you freaked out?" Asked Mike.

"I don't know, it just felt....you know, the burnt candles everywhere, it smelled bad, it was like satanic or something."

"Satanic? What the fuck?" Said Pat with his eyebrows raised way up wrinkling his forehead.

"So, what exactly was that place?" Someone asked.

"I don't know man, I felt like....I couldn't breathe in there, ha Mark?"

Mark made a face like he smelled something disgusting, "it smelled like shit in there."

He looked around, "sulfur or something, devil farts I'm sure."

"Oh, gross most of the girls said, some of the guys laughed.

"Seriously man," said Mark as he pulled his head back, "I don't wanna breathe devil farts." He looked at Judy, "you wanna breathe devil farts?"

"No! Gross!" Judy wrinkled her nose, "why would you ask me that?"

"Just checking." He said in a matter of fact way and paused long enough to see everyone looking at Judy.

She looked around. "Why are you looking at me?"

Roberto tried not to laugh, he went on.

"We got the hell out of there and ah," he took a long deep breath.

"Man, it felt good to breathe outside. So then, we walked back toward these little houses. We were gonna go in one, we walked right up to it. And out of the corner of my eye, I see these little grave-like holes, carved out of the embankment. Right next to the little houses". Mark and Roberto looked at each other.

"Shiiiit! Grave holes?" Joe looked at Mark hoping to get an explanation.

Mark ignored Him. "These holes are deep, man. Some had little doors on them."

"Little doors?" Asked Anthony.

"So, it's like a mausoleum?" Asked Cathy.

Mark asked, "maso what?"

"Yeah, man." Roberto quickly added, "we freaked out man." He did a quick look around. "Can you believe it? Right there next to the houses. I don't get it. It's like, back in those days people would be having dinner, look out the window, and see grandpa and grandma planted right there."

Some girls had questions, but after the devil fart thing, they wouldn't dare.

"Planted?" Asked Joe.

Roberto looked at him, "buried, planted man. Right there." He pointed at the wall right next to him. They all looked.

More people walked up. Joe looked at them and back at Roberto. "So, you really think these were graves?"

Mark couldn't believe the question. "What the fuck else would they be? A&W drive-through?"

Several people laughed. Joe made a face and stopped himself from asking another question.

Mark slowly looked around and let things settle down. After a few seconds, he went on with a different demeanor.

He shook his head slowly. "It is haunted man, I'm telling you. Why else would they have these maso whatever thingies right there?"

"Was there anything in them?" Asked Cathy. Judy's eyebrows instantly went up and gave Cathy a questioning expression.

"No. Somebody must've robbed them. You know, like the Egyptians." Said Roberto and caught a look from Cindy.

Joe looked around to see everyone's expressions, he looked at Mark and said. "Okay, I really want to see this." Joe looked back and forth from Roberto to Mark and repeated himself. "I really want to see this."

"You'd shit your pants." Said Roberto.

"Shit my pants? Why?"

"I'm telling ya," Mark said. Paused, and looked down thinking. He went on.

"It is haunted. There was this one little house." He looked around at everyone. "It looked like they still live there. Like today! Like right now!" His eyes went back and forth. "Everything, and I mean everything is right there."

Pat Dally raised his arms in front of him and looked at them. "Look, look at my arms I'm getting goosebumps, what the fuck."

"Me too," said Cathy.

"Well maybe somebody does live there." Said Cindy.

Mark looked at her. "No, no, it was old stuff. From the thirties." He looked at the group and paused just enough to let them think. "But..this place wasn't trashed. This place was neat, I mean it was like...."

He looked at Cindy as he thought of the possibility of someone living there. He then realized that he was believing his own story and regrouped. Mark's eyes went back and forth again. "It was like...they disappeared, you know. One second they were there and gone the next."

"Oh, my god, what do you think happened to them?" Someone in the group asked.

He pretended not to hear them. He looked slightly to his left and down as if he was thinking. "We walked up to this house." Mark looked at the group. "It had a little porch in front, I stepped up, the floor squeaked." He paused and tilted his head. "Yep, just like the movies." His eyes looked to the right and stopped. He went on. "I walked up to the door. Reached out, grabbed the doorknob, turned it, I couldn't believe it. I was like, what the hell?" He looked around in dismay. "It was unlocked. I pushed the door."

He paused, leaned forward, and pretended to look into the house. "It was like I accidentally opened the door to someone's house." He looked at the group and ever so slowly shook his head. "I see that everything is there and I almost closed the door. I looked at Roberto and...."

Roberto took over. "I said, what, what's the matter?"

Mark said. "I moved out of the way so he could look in and...."

Roberto went on. "I looked and everything, and I mean everything was in there. Furniture, there was a chair just a few feet from me."

He looked at Mark who wasn't sure if he was supposed to take over and frowned.

Roberto continued. "I turned back to look at Mark and he was looking at me with a weird expression and I said, what? And he said, 'what?' And I said, what, what?"

"What do you think? Is what I actually said" Mark said.

Roberto looked at Mark and quickly turned to the group. He went on.

"So we quietly and softly walked in. I opened a closet right there by the door and everything, and I mean everything was there. Clothes, umbrellas, even a cane. We walked farther in toward the kitchen and what do we see? Canned food, dishes, I mean everything was there. Even newspapers, from the thirties!! Can you imagine?"

"The newspaper?" Mark said and stopped. Everyone waited. He lifted his hand as if he was holding a newspaper, and pretended to place it on the table. "On the table."

"No shit?" Said Mike.

"No shit is right. Dishes?" He paused again. "Still in the sink. Dishcloth? Hanging there." He pretended to be looking at something.

They looked at him questioningly.

"Where?" Asked Joe.

"Right there," Mark quickly added, "by the sink. Like she was gonna show up any minute and dry dishes."

"No fucking shit?" Said Pat.

Mark looked around, not making eye contact with anyone as if he was looking through them.

"I felt like I was standing in her space. You know? I mean why am I here? This is somebody's home, and we're standing right here? Why?"

Roberto looked at Mark and asked. "How about the mirror and the razor?"

Cathy in a trance-like stare looked at Roberto and asked. "Razor?"

Mark sighed, looked down, and went on. "Oh, man." He looked at everyone. "I see this little mirror on the

327

wall." He slowly nodded. "On a little shelf, right?"

Some nodded, others frowned.

"An old razor, like in the old days?" He paused. "Right there!" Mark said softly.

"Even the soap....in the cup. Like you know, to make lather, to shave?" Mark paused to let them think.

"Fuck!" Said Pat and looked around to see everyone focused on Mark. Some with their mouths slightly opened, others wide opened. All on the edge, waiting for Mark to go on.

Mark looked at Pat. "Fuck is right."

Mark shook his head so slowly, that he looked directly into each person's eyes. Some felt uncomfortable and looked away. Others followed his face.

In a low slow voice, Mark repeated. "Fuck is right."

Mark looked slightly to his right and beyond the group, as if he was looking at something behind them.

"So I got right up to it. I looked down at the soap cup, thinking, shiiiiiit. This looks like someone shaved not too long ago. Right here!"

"Oh, my God," said Judy.

"Holy shit!" Someone in the group said.

"Right here! Right here, you know?" Mark looked and placed his hand in front of him as if presenting something. They looked at his hands. In a whisper Mark said. "Right here." He looked down. He took a deep breath and slowly exhaled and went on.

"I looked up at the little mirror, and suddenly I see something move behind me."

He quickly turned around to looked behind him. Everyone looked with him, and gasped.

"Man...I just about dropped my load." Said, Mark.

328

"What load?" Asked Judy almost to herself.

Mark gave her a look. Kelly whispered in her ear.

"Oh gross." Judy said under her breath.

"What did you see?" Asked Pat.

"Nothing. I turned around and...nothing. It must have been an old reflection."

"An old...refl...?" Someone asked.

"Yeah, like the mirror kept a memory. And showed it to me."

"Holy fucken shit." Said Mike.

"Oh, my god. You mean the mirror..." Judy said and stopped as she caught a look from Kelly.

"Fuck, fuck, fuuuuck!" Pat said.

Mark looked at Pat, "Exactly! Exactly what I thought." He paused for dramatic effect; he went on. "I, I....I'm not sure, but I think it was trying to tell me something. But it was so fast that," Mark paused. Everyone stared and waited.

Joe couldn't wait. "And what, what happened?"

"I'm not even sure. Things looked different. Once I looked in the mirror, it was different."

He paused again. Everyone exchanged looks. Pat leaned toward Mark thinking he might have missed something. "What was different?"

Mark slowly turned toward Pat and fixed his eyes on him. Pat leaned away, not sure of what was going on.

"I'm not even sure. It felt different. It was like I was looking at an old reflection, of the very spot I stood in. It was like I saw it through stranger's eyes and mine at the same time. Like it was superimposed or something." He paused again and looked at Roberto to see him totally captivated.

"Jesus Christ," said Kelly

"Superimposed?" Asked Judy.

"It was like the mirror affected my mind...it was weird, I'm not sure, I can explain it." Mark looked at Roberto again, trying to tell him to help.

Roberto took over. "Yeah, freaky, freaky, fucken freaky, freaky dude, I'm telling ya." He paused as he ran out of things to say.

Mark waited for him to go on and gave him a look. Roberto went on.

"I, ah, I was standing across the room looking at an old radio when this happened and...."

"An old radio?" Someone in the group asked.

"Yeah." Roberto said and looked down as if he was right back in that house. He took his time to reconstruct the scene.

"I was looking at this old radio...and out of the corner of my eye....I see Mark standing there. Just standing there looking at the wall. I looked at the wall and I saw nothing. I'm like what the hell? I looked at him, and he's still frozen looking at the wall. I look back at the wall just to make sure....and I see nothing, so I said, hey, hey, what are you looking at?"

To Mark, this was a queue to start acting. It was as if the director said action. He stood there in that school hallway with his eyes glazed over as if he was looking through Roberto. Roberto slowly looked over his shoulder to see nothing but a wall. The group had followed Roberto's actions and also looked at the wall. He turned to see them and went on. "He just stood there. Didn't move a hair."

"Why would he move a hair?" Someone asked.

Judy gave them a look. Kelly leaned toward her and

330

whispered in her ear, "That sounds like something you would say."

"At that point," Roberto whispered. "I'm telling you; I froze and didn't even know why. I felt something or someone. Some kind of energy or something."

Roberto paused and looked down as he tried to come up with more to say.

"So, what happened?" Asked Joe.

"So, I see Mark slowly turn his head and his body at the same time, right past me like in a trance or like a robot or something. I mean he didn't even see me." Roberto looked at Mark.

"I don't remember any of this part," said Mark and looked around. "Seriously, I don't."

Roberto went on. "Mark, walked past me toward the door as if I wasn't even there. I was like, why is he acting like that?"

He looked at Mark who raised his eyebrows and shrugged, like saying, don't know what to tell you.

Roberto went on. "I said to myself, whatever the hell is going on here, this, this it, this thing? I, ah, I, I, too, began to feel it. We both headed toward the door. And I was like, wait a minute. Why are we headed out? We weren't done looking. I thought we could look at more stuff but no, we were actually headed out the door at the same time. Like this reflection, this thing was forcing us to leave."

"Wow, it was like you guys were being controlled," Judy said and looked at Mark to see if he was going to react. Mark didn't flinch. As far as he was concerned, he was in character.

"Yeah," said Roberto, "it was like, it was controlling us."

Roberto let out a really deep breath and said. "And then, the fucking boots."

"What fucking boots?" Said Anthony almost like he was ready for the story to end.

Roberto slowly turned to Anthony. "There were these boots right there by the front door and....."

Mark interrupted him. "It was like, I don't remember these boots being here."

"Oh, come on." Said Joe.

Roberto and Mark turned toward him. Mark started to open his mouth, when Roberto raised his hand and stopped him. He went on.

"Hey, you think whatever the fuck you want man." Roberto pointed to himself and then at Mark.

"We were there. Remember that. Where were you, ha? Where exactly were you Joe? Watching The Partridge Family? Spanking the monkey in the bathroom?"

"Spanking the....?" Judy and Kelly said at the same time and stopped as they caught a look from Cathy. Kelly looked at Cathy and mouthed, "what monkey?" Cathy hushed her.

Pat covered his mouth to stop himself from laughing as he looked at Judy and shook his head. She wrinkled her forehead, and looked around to see some giggling, others laughed. She couldn't understand why. Roberto had to rub it in and asked Joe.

"It was the monkey thing wasn't it?"

Joe rolled his eyes. "I didn't mean to say anything. Really!"

"Okay, let's say the boots were there and we didn't see them when we walked in." Said Roberto.

"Oh no dude, It's cool, it is." Said Joe.

"You know what? It doesn't matter man!"

Said Roberto and looked down as if he was looking at the boots. "I'm standing there looking down on these boots and I thought, there's something not right here. Something is not right."

"Oh, fuck man. Oh, shit." Said, Mark.

"What? What?" Ask Anthony.

"Fucking boots, not a speck of dust on them."

A few people gasped while others were confused. Mark went on.

"We just stood there. I thought, did these people just come home? I looked at Roberto."

Mark paused and once again looked past everyone. He sighed deeply and lowered his voice. "It was like we crossed paths with them, maybe in that other dimension, but right here. And didn't even know it. We couldn't see them, but I felt something, I'm not sure what, but I felt it. And somehow, I felt like they could see us."

Mark stopped to listen to the silence.

Cathy had to ask, "what other dimension?"

Pat rubbed his arms. "Fuck you man, I'm getting chills...shit."

In a soft low voice, Mark said. "I could feel them. Almost hear them. Like the sounds and reflection of these long-ago people, had just come home."

Everyone looked at each other.

Roberto thought it was time to end this and said, "I couldn't handle it. I boogied man. I took off. I said fuck that. I'm out of here."

"What do you mean?" Asked Kelly.

Cathy started to ask Roberto, "did you...." Mark interjected. "He took off! He ran out of the house. Fucker left me there."

Everyone looked at Roberto. Roberto looked at Mark like saying, really? Mark was on a roll and he knew it.

And Mark had to go on, "I, ah, I couldn't run. I had to stay. You know? Out of respect."

"Respect?" Cathy asked.

"Yeah, I wanted them to know...I knew. That I knew this was their place, in this dimension and any other. And we were the ones intruding and we were sorry."

Mark sighed and paused. Roberto looked around questioning how long was Mark going to keep this up.

Mark continued almost in a whisper. "I then said," he paused. Everyone leaned toward him trying to hear him.

"I said, thank you, thank you. I then slowly and politely." He paused for one second. "Walked out, closed the door behind me, and that was it, I walked away."

Most had a sigh of relief and listened to the silence as Mark's captivated audience totally focused on him.

Mike slowly looked away and softly said. "I got to see this."

"No way man. Have you not been listening?" Mark asked.

Cathy looked at Mike. "Respect, respect!" She looked at Mark. "That's why you don't want them to go, ha?"

Mark pointed at her. "Respect is right. And, we don't want anybody getting hurt."

"Getting hurt?" Joe asked and looked around not believing. He looked at Mark. "By what?"

"Have you not been listening?" Mark responded. "How do we know what these yesterday reflections are capable of? I mean, what if you piss them off? Have you....."

"Give me a fucking break," Mike interjected.

334

Everyone's eyes darted back and forth. Kelly couldn't believe what Mike said. "What? What are you saying, Mike?"

Mike instantly responded. "That this is......"

Kelly interrupted him. "Do you honestly think they made up this whole thing? Mark and Roberto can't make up this kind of detail. I read books all the time Mike and this, this...." She stopped and looked around. "I mean really think about Mike."

Mike sighed and looked away thinking. After a few seconds, he turned to Mark and placed his hand on his shoulder to get his full attention, and said.

"Okay, she's right, you are definitely not capable of making up that story."

Mark exchanged a look with Kelly.

Mike went on, "I don't know what I was thinking. But you did say reflections, right?"

"Yesterday People reflections, yes."

"I tell you what?" Mike said, "we'll go there at night. No light, no reflections."

Mark was totally surprised by Mike's ability to come up with this idea, but as always, Mark had a quick comeback.

"These are not reflections of light; these are reflections of beings, of entities, reflections of people....DORK."

"What the fuck man why do you have to be such an asshole?" Mike asked.

"Because I am an asshole, what can I tell ya. No question there Mike. Don't want me to be an asshole, don't...."

Mike's brain almost exploded. He interrupted him. "Do you honestly think that these...these..."

"Yesterday people!" Kelly finished his sentence.

Mike continued. "These, these used to be people, these whatever people....., if they were people." His eyes were almost bulging out of his head. "Do you honestly think they're still there?"

"Are you serious?" Mark asked. He looked at the group. "Do you guys hear this? You see what I mean? How can you have respect, if you don't believe?"

Roberto leaned in and whispered in Mark's ear.

"We need to end this.."

"Oh, yeah, you're right." Said Mark, "I don't think they can handle it anyway."

"Couldn't handle what, what are you.....?" Asked Mike.

Joe stepped in and said. "Look, look, we'll be respectful. Okay? And we do believe. I mean look at us. We're all here listening Mark. We would've left if we thought you were bullshitting us."

"Fuck him." Said Mike.

Joe, who was now the calm one, put his hand on Mike's shoulder trying to calm him down.

Mike brushed him off. "Can't handle nothing my ass."

Mark rolled his eyes. "Talk, talk, talk. Mr. big shot, heard it all before, pussies, man!"

"Pussies?" Mike asked with his eyes bulging out of his head. "You're the asshole pussy."

"Asshole pussy? That's disgusting." A girl in the group said. Everyone looked at her.

"What?" She barked back.

Mike launched forward. "I bet you five bucks, five bucks we go out there day or night and handle whatever the hell is out there."

"Ooh, five bucks? Puss and a half, Mr. big shot." Said Mark.

Joe finally lost it and got right in Mark's face. Mark

stood his ground. Roberto stepped in between them, and put his hands against their chests separating them. "Calm down, calm down."

Mark and Joe stared at each other. Roberto took one step back. He looked at Joe. "Look, the day we just told you about?"

Joe turned his head towards him but kept his body facing Mark.

Roberto went on. "That day was....well the one thing we didn't tell you about is......."

Mark stopped him with a look and said. "Don't even go there, man. Don't EVEN!"

"What? What happened?" Asked Joe.

Roberto looked at Mark. "Maybe they're right. Maybe they should go. That way we'll have someone that can back up the other story. No one is gonna believe that one."

"What other story?" Asked Mike and Joe at the same time.

"Well," Roberto went on. "The next day we went back and it got dark on us, and, and, ah, ah...never mind......forget about it, man."

Mark and Roberto walked off.

Mike grabbed Mark by the arm. "Forget about what? What happened?"

Mark pulled away from him, "forget about it," and walked off.

"We'll do seven dollars and we'll go there at night....or day."

Mark and Roberto stopped. They waited.

"And we won't touch anything. We just want to see man. That's all." Said Mike almost begging.

Mark and Roberto came back.

"Okay." Said, Mark. His eyes went back and forth from Mike to Joe. "I tell you what. If you think you're so tough."

"I want to go." Said, Kelly.

"We're not taken some girl. Come on man," Joe looked at Kelly like saying get out of here.

Kelly looked at Cathy asking her if she wanted to go.

"Not me, not after Bigfoot, no way." Said Cathy.

"Seven dollars a piece, all three of you go, at night." Said Mark.

Everyone looked at Kelly. Joe looked at her with an expression as if to ask, are you sure?

"I...want...to...go." Said Kelly.

Joe continued to look at her, hoping she would change her mind. "You really want to go? After hearing that?"

"Hell yeah, I want to go."

Mike looked at Mark and said. "You're on."

Joe could not believe it. "Seven dollars a head and we're taking a girl? You gotta be kidding me."

"You know what?" Mark looked at everyone. "I'm out." They walked off.

Kelly gave Joe a look and pointed at Mark and Roberto telling him to fix this.

"Okay, okay." Said Joe. "All three of us are going."

Mark and Roberto stopped. They came back.

Mike smiled. "We have a deal."

Joe looked at Kelly. Do you have seven dollars?

Kelly made a face like she was just insulted. "Of course."

"Okay, I guess we're on," said Joe.

"So how do we know they were actually there?" Asked Cathy.

338

"We'll bring something back," Joe said, like no big deal. Mark thought about it for a few seconds. "Hum. Hold on. Give us a minute." Mark and Roberto walked away and talked. They came back. Mark looked at all three.

"Here's the deal. One of those little grave maso thingies? Has a cup in it."

"Mausoleums!" Cathy had to correct him. Everyone looked at her, like saying whatever. Cathy cocked her head and gave them their whatever look right back.

Kelly looked at Mark questioning. Mark looked at her, "what?"

"Why do we...." Joe interrupted her. "Okay, okay, and what about the cup?"

Kelly's eyes darted back and forth from Mark to Joe.

Mark went on. "Okay, you're gonna bring us that cup."

Mike made a questioning expression, like, is that all? He smiled, "easy, easy man."

Mark looked around assessing everyone and continued with his instructions.

"You're gonna walk all the way through town, past the house with the boots, to the very end."

"If it's at night, how.." Mark interrupted Kelly.

"You'll know, believe me. Your skin will let you know."

"My skin?" Asked Kelly, as her eyes deepened. She looked around as if to ask everyone if they heard this. Everyone looked at each other, but wouldn't dare say anything.

Mark looked at Mike and Joe. "Remember, only one cup, many little maso thingies so you're...."

He stopped and looked at Cathy hoping she wouldn't correct him. Cathy raised her eyebrows and shrugged.

Mark went on, "you're gonna have to open the thingies one by one until you find the cup." He stopped again, looked around to make sure no one had a question, and finished his sentence in a relaxed, not a big deal sort of way. "And bring it back. That's it."

Roberto made sure everyone was on the same page. "Seven dollars per head. That's the bet. If you bring that cup back, we'll give you twenty-one dollars, if you don't."

"You are on," Said, Mike.

Joe decided he had an important question. "What color is the cup?"

"Pink! What the fuck man?" Yelled, Mark.

"Jesus," said Joe, "what's your beef man? I wanna make sure we bring back the right cup."

"The right cup? Are you shitting me?"

"Never mind, shit!" Joe said, hoping this was over.

Mark shoved his right thumb in his pocket, he then shoved his left thumb in his other pocket and pushed down on his jeans. He had no idea why he did that and realized that everyone watched him do it. He looked around with his eyes keeping his head still. His nostrils moved to his rapid breathing. He realized that he was truly mad at Joe but couldn't understand why. He then thought, is this what you call acting? Mike brought him out of his deep thought.

"Hey, how do we get there?"

Mark looked at Mike. "Later." They walked off. "Draw you a map," said Mark as they walked away.

24. SHIT CAME CRASHING

Roberto and Mark had this whole thing figured out for a long time, and we're excited to finally put it to work. To them, it was like Halloween in the middle of spring. They had everything they needed, plenty of rope, fishing line, a huge chain, and all kinds of stuff to rig up. And most of all, three willing participants. It was time to scare the shit out of people and that made it a great day.

There was only one way to get everything there. They loaded everything into Mark's Dodge four-wheel drive Power Wagon. They drove north out of town on Highway 101. They turned left onto Highway 128 toward Boonville. About four miles later they found a place to park off the highway. They waited to make sure no cars were coming. They grabbed everything they could from the back of the truck and crossed the highway. They climbed over a short fence and headed up the hill. It was hard work, but it was fun work. It took about twenty minutes to make it to the top of the hill. They had no idea who owned this town and didn't want to find out. So when they got to the top, they looked through binoculars to make sure no one was around. It took about a minute to slide down the hill and into the backside of town. They sat everything down and it was time to play. After about an hour of setup, Roberto stood behind a bush that was about fifty feet from the big building. He held a fishing line they had attached to the front doors of the saloon, which was the main entrance to the hotel. Mark stood in the middle of town. Roberto pulled on the fishing line. The doors opened and closed, opened and closed.

"Holy shit," said Mark.

Mills popped up from behind a window inside the bathhouse.

"What do you think?" Asked Mark.

"I can see the trail of shit man between here and Eureka." Said Mills.

Mark ran toward Roberto, stopped, and yelled. "Perfect, perfect man. Okay, pull on the other one." Mark ran to the front again and waited.

Roberto grabbed the other fishing line and pulled. Two doors they had leaned against the wall of the bathhouse came crashing down onto the street.

"Man, you should see this Roberto." Yelled Mark.

Roberto ran up to them. "Did it work?"

"Hell yeah, it worked, perfectly dude." Said Mark.

"Good, good," said Roberto, "where's the chain?"

"Right there." Mark pointed to a huge rusty chain lying next to the Saloon wall.

Roberto grabbed it and a memory came to him.

It was a day after a storm back in nineteen sixty three

in Mexicali Mexico. Six year old Roberto, his eight year old brother Ernie, and their Dad drove up to an intersection to see a few cars stuck in the mud of the unpaved streets. Traffic was chaotic as cars made their way around the stuck cars and through the intersection.

"Mijo, grab the chain." Said Roberto's Dad.

Roberto and Ernie jumped out of the pickup. Roberto climbed into the back of the truck. He grabbed the chain, and lifted it as much as he could over the side of the truck. Ernie grabbed it and pulled it all the way off and onto the ground. Their Dad got out and grabbed the chain.

"Stay here, I'll be right back."

"Hey, hey Roberto!"

Roberto snapped out of his memory. "What?"

"What are you doing?" Asked Mills as he stared at him.

"Just thinking. What are you guys doing?"

"Watching you think." Said Mills as if it was the normal thing to do. Roberto made a face.

"So, what's next?" Asked Mark. "I mean now that you're all done thinking and everything."

Roberto looked down to see the chain dangling from his hands and said, "the chain, I'm on it."

He took off with part of the chain dragging behind him on the ground. He headed up the stairs to the second story balcony. He walked to the front of the building. He stopped and looked across the street at the bathhouse. He looked down at the dirt street and felt like he was in Dodge City, in the TV show "Gunsmoke". He felt like Matt Dillon. Or, one of the filthy, dirt in their teeth cowboys in the saloon. In almost every episode, the clean pretty prostitutes took filthy cowboys upstairs to the brothel. Roberto asked himself, I wonder if the girls made

343

the cowboys shower?

"Roberto, Roberto," yelled Mark.

"What?" Asked Roberto, irritated. He looked down at them.

"What are you doing?" Asked Mark.

"Thinking." Said Roberto and looked away to continue his thought.

"Again?" Asked Mills.

"Thinking about what?" Mark asked.

"Prostitutes." Said, Roberto.

"Prostitutes?" Asked Mark.

"Now that I understand." Said Mills.

"Why....." Asked Mark.

"Why what?" Asked Roberto and looked at the leaves and debris that had collected on the balcony floor.

"Why prostitutes?"

"Why not?" Asked Roberto as he processed his plan for the chain.

Mark looked at Mills as if to ask, can you believe him? Mills tightened his mouth and nodded. "He's right, why not?"

A few minutes later, Roberto stood behind a tree next to the hotel. He grabbed the thick fishing line he had tied to the chain he laid and stretched out on top of leaves on the balcony.

"Okay, start walking," Roberto said to Mark and Mills who stood on the street.

They started walking. As they got to the hotel, Roberto pulled on the fishing line dragging the chain on the leaves making the sound of wind. Mark and Mills stopped.

"Oh my god." Said, Mark.

"I don't fucking believe this," said Mills. He looked at

344

Roberto. "You've got to hear this. It's scary as shit, and confusing." He looked at Mark who was already looking at Roberto in dismay.

"Seriously man, how did you come up with that?" Mark asked Roberto. "I mean you hear wind, and it makes you think like you're feeling wind, but you don't and it confuses the shit out of you."

"Ass holes and elbows man, I'm telling ya." Said Mills

Roberto laughed and asked Mark, "so you like it?"

"Like it? Question is...did I shit my pants?" His eyes darted between Mills and Roberto. "Maybe I did." He leaned down and reached way back between his legs and patted his ass. "Nope, I'm good."

They laughed. Mark pointed at Roberto, "almost though, I did feel something – a little squirt in there. A little chocolate, maybe?"

Mills backed away. "I hope not."

Everyone laughed into a moment of silence.

"Man," said Roberto, "I can't believe we're finally here."

"I hear that." Said Mark.

Mills looked around and smiled. Roberto looked up. "Man, it's already getting dark. They're gonna be here pretty soon."

Mills asked, "did you put the cup in the thingy hole?"

Mark walked right up to him looked right into his eyes and waited.

"What?" Asked Mills.

"You're not serious, are you?"

Mills thought for a few seconds and it finally hit him. "You son of a bitch."

"That's right. They're not gonna get anywhere near that

345

moso, masoli, or whatever that damn thing is called." He put his arms out to the side. "So, what's the point?"

Mills laughed and felt dumb for asking.

"Hey, let's have a beer," Mills said with a huge smile.

"I have a good idea," said Mark, "let's have some beers."

"Why didn't I think of that?" Said Roberto. He walked up to a brown paper bag. He reached in and pulled out a six-pack. He looked back into the bag to see the other six pack with only four beers.

"Hey, what happened to the other two beers?

"The cost of doing business," said Mark.

"You're kidding?"

"Nope, Drunk George is getting greedy."

"I guess so," said Roberto. "Maybe we need a new source, like maybe a Drunk Tom or something."

"Oh well, I guess he was thirsty," said Mills, "come on, toss one over here."

After they had a beer, the sun had slid behind the hills that surrounded the old town, and the long shadows had cast themselves upon the landscape as they had for centuries. This meant that it was time to get going.

Roberto pointed to the tree. "Are you gonna take that spot, Mark?"

"That's the one with the wind, right?"

"Yeah."

"Great, I'll take it."

"Right on. Are you ready Mills?" Asked Roberto.

"Ready, as ready sir." He took off. He got halfway across the street and stopped. "Dude, I just copped a buzz man. On one beer! Love it!"

"Me too," said Roberto.

Mark looked at them pretending to be confused.

"A buzz? Is that like shaving the hair on your balls or something?"

"You shave the hair on your balls? Weirdo!!" Said Roberto.

"Ah, didn't say that." Mark quickly responded.

"You have hair on your balls?" Asked Mills.

Roberto and Mark sort of laughed as they looked at Mills questioning.

"What?" Asked Mills.

"Dude, you don't have pubes?" Asked Mark.

"I was kidding."

"Wait a minute," said Roberto. "You mean to tell me you're running around right now with the twins hairless?" Roberto laughed and took off.

"I was kidding." Yelled Mills.

"Mr. Sphynx, you better see a doctor." Said Mark and took off.

"I said I was kidding." Yell, Mills.

Roberto made his way to his spot which happened to be in the back of the hotel. He sat on a wooden box holding the rope he was supposed to pull and laughing about what Mills said. After a few long minutes, he looked around to see himself almost in total darkness. Surrounded by bushes, poison oak, some kind of ivy and god knows what else. The sound of his breathing seemed louder in the stillness of the night. His thoughts began to get the best of him as the Yesterday People snuck up on him. He wondered how Mark came up with that stuff. I was right there and there were no reflections of any kind. Yet Mark somehow came up with these ideas, and I went along with the whole thing. But other things were true. There was a

mirror for shaving, but no soap cup, and for sure no
yesterday reflections on that little mirror. Maybe that's all
he needed, the seed to the story. Roberto came out of that
thought and stood to look around. He instantly saw
movement in the far distance.

"What the fuck?"

His heart pounded as the story of The Yesterday
People played out in his head.

"It can't be, who or what the hell was that?" He said
under his breath.

Is it possible that Mark wasn't making it up? Being
behind the hotel all by himself was suddenly not such a
good idea and started making his way to the front. He
stayed low to the ground as he made his way to the very
front of the building. He peeked around the corner and
saw movement in the shadows next to the house with the
boots.

"Holy shit."

The movement stopped. The sound of his breathing
was too loud and told himself to settle down. He took
long deep breaths. After a minute or so, he finally settled
down. He slowly got halfway up and there it was again, the
shadow of a man moving by that same house. He asked
himself, how do I know that's a shadow and not the actual
man? And why would I think it's a shadow? And then - the
thought he didn't want to have. It's a reflection. A
Yesterday People reflection.

"Holy mother of all shits."

He dropped back down and kept asking himself, what
do I do now? What do I do? I've got to get out of here.
Still, on his knees, he turned around to face the back of
the hotel, crawled all the way to the corner, and stopped.

What if I look around the corner and see someone, or something? What happens then? Do I scream like a little girl and take off running? Or do I shit my pants, get that over with, and then take off running? What am I thinking? What am I thinking? He kept asking himself. I've got to man up for god's sake. He finally made himself peeked around the corner. "Thank god," he whispered as he saw only the wooden box and the rope lying next to it.

"Oh, good. No reflections, no whatever people."

He looked back to where he saw movement and to his relief saw nothing moving. "Good."

He crawled around the corner, sat on his box, and thought, boy, just wait till I...something came up behind him. He quickly turned, fell off the box, and heard Mark laughing as he stood over him.

"What the fuck Mark? What are you doing here?"

Mark covered his mouth and bent over laughing. "What, what happened?"

"You almost scared the shit out of my man, fucking idiot."

"Almost, are you sure?" Mark patted himself on the butt with both hands and said, "patted it down, patted down man, the last thing you want is a heavy load."

"What the fuck are you doing here?" Asked Roberto.

"Seeing what you're doing." Said Mark.

"You......" Roberto started to say.

Mark interrupted him. "You should've seen yourself. Man...god damn, you lost it, dude, what the fuck." Mark laughed.

Clearly irritated, Roberto asked, "where the hell is Mills?"

"Across the street. I think. Why?" Asked Mark.

"Why? Because I saw somebody over there." Roberto pointed.

"Over there?" Mark asked.

"Yeah, by the houses."

"What house?"

"Thee house."

"With the boots? House – house?" Said, Mark.

"Ah yeah."

"Are you sure?" Said Mark in a deep voice.

Roberto heard something. He looked toward the street held up his hand and whispered. "Ssh, hear that? I hear voices."

"Oh shit. How do we know it's them?" Mark whispered.

"It's gotta be them. Hurry, remember to wait until they get past the corner of the hotel." Said Roberto under his breath.

Mark took off. Roberto looked toward the boot-house and saw no movement. Good, he thought. He calmed himself down and got into position. The voices got louder with every second. Wow, Roberto thought, it's finally gonna happen. He stood and looked over the bushes. There they were, three human figure shadows walking toward the hotel. He heard himself breathing again and felt his heart speeding. Wait, he told himself, wait, they're almost there. They got to the corner, Mark pulled on the chain. The sound of wind in the quiet of the night was loud. The voices went silent.

"One, two, three," Said Roberto and pulled and released repeatedly. The front doors of the saloon opened and closed over and over, squeaking and banging up against the wall. He pulled on the other line, and the doors they leaned against the wall across the street came crashing down. Roberto heard Mike, Joe, and Kelly gasping as they took off. Mills pulled his line toppling over an old refrigerator. He popped up from inside the bathhouse and looked out a window.

"Assholes and elbows." He said to himself.

Roberto pulled on his next line, and the old spring mattresses came crashing down onto the street. Three shadow figures ran past the hotel and into the woods. The sound of breaking branches came next as they ran through the bushes and anything in their way. Their rapid breathing clearly heard in the silence after everything came crashing down. Three separate thumps echoed throughout town as their bodies collided with a fence.

"What the fuck?" said Roberto.

Squeaks, grunts, and other bodily sounds came next as they struggled to climb over the fence. A couple of bodies finally fell onto the other side.

"Wait, wait!" Was the clear sound of Kelly being left behind.

Over the fence, she finally dropped, as she heard the fading sound of Mike and Joe running through the high grass. The lone sound of Kelly struggling to get up the hill faded as she finally made it up and over the hill. Next came the silence. After that came Roberto's rapid breathing. He stood tall and looked over the bushes toward the hill.

"Shit, shit, shit," He looked around in all directions.

Mark came around the corner. "Holy shit man."

Mills came around the corner. "Did we fuck them up or what?"

"Oh, man." Said Roberto and they started laughing.

"Ssh..." Said Roberto. They laughed quietly.

"Did you hear them hit that fence?" Asked Roberto.

Mark bent over trying not to laugh. He covered his mouth but couldn't stop. "Oh, fuck, oh, fuck man. I have never......oh shit."

"Guarantee, trail of shit between here and Eureka, man." Mills said.

"I can't believe it. I hope no one got hurt. What do you guys think?" Asked Roberto.

"About what?" Mark asked through his laughter.

"Do you think anyone got hurt?" Roberto looked at Mills.

"It's just a fence man, relax."

"Yeah you're right" Roberto finally relaxed and they all laughed aloud.

"Dude," said Mark, "that refrigerator was so loud, I was like shit, is this thing gonna hit me or what?"

"What about the mattresses?" Ask Roberto. "They were so goddamn loud...I couldn't believe it. I thought, did I forget something or what?"

"Well, actually," said Mills, "we added more crap when we went back over there."

"No wonder."

Mills went on. "You think they were louder than shit? You should've been on the other side. Man I tell you, it was really loud for us."

They stood in silence for a few seconds and caught their breaths.

"Well, let's get the hell out of here before The Yesterday People come back." Said Roberto.

"What do you mean come back? Asked Mills.

Mark grabbed him by the arm and pulled him. "Come

on, you don't want to know."

Mills pulled his arm away. "You don't want to know what?"

Mark and Roberto looked at each other.

"Let's get the hell out of here, okay?" Said, Roberto.

"What about our things?" Asked Mills.

"Tomorrow, man, mañana." Said Mark.

They headed out of town in the opposite direction of their victims. To Mark, Roberto, and Mills, it wasn't if you believed but to choose to believe. To them, it was better to, than not to. After all, what is life without belief, but an empty page for the unread not to believe? Now begs the question, what was it that Roberto and Mark saw shining from that hill? And did they have a choice? There was no water tank, no tin roof. It was a forgotten little town nestled within the arms of Mother Nature herself. So how is it that Mark and Roberto came be at that very spot?

Is it possible that on that day, it was the little mirror that came calling and not the other way around? Was it an accident or coincidence that in that specific time and space, many forces came to be? The sun, the rotation of the earth and the location of that little mirror on that little shelf. What about the broken window the reflection from the little mirror passed through? Only to reflect from another window, on another house, to the exact location on the hill on which they stood. Is it too far of a stretch to think that reflections of a forgotten past somehow got trapped within glass? Waiting for the exact moment, the perfect conditions in which to escape? After all, it is light that glass reflects. And it is light, that will travel into space, only to be seen by those in its way. In this case, two curious kids on a hill.

25. DOCTOR IN THE HOUSE

Dr. Culpa, a sixty seven-year-old red haired man, Margaret, and Paul sat in the conference room at the Cloverdale Police Department.

"I'm glad you decided to come all the way out here, thank you," Paul said to Dr. Culpa.

"Oh, no problem. I retired a couple of years ago, and to be honest with you, it's driving me nuts. At my age, this is an adventure." Said Dr. Culpa.

Paul looked at Margaret. "Where have I heard that before?"

Margaret gave Paul a look.

"You're retired too?" Dr. Culpa asked Margaret.

Margaret looked at Paul with that stern, teacher expression. "Thank you, Paul. You know, Paul, that's pretty much like asking a lady her age."

Paul looked at her questioning.

"Except you're telling not asking." She added.

Paul looked at Dr. Culpa, pointed at Margaret, and said. "Use to be my teacher."

Margaret threw her arms up. "There you go again."

Paul and Dr. Culpa laughed.

Margaret went on. "Well, the word is out. I'm old and a retired teacher. I guess I'm an open book."

"She's......" Margaret interrupted Paul.

"Let's leave it at that shall we?"

"Don't worry, no more secrets." Said Paul. "She's the one that found our man."

Dr. Culpa looked at her in amazement and said, "really?"

Margaret smiled at him. "An adventure. As you said."

He nodded in agreement. "Oh, I understand."

There's a moment of silence as they look at each other.

"It's so beautiful out here." Dr. Culpa said.

"The last time I was here, in this neck of the woods was about five or six years ago."

Paul's eyebrows went up, surprised he had been here. "So, you have been here?"

"Oh, yes, twice, five years ago and fifteen years ago. As a matter of fact, the first time I stopped at the Shop and Save on the way in, and ah." He paused, questioning if he should tell the story. Margaret squinted wondering why he stopped. Paul leaned forward in anticipation.

"What happened?" Asked Paul.

"Well, do either of you remember that robbery at the Shop And Save?"

Margaret and Paul looked at each other.

"I do," said Margaret.

"I think I do, but over the years I heard all kinds of versions. Why do you ask?"

"April seventeenth, it was a Saturday, two thirty-seven pm. I was at the register when it happened."

Margaret and Paul's mouths slowly opened in disbelief.

"Oh, my god!" Said, Margaret.

"Is that right?" Said, Paul

Dr. Culpa shook his head slowly as he processed that memory.

"Yes, there I was buying a turkey breast and salami sandwich on a French roll." He stopped as his mouth watered at the thought of that sandwich.

"So what happened?" Asked Paul.

"Well, I got a pickle with it and..." He stopped as Paul leaned toward him thinking he might have missed something. The doctor looked directly at Margaret and added, "and potato chips of course." He nodded as he said, of course.

Margaret nodded with him and said. "Of course, got to have the chips."

Paul frowned as he looked at them. "The robbery, I mean, what happened at the robbery?"

"Oh, yes, the robbery. Well, it pretty much happened just like they said in the papers. Two guys came in and walked right up to the young man at the first register. Gary Whittaker was his name."

He paused to give them a chance to ask, you remember his name? But instead, Paul shook his head slowly and leaned toward him in anticipation. Dr. Culpa went on.

"Anywoy, they pulled out guns, and we all froze." He shrugged and made a face as if to say, what can I say? He quickly went on. "One of the guys went to the back, rounded up everyone, and locked them in cold storage."

"Wow, so it is true."

"What do you mean?" Asked the Doctor.

"Well, I was in the seventh grade when this happened and...." Paul stopped himself as he caught a look from Margaret. "I'm sorry," said Paul. "Go on, I didn't mean to interrupt."

"Oh, no, that's okay. So, after a few minutes of this guy going from one register to another, he came back to where I was and stood between me and the young man Gary. The man looked toward the back of the store and yelled. 'Is everything alright back there?'"

The doctor raised his finger and placed it next to the outer edge of his eye. He went on.

"Out of the corner of my eye, I caught movement. Your chief of police came around the corner and shot between me and Gary, striking the robber in the chest."

Dr. Culpa paused as he thought about hearing the bullet striking the man. His breathing became evident. Margaret and Paul leaned toward him, wanting to hear more.

He went on. "I'm telling you, no matter how many times you see it on television or in the movies, it is nothing like being there." He paused for a couple of seconds. "I had no idea how loud a pistol is. My hearing was gone. Instantly, my ears muffled. And to see a person get shot at such a close distance. I mean, he dropped instantly. There was no launching backward from the force of the bullet or anything like in the movies. He dropped straight down. And then the smell of gunpowder. I had no idea. Anyway, at that point, every cop in town rushed in, and it was over. The man in the back gave up right away."

Paul shook his head slowly and said, "wow, all these

years I've heard the story, and what are the chances of you coming here to tell it as a witness. I mean, what are the chances?"

Dr. Culpa frowned and asked. "So no one told you what happened? I mean, here in the station?"

"Well, by the time I got old enough, nobody was talking about it, so no."

Paul looked at Margaret and then at the doctor. "Weird, isn't it?"

Margaret made a face and tilted her head as if to say, I guess. She looked at Dr. Culpa. "Never mind all that, did you enjoy your sandwich?"

Everyone laughed. Dr. Culpa pointed at Margaret. "She is funny."

Paul nodded in agreement. "Yes, that she is." He continued to nod slowly as he processed the story. He went on. "Well, we have a lot to cover, but thank you for the story."

"Oh, my pleasure. So anyway, both of those times I stopped at the Shop and Save on the way in and at the gas station on the way out north of town."

"At the Texaco?" Asked Margaret.

"Yes, that's it." He said and nodded at her.

"So, tell us about him." Said Paul.

"Oh, sure, sure, well, when I got your call, I instantly remembered him." Said Dr. Culpa. "I remember the day they brought in."

"Really, after fifteen years?" Asked Paul.

"Oh yes, Roberto Tenna was one of those patients that made it hard to forget them. They make an imprint on you."

"In what way?"

"And, a mystery does always help you know. An

unsolved mystery." Said, Dr. Culpa

Paul and Margaret looked at each other questioning.

"That's another reason why I remember him."

"Really," Paul said.

"Well of course." Said Margaret and looked at Paul as if to say, you should've known that.

Dr. Culpa watched their interaction. Paul smiled and waited for him to go on.

"I've always wondered what happened to him. Extremely nice, polite fellow, very intelligent and..."

"If I may, who found him?" Paul interrupted him. Margaret gave him a look.

"Oh, I'm sorry, I didn't mean to interrupt you."

"No, no that's okay. Ah, he was found on the side of the freeway, staring into infinity. Nonresponsive."

Paul and Margaret looked at each other again.

"He was parked. No accident. Just parked there on the side of the road. And ah, he was brought to the hospital. Without any physical injuries. And I was called in to evaluate him."

"So, he was just sitting in his car?" Asked Paul.

Dr. Culpa nodded and went on. "Yes, just sitting there. I guess he ran out of gas." He paused and thought about how running out of gas was most likely the trigger that finally brought Roberto to his knees.

"That may have been the final event that put him over the edge. It doesn't take much, once they reach a certain point."

Finally, Margaret thought, I'm getting some answers to so many of my questions. "Any idea what might have happened in his life to cause this?"

Dr. Culpa sort of cocked his head and said. "No, not really." He paused for a few seconds. "A couple of days after he was brought in, I was finally able to speak with him. For the first two days, he just sat there. Then one day he started talking. But, as far as his past is concerned, I wasn't able to get much. It was as though he had none." He paused and looked down in deep thought. "But of course, we all do. He just wasn't ready to talk about it. However, after spending a few hours with him, I was able to assess some of his personality and as I said, very pleasant and highly intelligent."

"How do you mean?" Asked Paul.

"I could tell by his wit. He had that, ah, what I like to refer to as three-dimensional humor. Not too many people have it."

Paul looked at Margaret as if to ask, what is that?

Dr. Culpa went on. "For a while there it was as if nothing was wrong with him." He paused as he saw them frown.

"I honestly thought this guy was normal. That whatever happened to him was a one time event. Maybe a micro episode. But, all of a sudden.....he shut down...became unreachable."

He sighed. Place his hands on his knees and paused for a few seconds.

Margaret saw his reactions and had to ask. "This really bothered you didn't it?" Asked Margaret.

"It did, I have to admit...it did." He paused for a few seconds and went on. "It's one thing not being able to help someone, knowing that you did your best, another not knowing how, as with him. It's like a patient being physically ill, and dying on you, and not knowing why. I didn't get the chance to diagnose him, let alone help him. He was simply unreachable. Couldn't talk? Wouldn't talk? I wasn't sure."

He turned away as if embarrassed by not being able to help him. Margaret almost reached out and touched him. The urge to comfort him, almost unbearable. So much so, that it surprised her, and asked herself, why? How can it be? Here he is, this perfect stranger whom I've never met, and here I am feeling something. What, I'm not sure, but feeling it. After all these years he's still trying to help this patient that briefly crossed his path so many years ago. And as he, here I am on a mission of my own making. I too am relentless in my efforts to help this poor man, not because I couldn't, but because I didn't. So there lies the difference. He couldn't, I didn't even notice him. Shame, one hundred percent of undeniable shame flooded Margaret's body. After a few seconds of silence, the doctor went on.

"I thought it was gonna be temporary. But, after about two months and several attempts with different medications, it became apparent he was in for the long haul."

Dr. Culpa gave Margaret and Paul an expression as if to say, what can I say? Paul found himself captivated by the story and the clarity of this man's memory. These were long-ago events, and he spoke of them as if they happened a few days ago. Margaret watched Paul as he looked at the doctor with intensity and wondered, what is he thinking? As if forgetting he was holding the report, Paul looked down at it and his eyes went in search of his next question.

"Ah...hm...it says here he disappeared?"

"Yes, yes, it's a minimum-security facility. So, it's not difficult to get out."

Paul looked at his report again.

"Ah, may I ask?" Said Dr. Culpa.

"Yes, please."

"Did he commit a crime?"

"No, no, actually, he appears to be well-behaved with the exception of a couple of things."

Dr. Culpa waited for more information. Margaret interjected.

"We....we are...just trying to get him some help. As a matter of fact, he's so well-behaved that we thought we could actually make a difference."

"That's awfully nice of you guys." Said Dr. Culpa.

"Well, we do what we can around here," said Paul and wished he hadn't. Margaret fought the urge to look at Paul, as she thought of the night he left her all by herself at the theater with Roberto.

Dr. Culpa's curiosity urged him along. "If you don't mind me asking, how long has he been in town?"

Margaret looked at Paul as if to say, you take this one. He looked at the report in search of a way out.

"Fifteen years!" Margaret said really loud and looked around as if to say, can you believe it? "Yeah, it took us a while." She added.

Dr. Culpa laughed. His eyes darted back and forth and settled on Paul. "She's funny, you are lucky to have been her student."

Margaret looked at Paul. "Listen to this man. He knows what he's talking about." They laughed.

"Oh, I am, I am," said Paul.

"Yeah right," said Margaret. Dr. Culpa and Margaret laughed again.

Paul frowned and asked. "Are you sure you two don't know each other?"

Dr. Culpa continued laughing and shook his head, "no, no. Do I know you, Margaret?"

"Nope." She said laughing.

"Okay," Paul said and looked at his report. "I wonder how he got his car back? It says right here it was impounded."

Dr. Culpa leaned forward. "His car? How do you know he got his car back?"

There's a knock on the door. Paul ignored the knock and couldn't believe this man's level of curiosity, his need to know. Paul looked at his watch. "Hmm. It's too bad, I gotta get going." He looked at Margaret questioning.

"What?"

"Can you...." He stopped and pointed toward the direction where she found Roberto. Dr. Culpa watched the interaction with interest.

Margaret caught on and said. "Oh, I'll take him out there."

She looked at Dr. Culpa, he looked at her questioning.

"An adventure," Margaret said, "hope you don't mind?"

"Count me in." He said without hesitation."

Paul felt good about their meeting and felt even better about having someone for Margaret to go on her adventures.

Paul smiled and said, "Good."

He turned to walk out and stopped. He looked at them and said. "Now be careful."

Margaret raised her eyebrows, opened her eyes wide open as if to say, who us, and said. "Oh, we will."

Paul looked at Dr. Culpa, "I hope you don't have mute ear syndrome when it comes to being careful. As you know who." He pointed at Margaret with his head.

"Oh, I'm afraid that's a senior condition." Said Dr. Culpa. They laughed.

363

26. FROM RAGS TO MEMORIES
distance of space

A much younger Roberto stood in the back of his nineteen fifty-two Chevy pickup at the local dump. He tossed out a dresser and the last of the boxes. He jumped off and landed on a book. He looked down and thought it may be something interesting and picked it up.

"What the hell is this?"

He wiped off the cover and saw, nineteen seventy-two engraved on it. He opened it and saw a black and white picture of a little town with a man standing on the sidewalk. He felt a peacefulness come over his entire body. It was as if the picture was talking to him. Whispering was more like it. Next came the warmth, the welcoming feeling one would get when seeing relatives or friends one hadn't seen in many years. The caption read, Main Street, Cloverdale California. A huge smile came on to him as he zoomed in and found himself in what he thought was a dream. There he stood in the middle of that black and white picture, smiling. He questioned all that he saw and accepted all that he didn't.

Unsure of what was going on, he panned around and could not believe what he was seeing, as the black and white panoramic view began its metamorphosis. The Grey on the trees faded into green, the cars one by one transformed into colors only he could imagine. The once silent picture, all too real it became, as the sound of a soft breeze brought him unfamiliar smells he couldn't understand. And, as if that wasn't perfect enough, a bird flew by ushering in the full-spectrum sound. It was as if the bird was the conductor of the sounds of nature. From the center of his brain this must be, but how, and if not, from where?

"Good morning. How are you?"

Roberto turned to see a man smiling as he walked past him and quickly responded.

"I'm fine, thank you. How about you?"

"I'm fine, thank you." Said the man as he spun around, smiled at him, and continued on his way.

In total disbelief, Roberto watched as the man walked toward a gray horizon when consumed by his eyes, it turned a perfect blue.

"I don't understand," Roberto said to no one there. He looked up to see the deepest blue he had ever seen. He asked himself, how could this be? A trash truck drove up and stopped next to him. A man in his mid thirties by the name of Jim, jumped off of the back of the truck and saw Roberto looking up. He walked up to him and also looked up, but saw nothing.

"What are you looking at?"

"The sky, the beautiful blue sky."

"It is, isn't it?" He looked at Roberto and said, "beauty and everything aside. Are you done here?"

Roberto continued to look up.

Jim asked again, "are you done here? Hello, hello! Are you done? Sir."

Jim placed his hand on Roberto's shoulder and startled him out of his dream and back to the disposal site. He looked at the man standing next to him.

"Hey, buddy? Are you okay?" Asked Jim.

Roberto squinted as if trying to focus, and tried to figure out how this man ended up next to him.

"Is he okay?" asked a man in the bulldozer.

"Yeah, I think so. He's fine." Said Jim.

Roberto tried to smooth things out and said.

"Oh yeah, I'm fine, I'm fine."

Jim looked at the yearbook. "Let me see. Hey, nice little town."

He turned the page to see a vineyard and rolling hills.

"Wow lucky you. Wish I grew up here, I mean there." He pointed at the picture.

Roberto hesitated, not knowing what to say.

"So what are you doing here man?" Jim asked not believing anyone would move away from a place like that.

"Just getting rid of some stuff," Roberto said, not thinking about it.

"No, I mean here, here." He made a gesture as if to include all of southern California. "In this dump." Jim stopped himself and regrouped. "I mean, why aren't you living there?" He pointed at the picture.

Roberto frowned and said. "Actually, I just found this."

Roberto looked at the front cover and then looked at

the back of it as if to show him he had never seen it before.

"Ah, get out of here, no way,"

"I'm serious."

"Get out of town," Jim said as he shook his head.

The man in the bulldozer couldn't believe what was going on and yelled. "Hey, hey, you two, hey!"

They both looked at him.

"I don't mean to interrupt your little get-together or anything, but do you mind getting the hell out of my way? Both of you."

He stood up and put his hands on his waist. "What the hell? Jesus Christ, Jim, I sent you over there to get rid of this guy and you get stuck there with him?"

"Okay, okay already." Said Jim "Give it a rest."

"What is that, Penthouse?" Said the bulldozer man.

Jim gave him an angry look. "Penthouse my ass, we're looking at his yearbook, dog head."

"Get the hell out of my way. Come on man!"

Jim brushed him off and turned his attention to Roberto. "Boy, what an asshole that one, ha? But we do gotta get going here, so get yourself back to that little town will ya." He pointed to Roberto's pickup.

"Take it easy buddy. And send me a postcard, will ya?" He walked off.

Roberto looked at the picture with the vineyards and rolling hills. He smiled, closed the yearbook, and got in his truck. He placed the yearbook on the seat next to him and drove off. He looked in his rearview mirror to see the dresser, a few boxes, women's clothes, and a photo album he just tossed out. There they were, lying among the trash. His smile vanished as he saw the distance between him and the objects he threw away. A distance that would grow regardless of his state of mind. For this was a distance of space and not of the mind. He almost hit the brakes but fought it. He asked himself, what is it with us humans and things? How is it that things can be important one day, and trash the next? Margaret and Dr. Culpa stood outside the shack where Margaret had found Roberto. They looked through the opening of the door to see Roberto talking to himself.

"Take it easy, buddy. Send me a postcard we'll ya?"

Roberto, stood against the far corner of the room. He sensed something wasn't right and stopped talking. Margaret and the doctor waited. Roberto slowly slid down the wall to a crouched position. Dr. Culpa and Margaret quietly backed away. They made their way through the bushes and onto the trail. They stopped to catch their breath.

"He looks nothing like the man I treated. Are you sure this is the same man?" Asked Dr. Culpa

"As far as we know."

"How can you be sure?"

"Paul lifted a thumbprint from a thermos that I gave Roberto food in, and it came back a match. The person in your report and this guy is the same person."

Dr. Culpa looked away, slowly shook his head, and rubbed his face as if he had a beard. Margaret watched him.

"That is unbelievable." Said Dr. Culpa.

"Yeah, I mean, I know only of this man, so, for me...." She stopped herself knowing no explanation was necessary.

Dr. Culpa nodded and asked. "So Paul lifted a print ha?"

"Yes."

"Whose idea was that?"

"Paul's, sure wasn't mine."

"Very smart boy. You must be proud Margaret."

"Of what?"

"Of having been his teacher. I mean think about it. You gave society not only a good person but a policeman."

Margaret loved what she heard and waited for more. He thought of the implications of his words and continued.

"Often, if not most of the time, as teachers you have more influence on them than their parents."

Margaret smiled and said. "I am, I am proud of him."

"What about of you?"

"What do you mean?" Asked, Margaret.

"Not only should you be proud of him, but of yourself."

She thought for a few seconds but said nothing.

"Think about it, that's a great achievement. No matter how you look at it."

She made a face like saying, well, I don't know about that, but didn't actually say it and felt a little embarrassed.

He saw her hesitation and said. "Oh, come on, we deserve to acknowledge our achievements. To take a victory lap every now and then. It's good for us Margaret."

"I guess; you know now and then. You know he still calls me Ms Himes, which is cute."

"You're a modest woman Margaret."

"I don't know." She paused for a couple of seconds. "It's hard for me to take that lap. I don't know why."

He kept his eyes on hers and smiled. He nodded and said. "That's exactly what I mean, Ms. Himes."

They laughed.

She pointed at him.

"Which brings us back to this poor man. How he got here, and how he knows my name."

"Yeah, now that's a mystery in itself. He must have heard it, or seen it somewhere. A picture in a newspaper perhaps?"

"You're probably right." Said Margaret in total agreement. She thought about how she disagreed with Paul when suggested the same.

Dr. Culpa went on. "Possibly even met you. Our subconscious is powerful. If only we had total recall. Chances are you have crossed paths with him. Even you and I might have crossed paths. But we can't remember. The day I got gas at the Texaco station fifteen years ago, you might have driven by, or he might have walked by. Who's to say?"

Margaret nodded again in agreement. "Yes, there is that possibility."

"The day he said your name, he most likely had no idea that you were actually there, or not there, depending on perspective. He did, however, recognize you. In his psychotic episode, all is real and all is not. And....as you already know, he lacks the ability to tell reality from hallucinations."

"That must be terrible," Margaret said and looked away in thought.

"Our subconscious is powerful Margaret. Even at this distance, he could very well be aware of us, right now."

Margaret slowly turned to him. "You think so?"

He cocked his head to one side and said. "Not really, I'm just trying to impress you."

"Oh my god!" She tapped him on the shoulder. They laughed.

A couple of hours later, Margaret, Dr. Culpa, and Paul sat at the conference table at the police department.

"So, you're one hundred percent sure, that's the same man?" Dr. Culpa asked.

Paul nodded and said. "Yes, the system matched him to the owner of the car that was found fifteen years ago. Not far from where he is right now."

The Doctor smiled, looked at Margaret, and then at Paul, but said nothing. Paul looked at the Doctor, and then at Margaret. The Doctor's smile got bigger as he began to nod and said.

"So that's how you know he got his car back."

Paul smiled, "you caught me." Paul pointed at him and looked at Margaret. "Very smart this one. He should've been a cop."

They all laughed and then to silence. Dr. Culpa tapped the table with his index finger. Margaret frowned as she watched him and then looked at Paul.

"Where have I seen that before?" She pointed at Dr. Culpa's finger with her head.

Dr. Culpa stopped tapping and looked at her. Paul ignored her.

"Seen what?" Dr. Culpa asked.

Margaret pointed at his finger still on the table. "That."

"My tapping?"

"Yes." Said, Margaret, as she raised her eyebrows and looked at Paul.

Dr. Culpa looked at Paul, "he also does this?"

"Yes!" She leaned toward him to emphasize her yes.

"Must be a job hazard of some sort." Said Dr. Culpa and looked at Paul for agreement.

"I agree - totally."

Everyone sort of laughed. The seriousness of the moment presented itself. Everyone paused for a few seconds.

"Hm, what to do, what to do?" Said Dr. Culpa.

Paul waited for them to take the lead but realized that wasn't about to happen. "So what do you think is the best approach to this? How do we proceed?"

"I could prescribe him new medications, which could help him. But I should evaluate him before I do that."

"Why can't we give him a little medication in his food?" Asked Paul.

Dr. Culpa sighed and said. "That's what Margaret suggested, but that's very undoctor like."

"Well, he's very unhuman like..so."

"Paul!" Margaret gave him a look.

"Well he is. Before you started feeding him, he used to eat out of the trash like it was a buffet. Not that it isn't mind you. It's not like the guy is starving, in case you haven't noticed."

"Where is this going, Paul?" She felt embarrassed for him.

Paul stood up and suddenly became a comedian. "I tell you where it's going, dessert, trash style. You feed him the entree and he digs into the trash for dessert. I'm telling you. It's dessert for this guy. It hasn't killed him."

The doctor thought that Paul may have a point. The microorganisms in trash could be making Roberto stronger, building up his immunity.

"You may have a point." He thought about it again and added. "Well, this is against my better judgment, but."

He opened his medical case and brought out several bottles of pills. Paul and Margaret looked at him and then exchanged looks.

Dr. Culpa returned the look and said, "I volunteer in my spare time." He looked at Margaret. "Five days a week. I'm an adventurous guy. What can I say?"

Margaret laughed and said. "That you are."

"I suggest that we sedate him, and we can bring him back to...."

"To my place," said, Margaret.

"And at that point, I can examine him and....ah, we'll take it from there."

"Good, we have a plan." Said Paul and recognized the good chemistry between them, and felt good about those two being together.

27. IT'S WHAT WE DO

The next morning Roberto slept on the floor of his shack. He was wrapped up in several blankets Margaret had left him over the previous weeks. The sound of something hitting another something; came to him in what he thought was a dream. Within the norm of his dream, he analyzed the sound and concluded that this was the sound of two objects colliding, nothing else, but why? That was the question that intrigued him; causing him to further analyze the sound. There it was again, this time reverberating in slow motion just for me, he thought and asked himself. What kind of objects are these that are colliding? He opened his eyes just in time to see a drop of water splash up from the floor and onto his face. What are the odds, he questioned, and added, why not?

Over the years he had found the one spot that didn't leak, till this very moment. To Roberto, this was the norm.

Over time he learned to accept things for what they were, and not for what he wished them to be. That misgivings were just that, misgivings without intent for the living. It was a matter of timing in a world of odds and nothing else. In the first few months of his homelessness, paranoia was everywhere. The world was out to get him was his only conclusion, regardless of the good intentions of people, of animals and by all tense and purposes, even, Mother Nature herself was out to get him. But now, his delusional self-importance had relented to the mishaps that will follow regardless of the path to his limited existence.

He closed his eyes and laid there for a few more minutes. He clearly heard the sound of water stretching and asked himself, how is that possible? There it is, stretching even more. Why not, water is elastic, right? He opened his eyes in time to see it stretch even more and release as gravity took it from its grasp from the dilapidated ceiling. His eyes followed. No shape would the drop not take as it traveled through the air as if not knowing how its fall would end. The sound of his breath moving away from him in the cold morning air came next. After that, came the sound of birds chirping as if they had something to say. The sound of the highway followed, but to him, it was the sound of the ocean he chose to accept. He slowly sat up, looked around, and realized the stiffness of his external self. The sound of someone telling him to get up made him question who it was he heard. Over the last couple of years, this guiding voice had presented itself. At first, he questioned whose voice it was, but now it was someone to talk to and nothing else. He got up, picked up a blanket, wrapped himself with it, and walked out. He walked around the corner, under a tree between several bushes, and onto a small clearing. He looked to the spot where Margaret usually left the thermos and there it was against a tree.

Dr. Culpa and Margaret sat in her van drinking coffee conversing like teenagers. His eyes feasted on the dash of her beautiful van. He reached out and felt the chrome and the knobs on the radio.

"This van is wonderful. How long have you had it?"

Margaret also looked at her dash and said, "thank you, I love it. This used to be my sister's. She married a Wall Street guy, and he couldn't handle it. It was embarrassing to him."

"Are you serious?"

"Oh yes, it was either him or the van, one of them had to go. That was almost thirty years ago. They were married for fourteen months. I still have my van." Margaret laughed.

He watched her in disbelief and said. "People today, I don't know what's wrong with them. You know what I mean?"

"Oh, I do know. Believe me."

He added. "I mean...who could possibly think anything negative about one of the best-designed vehicles in history? It doesn't get any better than this."

"Oh, yes, I know."

"So what does she drive now?

"Another Volkswagen Van. Just like this one. She couldn't get herself to ask me if she could have this one back. Needless to say, I didn't offer."

"Good for you. I wouldn't have either."

"Well, you know for a while there she was Ms. Hot-

Shot. Driving around in her BMW." Margaret said and moved her body like saying look at me.

"Till she found him with the boy next door that is."

Dr. Culpa's eyes got really big and asked.

"Is that right?"

"I tried to tell her. A man who doesn't like a Volkswagen Van is no man as far as I'm concerned. I then said to her, I'd hide my underwear if I were you."

Dr. Culpa looked at her questioning but decided not to ask.

"I don't like sharing my underwear, not with a man anyway. But, from what I've heard, there are a lot of men who love wearing women's underwear. That doesn't work for me. I don't know you."

"Oh no, no, no. I prefer my own." They laughed. He shook his head as he processed that thought and added. "You're too much Margaret."

"Well, I call it as I see it."

"That you do." There's a break in the conversation.

"I hope he's hungry this morning." Dr. Culpa said after taking a sip of coffee.

She looked at him like saying, are you kidding me? "Hungry? Believe me. This boy is always hungry."

Meanwhile, as they sat in her van talking, Roberto finished the first lid of soup. He refilled the lid and started on the second. Paul and two men drove up to the van going in the opposite direction. Paul rolled down the window. Margaret also rolled down hers.

"So how's it going?" Asked Paul

"I think we're ready to go down there." Said Margaret, and looked at Dr. Culpa to see what he thought.

377

"Yep, he should be ready." Said Dr. Culpa.

"Okay," said Paul, "I'll park."

He took off and made a U-turn. Margaret and Dr. Culpa got out and looked around as Paul parked. Paul and the two men got out. They opened the back door of the SUV and pulled out a mountain rescue stretcher and a couple of duffle bags. They walked up to Margaret and the doctor.

"So, what's the plan?" Paul asked Dr. Culpa.

"We'll go down first," said the doctor, "and ah, you can follow a few yards behind us and...."

"Sounds good." Said Paul, eager to get going and didn't realize he had interrupted the doctor.

Margaret and Dr. Culpa looked at each other. Margaret made a face like saying, well pardon me. She looked at Paul, "Well look at you, Johnny on the spot over here."

Dr. Culpa laughed and said, "Johnny on the spot, haven't heard that one in a long time Margaret." He placed his hand on her shoulder as she tried to keep herself from laughing. He looked at Paul. "Johnny on the spot. That's a good thing, Paul."

"I guess." Said Paul, as he looked at them questioning. "So what's in the coffee?"

Margaret placed her hand over her mouth and whispered to Dr. Culpa. "Cop over here, be careful." She looked at Paul. "Coffee! Nothing but good Juan Valdez himself."

Dr. Culpa laughed again.

"We're early birds, Paul." Added Margaret. "It's a natural high, what can I say?"

The two men with Paul sort of laughed.

"By the way." Paul pointed to one of the men.

"This is Tim Harris, he's a volunteer fireman, and this is Tom Johnson, also a volunteer fireman. They shook hands and exchanged pleasantries.

"Well, are you ready?" Dr. Culpa asked.

"Absolutely." Said Paul.

They started down the trail. About seventy yards later, Dr. Culpa and Margaret stopped. "There he is." Said Dr. Culpa.

"Oh, my God." Said, Margaret. "Is he passed out?"

"I'm pretty sure he is. He's not moving, and I can see him breathing deeply."

Roberto laid on his back near the edge of the clearing with the thermos next to him. Dr. Culpa looked back at Paul and the guys and waved them over. They walked up to them.

"Wow." Said Paul. "He is totally out, isn't he?"

"He sure is." Said Dr. Culpa.

Tim and Tom looked at Roberto with great interest.

"So how much time do we have?" Asked Tom.

Dr. Culpa continued to look at Roberto and said, "It varies, but considering his weight," he looked at Tom, "I say at least a couple of hours."

They walked up to Roberto. Margaret picked up the thermos and turned it upside down. "I guess he was hungry."

"So he ate it all?" Dr. Culpa asked.

"Not a drop left."

"Good, that means we have plenty of time."

Margaret looked at Roberto and lost herself in thought. "how does a person get to this?" She asked Dr. Culpa.

"Well, you'd be surprised, Margaret. In a society like

379

ours, well most of us are pretty much one accident or incident away from...ah..from this." He pointed at Roberto and went on.

"I'm afraid that we live in a society that's...to put it mildly, unforgiving and primitive regardless of what you hear. History will not be kind to us. I can pretty much guarantee you that."

"That's pretty scary." Said, Margaret.

"Yes, absolute...reality has the tendency to be....just that." He paused and thought about the truth of his comment.

He sat his medical case next to Roberto and knelt next to him. He looked at him from head to toe and asked himself the same questions that had invaded Margaret. Whose child is this? How exactly did this happen to him? Where are the people in his life? His mother, his father. Other questions rushed through his head and heard himself say.

"My goodness." He signed and said. "You know it's one thing to see them at the facility, all showered up in clean clothes. But to see them in their natural habitat, sort of speaking, is a whole different thing entirely."

He shook his head and went on. "I mean...I have seen this before, don't get me wrong, but this somehow feels different to me."

Margaret teared up a little.

Dr. Culpa felt Roberto's pulse. "He has a good strong pulse." He opened his medical box and pulled out his clipboard.

"How can I help?" Asked Margaret.

He handed her the clipboard and a pen. "Here you go." He pointed to a spot on the paper. "If you like, you can write down the results of our examination for us."

"Absolutely."

Tom sat his medical case next to Roberto, opened it, and knelt to assist Dr. Culpa. He pulled out his sphygmomanometer (blood pressure device) and looked at Dr. Culpa, "may I?".

"Well of course."

"They don't get much action out here." Said Paul.

Dr. Culpa nodded, "I understand."

Dr. Culpa lifted Roberto's hands and looked between his fingers for needle marks and saw none. He pushed his sleeves up past his elbows and saw none, "wow, this is remarkable."

"One twenty over sixty." Said Tom.

"Okay." Said Margaret, and wrote it down.

"He is healthy." Said Dr. Culpa. "No signs of drug use so far."

"Told you, trash is his drug of choice and dessert," Paul said. Margaret gave him a look.

"And all the walking." Said Dr. Culpa.

They all looked at him questioningly. He explained.

"Oh, yeah, surprisingly enough, a lot of homeless men have strong vital signs due to all the walking. How many miles would you say it's to town?"

"About two miles, maybe more." Responded Paul.

"You see what I mean? If he walks into town once a day, and back, he's walking four miles a day and I can assure you he's walking a lot more than that." He paused and added. "Of course, his mental health is a whole different story."

Tom pulled out a small flashlight. He opened one of Roberto's eyes and shined the light into it. Tom and the doctor looked into his eye and saw pupil constriction. They look at each other.

381

"Good to go." Said Dr. Culpa.

Tom and Dr. Culpa started putting back their devices into their cases in almost perfect synchronicity. They both closed their cases at the same time. Tom stood and lowered his hand to help him. Dr. Culpa grabbed his hand and he was on his feet. It was as if they had done this a thousand times. Margaret and Paul watch in amazement.

"What?" Dr. Culpa asked.

"Oh, nothing." Said, Margaret.

Paul pointed toward where they were kneeling and said, "you two were doing everything in sync. I mean...."

"It's what we do." Dr. Culpa interrupted him. He looked at Tom and patted him on the shoulder.

"It's what we do." Said Tom.

Everyone sort of laughed. Tim had the stretcher ready to go. Straps neatly spread out, helmet for Roberto in his hands.

"And look at him." Said Margaret, as she pointed at Tim.

They all looked at him.

"It's what we do." Said Tim.

Margaret smiled and said. "Something must be either really right or really wrong, not sure which."

"Why is that?" Dr. Culpa asked as everyone waited to hear.

"It's what I do, or it's what we do. You know how many times I've heard that phrase in my whole life?"

They all waited.

"Four, five, let's say six times." She wrinkled her forehead. "But lately?" She looked at Paul who made a face questioning her. She looked around. "Just right now, three times." She pointed at Paul. "Four, you said it just the other day."

382

Dr. Culpa turned to face her and said, "to answer your question," he leaned toward her, "something is really right."

He looked at all of them. "We" he made a circle to encompass all, "have a common cause." He pointed at Roberto. "And there it is."

Everyone smiled, Margaret once again got a little teary-eyed and said, "You're right. Something must be really right."

Tom and Tim moved the stretcher next to Roberto. They placed him in it, placed the helmet on him, strapped him down and they were ready to go.

"Like a lean machine." Said Dr. Culpa.

"Impressive." Said, Margaret.

"It's what...." Paul stopped himself. Everyone laughed. Tom and Tim lifted the stretcher and started up the trail.

"What we do," Paul said under his breath. He grabbed Tom's medical case and ran to walk next to the stretcher.

"Let me know if you guys need any help."

Tom looked at him and said. "Don't make me say it."

A few yards later, Paul looked back at Margaret and said. "Can I get your keys so I can go ahead and open the van?"

Margaret tossed him the keys, Paul caught them and took off. A few minutes later they got to the van. Paul stood next to the open side door of the van. He crawled in on his hands and knees. Tom handed him one end of the stretcher. They positioned him with his head toward the front of the van. Paul got out.

"Looks good." Said Dr. Culpa placed his knee onto the van and got in.

Tom also hopped in; Tim closed the side door. Tim

grabbed the handle and pulled on it to make sure it was closed properly and said, "It's good to go."

Paul put his hand on Tim's shoulder, "thanks."

"No problem," said Tim. He picked up a few things and headed for Paul's car.

Margaret couldn't believe that it was actually happening. She turned to Paul. "Thank you, Paul, thank you very much."

"You're welcome."

He saw her expression; one he had seen before and knew a hug was coming. The hug came, and the hug went. They both smiled.

"I'll see you there?" Margaret said.

"I'll be right behind you."

They got into their cars and took off. She looked in her rearview mirror to see Dr. Culpa and Tom examining Roberto.

"How's it going?"

"He's fine." Said Dr. Culpa. "He's a strong boy." They smiled at each other in the mirror.

"His vitals are strong and steady." Said Tom with a smile.

Her eyes came back to the road. She inhaled a huge deep breath almost accidentally and held it for reasons she didn't want to reveal. As if the joy of a minute ago hadn't happened; insecurity became evident, percolating, simmering deep inside her, in search of the surface to her conscious mind. She heard herself thinking almost aloud. I hope we're doing the right thing. I don't see how we're not. I can't begin to imagine what it was like for this man, to have lived all these years out here in the woods, the streets, in these dusty hot summers. And how about the

384

cold wet winters? And now I have to ask, did we have a choice? She felt her mind slipping into a deeper state of thought which she wasn't prepared for.

She almost fought it but had to explore it. Are these real choices, or a sequence of events triggered by other events? Maybe these are a series of accidents as I thought before, and we're simply reacting. As humans, we like to think we have control. And if so, how much? And how much of that comes from random states of mind that at the end of our human day, we justify by reverse-engineering the otherwise common, into complex mathematical equations resulting in our illusion of free will. Which brings me to this. Does free will exist? If so, at what point do we interject? After all, the point of interjection is the determining factor. That will determine whether it's choice, free will as we like to call it, or something that's forced upon us, resulting in what we perceive as choice. She slowly exhaled her accidental breath hoping no one would notice.

28. THE LENS OF LIFE

Margaret drove into her driveway which led to the side entrance of her house. Paul and Tim drove up and parked behind them. They quickly walked up as Margaret opened the side door of the van. Dr. Culpa spun around to face the outside of the van, extended his legs out, and placed his feet on the ground, still sitting in the van.

"This is why I like this van. Look at me. Try doing this in a car." He leaned forward, stepped out, took a couple of steps, and felt a pinching pain in his lower back.

"Oh boy."

He stood straight, placed his hand on his waist, and stretched. He turned to a vision he had never seen before.

"What a sight." Said Dr. Culpa, "a man on a stretcher in a nineteen six five Volkswagen van."

He looked at Margaret to see her worried. He took a

couple of steps and stood next to her. He turned to see it from her perspective and said.

"Look at that. We have a whole team here."

Tom, still inside the van, was ready to move Roberto. Paul and Tim positioned themselves to get Roberto out. Margaret took a deep breath and held it as her head slowly moved from side to side.

"You gotta let it out, Margaret. Don't want you passing out on us." Said the doctor.

She slowly exhaled and looked at him, but her thoughts were somewhere else and he knew it.

He added. "This is the part where you're supposed to smile due to the overwhelming joy." He waited for her to say something but heard nothing. "Maybe we should've brought balloons or something."

"Oh, I'm sorry, it's just that..." She placed her hand on his shoulder.

"I know, I know." He said.

Tim grabbed the head end of the stretcher and pulled on it as Tom and Paul helped him. Tom grabbed the opposite end, raised it a couple of inches and they were out of the van.

"I'll grab the door." Said, Margaret.

She opened and held the door open. Dr. Culpa and Paul helped with the stretcher. They walked in through the kitchen, to a hallway, and into a bedroom. They laid the stretcher on the bed and removed the straps, and the helmet and carefully removed the stretcher from under him. Everyone took a breather and looked at Roberto.

"Well, we need to clean him up a bit." Said Dr. Culpa.

"I'll get some water and a few washcloths." Margaret walked out of the room.

"I gotta get going," said Paul, "but Tim and Tom will assist you in any way they can."

"Thanks, Paul."

"And," Paul grabbed his handcuffs and handed them to Tim. "You need to cuff him to the bed before you leave. We have no idea who this man really is."

"Got it."

"I think you're right." Said Dr. Culpa.

"Good, I'll be back in a few hours."

"All right." Said Dr. Culpa. "And thank you again. You're a good man Paul."

"Well, I don't know about that." Said, Paul. Dr. Culpa was about to say something else when Paul looked at the guys.

"I'll see you later." They both nodded.

Roberto got the only sponge bath of his life and his first cleaning in years. Dr. Culpa set up an IV and administered a sedative to keep Roberto calm and sleeping. He administered a new medication. The day finally came to an end with a feeling of accomplishment, exhaustion, and excitement all wrapped up into one. And then there was the feeling of change, nothing from this day forward will ever be the same. Margaret and Dr. Culpa knew it and welcomed it.

Dr. Culpa got in the shower. Margaret stood outside Roberto's room and lost herself in thought. There he is, the same man that a few hours ago, I couldn't begin to get close enough to see the white of his eyes. The same man that you could sit outside his shack for hours and not hear a peep. And now, here he is, in my home, cleaned up and sleeping like a baby. He could very easily have been my son. Would it have made a difference? Is his condition, whatever it may be, something that could've been prevented, or is it predisposed? If it is predisposed, can it be managed? And if not, are we wasting our time? But how do we know? We have to try. What point is there to life, if one does nothing?

Dr. Culpa entered the hallway to see her leaning against the doorway. He was so taken by her beauty, he could do nothing but to stop and look at her. To see her right there, with all her concerns, her worries, with her need to help a stranger so deeply intense, her inner beauty has managed to surface to her face.

And here I am, he thought, a man she had no idea as to who I was just a few days ago, and yet, here I am, and here she is. He asked himself, how is it possible that our paths crossed? That they have become one? Her level of intensity and focus told him of her deeper pain, which had become his pain. To bring joy to her at this very moment was the only state of mind.

She turned to see him. To see him see her, and with their eyes touching, he slowly walked up to her. As he got to her, all he could do, he will, all that he cannot, he will, to comfort, to ease, to erase her pain. And as he approached her, her beauty, more revealing than ever. How can someone have so much beauty, so much heart, so much to give? He slowly reached out, touched her face, and gently took her in his arms and knew this moment was theirs to be had.

Hours late, Dr. Culpa and Margaret talked about the road they had embark upon. He was well aware of all that was at stake in the first hours of long term sedation and was more than happy to stay awake all night. And with that decision, Margaret pulled in another chair. It was a long night that passed without mention. A lesson into their lives, as they asked each other about their paths to where they found themselves.

Roberto tossed and turned, talked, and at times even screamed. His conversations, sometimes clear enough for Dr. Culpa to take notes. Other times, his speech was unrecognizable. Like it was another language. Dr. Culpa actually thought that Roberto may speak another language, but how can a language be unrecognizable? They both had traveled extensively, so not to recognize a language was improbable, which led him to believe that Roberto's battles were scarring and traumatic. After a couple of long nights and very little sleep, Margaret and Dr. Culpa sat at the kitchen table. There was a long moment of silence as they both reflected.

"To save a man." Dr. Culpa said as he looked without direction. He looked at her. "Isn't that incredible? To save a man. That is why we are here. To save a man."

He turned away and lost himself in deep thought again. Margaret watched him with an intensity that made her question why.

Dr. Culpa, went on, "how often does one get to say that?" He looked directly into her eyes. "And you are the reason why we are saving this man."

"And you." She quickly added. "I couldn't have done it without you. And..." Her voice quivered. She stopped, looked away and slowly shook her head.

Suddenly confused, he asked, "what...I...don't understand, what's wrong?"

She looked up trying to compose herself, "I have my regrets."

"Regrets? How...can...that be?"

"Oh, believe me." Her mind traveled almost without

her. She looked down and questioned everything. "Regrets, decisions made, decisions not made, is more like it."

She looked up again, this time as if trying to see God. "This man has been pleading for help for fifteen years." She looked at him. "Fifteen years. And it is only now....."

"Don't be so hard on yourself." He interjected.

She looked away and quickly said. "No, no, I want to be hard on myself." She looked at him.

"Why not? All those years of selfishness. Stuck in my little world, with blinders." She brought her hands to her temples and quickly lowered them. "True and honest to goodness....self-indulgence. That's what was going on in my life."

"Self-indulgence? You are a teacher, how can..."

"Oh, just because I'm a teacher I'm not capable of egoistic behavior? Hate to tell you, but..." She pointed to herself. "This one right here, borderline narcissistic. I mean really, think about it. Fifteen years and I had no idea....this man..was even here. Let alone....oh, never mind."

She turned away. Paused, and went on. "I mean, don't get me wrong, I saw him, I think I did, but I'm not even sure of that." She shrugged her shoulders. "I don't know why!"

She looked at him. "And that bothers me. Damn right, that bothers me, and it should. Just a wee bit."

"But......." Dr. Culpa started to say.

She interrupted him. "And what about the other men before him?"

"What do you mean?"

"This man is just one in a series of men that have been the town bum, as they say, for....I don't know how long.

So I've heard. God knows I didn't know. And it is only now? That I have come to see, what had been in front of me for..oh...so many...years..I..I don't...I don't understand."

"But you know Margaret...." She interrupted him again.

"But nothing, Dr. Culpa."

"Please call me Charles."

"Happily." She made a face like saying it's about time.

"You're being too hard on yourself." He gently caresses her arm with his hand.

Margaret turned away.

"You are. You have no idea how much I want you to understand. The lens through which we see life is polished only by life itself."

Margaret slowly turned back to him as tears fell down her face.

He went on. "What's in focus today, wasn't in focus yesterday. You must understand that."

"That is my point!"

"But you had to have lived your life, your specific life, for you to see this. This!"

He looked around and back to her. And as he watched her, the need, the want to know what it was that tormented her, was almost unbearable. He slowly reached out and softly wiped her tears. She brought her eyes to him, reached out, and softly wiped his tears. With their eyes already kissing, she leaned toward him and gently placed her lips against his. With their eyes still touching, she slowly backed away.

"Thank you." He sighed.

Margaret covered her mouth as she turned away trying not to laugh. She looked at him and felt like she was looking at a young boy who for the first time finally kissed a girl. A boy who has brought out the emotions of a long-ago young girl. That young girl of long ago, held her breath as if doing so would help her hold on to those beautiful feelings a bit longer.

"That was so cute." She smiled through her tears. She went on. "In a thousand years, I wouldn't have thought of that response."

He tilted his head as he searched for words. "I'm sorry." Said the doctor.

"Oh, no, don't apologize. I mean that was, that….." She stopped herself.

He went on. "Kissing you has been my one and only thought since the first second I saw you." He started to shrug, stopped mid-point, and said, "I'm afraid I'm out of practice."

Margaret let out a little laugh, covered her mouth again and stared into the eyes of a man who had totally captivated her. A man that only a few days ago, she had no idea he even existed. All he could do was to ask himself, what is it about her, that makes her who she is? It seemed like a simple question, so simple in fact, that it confused him. He had been around beautiful women that cared for others as she, but there was something much deeper, more profound about Margaret.

He went on. "Tears and all, the lens in which I see life, more focused, never shall it be." He exhaled a slow deep breath that was held from a long-ago moment. And with that, another tear, and with that yet another. With their eyes deep within their hearts, he reached out, caressed her face with both hands, and kissed her as he had wished to do so many times before.

The next day they both decided to get a few things done. After all, they had brought home a baby of sorts, and things needed a bit tightening up. They washed her van, mowed the lawn, and started on the vegetable garden that Margaret had planted but had recently ignored. Margaret stepped into the house to check on Roberto while Charles got on his hands and knees and got to pulling weeds. Being the city boy he was, he couldn't believe how relaxing, and therapeutic it was. Just as the studies had shown but had never experienced himself. After a few minutes of weeding, he saw Margaret's shadow coming up behind him, but pretended not to. She got right up to him and just as she was going to straddle him, he rolled over causing her to fall on him. She pinned him down.

"I give up, I give up." Said Charles.

As if they were Adam and Eve in the Garden of Eden, without a single apple in sight, they laughed, locked eyes, and kissed. Later that night, Charles sat on a chair next to Roberto's bed and found himself in deep thought as he looked at him. He looked toward the door to see Margaret with a kind smile looking at him.

She pointed at Roberto and whispered "Our baby."

He smiled, looked back at Roberto, and lost himself in that very thought. And how wonderful it would have been to have married that beautiful, wonderful woman who stood just feet away. Right there she stood looking at me, at me!

The next morning, Margaret and Charles stood in front of the stove cooking breakfast. Roberto hesitantly walked up and stood at the kitchen entrance. Confused as he could possibly be, many thoughts and questions crossed his mind, as he tried to get his bearings. Who are these people? Where am I? How did I get here? My God that breakfast smells good, and with that, all questions went out the window.

Charles caught a glimpse of him and whispered in Margaret's ear. "Let's put our plan into effect."

She tensed up and stopped tossing the potatoes.

"Don't be alarmed," added Charles. "Just continue. Everything is fine, he's probably so hungry by now that your cooking has the best of him. So, let's stick to the plan."

Margaret slowly turned to Roberto and said, "good morning."

Charles turned around and said. "Good morning."

Roberto's only question was evident on his face, how do I get some of that breakfast? Charles slowly walked up to the table, pulled out a chair, and said in a matter of fact way.

"Here, sit down." Roberto sat.

Margaret sat a plate in front of him. "How would you like your eggs?"

"Scrambled." Said Roberto, without looking at her.

"Coming right up." Said Margaret.

Charles placed a cup in front of him and poured him coffee. He sat the cream and sugar on the table. A couple of minutes later, Margaret placed his breakfast in front of him and he dug in. She brought both of their plates to the table and they sat next to each other facing Roberto and pretended to eat their breakfast. They watched him eat and enjoyed every minute of it. He got done and looked up to see them watching him.

"Thank you."

"You're welcome." Said, Margaret.

The idea of not remembering someone who just served him breakfast confused, bothered, and embarrassed him.

"Do I know you?" Roberto asked.

"Ah, yes." She stopped not knowing if she should go on. She looked at Charles who added.

"I know you have many questions. Before we get into that, maybe you would like to have a nice shower?"

Roberto asked himself. A nice shower? Why would he ask me that? Who are these people? I just woke up in their house, in their bed, they served me breakfast and now they want me to take a shower? What am I missing? Roberto's confusion deepened with the events of the last few minutes. Before Roberto could say anything else, Margaret stood and said, "I'll be right back."

Charles stood, "Anything else I can get you?"

Roberto shook his head, "ah, no thank you."

"You're welcome, here, I'll get that."

Charles picked up his plate and put it in the sink. Roberto sat looking at the table, not knowing what to do. Charles sat again and waited for a question. Margaret walked in holding a pair of pants and held them out in front of her.

"What do you think?"

Roberto looked at the pants and then at the sweats he was wearing and then at Charles.

Charles pointed at the sweats. "They fit you pretty good ha?"

Margaret went on with her sales pitch. "These will fit even better. These are thirty-four waist, and thirty-six length." She placed the pants on his arm. He looked up at her. She grabbed the towel from under her arm and held it out so close to him that he had to take it.

Charles stood. "Here, let me show you."

He walked around the table and pointed toward the hallway with an open hand. Roberto slowly stood. Margaret slowly reached out and placed her hand on the back of the chair. He looked at her hand as she pulled the chair away from him. He kept his eyes on her hand the entire time. Margaret thought of the tremendous insecurity that he must be feeling. She pointed toward the hallway with an open hand. His stare went from her hand to her face and thought, why do these people want me to shower so badly? Do I smell that bad? He lifted his arm moved his nose to his armpit and smelled himself. His eyes fluttered and saw their reaction. Charles smiled without showing teeth, tilted his head, raised his eyebrows slightly, and made a face as if to say, yeah, pretty bad ha? Roberto nodded and started toward the hallway.

"Here, let me show you," said, Charles, stepped in front of him, and led him to the bathroom. Charles opened the bathroom door, walked in, and pointed to the shower, "that's the shower," he pointed to the toilet, "that's the toilet," he pointed to the toilet paper, "that's the toilet paper." he felt a hand on his shoulder. He turned to see Margaret smiling a couple of inches away from his face, conveying that she was sure Roberto knew.

"Oh, okay, sorry, I'll get out of your way," said Charles.

Margaret looked at Roberto. "We'll both get out of your way."

They walked past him. Roberto walked in and closed the door.

"By the way, I placed your underwear on the sink." She looked at Charles and smiled not knowing if she should've said that. She looked at the bathroom door as if she was looking at Roberto and said. "Well you know, they're not your underwear but they're new underwear and....." She looked at Charles questioning. She looked at the door again. "I hope they fit."

He took her hand and led themselves out of the hallway and into the kitchen. Margaret turned to face the hallway. "He looks so normal."

"I don't even believe it myself." Said Charles.

They turned toward each other.

"Am I glad I took his handcuffs off." Said, Charles.

"Oh my god, I didn't even think about that. When did you do that?"

"This morning. I figured we were both fully awake, filled to the gills with coffee, I figured we could take him on if things got ugly."

She placed her hand over her mouth as she laughed quietly and asked, "if things got ugly?"

"Yeah, you know? I mean..."

She placed her hand on his chest and said, "it was a good idea."

"I think so, can you imagine what would've happened if he woke up handcuffed to the bed? I know what I would have thought."

Margaret's mouth slowly dropped open. "Oh my god, I'm so glad you thought of that."

"Well, to be honest, I was just improvising."

"Good improvising."

"Thank you."

Excited about the outcome of their experiment, they stood in silence and listened to themselves breathe. Margaret wrinkled her forehead slightly and said, "I can't believe how loud we're breathing."

"I know." He looked toward the hallway and back to her. "I'm excited Margaret. You're excited. We're both excited."

She nodded slowly. "Yes, I am, and yes we are."

He looked away thinking and said. "I don't think I've ever felt this way before." He looked at her. "It makes me kind of sad."

"Sad? Why?"

"It makes me think of all that I've missed." He paused, she waited. "I mean, why didn't I feel this at the hospital?"

"I don't know." She stopped to think. "I...I mean this is my first. You know?" She paused again, "maybe it's because we're doing this together." They both nodded in agreement. She looked away. She looked at him and away again.

"What?" Asked Charles.

"This...this is our project." She looked at him as if to ask, can you believe it?

His eyes went back and forth as he thought about it. "I didn't think of it that way, but I think you're right."

She went on. "I have an idea."

"What?"

"I take that back. I don't think I should see it as a project. That doesn't sound right."

He nodded and said, "I think you're right."

Roberto stood in front of the mirror and could not believe that he was looking at himself. The long hair, the beard, the long nails, the smell, all was confusing. But the aging, how do you ask yourself, how old am I? How do you ask yourself, where did the years go? Why can't I remember? And that which I do, feels like I was watching someone else live. Like I was going along for the ride.

There he stood in a bathroom he had never seen and he was getting ready to take a shower? He looked down and around himself and became aware of the space around him. He heard a knock.

"Are you okay?" asked Margaret.

He quickly turned on the shower and said, "yes."

Margaret tightened her lips with concern and looked at Charles who stood behind her.

"I guess he's not gonna shave." Said, Margaret.

"What do you mean?"

"Well, I didn't hear the faucet running."

Charles shook his head with a little grin.

"What?" Asked Margaret.

"You and Paul, always one step ahead of me. I didn't even think of that."

"I'm sorry."

"About?" Asked Charles.

"For what I'm about to say."

Charles frowned.

"It's what we do." Said, Margaret.

She moved her head like a bubble head. They both laughed quietly. Roberto showered but didn't shave as Margaret thought. It was a bit much for him. All he could think of was to get done with the shower. He dried himself, put his clothes on, and walked out to see both of them waiting in the hallway. He stopped, surprised to see them. They smiled and stood in silence for a few seconds. She couldn't wait. She asked.

"How do you feel?" As if she was asking someone who just got over a cold. He nodded.

"Good." Said Charles.

"I bought a pair of socks and shoes for you," said, Margaret and took off.

Roberto followed her with his eyes as she exited the hallway. A second later came the sound of the exterior door opening and closing which told both of them that she left the building. He looked at Charles questioning.

"I know, I know, efficiency is not one of her problems. Come on." Charles led him into the kitchen. He pulled out a chair for him. "Here, sit down."

Roberto sat and to his surprise, Margaret was suddenly back in the kitchen. Charles and Roberto looked at each other.

She held out the shoes. "What do you think?"

Roberto once again thought that her voice sounded familiar. She sat the shoes next to his feet and handed him the socks. He looked down at the shoes and stared at them. He felt nothing, therefore he did nothing. But there was something about the shoes that triggered a memory. He saw himself walking, walking, and walking.

"Why so much walking?" Asked Roberto.

"What do you mean?" Asked Charles.

Oblivious to his question, Roberto desperately tried to remember how he got to where he was. But the only thing that came to mind was walking and more walking. Next came the vision of a bridge. After a few long seconds, Roberto asked.

"I don't understand. Why am I here?"

"Ah..." Said Charles. Roberto interrupted him.

"I mean, you're very kind, but do I know you?"

"What do you remember?" Asked Charles.

"How did I get here?"

"Well, maybe we can start from there. Do you have any recollection of how you got to this town?"

"This town?"

Charles closed his eyes tightly and quickly opened them. "What is your last memory?"

"What do you mean this town?"

"We'll get into that in a bit." Said Charles as if it was no big deal. "Let's see if your shoes fit."

Roberto looked around with his eyes but kept his head fixed. He swallowed. He slowly began to shake his head. Charles watched him and thought it would be best to let him explore his thoughts. Roberto looked down and slightly to his left as if he was looking at something. Charles recognized the behavior as something we do when replaying events in our heads before verbalizing. Roberto was most definitely looking at something.

"What do you see?" Asked Charles.

"Did I wreck my car?"

Charles looked at Margaret who sat just a few feet away. Roberto also looked at her. She slowly nodded.

"Yes." Said, Margaret.

His breathing intensified and looked down.

"Roberto, what were you looking at? Just a little while ago."

"What town is this?"

Charles felt himself getting emotional and reminded himself not to. To relax and to pretend he was back at the hospital.

"Cloverdale," said Margaret.

"Cloverdale?"

She nodded and looked at Charles asking with her expression if she should have answered. Charles kept his eyes on Roberto and asked, "does that sound familiar?"

"I'm not sure." Barely audible.

Roberto saw Margaret's eyes tear up and looked

directly at her. He shook his head slowly. "I know you, don't I?"

Margaret covered her mouth and nodded. Charles also got teary eyed, smiled, and said, "this is good."

Roberto felt emotions coming from all sides and began to tear up. "but I don't know why."

He got up. His breathing intensified. His frown deepened and walked out of the kitchen and into the bedroom. Margaret brought her hands to her face and tried to compose herself, but it was too late. Her tears rolled off her face and said, "My God that must be terrible."

"Yes, yes," said Charles. "Can I have a little time with him?"

"Of course."

Charles walked out and into the bedroom to see Roberto sitting at the end of the bed with his head hanging. Charles pulled up a chair and sat facing him at about six feet.

"Roberto, allow me to apologize, I, ah...."

Roberto interrupted him with a look and looked back down.

Charles went on. "You see, it was not my intention to do this in this manner. Margaret and I...."

"Margaret? Is that her name?"

"Yes, you see...." Roberto interrupted him.

"Why am I here?"

"You are here because you needed help."

Roberto looked away and tried to remember what could've happened to cause someone to think he needed help.

Charles went on, "you see..." Roberto interrupted him yet again.

"How old am I?"

"Please Roberto allow me to say a few things and then we'll get into that, please."

Roberto kept his eyes on him, telling him that he was ready for an explanation.

"It was my intention to introduce myself the second you woke up and as you've seen things didn't go as planned. And for that, I'm sorry. I'm a doctor, a retired Doctor and I'm here to help Margaret, help you. My name is Charles"

Years of experience kicked in for Charles. He put his emotions in a box as if he was back at the hospital and looked forward to helping this man. He knew as Margaret did, they were in for the long haul and welcomed it. After several sessions of therapy, they took him to a doctor for a physical and to the hospital for a CT scan of his brain. They concluded the car accident had played a role in Roberto's memory loss and contributed to an existing condition.

Charles and Margaret now knew more or less what they were dealing with. Months passed, and with every day, Margaret and Charles became closer and closer. They couldn't begin to imagine their lives without each other. Roberto's need for answers gave him the tools to make tremendous strides. And now, with their lives intertwined, a family was in the making. As if Margaret was his mother, if Roberto disappeared, she would find a reason to look for him. She turned the corner of the house in search of him and saw him sitting on a bench in the backyard. His head hung low as he cried. Wanting to console him, she started toward him. Charles walked up behind her. He gently took her by the arm and walked her away to leave Roberto to his healing. She leaned against the house and looked up as if searching for answers. Charles brought her to his shoulder.

29. DISTANCE OF MIND

Eighteen months later, against Dr. Culpa's advice, Roberto decided to go back to Arlington Heights. To face the music, as he had told Charles who tried to discourage him. He told him that going back to a place that had powerful memories may throw away our progress. He told Roberto as they sat in the backyard, "you may think you want to face the music, but in this case, the music may want to face you." He paused to get his reaction, instead, Roberto looked away.

"Don't take this lightly Roberto." Charles went on with his discouragement.

"Think about it, you may not even remember your so-called music, and by that, I mean events that have led you to this very spot right here. It's difficult for our brain to stitch back events that are out of sequence. Without a foundation, events, places, even people, will seem foreign to you. As if they were someone else's memories. You may find yourself in a familiar place you have never been. And then what? I'll answer that for you. Questions and more questions will come rushing in unraveling you to the core. Sending you right back to where you were. In some cases, farther back into an abyss. And that, I can assure you, is the last place you'll want to be."

He paused again to give Roberto a chance to respond, but Roberto continued to look away and said nothing. Charles went on hoping to change his mind.

"To reestablish linear thought out of random chaos is something that I wouldn't recommend to anyone. Let alone to someone who has lived what you've lived through, for as long as you have."

Charles was so concerned that he offered to go with him, including Margaret. But Roberto's thirst for the truth left him no option. Facing his demons with this level of exposure, with someone other than himself, made him uncomfortable. And, it would make it impossible to confront not only that which shaped him, but traumatized him for years. He had traveled through the tunnel of destitution, and now, only one option was at hand, the truth. This was something that he had to prove to no one but himself.

But late at night, after the conversations had stopped. When the smell of Margaret's great cooking had faded. The distance between his now and his thoughts, vast, confusing, and often empty. The totality of silence would sneak in and chip away at him one second at a time. And with that, came insecurity, which made him question if Charles had a point. But to him, he had reached the point of no return. Changing his mind would bring forth more insecurities. At which point, he would have to ask, am I capable of making decisions on my own? So what's a grown man to do, but do what grown men should, and that is to face their fears and to overcome them. So, a few days later, Roberto rented a car and took off.

His journey back to southern California was one of discovery. Everything as if he had never seen it. Nothing brought back any memories or reactions of any kind. But as he passed Bakersfield on Highway Five, finally a trigger. But of what? An unattached emotion? A response to a trigger without reason? Why would that happen? His brain was like a sponge left in the desert to die but somehow survived. And now, he was on a mission to find the trail that took him off course. To retrace his steps to a Roberto that had betrayed him. He needed to challenge his past self, for him to understand his now Roberto. Nothing would escape the portal to his brain. As he descended the Grape Vine, familiarity began to work its way to him. But as he got closer, it was as if the walls of his past ascended to protect him. Not one thing called out to him. He began to question everything; the report that Paul showed him, Margaret's story in front of the theater the first time she engaged him. And most of all, Charles's conclusions of something gone terribly wrong in his life.

This was a sign of paranoia. As Charles told him, this was something he would wish on no one. Roberto told himself that if anything was going to make sense, it would be the neighborhood that he lived in.

"I can't wait to see it," he heard himself say, but then questioned as whether he heard it, or said it. He felt and heard the echo in his chest as he drove onto the street he used to live on. He looked around. He heard himself breathing in the thickness of sounds. He felt nothing and remembered absolutely nothing as he looked around.

"How can this be?" This time he clearly heard himself.

He pulled over and parked. He looked at the map and realized he was a couple of houses away and across the street from his old house. He felt fear as he realized that things were not falling into place as he had hoped. He decided to sit in his car and simply relax. A few minutes later, he heard himself say, "I have to face the music." He then heard Dr. Culpa say, "the music may want to face you." And now that he was here, one question came to mind, why? Suddenly, the need to face the music didn't seem all that important. A stupid idea at best. So what was it? What was his state of mind that caused him to make this trip? He tried and tried to remember, and nothing rose to the level of urgency. And with that? Tremendous insecurities about his decision making came calling.

He looked at his former house across the street and remembered nothing. But there was something about the mailbox on the left side of the garage. A memory jumped out at him. He saw himself installing that mailbox. He had a drill in his hand, and then a hammer. It was like a short-edited version of an event. As if he cut away the parts he didn't need, but kept enough to know he installed that mailbox. He looked at the other houses and none had the mailbox next to the garage door. Another quick flash of him driving up to the garage. He opened the mailbox and took the mail. He thought, what a great idea. And then, as he sat there thinking of that. A faded memory played out. So faded, that he questioned if it was a memory, a dream, or an obscure thought that came out of nowhere. He saw his car on a trailer. I brought my car home on a trailer? From where? Why would my car be on a trailer?

408

A quick flashback of him getting his car out of a storage unit came next. What is that all about? How is that possible? Under what scenario, would I put my car in storage? The tremendous need to see his car came over him. It was direct and present as if he still had his car. He snapped himself out of that and the questions kept coming. Wait a minute. I don't believe this. This must be a test. More like a trap to see if I'm capable of deciphering a dream from a memory? And if so, what happens if I fail? More importantly, who is testing me, and why? He then saw himself working on his eight-track tape deck. Why did I have to fix my eight-track? Gaps and more gaps, why so many gaps? When all is followed by questions, you have to ask, why? There it is that vicious circle of circumstance. He thought he said it, but they were words from long ago.

A sudden need to get out of the car overwhelmed him. The next thing he knew, he was standing outside his car staring at his old house. He looked around to see his rental car behind him and realized he had no recollection of getting out of his car. And then, what he thought was a memory of a movie or something. An elderly man in denim overalls leaning against an old truck. As that crossed his mind, he felt as if the old man was leaning against his car right now next to him. He almost looked for him but stopped himself. These are thoughts, nothing but thoughts, he told himself. But the thoughts kept coming. As if these memories were on a reel of film. His next memory was of him driving his old truck on a dirt road. "Oh my god," was the next sound he heard, "that was my truck. What happened to my truck?"

"Is that you Roberto?" He snapped out of his episode and saw a man walking toward him.

"Is that really you?" He asked again.

As if tumbling off of a mountain peak, Roberto's brain took a deep dive into the hell of confusion. Another memory came out of nowhere. In and out of his head in a millisecond. A man in a gas station asking, is that you Roberto?

"It's me, Dale, remember me?" Roberto heard, and hoped it was coming from his head.

"I'm Dale from across the street, remember?"

Roberto forced himself out of his head to where he stood. The man's hand reached out, a huge smile on his face. Roberto did the only thing he could. He reached out and shook the hand of a perfect stranger he had met before.

Not wanting to accept that Roberto had no idea who he was, Dale asked himself, how can this be? "You, you don't remember me?"

Not wanting to reveal that he didn't, Roberto said, "Dale?"

"Yeah, yeah. You used to live right there?" He pointed at Roberto's house. "I used to and still do, live across the street from where you used to live."

He turned and pointed to his house. Roberto's head followed his finger as if it was on a leash.

"Oh yeah...." Said Roberto pretending to remember.

Dale saw the resemblance of truth through his pretense. "You, you don't remember, do you?"

"I'm ah...I think I do."

Dale questioned himself if this was the same man. The image of the first time he saw Roberto's RoadRunner popped into his head.

"Yeah, you used to drive that RoadRunner. You talked me into buying a Challenger, remember?"

Roberto looked away and tried to remember. Dale watched him. Roberto remained in the void of absence much longer than he realized. Dale's next thought was that this man may be battling something. He had no idea what, but concern was his next feeling at hand. After all, this was the man he had tailored himself after so many years ago.

"I'm sorry....I'm having a hard time...." Said Roberto in a low voice.

"Oh no, no, it's okay man. It's been a long time," said Dale in an effort to help his old friend. "I probably remember you because I haven't moved. I'm still in the same spot, you know?"

Dale did a quick look around. Roberto looked from one house to the other, over and over. A quick flash came and went, of what seemed like an argument or something with a woman.

"You're married right?"

"Yeah, yeah, hey you do remember. I used to be married, but not anymore...thanks to you."

Roberto felt a little fear and asked. "What do you mean?"

"Remember that argument with my wife? You had an argument with her."

"I....I remember a lot of drama." Said Roberto, not wanting to be specific.

"Yeah, yeah, boy things changed after that. And...." Dale stopped himself as he thought about seeing his wife at his reunion a few weeks ago. And now, here's Roberto. He couldn't believe it. His face lit up.

"You know what? We have a lot of catching up to do. Let's go inside. Not only that, I have something that came in the mail for you, after all these years, can you believe it?"

He turned around. Roberto saw him walk off and instantly fell into one of his thoughts. Dale took a few steps and realized Roberto wasn't following. He turned back to see Roberto leaning against his car looking down. Dale asked himself, what is he doing?

Roberto saw himself in a warehouse of memories, dreams, and thoughts. Why so many? He asked himself as he desperately tried to organize each into its specific slot. This is a dream, it goes here, this one is a thought, it goes there, this one is a memory, it goes.... He heard something behind him. He looked over his shoulder to see thousands of memories as they came over a fence and into his now. It was like they knew he was in town and this was their chance to cling on to the person that created them. He thought about the metal bridge where he encountered memories left behind.

"You know what?"

Roberto heard and snapped out of his thought to see Dale looking at him.

"Let me bring it out to you." Said Dale. "I'll be right back."

Roberto saw him walk off again. At first, he had no idea this was the second time he saw him walk off. He thought about the memories coming over the fence. The scene replayed exactly like the first time. The scene on the metal bridge played out again. Wait a minute, Roberto said to himself. Everything is like an echo. I did see him walk off. Everything is replaying over and over, but how many times? How long was I in my head? That too was like an echo. How long was I in my head? It was as if he had spoken those specific words but couldn't remember why. How often does one ask, how long was I in my head? Why

412

am I asking that anyway? That's ridiculous. I'm always in my head. He felt angry and irritated but didn't know why. He snapped out of that to see Dale coming. He looked down. As if looking down was going to change all that had presented itself. And then, complete silence. And that he liked. It was a silence one would think impossible in southern California. But to Roberto, as he knew all too well, silence can be achieved anywhere at any time.

"You know what?"

Roberto heard.

Dale walked up to him. "I can't find it, but...."

Robert interrupted. "It's okay, it's ah....I'll come in."

"Good, good," Dale said, patted him on the shoulder, and quickly pulled his hand back not wanting to make him uncomfortable. "As you can see," Dale went on, "the neighborhood hasn't changed much."

They both look around. Dale ushered him toward his house. They walked in. Not knowing that he had never been inside Dale's house, he looked around hoping to remember something, but nothing came to him.

"Here, have a seat." Said Dale and padded the cushion on the couch. Roberto remained standing and searched for memories he never had.

"Let me see if I can find it," said Dale. "It's around here somewhere."

He went behind the breakfast bar, pulled open a kitchen drawer, and searched.

"Here it is." He walked up to him. "Look at this, I got this reunion invitation for you. It came to my house."

He extended his arms out, like saying, can you believe it? He flipped the invitation from back to front a couple of times.

"It's gonna be," he opened the invitation and searched for the date. "Wow, it's this weekend." He looked at him, "are you here for your reunion?

Roberto heard Dr. Culpa's words, "the music, in this case, may want to face you."

Dale realized he wasn't getting an answer. He turned the invitation to show Roberto a black and white picture of Arlington Heights High School in nineteen-seventy-six. A striking resemblance to Cloverdale High school. Dale looked at the invitation, frowned, and asked.

"I thought you went to school up north?"

As soon as the words left his mouth, Dale regretted asking and saw Roberto sigh and looked down. Instantly, Dale became concerned for his old buddy and said to himself, maybe I ask too many questions. I mean, after all, it has been many years. But something isn't quite right.

"You know what? We'll... we'll look at this later." Dale said and looked around for a spot to place the invitation. He placed it on the coffee table. He looked around to get rid of the next couple of seconds and decided to sit on the couch.

"Come on, please sit down."

Roberto sat. He saw a picture on the coffee table. He started peeling away the layers. Trying to come up with a connection to what he saw.

"Are those....your kids?"

"Yeah, those are my kids."

Dale found himself trying to keep himself in the moment. But it was almost impossible as his thoughts took him back to the night Roberto left all those years ago. Dale had wondered for years what might have happened to him. And now, here he is, but questions will have to remain unanswered for now. He brought himself out of that in time to realize his sigh.

"Yeah......you know they asked about you. For a long time."

Dale sort of cocked his head. A response to the emotions invading him. He looked away. He told himself to get it under control, but couldn't help himself.

"You made a hell of an impression on them. And on me."

Dale turned the picture to look at it. He grabbed it and handed it to Roberto without looking at him. As if to say, at least try to remember them. Roberto looked at it and heard Dr. Culpa in his head, something about stitching back pictures that are out of sequence.

In an effort to move things along, Dale asked. "Hey, how about a beer?" He stood and started toward the fridge.

"Oh, ah,...I'm fine, thank you. I'm on medication now....days." His voice faded.

Dale came back and sat as quickly as he got up and said, "That's okay man, we're all medicated." Hoping to get a laugh.

Roberto looked at the picture with intensity, trying to remember, to see the little faces of long ago. Dale nervously rubbed his hands and leaned over to look at the picture as Roberto held it.

"They're all grown up now. Married, and I have six grandchildren. Happy as hell about that, I tell you."

Dale looked away, and went into deep thought for a few long seconds. He then said, "you know, I get along with her now, their mother." He paused. "It's just that she was going through a rough time back then. You know? She's a good person."

Not knowing what to say next, Dale looked down to see his hands rubbing his thighs. He stopped, turned his hands over, closed, and opened them just to do something. He went back to rubbing his thighs and sat up straight stretching his back. He watched Roberto as he looked at the picture, and wondered, what could he possibly be thinking? He reached out, and grabbed another picture of the kids, just to have something in his hands. There was another moment of silence as they both stared at the pictures.

"Yep, she's a good person." Said Dale and looked away.

There's another pause. Dale placed the picture back on the coffee table, and rubbed both knees with both hands. He looked at Roberto and sort of smiled not knowing what to do. As if a memory heard his call for help, Dale smiled.

"Hey, remember the little vacation we went on? We met those two girls in the Jacuzzi?

Roberto lowered the picture and thought about his question. A snippet or two of the events of that day came to him. "I think so. But I thought we were going to go, but...."

Dale interrupted him. "Oh no, yes sir we went on that vacation. Boy, those girls were something else, weren't they?"

Roberto reached back into the void and tried to come up with something else of that day but couldn't. He sat the picture on the coffee table and slowly stood. He took a couple of steps and stopped. Not sure of what's going on, Dale simply looked at him.

As if they needed more silence, there it was again. Dale had never been so aware of silence before this day. Raising three kids and now having six grandchildren, silence kept itself at a distance. But now, it was an in your face silence, he thought, intrusive, and loud in its own way. He didn't want to hear it, but could do nothing but wait for it to end. Roberto began to shake his head. He looked beyond the walls as if he was capable of escaping with his eyes. But his eyes were busy holding back tears. "Jesus.....Jesus Christ, how can someone forget so much?"

Dale tried like hell not to get emotional but his old buddy's pain had become his and he too found himself holding back tears. "That's okay, that's okay man, I too forget things man, all the ti...." Dale's voice cracked as he tried to finish the word, time.

Roberto tried to fill in the blanks. "I remember...the night I left..I remember the rain....but....I don't remember why or anything else." He inhaled a deep breath, held it for a few seconds, but his quivering jaw refused to hold it. He looked at Dale as if to ask for forgiveness, and shrugged, not knowing what else to do or say. Dale stood, walked up to the fridge, reached out, and touched a picture of his old car. A day of long ago came back to him. He sat in Roberto's backyard drinking beers, upset crying because of an argument with his wife. Roberto helped him get through that and much more. He had changed the trajectory of a family's life and disappeared without a trace. That was something Dale could never accept. After a couple of days, he called the police who refused to take a missing person report. They thought he was most likely a man on some kind of secret getaway and not missing. But Dale couldn't let it go. He called time after time and got no help. One day he showed up at the police department and spoke with a sergeant who investigated. A few days later, the sergeant came to his house. He told him that he found Roberto and that he was in the care of professionals.

Dale's attempt to find his friend or answers to his many questions led to more questions. But due to him not being a relative, the sergeant told him that he couldn't go into details. For all those years Dale wondered what had happened to his friend. A few months after Roberto's disappearance, the bank took over his house, sold it and life went on. And now, the mystery thickens as they say. So many questions. Dale came out of his deep thought to see Roberto still looking down. He thought of how shitty life could be and heard himself say.

"Life is like a shit sandwich, some days we get bigger bites than others." Dale smiled. "Remember that? The shit of life thing?"

Roberto forced himself to smile through his tears and was surprised to hear himself say. "I do, I do remember something about that."

Dale smiled from ear to ear, happy to hear that his buddy from long ago remembered at least one of their experiences. And with that, there's hope Dale thought. He patted him on the shoulder, this time more at ease, and said.

"Remember? Run, it's the shit of life."

"I think so, that does ring a...yeah, yeah," Roberto said and felt a little smile coming from within. He turned toward the door not knowing why. He took a step and heard Dale say.

"Hold on." He picked up the invitation and handed it to him. "Don't forget this."

Roberto looked at it and hesitated.

Dale added, "don't, don't....look at it right now."

He folded it and placed it in his shirt pocket.

Dale thought, finally, a true smile and now, a small but

real laugh out of both of them.

Dale added. "I know, I know man, believe me. I went to my reunion a couple of months ago, and I was like, who the hell are these people?"

Roberto made a face as he heard the echo of a long ago memory as they sat in his car on a hill. He questioned the memory because Dale was driving and couldn't understand why that would be.

"But you know what," Dale added, "that was me. I'm sure you'll enjoy it."

Dale opened the door and they walked out. On the way to the car, Roberto decided not to look around. Just walk, he told himself. They walked up to the car, Roberto opened the door and paused.

Dale couldn't help himself, "here, give me a hug man." He grabbed him by the shoulders, pulled him in, and hugged him. He backed away a feeling came over him as if he was looking at one of his children. "You be careful out there, okay?"

Another echo, in and out of Roberto's head.

"I will...you too."

He turned toward his car and stopped again. Emotions flooded in. He turned back to Dale and said.

"I'll be back....I am feeling better...I am..and ah, you know....I'll be back."

"Good, good." Said, Dale, as tears filled his eyes.

Roberto fought his tears to no avail. He got in and as he drove off, he looked in the rear view mirror to see his awareness of the growing distance. It was that thing that occupied the between of things. In this case two people. It was a distance that would expand regardless of his physical world. With that awareness came finality. And with that, came a sadness to the moment that made him question the acceptance of finality and did what most would do when nothing will suffice. To write an alternate ending to an otherwise tale of no return.

30. A DEBT OWED

A few days later, Roberto sat in his car looking at the black and white picture of the house on the reunion invitation. If there was ever a place to face the music, this was most definitely it. His vision of questions coming over a fence rushed through his head. He looked up from the picture to see the same house almost unchanged except for a sign that told you it was now a restaurant. His eyes went up to the reunion banner that hung from the second-floor balcony. A quick memory of him sitting in his car across the street from the Owl Cafe darted in and out of his head. He tried to make sense of it, but it was so quick, he wasn't sure if it was an actual memory. He hesitantly exited the car. As he walked up to the house, emotions, feelings of having been there came to him. He remembered something about another reunion, but how can that be? The resemblance between this house and the one at the

421

Cloverdale reunion he stumbled into many years ago when he was homeless, almost too much and dangerous for Roberto. The need to turn and walk away, almost unbearable as confusion began to work its way to him. He forced himself to continue, to follow the arrows someone had painted with chalk on the walkway next to a hedge. His hearing began to mute on and off. One of his high school buddies, Gary, popped his head over the hedge and saw Roberto.

"Roberto? Asked Gary.

Gary looked back at the group and yelled. "Hey, you guys. Hey Anthony, it's Roberto! Hey, guys, Roberto is here."

Roberto's hearing muted on and off again as several people looked over the hedge.

"Is that him?" Asked Pam.

"Holly shit, Roberto? Hey buddy." Said Anthony.

"Roberto?" Asked Cathy, his cheerleader friend. The gate opened and Judy ran to him and hugged him.

"Oh my God I can't believe it," She grabbed him by the hand and pulled him through the gate.

Roberto walked into the backyard to many hugs, kisses, and as always, many questions. After a few minutes, the conversation went on without him. He stood close enough to hear, but far enough not to be included.

"Well, Mrs. Johnson's house is the last one of the Victorians," Cathy said.

"Who......?" Jerry asked.

"Mrs. Johnson, remember? She used to work in the office, at school."

Roberto looked away trying to remember. Cathy went on with her history lesson.

"This is the last of the biggies. Everything that was here when we grew up is gone. With the exception of a few of the old track homes of course, but you know."

Jerry couldn't believe it and asked. "When did she turn this into a restaurant?"

"God, right away. As soon as the property values went up everybody sold, except for Mrs. Johnson. She turned it into this."

"That's sad." Said Jerry. "I can't believe it. This means we can never go back."

Kathy placed her arm around him and said.

"But you know what? It's all still in here." She pointed to her head. "They can never take that away from us."

Roberto looked away.

"That's true. Our brain is ours." Said Mike Davison.

Not convinced that a memory was an alternative to the real thing, Jerry said to Mike. "It's still sad. No matter how you look at it."

"We can relive it all in here." Cathy pointed to her head again. "Ha Roberto."

She looked at Roberto who had lost himself doing that very thing she was talking about. To stitch back the pictures, events, and emotions. Most of which were out of sequence, unattached, floating in his head.

"Ha Roberto." Repeated Cathy, hoping to get him involved. Roberto nodded in agreement.

"What about city hall?" Asked Richard Doyle.

Cathy waved to him as if she was waving goodbye and said. "Bye, bye baby. Finito."

Richard tried to get a grip on everything being gone and couldn't. "How can that be?"

423

"The city doesn't exist. They now call it a district. I guess you didn't drive around before you came here?" Asked Cathy.

Richard shook his head in disappointment and said. "Nope, I just got here, I was running late."

Roberto looked away as the conversation went on without him. Jerry saw Roberto looking away and said. "Hey, you, Roberto, remember us?"

Jerry walked up to him and tapped him on the shoulder. Roberto turned around to see a few people looking at him.

"Gee, where were you?" Asked Jerry.

"Oh, I've been around," Roberto responded as if it was no big deal.

"No, I mean just now. What were you thinking?"

Roberto looked beyond Jerry to see a couple of people walk up and join the group.

"Ah, nothing."

"Hey Roberto, remember the ghost town?" Cathy asked with a huge smile.

Pat Dally heard ghost town and said, "holy shit, I haven't thought about that in years."

Mike raised his beer. "Hey, I was there and," he looked at Roberto, "thanks for scaring the shit out of us."

Cathy waited for an answer but didn't get one. She walked up to him. "Well, do you remember?"

"Yeah, yeah I do." Said Roberto with a new bright eye expression.

Cathy wasn't buying it. "Are you sure?"

Roberto clearly heard her, but hesitated. "Ah, yeah I do."

She persisted. "Are you sure?" She looked into his eyes as if to challenge him. "Do you remember Mark?"

"Mark, Mark?" Asked, Roberto.

"Bennett!" Said Cathy with her eyes bulging. "He was there that night. With you, you know? Rigging the ghost town."

"I think I do." Said, Roberto.

She looked at the group.

"You know we searched and searched for Mark, but we couldn't find him. Mills should be here though."

"Mills?" Said Roberto and wished he hadn't.

Cathy turned directly to him, not believing that he couldn't remember.

"Yeah, he was also there that night. He also helped you rig the ghost town." She waited.

"Oh yeah, he's gonna be here?" Roberto faked it.

Mike shook his head as he listened and thought about everything. "That story you guys made up was too much man."

Roberto looked down attempting to recapture some of what was being said.

"Oh man, I remember hitting that fence?" Said Mike and put his hands on his belly.

"You know what?" Cathy said to Mike.

"What?"

"Kelly told me just the other day that she still has a dent on her hip from hitting that fence. All these years later."

"I believe it. She hit the fence hard," Mike said. "Is she coming?"

"Yeah, she should be here any minute." Said Kathy.

"Why didn't I go on that?" Asked Judy.

Pat poked her on the shoulder. "Because you don't have the balls, that's why."

Judy made a face and asked. "Balls? What does it have to do with balls?"

Pat ignored her and looked around for David who was known as a kid for his Playboy magazines in his treehouse. "Talking about balls, hey David?"

David looked at him. Pat went on.

"Hey, remember that one day you hung those girls a B. A.? Remember? You stuck your bare ass out the window."

"That never happened." Said David.

"Fuck yeah, that happened." Said Jerry.

"Hell, yeah that did happen." Said Anthony.

Jerry gave David a look. "We were in Fullerton, right?"

Pat Dally nodded. "Yeah and....."

Jerry interrupted Pat and said," so we see these girls in a car next to us, and....."

Pat interrupted him. "David pulls his pants down to hang them a B.A. and stinks up the whole car."

Cathy made a face. "Oh gross!"

"What? What do mean?" Judy asked.

"He stunk it up. The fucker stunk." Said Pat.

Judy frowned. "You can't be serious." She looked at David, placed her hands on her waist, and said.

"You pig."

David perked up, stretched his neck up really high, and said. "Hey, hey, in my defense." He lowered his head. "Okay...I..have no defense."

Judy thought it was time to give David some advice. "Next time fart outside the car, will you,"

Everyone laughed and grossed out. Pat looked directly at Judy.

"He didn't fart. His ass stunk. Don't get me wrong, the fart wouldn't have helped, but he stunk it up because of butt funk. Get it?"

Everyone laughed again, the girls totally grossed out as Judy tried to make sense, but couldn't begin to relate.

"But....?....what....Oh my God." Judy finally understood.

"God had nothing to do with this," Pat said.

"Man, that was nasty!" Said Jerry, still laughing.

"Nasty? That's a nice way to put it. Man, am I glad I missed that one." Said Richard.

Cathy laughed with her hand over her mouth and pleaded. "Okay stop. No more please, stop."

David shook his head slowly as his face turned beet red. "That was a long time ago."

Cathy finally stopped laughing and looked at David. "When was the last time you showered David?"

David looked around searching for support as if to say, can you believe this? "That was a long time ago. I shower every day now. How about you, Cathy?"

Cathy frowned. "What about me? I didn't stink, and I don't stink."

David shot back. "I didn't say you stunk. Your bare ass sure was hanging out the window though."

Cathy felt her blood rush out of her head as her perfect memory played out that day. "I don't believe this," she said under her breath.

Judy held her wine glass to her chest and dropped her mouth slightly open as she looked at Cathy.

"You did what? Shut up. I don't remember hearing about this."

Pat went on. "Oh, you don't remember? It was on the news? Cathy hangs a B.A., film at eleven." Everyone laughed.

Roberto at this point had checked out. To him, it was

just another conversation without reference, unattached, more like distant voices from who knows where. He quietly walked away.

"Oh, yeah I remember that." Said, Jerry, as he rocked back and forth on a stool.

Cathy decided to embrace it and said. "Yeah, yeah, but you know what? At least I didn't stink it up like you know who." She looked at David.

"Wait a minute." Said Judy, "you dropped your pants with a bunch of guys in the car to hang a B.A.?"

Jerry smiled and said, "that's right baby!"

"Oh my god. Who was in the car?" Asked Cindy Jepsen, who had been on the sidelines listening.

Pat Dally proudly stood and said, "guilty as charged, I was in that car, yes I was, me, and ah."

He pointed at Jerry. "And Jerry, David, and Roberto. Yes you heard that right."

He put his arms out like saying, there you go. Some laughed, others were confused, Pat went on.

"Cathy." He paused and looked at her. "Was the very first girl I ever had in the car naked...baby." He grabbed his beer off of the stool and raised it above his head. "That's right baby." Everyone cheered.

"I wasn't naked," Cathy said, sort of trying to put up a defense. "I dropped my pants....down....a little. That's all!"

"A little?" Pat's eyes bulged out, embellishing the story.

In the far background beyond the conversation, Roberto walked toward the gate.

Richard leaned toward Cathy. "But you had your pants down. With four guys in the car. I mean come on man."

"Yes, yes," said Cathy, she paused, and tilted her head. "But I told them to look away."

Judy looked around to see everyone's reaction. Some laughed, others rolled their eyes. The guys who were actually there looked at each other.

"Yeah right." Said Jerry.

Cindy looked directly at Cathy in disappointment. "I can see it all now." She looked at the guys and made an innocent face and in a little girl's voice said. "Guys, can you please turn away because I'm gonna pull my pants down, okay?" She came out of the little girl's voice. "I mean really?"

"Well, they did," Cathy said, somewhat trying to defend herself, but not really caring at this point.

"Well, if that's the case, why did I hear about your turquoise panties?" Said Gary.

Beyond the conversation and beyond the memories, Roberto walked out the gate to a more comfortable space.

Pat looked at Gary in confirmation. "Oh yeah. That's right."

Judy looked at Cathy questioning. Cathy gave her a little smirk. As if to say, whatever.

"So much for looking away. I remember your turquoise panties." Said Judy.

Richard and a couple of guys looked at Judy. Richard frowned and asked her. "Why do you remember those? What's going on here?"

Judy placed her finger on Richard's temple. "Gym class. Get your head out of the gutter, jeese."

"The gutter was the last place my head was at." Richard quickly responded and laughed.

"Hey, remember the car chase?" Jerry asked.

David raised his eyebrows. "Man, do I remember that? That was nuts man."

429

"Oh yeah, we were chasing these guys from out of town, I remember," Pat said.

Jerry pointed at David. "Fucking, David over here, he was pounding the shit out of those guy's car, with a broom!"

"Not only the car, I smacked the shit out of a couple of the guys." Added David.

"Who's we?" Asked Bruce Collins.

Pat looked at David and said. "Me, David, and Lisa, she was driving.....we were in her Mustang right?" He asked David.

"Yeah, man that was a fast car. She could drive that thing too. I tell you what though, she used to scare the shit out of me sometimes."

Jerry went into thought as the memory played out in his head. "Yeah, me and Roberto, we were behind you guys in his RoadRunner. Man, that thing kicked ass!"

Pat thought about that crazy night as details came back to him. He looked at the group. "So we were chasing these bastards and we pulled up right next to them and..." Jerry interrupted him.

"We see David climb out of the window, with a broom!" Jerry looked around as if to ask, can you believe it?

Bruce looked at David. "Why did you have a broom?"

Cathy looked at Bruce. "Who cares?" She looked at Jerry. "Go on." Cathy couldn't wait to hear the story.

Jerry's mind went into overdrive and relived that night as if it had happened days ago.

"So David climbed out of the window with this broom and started hitting the shit out of that Camaro." Jerry jumped off of the stool. "I mean like he was way out there. His whole upper body was sticking out of the car. Roberto and I were like, what the fuck is he doing? Look at him. So he takes this huge swing, misses and almost falls out of the car. We were like what the fuck?"

Jerry looked at David. "Remember?"

David slowly shook his head as he questioned his childhood reasons for actions he now couldn't begin to understand.

Jerry went on with the story. "So he recovers, winds up, and I mean he pulls way back, and unloads on that Camaro. Man, I couldn't believe it. He banged the shit out of that Car."

"Oh, shit, remember the driver?" Pat looked around. "He tried to grab the broom and David was like, come on, come on, you want my broom, come on." Pat did a quick look around as if to say, get ready for this. "The driver...actually went for it. Dumb mother fucker. So, this idiot reaches out, David waits for his head to come out just far enough and WHAM, David nails his ass."

"His head you mean," Bruce corrected him.

"Actually, in this case, his head was his ass. That stupid son of a bitch." Everyone laughed. Pat shook his head as he looked around. "It was crazy man." He looked at David, "remember David?"

David laughed, some questioned the truth of the story, others just took it in.

"Oh man," said David, "that was nuts, ha, Rober..." He looked around. "Hey, where's Roberto?"

Anthony was thinking about the story and snapped out of it when he heard David's question. "I saw him earlier. He was headed that way." He pointed toward the gate.

Cindy and others looked in the direction of the gate and asked. "Where was he going?"

"I don't know," Anthony said.

As if dragged by the magnet for truth, Roberto stood

431

like a statue looking at the front of the house. He processed the image and tried to reconcile it with the Cloverdale Reunion house. A memory that came out of nowhere so he thought. But the images collided, nothing seemed right. Dr. Culpa's words snuck in and out of his head. A sudden change of mood flooded the group in the backyard. Everyone slowed down, took a pause, and reflected. Jerry's eyes darted back and forth as he said.

"Man, I shouldn't have said anything about the chase."

"I don't think he heard you." Said Mike and made a face like saying no biggie.

"I hope he's not leaving." Said Judy, as she looked around hoping to hear that someone was going to go check on him.

"No, he'll be back," said Mike, "don't worry."

Judy thought of the hell they lived through many years ago. "Oh God, I hope he's okay." She looked around almost pleading.

Cindy softly said. "I haven't thought about her in years. It's so devastating."

"Who?" Asked Bruce.

"Lisa," Cindy said, almost in a whisper.

"So, she died right?" Asked Bruce.

Cathy sighed deeply, paused, and softly said. "She was murdered." She paused again and looked away as if she hadn't said anything. But already knowing the next question, after a few long seconds, she quietly said. "Just a few years after we graduated."

Bruce froze and held his breath as he tried to understand.

Judy tried to control her emotions. "Oh, it was terrible. I couldn't believe it. I still can't."

432

There was a long pause as everyone took in the unwilling turn of the conversation.

"Oh boy, he was a mess," Cathy said with her breaking voice as she looked beyond the crowd toward the front of the house. "We all were, but, for him? I can't begin to imagine."

Roberto stood without expression. After several minutes of failing to reconcile the images, he walked away and sat on the curb facing the street. In his mind, no reason was necessary for actions taken. Sitting on the curb was an action preceded by another, nothing more. As Roberto raveled in his many worlds, his friends unraveled in theirs. It was an emptiness one could only hope didn't exist. For those who left town after graduation, the questions were too many to remain silent.

Gary sighed deeply. "So, what happened?" He looked around. "I don't understand. I mean, I heard that she was being photographed? Is that true?"

"Yeah, well, the guy was supposedly a photographer for a car magazine and...." Cathy's voice faded.

Judy finished Cathy's thought. "He was shooting her and her car."

"So that's the guy that killed her?" Asked Mike.

Cathy nodded. "Yeah, yeah," she looked away. Even for Cathy, who had lived in town all her life, these were events without passing. All it took was the sound of a passing car, a once happy song on the radio, and it all came back like it was yesterday. Here it all is, again, she thought. Her emotions now reeling out of control, she held on as she tried not to cry. But the story had to be told, so she went on.

"Roberto," Cathy cleared her throat as she felt her

433

tears coming. She raised her shaking hand to wipe her first tear. "And, ah, Roberto." She wiped her second tear. "He blamed himself for..." Her tears now out of control, both of her shaking hands came up to wipe them away. She looked around knowing she had crossed the point of no return in a tale she had hoped not to relive again. "He....blamed himself for not stopping her."

"What do you mean?" Asked Gary.

"Oh..." Cathy took a deep breath and held it for a second or two. She exhaled and said. "They had a huge argument about her going on that photo shoot. And ah, she went anyway."

Some looked at each other. Others looked down or away hoping to have the strength to hold back the tears. There was a long pause.

Cathy went on. "The last conversation they ever had,...was that argument."

Roberto had no idea he was the topic of conversation, as he sat on the curb, encapsulated in his silence. He looked down hoping to see nothing. The absence of everything felt good to him, but he questioned if it was good he felt, or nothing. What's the difference? He asked himself. If it's hard for me to tell, what exactly is the difference? Nothing felt like nothing.

The sound of a Mustang raging in the far distance caught his nothing. How can that be? There are many Mustangs out there, so why not? But this sounded too much like - he stopped himself. He closed his eyes and covered his ears. The sound of his breathing became louder as if to keep him from hearing that Mustang. He thought of how much one breath was like another. Yet, they claim that all breaths are different. It is the depth of observance that determines the difference, as with the sound of that Mustang. Something about it, not only called out to him, it sought him. He knew the sound of that exhaust, the gear ratio of that axle, the sound, and feel of that shallow clutch. It was exactly as he had adjusted it. Dr. Culpa's words interrupted that beautiful sound. He rejected his words. The sound of the Mustang raging came back. He thought of the night they chased those kids. Lisa, Jerry, David, Pat, and Roberto driving like maniacs. Hot rodding as Rock n Roll filled every square inch of their cars.

The sound of the Mustang snapped him out of that. There it was, a quick shallow clutch. She grabbed second, the Mustang screamed. She hit third, two seconds later she grabbed fourth. She must be in a straightaway, he thought. She eased off the gas, coming into a curve, Roberto was sure of it. She grabbed second and slammed the pedal to the metal as she came out of the curve sideways. There it was that Mustang screaming like a mountain lion. He saw Lisa's boots as she clutched, grabbed third, and pulled her Mustang out of the slide. The Mustang once again screamed. She hit fourth gear catapulting her into that straight away. Now that's the way it's done, he thought. He inhaled a quick breath and almost looked for the Mustang. He fought it and kept his eyes on the pavement. The shaking of his head caught him off guard. He stopped it and closed his eyes. The sound of the Mustang got closer. He asked himself, why is this happening? Dr. Culpa's words almost found their way back to him, but he rejected them. The sound of the Mustang came around the corner. He opened his eyes and there, on the pavement, and on his shoes, light that could only be from the Mustang.

A quick memory of him sitting in his old truck looking down at his feet on the pedals rushed through his head. The Mustang came toward him. It stopped, backed up, and parked. The engine revved up two quick times and turned off just like Lisa. Roberto's heart sped out of control but forced himself not to look. The door of the Mustang opened. There was a moment of silence. As if she stopped to look at him. The door closed. There was another moment of silence. Roberto looked down the entire time. The sound of footsteps started toward him. No, no, this is not happening, he said to himself. As if his friends in the backyard and Roberto were attached by a string of mental telepathy, the horror of their yesterdays played out at the same time.

Cathy went on with the story. "Their last conversation, the very last thing they said to each other, was that huge argument," She turned away. "Can you believe it? As if it wasn't bad enough."

Some fought back the tears, others gave in to them. Judy wiped away hers, but these were tears to be had.

"God it was awful. I should've stopped her, he, he..." Judy said, and couldn't go on. Those who didn't know what had happened looked at her almost begging. Judy went on, "I should've stopped her, he kept saying, over and over."

Anthony walked back to the group after looking over the hedge for Roberto.

"Did he leave?" Asked Cindy.

Anthony shook his head. "No."

"What is he doing?" Asked Judy.

"He's just sitting there," Anthony said as he saw Judy's tears falling off her chin.

"Where?" Judy asked.

"Out front, on the curb." Anthony tightened his lips as he too fought tears.

"He's sitting on the curb?" Asked Bruce.

"Yes," said Anthony and dropped his eyes to the ground.

Roberto's attempt not to stitch back the pictures had failed him. As the steps got closer, the need to look no longer escaped him. There she is, he heard himself say. That tall beautiful silhouette of hers with the streetlight shining through her hair. He fought back the tears, but like the tears his friends endured, these were also tears to be had. As if he was at two places at the same time, his other self stood across the street. He watched Lisa walk up to him and stopped. Roberto questioned, why am I seeing this from across the street?

His next perspective came from above. Roberto saw himself sitting on the curb as Lisa turned to face him. He waited. For what, was the question. And out of nowhere, as if tearing through the cloth of time, sound from another time, from another place. The argument they had on that very last day. Loud and clear the argument raged on. The sound of his voice bothered him. The sound of him telling her not to go bothered him even more. The idea of not grabbing her and holding on to her for dear life, a deadly mistake. The argument stopped. He opened his open eyes, this time to see her from her knees down as she stood in front of him. There they were, her boots right there.

She kneeled in front of him. He saw her from the neck down and told himself not to look up. If ever there was a silence to be seen, this was most definitely it. She reached out, raised his chin slightly, and tried looking into his eyes.

He fought her and closed his eyes. She grabbed his face with both hands, leaned toward him, tilted her head, and softly kissed him. With the walls of time and space nowhere to be found, her soft beautiful lips embraced his. The touch, the sound of her lips touching his, the heat of her skin next to his, he will always miss.

And then, the memory he will always regret. She begged him to fix her car, but he had refused. He finally gave in and she was off to her photo shoot, another deadly mistake. Roberto came out of that memory to see his tears falling onto his shaking hands. This was the debilitating fear that out of nowhere, so seemed, visited him throughout the years. There he was again, that third person, looking down on both of them from above. Still holding his face, she pulled her hands back and ever so slowly stood.

Next, came the memory of her waving as she drove off in her Mustang, happy, smiling. This was the last snapshot; the last frame of an event he was convinced was not only out of place, but shouldn't have happened as it did. He remembered it well. As that moment expired, as his hand came down from waving to her, in his mind and in real time, he saw her coming instead of leaving, as he had seen in a dream the night before. In that constant, there was no argument, there was no photographer, and there was no leaving. He had tapped into that human consciousness in a state of genetic evolution he had struggled with, thought about, dreamed about, and questioned for many years. He wondered how and why he found himself in this constant and not the other. Was it choice, was it random, or was it the end result of the forces at play? As they say, the tossing of the dice. Is that what life is? The end result of forces colliding? The impact of nothing becoming something? He brought himself out of that, to the memory he wasn't about to birth. Without

making a single sound, with an expression unwilling to be formed, the extensions to his brain brought him to his feet. He turned, took a few steps, stopped, and turned back to look at his then, his used to be. His hand started to come up to wave goodbye, yet again, but his now fought him. Without waving, he walked away.

As if coming out of that alternate reality, Roberto at that very moment saw nothing but pavement as he still sat on the curb looking down. But his unwillingness to accept what wasn't, took over and there he was, that third person walking away. He stopped, turned around again and there she was, that beautiful silhouette of hers walking away into the luminance of the streetlight she earlier came out of only to disappear into. And there he was again, still sitting on the curb questioning everything. The urge to see if she was truly gone, stronger than he was able to resist. He slowly raised his head to see no one there. As Roberto fought his demons, his friends fought theirs. Tears running down their faces, endless effort to console each other.

"Should we go out to talk to him?" Cindy asked.

"I don't think that's a good idea. Let's leave him alone for a while." Said Mike.

"What a terrible thing to have to live through. Jesus." Said, Richard. "Maybe it's best not to talk about it." Added Richard, wanting to move away from this.

"But we haven't had time to heal with him. In many ways we have." Said Cindy, as she looked around. "Us, but not him with us. I mean, I can't believe that he's actually here. We haven't seen him for so many years."

Judy went on. "We thought he might have died. He was in such pain just before he disappeared."

Cathy looked past the gate as if she was looking at him and said.

"I bet it feels like yesterday to him. Seeing us for the first time in all these years."

"Where has he been? I thought he was here the whole time." Gary said.

The confusion in Bruce's head was closer to the truth than he realized. "I actually heard that he had died in a car accident."

Everyone stopped talking as they saw Roberto walk through the gate and toward them. Roberto lifted his head to see sadness, tears running down their faces as he slowly walked up to Cathy. He looked into her eyes and gently hugged her. Her tears rushed out and on to him, as their faces touched. Roberto tried to console her and found it impossible to fight back his tears.

Judy gently placed her hand on his back to comfort him and asked. "Are you okay?"

Roberto backed away from Cathy but held on to her hand. He looked around to see more tears than anyone has the right to in a lifetime.

"I'm ready," Roberto said with his voice trembling.

They looked at him questioning, not sure if they heard him correctly, but said nothing.

Roberto released Cathy's hand and turned to them. "I'm ready to discuss her, to talk about her. I have to. I can't take that away from you, from her, from me. I want to feel...good about her. You know? I want to be able to talk about her."

Judy wiped away his tears and hugged him. Jerry moved closer to them as he fought back tears, but it was too late.

He reached over Judy and rubbed Roberto's back. Roberto released Judy.

He inhaled a trembling breath, wiped his tears and nose. He looked at each of them and realized the pain of their suffering.

"You know, for years......." He stopped.

"Ah, I tried, so, so hard to......" He stopped again.

He reached deep in an attempt to console them, but instead, they heard his trembling voice.

"It's just that....sometimes....I still feel her right here." He brought his hands to his chest. Everyone's heart sunk into the abyss of the pain they felt for him. Roberto moved his hands away from his heart looked down and said. "But it is time."

No one knew what to do or say. Cindy could not stand the sight of him crying looking down like a lost soul. His tears fell like rain. She hugged him tightly and whispered in his ear. "It is, it's time, and we will. We will talk about her, and we will never forget her."

She released him from her embrace, but kept her arm on his shoulder, turned to the group and repeated the words she had said to him. "It's time to talk about her." She looked at Roberto to make sure he was listening. "And we will. We will talk about her and we will never, ever forget her."

Anthony raised his beer, they all raised their glasses, and they all said. "To Lisa."

David said. "To Lisa and her Mustang."

"To Lisa and her Mustang." They all said.

They all came closer with the need to touch him, to ease his pain. Mike came closer and put his hand on Roberto's shoulder. There was a long hug between them all as silence found its way to them.

Pat, who went to get a beer, came back to see everyone crying, and hugging. He stopped short of the group.

"What the hell is going on here, some kind of orgy?"

Everyone looked at him. Pat raised his eyebrows and pulled his head back. "What the fu...."

Judy and Cindy turned to Pat, and opened their arms asking for a hug.

"You're not hugging me you son of bitches."

Some laughed through their tears, others too deep in their pain to hear.

David extended his arms to Pat. "Come, man, bring it in, come on man."

With his eyes fixed on the group, Pat shook his head and backed away. "Fuck you, hell no!"

He did a one-eighty and took off running. Richard, Jerry, David, and Anthony ran after him.

Roberto, for the first time since her death, listened to them. To their stories, their reality of events he had known only from his perspective. In his heart, the sadness will always be. But there was something about hearing their stories out loud, in their voices that eased his pain. It brought her back to life. In a limited way, but she was back and that gave him a little joy.

As all this was going on, a waiter picked up a few glasses and dishes and headed for the kitchen. As he walked past a couple of waitresses, Jenny and Olivia, the sound of sniffling and crying stopped him. He saw them holding a yearbook. He looked over their shoulders to see a picture of a blond girl standing in front of a store. Her name was Lisa Higgins. She was Roberto's true love and later became his wife. At first glance, the difference between her and Joan Briganti, Roberto's anti-gravity girl, almost undetectable. This was Roberto's favorite picture in his invented past. The image that brought him joy and kept him in his pain.

A few years after her death, he forced himself to move to another town. To rid himself of the pain his surroundings brought him. He loaded everything that connected his past to his present onto his truck. Her clothes, her jewelry, her pictures, and most of all, his yearbook with that beautiful picture. He drove to the disposal site. He cleared his mind and threw everything out. He stepped off his truck and onto what he thought was a book. He picked it up and drove off. When he got home, he dusted it off and realized that it was a yearbook. He felt apprehension and a little fear. He tried to throw it in the trash, but his curiosity got the best of him. He opened it, and there it was, an almost identical picture of an almost identical girl to his wife in an almost identical yearbook. At an instant, he felt joy. Her name was Joan Briganti. He embraced that joy and his new world was born. And now we have to ask, whose past, whose world did he come home with? And did he have a choice? Everything was almost identical to everything he lost. And how is it, that on that very day, at that very spot, as he tried to walk away from his pain, someone came to that exact spot, minutes before him in an attempt to walk away from their pain? In Roberto's new constant, he chose that yearbook as his means of survival. A means of getting through the day and nothing else. In his mind, everything was like it used to be. She and all were alive, all young, all, and everything unchanged. It was his slice of yesterday that had presented itself. So what could he possibly do, but to hold on to his slice of yesterday.

While the waiter looked at the yearbook, Jenny, one of

the waitresses, looked back at the waiter and pointed to Lisa's picture.

"That's her. It's so sad."

"Who?"

"The girl that was murdered." Said Olivia.

"What girl?" Asked the waiter.

"The girl..they're talking and crying about." Jenny pointed to the group with her head.

The waiter looked at the group and back to the girls.

"Why are you guys crying? You didn't even know her."

"Really? So you have to know someone to feel sad about them dying?" Said Jenny.

"Well....." The girls stopped him with a look. "What?" Asked the waiter.

The girls shook their heads and looked back at the picture.

The waiter frowned and said. "Hey, turn the page, I want to see what else is in there."

"So you want to move away from her just like that?" Said Olivia.

"Okay, I'm sorry she's dead. Okay?" He pulled his head back. "Come on, turn the page."

The girls rolled their eyes and turned the page to see the old metal bridge that Roberto, his brother Ernie, and their friend Claude used to jump off of and swim under when they were kids. This was another of many memories Roberto had transferred to his new life, his Cloverdale, and was convinced that this bridge was on the Russian River.

"Wow, that is beautiful." Said Jenny

"Are you kidding me?" Asked the waiter. "Was that here? I mean like in this town?"

"I don't know, I guess," Jenny said.

"I wonder where that was?" Asked Olivia.

"Are you sure this is the right yearbook? I don't remember ever seeing anything like that around here." Said the waiter.

Pat ran past him and the waitresses. Followed by a bunch of laughing men. They caught up with him and the group hug ensued.

"Get away, don't touch me you bunch of loving hippies," Pat yelled.

Randy flew in from a small town in Colorado to the reunion. After the dinner, he walked up to the fence next to the freeway. He couldn't believe all the houses that got taken out to make room for that freeway and the Mall on the other side. He looked at the bumper to bumper traffic. This was something he could never understand. He heard Pat screaming and looked back just in time to see another group hug. He smiled. He looked at the freeway again and saw a light moving in the bushes a few yards away on the other side of the fence.

"What the hell?"

He took a couple of steps toward the light.

"What are you looking at?"

He turned around to see Toby walking toward him.

"What are you looking at?" Toby Asked.

"I'm not sure. I just saw a light moving in the bushes."

"Where?"

He pointed. "Right there."

"What is it?

"I don't know."

"Is that a tent?" Asked Toby.

"Where?"

Toby pointed, "right where the light is. It's green."

"Oh, my god I think you're right. Do you think someone lives there?"

A radio came on from inside the tent.

"Oh my god, someone is living there." Said Toby.

"Can you believe it?" Asked Randy.

The zipper on the tent opened. A man stuck his head out, reached out, and grabbed a bottle of water from the ground. He saw Randy and Toby staring. He gave them a smile, a wave, dropped back into his tent and zipped it up.

Randy and Toby looked at each other.

"What just happened?" Asked Toby.

"That was cool." Said, Randy. "You see, who needs a condo?"

Randy's cell phone rang. "Hello?"

"Hello, Randy?" asked Mills on the phone.

"Yeah, what's going on Mills?"

"I don't think I'm gonna make it."

"Why not? What happened?"

Toby looked at the bumper to bumper traffic and saw a man in a car on his cell phone.

"I missed my flight." Said, Mills.

"Oh, that's too bad." Said, Randy.

Toby looked at Randy as he responded to the call. She looked at the man in the car.

"Yeah man, I don't believe it." Said Mills.

"Take a later flight, we can get together tomorrow."

Toby tried to put the two together.

"I don't know if I can catch another, but I'll try." Said Mills.

Toby's eyes darted back and forth from the driver to Randy. A memory came into her head of the time Mills came into the hallway at school with his guitar strap to his back, black beanie, headphones, and that eight track

446

hanging from his neck. She came out of her memory to see the driver and made the connection and at that very moment, decided not to tell Randy.

Mills looked out to see the Reunion Banner. He saw the two people standing on the other side of the fence. He thought that was weird, but didn't think for one second, that it was Randy and Toby. Mills had been stuck in traffic long just enough to change his mind about coming to the reunion.

Randy pleaded. "Come on! Just do it, man."

A few hours later, the events of that night became memories, and the seconds that didn't want to pass, like the seconds of countless nights, moments later, they were nowhere to be found. And the people who swore never to let go, who promised themselves to the night, only the dreamers had the ability to hold on. Still drinking, still holding on to that timeline, that if you pull on hard enough will lead you to your comfort, your familiarity, to your perception of your reality. And just like the seconds of a moment ago, eventually, they all had to let go. The lights in the restaurant went off. A couple of young waiters walked out and locked the door. A car drove up, and the two kids headed for the garbage bin. And yes, they pulled out a case of beer, got in the car, and drove off into a night of partying, in search of memories waiting to be had.

Roberto had one or two more bones to pick with his past. It was a past that anchored him to a reality that owed him an array of explanations. After the reunion, he drove on to Main Street as he had so many times, so long ago. The same Main Street that when he was a boy, had everything one could possibly want. Hot rods, girls, rock and roll as loud as your stereo could go, and the endless night to cruise it all, if only he could bring it all back and relive it exactly as they used to do. Each car with its own soundtrack, with its own story to tell. But Roberto didn't need to bring it all back. If nothing else a slice will suffice. He drove around in search of that little slice, but his unforgiving past of not so long ago was unwilling to let him go. He stopped at the same stoplight he used to stop at all those years ago. He waited for that feeling, that emotional connection. But remnants of that long ago was all his mind was willing to accept.

And with that, came a feeling of loss. Followed by sadness, which brought forth the question, why hold on to something that will never be? The light turned green. He made a left turn to get off Main Street and then a right. It was a part of town that had the last of the old neighborhood form the forties and fifties. A couple of blocks later he saw one of the remnants, the back of Arlington Heights Liquors.

He made a right turn onto the parking lot and there it was, that brick wall, that neon sign, Arlington Heights Liquors still shining like a beacon. A beacon that when you found yourself in a dark place, could take you places where you don't belong. He parked, got out, and leaned against his car. His head slowly began to shake as he took it all in. After a few minutes and many sighs, and questions to no end, he reached into his car and grabbed his yearbook. He opened it and turned to the Cloverdale Liquors in Northern California. He slowly shook his head at the incredible resemblance to where he stood.

A few minutes later he drove onto a hill overlooking millions of city lights, where in younger days there were only a few. It was one of their favorite spots when they were young. It was a place to drink, to smoke, where many babies were conceived. He got out and stood against his car. There was a hum to the city he didn't remember being there. As he thought of that, the sound that could only belong to one, made its way to him. There it was, that beautiful sound of her Mustang. He couldn't see her, but he could most definitely hear her. Lisa and her Mustang, their destiny some would say unfulfilled, unknown, forever on the streets of this never to be forgotten town, where Roberto was not only born but where his distant past resides.

31. A MISTAKEN LIFE

The very next day, Roberto drove north. This time, he took life in with eyes wide open. Instead of rejecting thoughts he embraced them. It was refreshing to see them as a thought and nothing else. As he came to the Golden Gate Bridge, he had a couple of flashbacks. Something to do about a gas station, but he couldn't explain it. He heard "Dr. Culpa say, the inability to explain the everything of everything, is normal. After all, not all that presents itself should have to be explained." This made it possible for Roberto not to have to explain everything. The next time he couldn't explain something, he would label it as one of the unexplained. This one he would say to himself, I will put in my list of the unexplained and walk away.

An hour or so later he watched the sunset and enjoyed it, but felt sad to see it go. Why is the day so short? The cycle of life came to mind, but he let it go. Driving north felt different than driving south. He felt a feeling of familiarity that confused him and found himself thinking about that very feeling. The rest of his journey, almost parallel to a journey he had taken more than fifteen years ago but had forgotten. There was a striking resemblance to the sequence of events. The time of day in which those events were taking place. The sound of the road and the wind on his face and hair from the open window. How long he had been on the road, and where he found himself along his journey after sunset. It was the totality of all, which made him question if he was driving a familiar road he had never traveled.

Was this an echo of that other constant? Or was this an unattached emotion? As if telling him to move along, the stripping on the road triggered the ticking of a clock in his head. As he sped up, so did the clock, as he slowed, the clock did as well. The questions started coming, the confusion right behind them.

He came around a long curve onto a tree-covered stretch of highway he swore wasn't there on his way south a few days ago. Amazed beyond belief, he leaned over the steering wheel to get an unobstructed view. It was as if everything that was perfect came to feed his hungry eyes. Nothing will escape this portal to my brain, he said to himself but didn't know why. Still leaning over the steering wheel, he looked up to see the trees moving toward him, past him, and disappeared onto the roof of his car. A quick flashback of streetlights doing the same, came and went at an instant. He thought of how incredible it was to see something right in front of him and have it disappear. Here one second, gone the next. How something could be

451

here and not here at the same time. One second his wife Lisa was with him, gone the next. He caught himself shaking his head as he felt his brain trying to escape. He put all that out of his head as he came out of a long curve into another tree covered tunnel of highway. And there it was in the far distance, the light at the end of the tunnel, the neon to his calling, the Owl Cafe. This is what he was thinking about. How the Owl Cafe was not here and here at the same time. The ticking of the clock vanished. He felt a new sense of journey. The questions, now irrelevant. He found himself in the midst of one of the deepest breaths he had ever taken. As he exhaled, he asked himself, what is it about this beautiful light that makes me feel what I am feeling? He couldn't explain it. All he knew was that it felt good, warm, welcoming. And just before he placed it in the list of the unexplained, he stopped and heard himself say. "This one I will put on my list of the no need to explain."

Little did he know that in his homeless forgotten past, he came to rely on that light. There was a reassurance, a commitment to and from that neon that developed over the years. It became his anchor, his compass when venturing out in the wilderness, and couldn't make it back before nightfall. Lost and confused, there it would always be. Its glow hovering just above the trees, its beautiful colors reflecting from the low hanging clouds. Showing him the path to his destination. On this night, it was no different.

He drove up to the Owl Cafe and parked right in front and there it was again, that feeling of a past life. As if he had parked on this very spot many times. He sat in his car and enjoyed his unexplained feeling of joy. A few minutes later, he got out and walked toward the door. He felt the urge to turn around and look at his car. It wasn't his sixty-eight RoadRunner, but it was his car. He took a quick look, smiled, and walked in. He saw Margaret and Charles sitting at a booth. Their smiles as beautiful as everything around them. He walked up to their warm hugs. This must be what it's like to come home, he thought. He sat, he looked out the window and all around. Margaret couldn't wait to hear it all. After a few minutes, the story of his journey started pouring out of him. Margaret lit up with pleasure.

As that was going on, the manager of the Owl Cafe and a newly hired waitress sat in the office. He reached into his desk and pulled out a box with several name tags.

"Ah, go ahead and pick one."

The girl frowned and hesitated.

"Go on," said the manager.

"What do you mean?"

"Look, if every time we hired a new waitress, we'd pay for a name tag, well." He shook the box. "You get my drift."

"Your drift?" Asked the girl.

"My drift, yeah, my...you know what I mean."

"Ah, you mean..."

"Yes, yes, pick one."

"Hmm let me think." Said the girl.

The manager grabbed one and pinned it to her blouse.

"Amanda?" Asked the girl as she made a face. "Do I look like an Amanda?"

"You know what? Here." The manager grabbed a few name tags and held them out in front of her.

"What, what do...." She started to ask.

The manager dumped the name tags into her apron pocket.

"You can pick another name later if you like."

He got up, opened the office door, and looked around. He pointed to Roberto's table.

"There, you see that table?" She nodded. "You see how he doesn't have coffee in front of him?" She nodded again. "Go on and see if that gentleman wants coffee."

She looked toward the table, but said and did nothing. The manager looked at her.

"Grab the Coffee pot, and a cup and walk up to that man and ask him if he wants coffee. If he says yes, pour him a cup."

"Oh, okay, okay."

She walked off, grabbed the coffee pot and cup and walked up to their table.

"Hi, would you like some coffee?"

Roberto looked at her name tag, and instantly felt joy but wasn't sure why. He asked her, "your name is Amanda?"

And then asked himself, why do I know that name? Where have I heard that name? He couldn't take his eyes off of her and once again asked himself, why? The waitress smiled, sat the pot and cup on the table, reached into her apron, pulled out a bunch of name tags, and placed them on the table. "For tonight? Yes."

She made a face like; can you believe it? Everyone laughed. The manager heard the laughter, looked their way, and smiled, happy to see her making them laugh on her first table.

"I just got hired." She said.

"Well, congratulations." Said Charles and Margaret,

Roberto smiled at her and said. "You know what Amanda, I'll have coffee, thank you."

"That felt weird," said the waitress.

They laugh again. Margaret leaned toward her. "What is your real name?"

"Christie."

"So we're gonna call you by your real name. Okay, Christie?" Said, Margaret.

"Oh, thanks." They laughed, she poured Roberto his coffee.

"Thanks, Christie." Said Roberto.

"You're welcome. And what is your name?" She reached out.

Roberto shook her hand. "I'm Roberto, and this is Margaret and Charles."

"Hello again." Said Margaret.

"Nice to meet you, Christie," said Charles.

"Nice to meet all of you."

She looked past them and out the window. "Oh wow, a Greyhound bus just pulled up."

They looked out to see the bus across the street. A few seconds later it pulled away to reveal a man with a trash bag filled with his belongings over his shoulder.

"I didn't know they did that, you know? Just stop and drop people off anywhere?" Said Christie.

"Yeah, you know that is kind of weird, isn't it? But...." Charles stopped himself. Margaret looked at him and nodded. Christie frowned as she wondered what was going on.

"As you can see Christie," Charles added, stopped and looked out the window. "He looks like he may be homeless." He paused as they all looked at the man. "You can usually tell by the trash bag. His whole life is in that bag."

"That is terrible." Said Christie. Margaret nodded in agreement.

"Patient dumping. You just witnessed Patient dumping." Said Charles.

The homeless man looked across the street to see the bright neon, people inside conversing and eating. He felt his empty stomach growling. He thought about how he may be treated if he went inside and asked for food. These were questions in the mind of a man who recently became homeless. The veterans knew exactly how they would be treated, and learned to endure it.

"You know what Christie?" Said Roberto,

"Yes?"

"Let me buy him dinner if he comes in. I'm sure he's starving."

"Oh, how nice of you. I'm sure he'll appreciate that."

Roberto looked at Margaret and Charles. "You know what, I'm gonna go out and say hello to him."

Christie looked at Roberto and then at Margaret and Charles as if to say, can you believe this? Margaret and Charles smiled as they looked at their Roberto. Their not so newborn, as they used to joke about when they first brought him home. Roberto got up and walked out. He came to a spot in the parking lot, and a tremendous need to stop and turn around came over him. He had stepped on the map, the exact footprints of his previous homeless life. A map forever imprinted in his brain, despite his willingness to forget those memories, those unattached emotions that felt as if they belonged to someone else.

He stopped as if he had no choice because he had no

choice. He turned around and froze. There it was, the Owl Cafe in total darkness. No neon lights, no Amanda, and no one inside. A jolt of fear rushed through him. But this fear was different. He not only felt it, he knew this fear. It was a bodyless entity that had presented itself into his timeline over the years. It was a defined, but undefined feeling just like the feelings triggered by his dreams of the people in mistaken bodies from previous lives, as he used to think.

He asked himself, is this one of the unexplained? Before he was able to answer, he looked across the highway and saw himself as the homeless man looking back at his now, the now Roberto standing in that parking lot. But this time, the Owl Cafe was all lit up, its neon calling out to him. Margaret, Charles, and the new waitress waved to him as he stood across the highway. He waved back and there he stood right back on that parking lot as that feeling of belonging came to him. The feeling that everything is going to be alright. It was in this little town, in these streets, where Roberto had built his now self, his now past. Is it possible to have been born to the wrong place? To have been born to the wrong people. Is it possible to have lived a mistaken life? To have a mistaken past? And if so, what was that place I used to call home?

Who were those people I left behind? Are they my past friends? And if so, is it distance of space or distance of mind that makes them so? And out of nowhere came this. What happens to solitary souls? Is that what I am, a solitary soul? And if I am, where will I find myself, the next time I can't find my now?

To the voices in my head...

I thank you for allowing me to use your voices. The voices that I heard throughout my childhood and in my head as I wrote this book. I not only heard you, I saw your faces, and your reactions to emotions that often caught me off guard. And through that process, you reminded me of the person I used to be. As a young man, I saw life through a lens in which everything seemed better, sweeter, brighter. I'd like to think that I'm still that guy, and in some respects, I am, but as we know all too well, life takes its toll on all of us. I still have a positive outlook, but the cracks are now self-evident. As we grow older, the way in which we achieve true happiness narrows.

Our past is dear to me; it is the one constant that can never change, regardless of the present we find ourselves in, and no one or anything can take it away from us. I had convinced myself that I would never return to Cloverdale. To do so, would present the danger of forever changing my perspective of that beautiful past. I had placed my memories in a pristine place deep within my mind, where no one or anything could taint or expose them to the changes that would ultimately come about.

But as time went on, I was reminded of the finality of life. Of the place I used to call home, and of the people I left behind. And with that, curiosity came calling on a friend. I picked up the phone, and yes, I called the Owl Cafe. She said, "hello, Owl Cafe, can I help you?" And in that space that exists, in the between of things, was my inability to respond. And in that space, was the sound of that other place. At that precise moment, I came to the realization that it was not only distance of space, but distance of mind, which existed between my now and that place I used to call home so many years ago. And with that, came the feeling of familiarity that everything was going to be alright. That everything was like it used to be. All alive, all young, all, and everything unchanged.

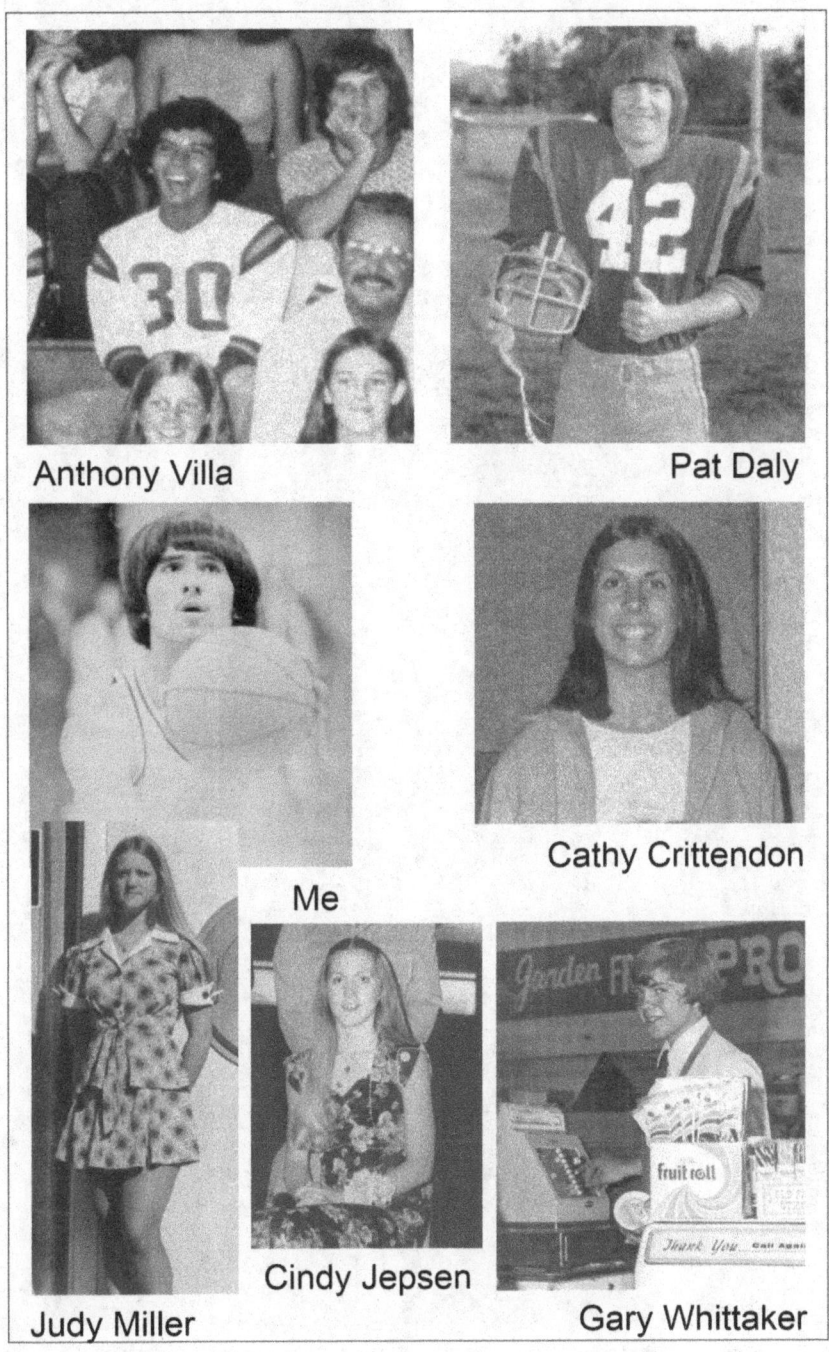

Anthony Villa

Pat Daly

Me

Cathy Crittendon

Judy Miller

Cindy Jepsen

Gary Whittaker

THE END....

Coming soon by Antonio L. Bugarin

THE DIGITAL DIVIDE

A story about the next genetic mutation: Kids are turning up comatose while on their computers and no one knows why. Some regain consciousness, while others, only their bodies survive.

www.ingramcontent.com/pod-product-compliance
Lightning Source LLC
Chambersburg PA
CBHW010650100726
47901CB00012B/2500